'The Lady and the Rooks, Edward Calvert, 1829—© Tate, London 2012'

OUT
OF THE
EARTH

JOHN AVISON

Order this book online at www.trafford.com
or email orders@trafford.com

Most Trafford titles are also available at major online book retailers.

Rook image on front cover courtesy of Margaret Holland

Printed in the United States of America.

ISBN: 978-1-4669-7241-4 (sc)
ISBN: 978-1-4669-7243-8 (hc)
ISBN: 978-1-4669-7242-1 (e)

Library of Congress Control Number: 2013901387

Trafford rev. 03/05/2013

 www.trafford.com

North America & international
toll-free: 1 888 232 4444 (USA & Canada)
phone: 250 383 6864 ♦ fax: 812 355 4082

For my father, George, who didn't live long enough to see his son do what he had always promised—write a book

There are more things in heaven and earth, Horatio,
than are dreamt of in your philosophy.

—Shakespeare, *Hamlet,* Act 1, Scene 5

PART ONE

1

IN THE DEAD OF NIGHT, one muscular pulse of a wing. It seems to lift Richard bodily, flinging him sideways in the bed. As if it is part of him, massively outgrown, black, sheathed in feathers. As if he has slept on his arm and numbed it and something else, something from the furthest blackness, has crept into the insensible skin, muscle, nerve, gristle, and bone.

Hands curling arthritically, fingers long and blue and gnarled, nails hooked and flaky, flesh and nerve pared away. Face straining forwards into the armour. I'm inside the scold's bridle again, the Serotonin Maiden's. Shoulders massively muscled, Quasimodo on speed and workout. Eyes out to the side, nictitating membrane installed, vision black, blue, grey—and mind-numbingly, I can see all but twenty-seven degrees of the wide world.

At first, Richard is terrified, fearing that what has grown into his bedroom might wake Sarah sleeping beside him; then he's furious it has arrived unannounced, that Sarah could not possibly understand if she saw . . . if she knew . . . and that she would leave his house and his life, tearful and horrified, as if he had raped a child, one of his pupils perhaps, and he would be alone with whatever possessed him.

Then he thinks, *It's only another dream.* The oft-repeated dream of rooks that seem to watch his every move as he lives and works in this ordinary Pennine village of Kirkbretton. They fall quiet in the trees as he passes and accusingly look down on him in silence as he looks up. Sometimes, at his approach, they circle the rookery in Saint Bride's churchyard in anger and frustration, screaming down at him, "Don't you understand yet? Can't you see it?" He wants to invite them to sit on his arm, to hop clumsily up to his shoulder, to whisper in his ear and tell him what they have seen and know, to give him the word. In his dreams, they might be guardians or messengers.

We rise, unnoticed, in the Triassic as the great reptiles struggle to find their feet. I trace my avian genes back fifteen million years to archaeopteryx, but this is a game with no beginning or end; the chemicals of life endlessly unravelled, simplified, brutalised. This pushing forwards is a force as basic as gravity, the inevitable in action like heat death, entropy. I haven't detected a change in the genes, though I've watched many a thousand generations of rooks try everything their intelligence has fitted them for. We're still the same creatures who watched the filthy Pict shiver in his furs and, before him, the Aryan stumble his way across the deserted plains east in Asia, west into Europe, and before that, Africa, and before that . . .

But this isn't a dream, unless life itself is a dream from which everybody waits to waken.

Out of what line did I step? The product of a promise as old as the rock on which Abraham strapped his son Isaac—the rock doused in oil, the rock on top of the highest hill, the Beltane fire-wheel, the cross rock, rock of ages. She called, She moulded, She created a lovely hybrid. "Time shall have no dominion," She said. "You shall see like a god, both man and bird."

Now facing the mullion windows and what little moonlight filters through the net drapes, he sees Sarah's very human arm beside him, long and still and peaceful, each tiny hair alive with light, resting on the duvet cover. He sees the bridge of her nose outlined as if in silver wire, the slit glitter of her sleeping eye.

He has the newly wakened intricate awareness of the little things—disturbed dust motes twinkling like free stars in the cold light from the window, the musty ancient smell of feathers, the softness of the laundered pillow on his cheek. But mostly he is aware of the bulky expectant avian creak of whatever is now in the room, fidgeting, breathing, waiting in the darkness beyond his human sight.

An angel? No. Angels bring light. Whatever woke him has sucked the light out of the air. But then Richard realises countless angels are dark, fallen out of the light an age ago, and maybe this is one.

We were never lovers. What, crow-man and queen of heaven and earth? But neither was I her slave. I am made this way to sit on her shoulder, to whisper from the fifteen-million-year wisdom of my kind, and she to whisper from the eternal myth of hers.

He should feel fear, but something deep within him is reassured.

There's a sudden impatient primeval croak that stirs Sarah in her sleep. It is not the sound an angel makes, Richard is sure.

He has heard the voice of an old and constant friend. No menace, just a statement.

"I'm here."

But then he thinks of himself as asleep again because he is not in his bedroom in Kirkbretton lying next to Sarah. He is in the Air. He thinks of the air as Air because it is the element in which he is most at home, the way humans think of their home as Earth, not earth. This would cause him to smile, but he can't because his face is not built to smile; instead, he opens his heavy beak and emits an exultant rasp. The Air wraps him and comforts him. He controls it with every feather and bone and muscle.

I can feel where my feet became claws, lengthening and curling round the branch. I can feel where the first black and dusty feathers grew, wrapping and tightening around my fingers, impossibly bending my arms, stiffening my joints for flight. On my shoulders sprout the first scapulars, glossy shields; and beneath them, the greater and lesser coverts; and beneath these, the long primaries and short secondary, the powerful remiges, rower feathers for each turn and trace I make, driving and steering the Air. My face, a face that looked and smiled on the gods of the Keltoi and Galli, the dreaming tuath, *and, on their mortal servants of high and low birth, stiffens. Out of the death-grey mask and a brutal beak capable of blinding—and in some instances, murder—nostrils rise to sit like caves in which the stews of the world miasmically circulate.*

He tries to remember what dreams of flying mean. Do they mean you feel free, or do they mean you want to be free? Who would want to be human, when the Air is your domain? He remembers the name rooks give to humans—upwrights. Or at least, that would be the translation. He can hear only the rook word. In the part of him that is human, he hears *Homo erectus, Homo sapiens.* Standing man, clever man.

As he beats his ragged wings and glides, he can see a bulging panorama of the world below him. It is like a landscape seen through a fish-eye lens. It is picked out in blue, grey, and black, though the blue is an inhuman colour, perhaps in the ultraviolet. Other traces, like the weaving lines of a map, are projected onto his vision—the whispers of stars invisible in daylight, the earth's magnetic pulse, thermals, a knowledge of where food can be found and where others of his kind live and move.

He thinks of this as a second language in which he is utterly at home. Yet he knows this is not the language into which he was born. The two race in his mind, and he wonders what he truly is.

Way below his wings, a pristine world glitters in early morning sunlight. It is not Kirkbretton. Perhaps it is his ancient congeries in the Lammermuir Hills of southern Scotland or his human ancestral home in the Yorkshire Dales. But again, it may not even be of his time. He recognises no feature of the world, no wall or field or stream or settlement. For a moment, he falters, scared, and the Air gives way beneath him.

These manifestations of my earthliness—this ancient mute-spattered nest I call home and throne, greatest in the length and breadth of old Pretan, as the misty land mutates into Pryddan, then Prythain, then Brithan, then Britain—serve only to remind me of my duty to the gods, which is a duty, of course, to life itself. Together, we spin through the emptiness of space while the world grows old around us. For as long as I choose to live in these twisted mist-limned boughs, weaving my days with thoughts that mix the past, present, and future, this tree will live, as impenetrable and eternal as the Northmen's Yggdrasil, old Mimameidr.

In that moment, he realises, as he has realised before and thrust it away, that he is being called. He is under contract. He has a commission, and the Being that commands him is as old as the earth. The Being has many names and is life and death.

What does She want?

"I want you, of course," says Sarah sleepily. The same early morning sunlight now filters into the room. It shines on Sarah's billowing ruddy hair and turns her skin to gold. She's smiling. Richard raises himself on his elbow and strokes her freckled forehead. Her arm reaches to Richard's shoulder and draws him downwards. Her breath is morning breath, and her breasts are warm.

"Where've you been?" she says, frowning.

He wants to say "Flying" or "With the Goddess" but, even with sleep in his eyes and mind, this wouldn't be right. "Just dreaming," he says and kisses her gently on the lips. Her hand goes to the back of his tousled head and pulls him closer. She kisses him more urgently.

A feather, the gentlest reminder that all is not as it seems, drifts out of the sunlight to the bedroom floor.

2

CARTIMANDUA, QUEEN-TO-COME OF THE FIFTEEN Tribes of the Brigantes, Bright Arm of the Goddess, is also in a waking dream of her own. Her watcher and teacher is Aduna, grey and ancient, a stringy witch, the girl's chief flamen, druid, wise in the ways of Earth.

Aduna, wise in Earthly things, is herself the inheritor of a worshipful tradition as old as the hills. But she is also known by and knows of things not immediately evident in the waking and living world. It is she who concocted the potion that courses headily through the young princess's body and brain tissue.

And watching too is the Goddess Brigid, invisible guardian of the Brigantes. How do I, Her oldest confidant, know that the deadliest force in the worlds of the living and dead is alert and watching?

Because I am Her, and She is me. I am Her bridge. I can see and feel what She sees and feels. They call me a the bird of ill omen, but I am only a humble guardian of the sacred, channel for the triple Goddess—virgin, mother, and harridan—in what the unwise call the "real" world.

It seems to me today She is in the third and most dangerous of her manifestations, the hag, turning the world pensively in Her hand, as likely to dash it to the ground or swallow it and kiss it alive.

It is for Her that the cold world now hangs on a knife-edge, holding its breath.

Not a bird sings evensong. Above the valley mists, the Dog Star is a spear point of light in a still sky sinking bluer, bluer into night. It is a bleak evening—not a breath of wind but bitter and crisp.

It is Her own festival of Imbolc, ewe's milk eve, a moment of change dedicated to the first stirrings of life in a world enfeebled and trapped in a long season of death and misery. After the winter, it's time to renew the promises, rekindle the fires of life, marvel anew at the thrusting green life of stem and bud.

Time to commit a life to the Goddess's service. The latest in a long line stretching unimaginably far into the past.

I, Hroc, Master of Flocks, watch from my hawthorn bush as unseen hands push open the leaning gates of Uellacaern, the palisaded fortress that the Romans will storm and reduce to ash mere years from now. Here, they will build their own fort and town of Olicana, Ilkley.

In summer, this is a garth, a pretty place on a gentle rise above the rushing river Isara, a haven in the midst of skirmish-torn Brigantian territory. But now, in February, it is shrouded in mist. Out of the stave-ringed fort emerges a single file of priestesses, angry light flickering orange at the head. Aduna, high flamen of the Great Goddess, holds a scion of the eternal fire aloft in its iron cresset.

Taranis, Thunder Man, turner of Heaven's mighty wheel . . .

Twelve grey-cowled children of the old faith follow, chanting arhythmically—each speaking to their own patron god or goddess, each with a glimmering, smoking brand, each brand parting the mists like an eyot in a swirling river. And the fog clamps shut behind it.

Then comes the child-woman Cartimandua, nicknamed Sleek Pony by her tribespeople after her intense passion for and knowledge of horses. She is princess of the Fifteen Tribes of Brigantia, only daughter of Queen Cybella, the latest in a line stretching way beyond her present assumed nobility. Her genes are borne aloft, not always on the unsaddled horses of the mysterious Aryan, but from the unknown and unacknowledged tribes that rose before them, generation after generation, some the pursued, others the pursuers.

Her dazzling blue eyes are glazed and unseeing. Though her companions stumble occasionally, she walks proudly and sure-footedly, as if guided by inner lights. The potion administered to her before the stone altar in the sacred enclave of the stronghold is working in her mind, and she is travelling in another world, where the Goddess whispers in her ear and moves her soul silently on unknown paths.

Thirteen more of the torchlit faithful follow. Then the mists close like a tomb door, and Uellacaern is folded in the evening gloom.

I fly with them above the void of the mists.

The column weaves steadily out of the valley fog on to the bald moor on a path worn by time and tradition. A curlew's bubbling lonely call, the spirit-voice of one long dead and buried in some moorland cairn, harries the dead silence.

The sacred circle they approach was built by unknown hands many lives earlier. The monoliths are roughly carved, giving the appearance of having only lately thrust themselves out of the gritstone and heather. But only those with the minds of brutes and savages can fail to hear Earth's song in this spot, the crossing of lines of power so strong the ground almost vibrates.

Aduna and the leading twelve turn left; the thirteen following bear right; and both arms form a complete circle inside the standing stones.

But Cartimandua stops of her own accord before the flat carved central altar.

She is clad only in a simple shift of white linen tied at the waist, yet she is impervious to the chill. For her, the moors are alive with lights and whispers and the sky with the cruel omnipotence of her Goddess.

Her sole ornament is the torc that denotes her total allegiance to the service of the Great Mother, Brigid. It is of fine gold, wrenched from the beating heart of Gaia in times so ancient as to be unspeakable, beaten and twisted by saints into the likeness of the black rook, Hroc, symbol of life and death, perfect startling rubies inlaid for eyes. Among the grey hoods and undyed homespun of the druids, Cartimandua's white robe gleams in the dusk, a perfect foil for the torc, which now seems to pulsate with the swelling power of the ley lines at whose nexus it is poised.

The princess carries a phial of her own menses, a token and sacrifice of her emergent womanhood.

The muscles of her pallid face are taut. Her long raven-sheen hair is tressed. In the waiting silence, her eyes seem suddenly to focus on the intricate carvings before her, their swirling symbols of eternity, their double fylfots intertwined and surrounded by a tau of cupholes and, at their head, the Crookstone, over which the Dog Star now hangs in the silent indigo sky.

She breathes deeply, reaching her full height.

O blessed Medb, would that I were safe among your sacred groves now . . . , she thinks, but she says, dreamlike, "O blessed Brigid, Mother of All, give me strength to accept your will . . ."

High priestess Aduna begins the ceremony.

And so it is that Cartimandua dedicates herself to the Goddess of many names, just as I do now and a million times in the past and future. The line is unbroken.

But something is not right. The Goddess is disturbed, doubtful and so, therefore, am I. What is wrong? It eludes us both. As sentry and servant, I watch with foreboding.

3

I T WAS RAINING—NOT THE ANGRY storm rain that provokes the spirit to rise and resist nor the drizzle fit only to irritate, but persistent heavy bone-wearing, bone-weary rain that seeps into the soul, curdling and disfiguring.

In the antechamber of Cartimandua's square house in the centre of bustling Uellacaern, a column of smoke rose into the hut's rafters and was whipped away into the cloudy night through an opening in the thatch. Drops of rainwater occasionally hissed and spluttered on the brands or hot stones below.

A huge wattle double screen, the gap between packed with insulating wool, divided the antechamber from Cartimandua's throne room. It was lined on both sides with a glittering array of shields, spears, harnesses, and swords—not the workaday kind, but of the weaponry and tack created by the Celts' most talented craftspeople, highly decorated with gold leaves and gemstones, filigreed and inlaid—in an arrogant and casual display of wealth.

Two men—one elfin, handsome and tall; the other, stocky, squat, muscled and brutal—stood warming their hands and drying themselves by the large iron brazier in the antechamber. The shorter of the two, Vellocate, had been initially attracted to a detailed examination of the wall-mounted arsenal but had exhausted his professional curiosity as an armour-bearer and was now showing signs of irritation and impatience.

The slimmer man, Venute, was holding back the first with soft words and subtle bodily signals as one would cautiously leash and hobble a blooded mastiff.

Though the two men were friends, comrades in arms, the slighter warrior was clearly master not only of the bull-muscled creature but of himself. His companion gave the appearance of being a servant to a master and a slave to his emotions.

Venute was lithe and hard-muscled, pale-skinned, bronze-haired, and dark-eyed, indicating a genetic part-inheritance from the pre-Celtic Beaker folk, those the Celts themselves named *tylwydd teg,* "the beautiful people," "the fairy-blessed." He moved with graceful confident economy or not at all; though even in perfect poise and stillness, his sharp eyes took all in, and the complex muscles of his face fleetingly echoed the faintest intimation of his thoughts.

Long flowing hair, plaited and held with a bronze pin grip, curtained a high, unlined and youthful forehead. He was in his midtwenties. His full, sensuous, almost sneering lips and prominent cheekbones, over which brown eyes burned like sleepless sentinels, spoke of control—of self and others—and of intelligence untrammelled by sentiment.

He wore an intricate patterned leather tunic, the baggy strong linen breeches dyed plain dark blue, the colour of royalty or at least of considerable wealth. His strong twin-ply leather moccasins were tall-sided like boots. He was bareheaded, and a large black cape fastened with silver clasp was thrust well back off his shoulders to reveal a wealth of bronze armbands and a large richly patterned gold torc round his neck.

Venute was young chieftain of the Denovii, a tribe or clan of perhaps fifty interlinked families, farmers, and herders from the South Pennines. Hardy secretive mountain and moorland folk, they were in the first wave of settler Celts many generations ago, who mingled and interbred with the ancient ones, the small dark-haired residents of the island of Pretan. Thus, they were linked with the Brigantian royal bloodline, which claimed ancestry almost as old as the soil and of which Queen Cartimandua was the corporeal and spiritual head.

The weave and pattern of their cloth and stitching of their leather gear identified the two men as tribal brethren. What ultimately separated Venute from his bucolic companion was not the wealth of his jewellery but an almost indefinable arrogance and sophistication—the dust of a culture that had stepped irrevocably beyond the tribal.

At his father's behest, Venute had been educated in the southern fortress town of Camulodunum, Colchester, capital of the Catuvellauni, where his cousin King Cunobelin reigned over an ever-growing empire. King Cunobelin courted Roman culture and aped its architecture—a trait rebellious northerner Venute and his childhood companion Caradoc, Cunobelin's eldest son, encouraged each other to despise.

The second man was Vellocate, armour-bearer to the prince, chosen for his compactness. At war, Venute needed to see past and over his armour-bearer, who was also his charioteer. Bulk obstructed his view, his aim. But no warrior of the noble caste would be driven by a weakling; an armour-bearer and charioteer was expected to hold his own in the thick of skirmish. And Vellocate was more than capable of that.

The charioteer was simply dressed in a linen vest, leather and bronze embossed skullcap, brightly dyed laced-up jerkin and coarse woollen trousers tied at the knees with thong. He was blond-haired with a huge moustache and eyebrows, square in forehead and shoulder, tanned, and built like a shaggy northern ox.

"How much longer must we wait?" he asked. "This arrogant queen humiliates us. By what right—"

"By the right of the Great Goddess," said Venute quietly, his hand on his armour-bearer's chest. "Have patience. Go check the horses. There is no need for you to stay by my side." Venute glanced at the guards, posted at either side of the leathern doorway to the throne room. "As you can see, I am in good hands. I give you leave to enjoy yourself. We passed an ale hall on the way from the gatehouse. The night's young. When you've seen our animals are being looked after, go find a wench there. Think of ways in which you might cement the Brigantian confederacy."

After a moment's consideration, a broad smile broke out on the royal armour-bearer's face. "You mean . . . ?" And he made a crude sexual gesture. The prince nodded slightly, mirthlessly. "Then I'm gone," grinned Vellocate.

Alone, Venute reviewed the reasons he and Vellocate had made the trip to the nerve centre of the Brigantian confederacy. Queen Cartimandua's passion for horses was well known among her people, among whom she was known as Sleek Pony. She was an inspirational horsewoman.

Knowing these passions they had brought as gifts a string of fine-bred ponies from the Dark Peaks, the sandstone hill country south of Uellacaern—war animals they could ill spare.

Sometimes you must give much to receive much, he thought, consoling himself. This way we test the woman's mettle. If, in the future, we need help, she must respond. If she fails to do so, we will seek alliances with . . . others. The North Cymri, for instance, or the Cornovii or Deceangli. She must understand the difference between friend and foe and that our loyalty has its price.

"Venute!"

Vellocate tore back the hide that protected the antechamber door from the miserable rain outside. His eyes were wide.

"Come quickly!"

Drawing his heavy sword, the prince rushed out into the muddy night. Vellocate was running backwards, pointing to the huge thatched roof of the palace. Venute was just in time to see the dark shadow of a bird's wing in the light from the roof's open smoke hole and hear the scratch of claw and feather as it disappeared into the palace.

Vellocate had placed both hands over his chest, warding off evil spirits. Venute smiled at the superstition, rested his long-fingered hand on the fighter's shoulder. "The High Queen's consort is Hroc, the Black Rook, Vellocate," he whispered sarcastically in the warrior's ear. "I thought you knew. This bird from hell speaks to her, tells her which way the world turns. Don't be surprised, my fine soldier, if she should choose its company over ours."

Louder, he added, "And by your noise, I believed at least two legions from Rome were outside the gates, knocking to be let in. Off you go a-wenching, Vellocate."

Unlike the many traditional roundhouses inside the triple-walled fortress of Uellacaern, the palace was square-based, with immense smoke-stained timbers of oak reaching at an angle upwards to meet forty feet above the hearth. Thatched, it was adorned externally with black-eyed skulls skewered on high poles, the fallen warriors of the Carvetii, a northern tribe outside the Brigantian federation of fifteen, whose recent raids into Brigantia had been annoying the queen.

Inside the palace, a soot-bellied cauldron simmered centrally on the end of a chain slung from the massive beams above the fire's heat, the cauldron's shadow shuddering in the uneven dance of flames. Fumes rose from it into a golden mist that hovered way above the tallest head, a strange weaving cloud that distorted the vision.

But a cold odour of lamb's fat mixed queasily with the smell of damp wool, bringing the wanderer back to earth, and all was tinged with the acrid odour of ash and wood smoke.

In the dim light, remains of a meal enjoyed recently by the queen's servants and regrettably missed by her guests outside lay scattered on a long low table among wooden platters, soiled iron daggers, and wooden spoons and bowls.

Further into the shadows, three looms stood, casting huge black forms on the wattle-and-daub walls, their shuttles silent, their feeder spinning wheels in heavy shadow, laden with the next day's warp and weft. Over racks were stretched unfinished blankets, mats, a thick, luxurious cloak some house slave was weaving for her dowry. More mats littered the floor—some rough plain beaten flax, others cleverly patterned and soft underfoot.

Cartimandua's only attendant that night was the red-haired daughter of a Cymric chieftain, a child of the Ordovices, to whom the queen had promised a Brigantian husband. As was the custom, the thirteen-year-old was learning housecraft in a noble household before betrothal. The queen had dismissed her other attendants, and the girl was preparing her mistress for a late audience with her southern visitors.

"You, my dear, are my only hope."

Brigid, Great Goddess of all the Celts, stood behind Cartimandua, stroking the queen's glossy hair.

The child servant saw only vague movement in the flickering shadows, a trick or play in the air where the Goddess stood. She felt, perhaps, a tingle of electricity, a shiver of unease. A child of the Earth, she was unsure whether to interpret the sparkling coldness of the air that swirled silently round the Goddess as a clammy breath from the grave or the clean freshness of Elysian fields.

Warkk.

On the Goddess's shoulder stood Hroc, the great rook of foretelling, his beady infinite eyes glittering in the firelight.

Occasionally, he buried his slate-coloured beak with its ugly pouch into Brigid's hair, as if whispering to her. Occasionally, his wing stretched, a looming ragged shadow on the lamp-yellow daub walls behind the royal seat.

"*My only hope. Things are not as they used to be,*" the Goddess mused. "*In times long past, we used to walk among you—gods with men, men with gods. We would feast and carouse, make love, go to war riding at each other's side.*

"*Now all which must be done must be done by human hand. But do you remember your initiation ceremony at the Stones? Eve of Imbolc, under the light of the Dog Star, when you poured the first blood of your womb onto the altar, and the Earth received it? Your mother, Cybella, dedicated you to me when you were born, but it was only then, at the Stones, that you became mine utterly, only then when I began to love you as I love my own daughter, Arianrhod, beautiful Silver Wheel. Am I boring you?*" she said sharply.

Cartimandua's blue eyes shot wide open. "Heavens, no, Mother. Your touch is so gentle. I was wandering."

"Pardon, my lady?" The red-haired girl stopped, bowl in hand. Her mistress was talking to the air.

"*Then listen. A prince awaits you outside. He is offering the fealty of a small southern tribe, one of the fifteen. He is a clever man. He is the first of several emissaries. They will offer their loyalty in exchange for your protection. Queen Cybella let many of her alliances rust. You must not. The defence of the entire Northland depends on you. The Belgic tribes have melted like snow before Rome and its heathen hordes of bull and boar worshippers. These soldier boys have bled the flatlanders dry with demands for tribute and, in return, have offered them "kingdoms"—kingdoms they already owned before the legions landed!*"

"*Do not be fooled, my sweet, by Rome's promises. Bind your Brigantes together. Press Rome and its idolaters into the flat South and keep them there. Then one day, we may rule again . . .*"

The Goddess gripped Cartimandua's hair and tightened it. The queen struggled a little, grunted.

"My lady! Are you all right?"

"The Picti are raiding from the north, and the Scoti are landing in the west from Eireann. This prince and others after him will seek your armed strength to drive them out and offer, in return, their own force. Let the threat from the Pretani take second place in your thoughts. Who is the enemy? Who?"

"Rome is the enemy," said Cartimandua sullenly, as if in the classroom with an overbearing teacher.

"If my lady says so," muttered the Welsh maiden, curtseying.

"Rome, Rome, Rome is the enemy! And to destroy them, you will find that the strength of all is greater than that of the parts. If help is offered from further afield—from the Pretani in Cymru, for instance—take this too. But remember that honour can be costly."

"You are the clean, pure receptacle of the faith, the chalice of the old religion. I believe in you, trust you. You are my envoy on Earth, my bridge, my voice. Remember your Imbolc vows?" Brigid breathed in the queen's ear.

"I do, Mother." Cartimandua fingered the slim torc around her pale neck, unclasped it. She turned it in her lap, and it gleamed in the firelight, living golden fire, the eyes of the rook Hroc piercing her soul. The jewellery seemed to writhe, to grow bigger, to fill her vision.

She was unaware that the maidservant had crept closer, mouth agape. Who *was* the queen talking to? She reached out her hand, soothingly, for it seemed to her the queen was distressed.

"You keep the torc close by you, I see. Remember your promise always. No harm shall come to you if you keep the faith. The torc is the symbol and sign of our bond. Now use our strength, our union, to bind the tribes together, my sweet. Hold the torc before you at all times. Bind them."

Hroc's wings spread, and his shadow filled the hall. A log crashed, and a shower of sparks rose into the thatch. Cartimandua, released from the Goddess's grip, leapt to her feet and turned, screaming. The handmaiden shot backwards, eyes wide in fear.

Cartimandua snatched a shortsword from the wall behind her. "Bitch! You are not the Goddess! How dare you touch me!"

In the antechamber, Venute and the guards exchanged glances. A horrific scream tore the air. All three rushed into the royal hall, swords drawn.

The child lay in a spreading pool of her own blood, her eyes dimming, her slit throat pulsing ever slower. The prince strode to Cartimandua.

"Lady, are you all right? Was this creature a traitor?" he said quietly, scanning the room's shadows. "How did this happen?"

The queen flung her bloodstained sword to the ground. Her fingers urgently stroked the torc. "A traitor? No no. Yes! She pretended to be—someone else. She tried to strangle me. How dare you question me! On your knees before your high queen!"

"Lady." Venute knelt briefly, signalled the dumbfounded guards to attend to the stricken child. Then he rose, eyes glittering.

"You have wasted a life," he said without flinching. "I have no doubt in such a privileged household she was a noble's daughter. These things, once done—"

Cartimandua held out the palm of her hand imperiously, silencing him. Seconds passed.

"You need to remember, prince of the Carvetii, that you are in the presence of one blessed by the Great Goddess," Cartimandua said menacingly, composure regained. "If I choose, or if She choose, you could leave this life as quickly as the red-haired child did. I regret the girl died. There was a misunderstanding. I may have no similar regret for the death of one who questions my motives and authority, for they will have earned their death. What do you say?"

The prince smiled. But it was frozen, calculated. Cartimandua was caught in its glare. "You are entirely right, lady," said Venute and let his gaze drop. "I have offered advice without warrant. I have not spoken as one ought in the presence of my queen."

Do I detect sarcasm? Cartimandua stared at the bowed head of the man in front of her. How his hair gleamed in the firelight! She noted down the perspective of his strong nose, and behind the disguise of his thrusting moustache, his lips still curled in amusement. A warrior's face. A nobleman's face.

A dead man's face. If I so choose.

As near a match for her in cleverness, subtlety, cruelty, thirst for control, perhaps. An ally.

A competitor.

"*He's yours if you want him,*" said a voice inside—the Goddess? Excitement rose in Cartimandua's throat. Her buttocks tensed. "*You can have anything you want. You are the high queen.*" She felt her back start to curve like a stroked cat's, her nipples suddenly exquisitely sensitive. She became aware of a warmth between her thighs, beneath the folds of her skirts. *The violence, the iron smell of blood. I need his hands in my hair, his head between my breasts, his lips . . .*

"*Then take him. He is yours.*"

"Thank you, Blessed Goddess," she murmured.

Wings flapped dustily in the throne room's distant gloom. If Venute heard them or Cartimandua, he gave no sign. She spoke louder, though there was a quiver of desire in her voice.

"It is late. You have travelled far in bad weather. I shall inspect your homage tomorrow, and we'll discuss what you expect in return. We'll ride together." Cartimandua made a little gesture of dismissal. Venute saw it and, annoyed, toyed just long enough with the notion of an insolent response for the queen to notice. She coloured, her lips hardened. The prince took her hand and kissed it.

"As the queen commands," he said and left the chamber.

4

CARTIMANDUA, DRESSED LOOSELY IN PURPLE flax with a gold-threaded woollen shawl, idly studies her armoury in the high echoing hall of the palace of Uellacaern. Though it is yet spring and rainclouds hang low overhead, she has the summer slinking indolence of a cat on a roof.

Epona, mare Goddess, rides sidesaddle. Her long-maned pony raises a foreleg high. The Goddess too is long-maned like her mount, with staring remorseless eyes. Cartimandua strokes the brass with the tip of a long manicured finger, thinking, *I can ride better, faster than the Goddess. When I ride, I am the Horsewoman, Woman Horse, Mare, and the wind flies through my hair. I went to the oak grove and worshipped with Aduna, and Epona blessed me. But I am, of course, still bound to the Lady, and Epona knows this, respects this. All my stables shall bear Epona's likeness, and all tack shall carry her likeness also, either in brass or carven in wood or embossed or hammered in leather. In this way, the Goddess will make fertile my animals, give them easy labour, and give me horses for war and trade and breeding that will be known throughout the land.*

Aduna says, "My lady."

Cartimandua turns with a sharp intake of breath. The high priestess has arrived silently at her bidding, though the queen cannot for the moment remember why she called her. The two women, Aduna and the Cartimandua, salute each other with short bows; the druid, she who understands the oak, is the high priestess of Brigantia, and Cartimandua is queen. Both serve the Goddess. In the eyes of the Goddess, both are equal.

Aduna, sharp face in shadow beneath her cowl, bronze sickle knife tied at her waist, is grey-haired as a badger, slightly stooped; the dark eyes that burned with a lifetime of passion in the service of the Great Mother are heavy-lidded now, if no less piercing.

"I called you for a purpose. There is a question in my mind."

"Then, as always, I shall attempt to answer it, my lady."

"Is this a good time to be handfast?" Cartimandua takes the druid's hand and places it on her forehead briefly, as if asking a blessing.

"Ask those who are handfast, my queen," says Aduna cautiously. "I am bound only to the Goddess in all Her forms."

"No no, Aduna. Is this a good time to *get* handfast?"

Aduna clicks her tongue disapprovingly, holds the young queen by her slender hard shoulders.

"To the tall one, the horse trader? Venute? This is what you want to know? I can tell you this for nothing—he is a shrewd and strong man, and he will become wiser and more powerful. He is of noble lineage, and though his people are small in number, they are proud and true to the faith of Pretan. For the rest—for the future—let the world beyond tell it. Come with me. Come with me."

The women fling on cloaks—Aduna, the uniform grey of her high priestess calling; Cartimandua, a sumptuous woollen sagum with a fine gold snake clasp. Guards hold open the leather doors of the palace, guards salute at the high entranceway of Uellacaern. Two bodyguards follow at a discreet distance as the women make their way along a sheep-cropped path by the river Isara, the Winding One, that in later days would be called the Wharfe. But

Aduna turns and sternly warns them against following further as they approach the alder grove.

Aduna finds a narrow winding path. Cartimandua follows closely. Briars tug at their clothes. The queen is soon disorientated. "Aduna, slower," she calls, and the druid grimly notes the anxiety in her voice.

The sky is lowering but bright with diffuse sunlight; Aduna is sure that the day will clear. The ground is sodden and a fresh earthy smell rises invigoratingly from it. The sun is glowing somewhere in those banks of cloud, and birds are singing; *the Goddess is near.*

The path opens out into a green hollow. At the far side, a small rock face is topped by an ancient oak, whose roots seem to clutch the stones like coiled snakes, crushing them together. Beneath, a large flat stone has been slightly hollowed to form a natural altar. Aduna sits down on it and gestures the queen to join her.

"Is the Goddess here?" whispers Cartimandua, looking around apprehensively.

"There is something so unbearably naive about you," chides Aduna. "The Goddess is in your blood. You have known this since childhood. You are not afraid to use Her power. Yet you seem to forget that She is three in one, the Macha, the Morrigan, as our cousins in the western mountains and over the western seas call Her—virgin, all that is lovely and innocent and pure; earth mother, bountiful giver of harvest, protectress of mothers and their children; and harridan of the battlefield, death on wings, corpse maker, the hunter of souls, vengeance.

"Only when you can embrace all three aspects of the Goddess will you really worship Her."

"I'm sorry," says Cartimandua, a tear in her blue eye. She is like a child again, affected by the spring air and the smells and sounds of growing things. Or perhaps she is in love. "You have taught me this so often. But more often than not, I hear only the Hag's voice, the voice of doom."

"And what does She tell you?"

"To make alliances with our separated and distant kin. To fight Rome. To protect Her land with blood and fire if necessary."

The priestess sighs. Suddenly, she turns and grips Cartimandua's arms, stares into her blue eyes. "Listen to the Goddess, child. Listen to Her quiet voice, the voice that speaks of love, of union with the blessed Earth."

Aduna is thinking, *Can this child be the Blessed One, the one chosen by the Goddess? Why, then, can she not hear the messages that shout from every skein of life? She is old enough.*

Aduna reaches to touch the roots of the oak and begins a low prayer chant. "O-ooozhah-zhah-zhah. O-oo. Mei. Me-me-me-mei-oooh. Zhah!" As she sings, a shaft of light breaks though the clouds and pours into the grove. Everything is golden.

Cartimandua closes her eyes, raises clasped hands to heaven in the way she has been taught. But no revelation comes to her. When Aduna has finished, she fidgets.

"What is it like—serving the Goddess?"

"Oh, child. What is it like being alive? It is like—holding hands with the Earth. All life has its rhythms and cycles. Sit still somewhere. Think about nothing. Feel how the world flows through you first; recognise your hunger and cramp, where the sun burns your skin and where the wind numbs you, then find the place where all of this no longer matters. You may find it above yourself or below yourself. But it is there—always there.

"Now watch how the flowers blow in the breeze or how the silver fish move in the stream, how the flocks of chaffinch or starling wheel and turn or how the clouds travel, some fast, some slow, some dark, some light, like the music of the pipes, the shells, the horns and the lyres with the drums, all together. Or lie on your back and watch the heavens racing past and feel the Earth's deep song. Or put your back to one of the ancient stones our forefathers buried and blessed. And just listen.

"The elders of our faith in years gone by learned to be so quiet inside they could tell where the Earth's lines lay—where the power flowed, where to find hidden water, where to find the clay for fine pottery and metals for swords and coins and ornaments. The Earth holds secrets only to the blind, the daylight fool. For the wise, everything is visible—the sap in the leaf and bole, the blood in the veins, the thoughts in the head, the lie of the stones in the soil.

"The wise can see what the daylight fool calls the dead. The dead are all around us in a world separated from what we call our own by the thinnest of barriers. Nothing dies. The stuff of the Earth endlessly reforms. Nothing dies."

Aduna strokes the child queen's soft face. "Let's go back."

"See how lightly my finger touches the mirror. See how my breath clouds the mirror then disappears. See how the mirror *bends*—"

"Lady!" Aduna was shocked. Finest Belgic bronze with beautiful scrollwork, tiny inlaid mother-of-pearl stars, a queen's ransom . . .

"But who's behind the mirror? My dreams, Aduna. I could hardly sleep. What do you truly think of the prince Venute, newly arrived with war ponies?"

"A head turner, I'm sure," said the high priestess haughtily. "But I am no old alehouse gossip or matchmaker. I am the servant of the living Goddess. It is the festival of Medb this full moon, and I have much to prepare. I haven't time for this," she said, brushing Cartimandua's hand from her robe then, almost absently, stroking her royal mistress's lavish hair. "Don't bother me with your lusts."

No one but Aduna could have got away with such insouciance. But for Aduna, Queen Cybella's closest aide and nursemaid to the young Cartimandua, her druid guide, there seemed no line to step over. They had never been parted, not for a day. Both accepted this easy relationship without thought.

"Matchmaker?" Cartimandua spun round on her bench. "Who said anything about matchmaking? I speak of alliances."

"Then speak to your mareschals, my lady."

"That may be necessary. You may go now."

The queen called for a large bowl of warm water and soap and washed thoroughly, more thoroughly than she had for weeks. She chose oils and herbs from her array of jars and anointed herself as if preparing for a religious festival. She had slaves comb her long dark hair and braid it. She applied a little ruan—a reddish dye made from a herb—with great care, highlighting the smooth skin of her high cheeks with practised skill; darkened her eyebrows with berry juice; painted her fingernails.

She chose her riding gear, and as she broke fast with porridge, bread, and fruit, called her mareschal-in-chief, a stocky dark Brigantian named Ewan, to bring her up to date on the infuriating incursions of the Parisii on her eastern frontier that were at the core of Venute's diplomatic mission.

"And tell Venute I will meet him at the stables," she finished carelessly as Ewan backed away to leave. "I shall inspect his gifts."

"These are excellent ponies," said Cartimandua. "Strong, young, well broken. The mares will breed well with our own bloodlines. This one"—she indicated a narrow-headed, somewhat fretful stallion—"will be a challenge. He is strong-willed, and his eyes speak of unpredictability. I shall ride him myself today. He wants his own way. But there will be only my way." She stoked his long muzzle. "I'll call him Kestrel. He has the look of a predator."

"These animals have cost your people dearly. You have my gratitude. But you want something else."

Venute smiled. The queen, tall and lithe, was only an inch or two shorter than Venute and held herself like a warrior. Her eyelashes were long and dark and bowed. Her scent, of open fields and the shade of hedgerows in summer, mingled with the warm odours of straw bedding and manure in the stable and the drift of smoke from a brazier in the yard outside. For a moment, Venute forgot his mission and fumbled his reply.

"I, ah, want something else."

The queen's lips pouted. Venute looked into her eyes and drowned in their dazzling blueness.

"And that would be?" she asked softly.

Venute struggled to regain his composure. "The gifts symbolise my people's loyalty to the house of Brigantia and our desire to throw in our lot with the confederacy, obviously," he said, clearing his throat. "But yes, we do need your help. Specifically, over the continuing attacks from the Parisii on our eastern front. We would ask that our warriors carry the colours of Brigantia on their shields . . ."

"It's granted."

"And that, if the Parisii should launch a major attack on our territories, that the Brigantes should rally to our cause in such numbers as to drive the eastlanders back with such force they do not return in our lifetimes."

"You have that undertaking. I swear by the Goddess Brigid Herself. I shall train Kestrel here to crush skulls with his hooves, and he and I shall lead the cream of Brigantia into battle ourselves. I look forward to it. But tell me this, Venute," she said, touching his forearm. "If the confederacy should find itself under attack, may we expect the Denovii to send warriors to our aid?"

"That's the deal."

"And if a queen should call on a prince's personal allegiance . . ."

She reached closer to him, her breath on his cheek. Her raven hair touched his lips. For a moment, he could scarcely breathe.

Then she spun away, holding her skirts above the stable floor and began to saddle the stallion.

"Ride with me. Where is your man?"

Venute was taken aback by Cartimandua's sudden change of direction. *How does this woman's mind work?*

Venute's dark eyes narrowed. "Vellocate? I dismissed him to the house by the gate last night and have not seen him since, lady. As far as I know, he's still with the women. That, or sleeping off the ale." He tapped a small horn at his side. "He will come if called."

The queen laughed. "I don't want your man around. I just want you."

Venute saw the look in her eye. A riot of thoughts passed through his head, and he shook it vigorously. Finally, he turned to what he knew best, slapping a pony's rump. "These are fine animals. Chariot-broken but excellent for riding. They will serve you well."

"So might you."

"So I might." He threw a saddle on his own mount and turned to face her. "Just how close an alliance might the queen be looking for?"

The same wry smile as last night. Cartimandua screamed with delight. "The race is to the Cow and Her Calf." She pointed to the misty hills where, a mile away, an outcrop of rock broke the moorland skyline. "I'll show you how close an alliance I'm looking for when we get there."

"I have no dignity. Only power," she breathed. They stood on the crags looking down on Uellacaern. Wisps of smoke drifted away from the miniature town on the banks of the Isara and were lost the moment they passed over the palisades. Yesterday's rain had freshened the air and repainted the river meadows, the alder and birch groves at its side, and the blue hills beyond with clean colour.

"Naked cruel power in this world and the next. The Goddess is always at my side. We walk together always. Remember this." She touched his sleeve, the slightest touch, palm out then down, chiding yet intimate. "I need someone like you. Someone strong, imperious. I need a warrior as skilful as myself. They are all cowards round here. I know when a swordsman is feinting. I know when my opponent's stone or arrow falls short or fails to hit a strawhead target, that I am being condescended to."

She looked at Venute slyly. "You are not that kind of man. I feel it in my bones. I can wrestle—" And so saying, she darted a foot behind Venute's heel and threw him. As Venute, surprised, tried to struggle to his feet, she whipped from her jewel-studded girdle an ivory-handled dagger and held it to his throat, her knee between his shoulder blades.

Venute raised both hands, palms on the ground above his head. "I yield, lady," he said.

But in the instant Cartimandua relaxed her grip, Venute's reached back like sure lightning, grasped the queen's head firmly and hurled her over his shoulder, turning and rising as he did so. The knife slithered across the ground. The queen screeched as, with a snake's speed, Venute pinned her to the ground with his knee and held her jaw tightly between thumb and forefinger.

"There's one thing we should understand from the outset," he breathed through clenched teeth. "There will be no feinting, no mercy, no tolerance. In one respect only do I recognise you as a woman."

Cartimandua's eyes fixed on her oppressor. This was the game, *the* game. Venute's smoking brown eyes challenged the naked blue of Cartimandua's for what seemed an age.

"This is no place to talk about alliances, lady," he said, relaxing his gaze finally, helping her to her feet and gripping her forearms tightly. "If you would care to return to the square house, we might dismiss your servants, and I will help you out of your dirty clothes."

"How very informal you've suddenly become, Venute," she smiled, her eyes flashing with victory.

Venute gently unclasped Cartimandua's copper-studded leather riding tabard, and she slipped deftly out of it, loosening her hair and swirling it. She touched his nose provocatively.

"You shall be my foremost slave, I think."

"I think not, lady," said Venute quietly, grasping her slim wrist. "No Denovii was ever a slave."

"You are hurting your queen."

"Lady, I came here as an emissary. The elders of my people were curious to know what kind of woman our new queen was. I came to do business, trading like for like, war ponies for military support in time of trouble, loyalty for loyalty, debt for debt." He was breathing hoarsely in her ear, her wrist still suspended. "This"—his finger traced the smooth skin at Cartimandua's naked shoulder, making her shudder—"is new, requires thought."

"You are a warrior, Venute, and a prince of high blood. Don't tell me your seed has never been shed in pleasure or to honour the Goddess or both."

"You may find it hard to play queen on your back, lady, just as I may find it hard to play emissary or humble outlander princeling."

And should we go further—should the impossible happen and our dynasties are fused—what then?

With a subtle twist, he brought Cartimandua's hand down to her side, held her from behind round the narrow waist, kissed her neck so gently she half-turned to confirm his touch; and he held her cheek, felt her breath, kissed her parted lips firmly. Their breathing deepened, moved in harmony.

He slipped the straps of her brushed woollen shift from her shoulders and helped it smoothly to her waist over the long soft curve of her thighs and buttocks.

Cartimandua turned regally to face him. Her body had been blessed by the triple Goddess; it was without discernible blemish, save for the tattoos of her caste and dedication to Brigid—silk smooth, athletically muscled. In the shadow beneath her dark-nippled right breast was the blue-tattooed double fylfot, the Goddess's sign of eternal life. And at her neck was a golden torc with a spread-winged bird, whose ruby eyes stared unblinkingly at the prince. He moved towards her.

"Let me take this—"

"Touch this and you die," she said harshly, stepping back, clutching the torc to her neck.

Venute spread his hands, smiling. "I'm sorry. A taboo. I could not have known—"

Cartimandua stepped forwards, began to unlace his tunic, tiptoed to breathe in his ear, "The Goddess's gift. I wear it always. No one touches it but me. You could not have known." She kissed the bronze whorls of hair on his chest.

"Should we sacrifice?"

The lamplight flickered its seductive bronze over their glistening bodies. The queen's leather-stitched wool-packed bed creaked.

"I think not," whispered Venute. "The gods may be kind and cruel in turn. Let us be likewise. I shall be Borvo and you Damona, healers both. Tonight, let all live. What do you think, lady?"

Cartimandua laughed. "Let all live. I have no prisoners, no slaves who are sullen and work-shy, no handmaidens who have offended me—now, not even the young brat who assaulted me. Let all live. But you must take this. It is my custom. It brings me nearer the Great Mother." She handed him a shallow bowl in which dark herbs had been crushed. The odour was of fennel and mould.

"I take nothing. I go into this clearheaded. Not even wine, mead. Afterwards—who knows?"

"For this insult, this rejection of Her liquor, the Goddess will turn your rod to jelly."

"Now I think you have found for yourself that this is not true. Enough. You have a man's grip."

"A man! And how would you know how a man's grip felt—here? So Vellocate is more than an armour-bearer. The rumours are true!"

"What rumours? Ah. Ah-hah. Don't play these games with me, woman."

"Who is dearest to your heart?"

"I have no spouse, no lover."

"I would have her killed. No, I meant, of the gods. Who rides with you as the Mother rides with me in my fine chariot, as Epona sisters me on the wild moors?"

"Cernunnos. The Denovii's chief god, the stag king of the forest. To him, we owe our livelihood. He leads us to the fruits of the forest in due season, shows us the lair of the wolf, the sett of the badger, the form of the hare on the moors. He is in the changing light of the groves and makes the fountains sing and shine. He leads us to the sacred toadstool for the autumn rites. There are some who worship Artio, and she is indeed a powerful goddess, others Borvo or Taranis or Medb, but all ultimately acknowledge our Lady Brigid as queen." Venute raised himself on his elbow. His eyes sparkled in the firelight. "Cernunnos appears in many guises. For him to appear as himself, I wear the horned helmet."

"And then are you he?"

"You ask a strange thing. How many dance at Lughnasa? Let us count the stars—are there more than there are grains of sand? Why does mistletoe grow on oak? Are you the Goddess Brigid?"

"That I am. There are times when She and I are one or when She and I are mother and daughter. Or sisters, twin sisters."

"Then if I do this—or this—to my queen, I do it also to the Goddess?"

Venute kissed her on the lips, the breasts, the belly, and in the salt of her groin, where his tongue gently probed the hardness that was the seat of her sensitivity. She arched and moaned. "Surely you can feel Her? She runs in my blood, in the heat of my cheeks, in the scent of my skin and loins. You can—feel—the hot rivers She sends to greet you."

"Then this is in honour of the Goddess," breathed Venute, his eyes glittering in the firelight. And he parted her thighs and thrust home.

Feathers shuffled uncomfortably in the gloom above.

5

AD 48, Corinium Dobunnorum (Cirencester)

"HOW LONG HAVE WE BEEN in these bloody islands?" Ostorius Scapula, successor to Aulus Plautius as governor of Britain, slammed the leather shutters on a windy, shower-strewn night that was dragging slowly towards dawn. He turned to his drinking companion Julius Constantius, the *legatus juridicus* and governor of the newly founded fortress town of Corinium in the heartland of the docile tribe of the Dobunni, in whose enclave he was guest.

"Five years, sir, give or take," said Constantius.

The two men could hardly have been less similar in looks and build. Ostorius Scapula was altogether a dark man—drab-skinned and pockmarked of face with cropped but obviously curly black hair combed forwards in the current Roman senatorial style, hair neither long nor luxuriant enough to cover the bald gleam of a sword scar that started above his left ear and tapered out in a cluster of disfiguring lumps at his chin. He was long-nosed and thick-lipped and covered in body hair, yet despite his obvious physical disadvantages, he remained an awesome bulk of a man at forty-two years in his military prime. He carried himself regally and was known as a brutal and uncompromising commander, even among those who had conquered most of the known world with unequivocal brutality, yet he was liked by officers and respected by the men.

Julius Constantius was tall, graceful, slender, with the athletic appearance of a runner and the bearing of a patrician. Yet there was a kind of slow, lethal menace in his movement, the flicker of his cold grey-blue eyes, the way his long slim fingers arched and played cat and mouse with thoughts. He reclined on a couch, one of the Spartan room's few luxuries; furnishings to his express order were on their way from Italia, Tarraconensis—northern and central Spain—and the craft houses of Germanica.

Scapula, on the other hand, was restless, ticking off what was known and acknowledged and supposed and imagined.

"And all the Celtic tribes of southern Britannia are subjugated or driven out, west and north?"

"They are, sir."

"This is good." Scapula scratched a tooth pensively. "Yet we are undermanned and undersupplied, and our outposts are constantly at risk. And not a day's march away, there lives the biggest flea that ever vexed a dog."

Constantius nodded.

"So what should we do, Constantius, constant friend? How do we persuade that noble prince of the subjugated Catuvellauni, Carad—Caroc—"

"Caratacus, sir. The natives call him Caradoc."

"Whatever, to hand over his sword?" Scapula gestured vaguely in the westwards across the shrouded Cotswolds in the direction of the land of the Cymri, high mysterious Wales, beyond the shutters that hissed and clattered in the wind.

"He will never do that, sir. He's too much in love with his own image, the roving pirate, Mr. Charisma of the loyal tribes." Constantius used the Greek *khárisma*, his lip curling in sarcasm.

Both men, experienced soldiers, were playing down the resistance leader's significance as a major thorn in the flesh. Both understood the paradox posed by the prince's continued rebellion; Caratacus could no more stop the Roman Empire's juggernaut than a cup of water could douse a forest fire. But the man's presence just out of Rome's grasp, stirring insurrection and unrest among the tribes of Wales, whence he had fled following his defeat at the crossing of the Medway, was as an immense irritant and a frustration. He was a sore that could not be salved, a drain on resources that for the present neither man could afford. They were extended to the limit, exposed to the point where a continued war of attrition or a full-frontal assault could break them.

And both suspected that Caradoc, Caratacus, was set on a course they could do little to prevent. Alive, the Celtic hero. Dead, the Celtic martyr.

This was a career issue for Scapula just as, 102 years earlier, it had been for Julius Caesar.

Both Romans knew the military cost of guerilla warfare. Scapula had seen it firsthand in the foothills of Pannonia, Hungary, under his commander Aulus Plautius, whom he followed to Britannia; and Constantius started his service in Judaea, both territories seething with rebels, fanatics, and suicidal zealots.

"Aulus Plautius was too soft," said Scapula. "He did well to play the Atrebates tribe off against the Catuvellauni, but he should have gripped that bastard—Caratacus—round the neck and squeezed. He had him at the Medway when Flavius and Sabinus Vespasianus made a mess of things and Hosidius Geta had to sort them out. He had him"—Scapula shuffled the untidy pile of campaign maps on the table before him and stabbed a finger at Durobrivae, Rochester—"here, and the slippery son of Hecate slithered out from under yet again."

Constantius sipped wine pensively from a Celtic cup, stroking the intertwining patterns of its silver with the long white pad of a thumb.

"We've gone from east to west, right across the country, and he's fallen all the way. We've pushed him to the edge of the land of the Silures, but we can't bury him in Cymru. The hillmen run to him like cats to rotting fish."

Scapula's brow gathered like thundercloud.

"He has persuaded the Silures of southern Cymru to fight and die for him, and when we have beaten them, he will run north to the . . ."—Scapula pushed maps and documents to one side—"the Ordovices, and when they are all dead . . . where will he go?"

"He will attempt to turn the Brigantes to his cause, I guess," said Constantius. "As I've argued before, we don't think he'll go to the Scoti in northern Hibernia, Ireland, the Pretani in Gaul, or the Pictii . . . at least, not while his best chance of preventing our penetration north is to use the Brigantian confederation—"

Scapula finished his sentence. "As a buffer state. That host of hairy Brigantian brutes and their mad queen. Hmm."

His commanders, and especially Constantius, had warned that a strong push from the north and west—from the remnant of the Silurian forces and the as yet unconquered Ordovices, together with the Brigantes—could at best set colonisation back by years, at worst, push him off the island.

He didn't believe they were strong enough, united enough, but he saw no reason to stand idle and let the opportunities for rebellion be created. He saw genuine trade opportunities with Cartimandua, queen of the numerically largest of the northern confederations, the Brigantes; they smelted lead, iron, and copper; produced quality wool, leather, and furs; bred ferocious hunting hounds; and created intricate and beautiful jewellery, all of which needed the kind of markets Ostorius Scapula was talented at manipulating.

But he would not make Cartimandua rich so that she could bite the hand that fed her. He would not arm her forces, which spies said could number fifteen thousand warriors. The key was neutralisation.

Caratacus out of the picture. Her strategist husband Venutius too. If those two got their heads together . . .

Cartimandua, he felt intuitively, held the key. There was a pressing military reason why he should woo the queen. He, like Caradoc, wanted the Brigantes to act as a buffer between the "civilised" south and the wild north. Unlike Caradoc, though, he wanted Cartimandua to absorb the Pictish reivers and the Irish landing parties to protect his right flank as he hit the Cymri hard.

For this, it was necessary at the very least to neutralise the Brigantes. Such tactics—deceit, bribery—were vital, unavoidable. He could not subdue the north by force. Yet.

And Scapula was under no delusions; if Caradoc ever reached the Brigantian heartland, the prince of the Catuvellauni's brutish charisma could undo months, years of subtle persuasion. He said as much to his legate.

Constantius agreed and added: "Our intelligence is that the Queen Cartimandua has the greatest of scorn for those British kingdoms she believes are puppets of Rome." But Constantius's mouth twisted, and his eyes glittered with amusement.

Scapula leaned back on his canvas chair and laughed sarcastically. "And, of course, she is not a puppet. She is strong and independent. She will never accept a bribe."

He needed Cartimandua under his control until he could create further legions from auxiliaries—the Belgi, for instance—and summon the legions' strength for further conquest. There was much political work to be done there with Rome, and communications were so slow these days, so slow.

Scapula's eyes glazed. The governor's sudden stillness caused Constantius to hold his breath. The crackling of the fire, the muted thump of sentries' hobnailed sandals on the walls, and the whine of a distant wind on the stone quoins of the rough-built fort were an intrusion that the legate would have wished away if he could.

"I have a plan, Constantius. I wonder ... let's make her stronger and more independent by sending her gifts."

"Gifts, sir?"

"Gifts. Make a note! Young slaves. Belgic children. Arretine ware—a cartload. Wine. But the cheapest. These savages will not know the difference. Other things the creatures are unlikely to have seen before. Zebra and leopard hides. Concentrate on items of splendid appearance rather than content or quality. I'm sure you understand."

Constantius snapped his fingers. No room in Roman high command was ever devoid of servants, however empty and private it appeared; and from behind a screen emerged a bleary-eyed little ferret of a Greek scribe, opening a parchment and unclipping writing gear from a rosewood box as he scurried to a corner desk. As the Greek worked to Constantius's direction, Scapula reviewed the position.

Despite his humour, it was not good.

From Publius Ostorius Scapula Governor of Britannia in the name of The Emperor of Rome, Tiberius Claudius Drusus Nero Germanicus, to the mighty Cartimandua Queen of all the North—

Greetings!

"I would never have believed I could sink this low, Constantius."

"Your Majesty, please accept the accompanying tokens of our esteem in the spirit of friendship in which they are sent and in the knowledge that they but poorly represent our emperor's regard for your realm and person.

"It is our earnest wish that the empire and the people of Brigantia should live together in peace and that we should explore the many possibilities of trade and cultural exchange that such a peace opens before us.

"It would be a personal honour if you would use my emissary to respond to this letter by return.

"There is no need that our interests should ever conflict. Rome has much to offer you."

"Oh, and do make sure to send a translator. That illiterate heathen will know no Latin, and we can't be sure her southern-educated lover boy—what's his name? Venutius—will be home from his rather unfortunate attempts to create a Brigantian tribal union. Thank the gods the Fifteen Tribes spend most of their time at each other's throats."

The governor stood up and stretched his stocky frame until bones popped in their sockets. "I'm old and tired, Constantius," he sighed. "I have no taste for courting this northern horse-trading queen and her cold-fish husband. The truth is, all I want is Caratacus captured. Alive, in this hand, so that every savage in this soggy, cold godforsaken island can see their hero winched into the sky by his testicles."

6

I T WAS NIGH ON MIDSUMMER, the feast of Lugh of the many talents, the "Long Hand". A propitious time, most said, for handfasting.

In the stone circle, Venute stripped off the handfast regalia, weapons, and clothes. He stood naked before his armour-bearer.

"Take care of these, Vellocate," he whispered, holding out the bundle. "It's required at this time that I carry no armour."

Vellocate glanced down at his master's loins, grinning. "You, er, will be keeping the spear, though, my lord?"

"Very good, Vellocate. Very witty."

Vellocate coughed, glanced round at the assembly—the druidic elect and acolytes, visiting chieftains and their retinues, warriors of all Brigantia and their spouses, Uellacaern's elders and slaves, even some of the older children. Over the silent crowd, a soft unearthly harmony of druidic voices hovered, almost beyond human hearing—the Song of the Stones.

"May the gods' luck be with you, m'lord. She is a beautiful woman."

Cartimandua stood, arms folded, dressed simply but gloriously in a soft flowing purple sagum, her unbraided hair heavily garlanded with summer flowers and flowing gently in the breeze. Like a statue she was, near the Dog Stone, guarded by grey-cloaked adepts. Her eyes were turned skywards; bronze light struck from her high cheekbones; the gold and mother-of-pearl clasp of her cloak gleamed in the evening sunlight.

Lost in some parallel world, she ignored her husband-to-be as he was led to the altar stone and laid gently across its multitude of carven whorls and mazes. Venute felt the gritty sun-warmed stone beneath his shoulder blades, buttocks, calves, and heels; lowered himself into the cradle of the Earth, the Great Mother; calmed himself; and waited to hear Her voice.

A shadow passed over him. Aduna—her face a ceremonial mask of woad and lime, an intricate swirling map of blue and white—presented the razor-sharp ceremonial knife before his glazed eyes.

"As queen's consort, Prince Venute, it is the custom you should carry the Mother's mark on your flesh. Do you agree to this?"

"I agree."

"Louder, my lord."

"I agree."

Aduna placed the bowl of dye on his taut stomach. Chanting softly, rhythmically, eyes closed, Aduna dipped and pierced, dipped and pierced. Venute clenched his teeth, bore the pain as the blade stitched a pattern into the skin of his chest.

Finally, the dedication was over. Some drug, probably in the dye, had started to work insidiously on his consciousness. The wounded area burned like fire. Venute felt it would eat into his heart.

The westering sun cast long purple shadows across the moorland grasses. In the stillness before the handfast ceremony began, it was difficult to determine which were those of humans and which of the standing stones. Supine on the altar stone, naked, Venute breathed steadily, deeply as he had been instructed by Aduna. The great cobalt vault of the sky had begun to rotate around him as she had predicted; though the prince could not see

Taranis, he could hear the great god of the sky whispering and the wheel of the world turning upon the single point, the axle and zenith infinitely above his head.

The dry smell of cooling gritstone sand, the wild tang of early heather, the bruised and heady odour of bracken, all began to fade from his nostrils. A breeze was springing from the south, where the low hills were dipped in summer heat-haze grey. The slow chanting of the adepts and their intricate weaving-column dance was joined in ragged fashion by the marriage witnesses who crowded the slopes of the shallow depression in which the Stones lay, and a skin drum thudded rhythmically like a heartbeat.

"Mighty Taranis, who orders the stars and the sun on their invisible courses, speak now!"

The drum notes and dance abruptly ended.

Silence.

Then after a pause so long Venute thought his heart would stop, the crippled rumble of the thunder god's hammer beat across the distant horizon.

"Taranis has spoken. In praise and thanks, let the Earth be watered."

Ministrants sprinkled water over the warm sandy soil and magical stones; a scent of summer rain rose up, so sweet Venute felt like weeping.

"Beloved Arianrhod, queen of heaven, daughter of Don, the maker of all that breathes, let your son, dexterous Lugh, upon whose festival day we forge this royal union, now drive the sun chariot to the world of the dead, taking with him these two souls for burial, that they may pass through the death of self and be reborn as one in the new light of the morrow. Bless them, beloved Arianrhod, with fruitful loins. Let fecund Rosmerta, many-breasted, suckle and infuse them with new life."

Aduna's voice, deep and powerful, was thickening and cracking with emotion, rising to crescendo.

"And may the Great Mother, our goddess and guardian and life-giver, descend upon you and protect you now and forever!"

The high priestess stretched out her arms, beckoning Cartimandua forwards. The adepts parted like a grey cloud. Queen Cartimandua moved to the altar stone.

Aduna's voice was furred, soft. "You may now break the seal."

"Venute. Venute!"

At Aduna's urgent whisper, Venute opened his eyes.

Cartimandua had unloosed her cloak, and it had gone, taken by some ministrant. She was naked, her skin glistening with perfumed oil. Her face, looming over Venute's, was in deep shadow, her hair sparkling, the sunlight catching blue fire from it.

She touched his lips with her finger. "They must watch us break the seal."

"There is no 'seal' to break. You know that. They all know that."

Cartimandua's cheek twitched with the faintest of smiles. "Nevertheless, it is the custom of both our peoples."

The drums began to beat slowly and a chant began, behind which could be discerned the twittering of women's laughter and the animal growl of the men. The queen leapt agilely across Venute's body and knelt, thighs apart, taut across his loins.

Carefully, she lowered herself. The drums beat stronger, louder; their tempo rose slightly. The chant became more insistent—"Brig-id, Brig-id, Brig-id, Brig-id, Brig-id!"

Over the queen's head, there arose the huge figure of Hroc, his talons embedded the muscles of her long graceful neck. Venute felt his own heat rising as Cartimandua—breathless, flushed—moved to the beat of the drums and started chanting, backwards and forwards, backwards and forwards.

And then he was inside her—deeper, deeper—and the altar stone seemed to be pushing his taut buttocks upwards until his whole groin seemed consumed.

"Brig-id, Brig-id, Brig-id, Brig-id, Brig-id, Brig-id, Brig-id, Brig-id, Brig-id, Brig-id, Brig-id, Brig-id, Brig-id, Brig-id, Brig-id, Brig-id, Brig-id, Brig-id—"

Venute thought, as the streams of seed shot from his body into hers, that there would be no ending, that he would exit the world, drawn after his seed and crushed and swallowed by the seemingly endless spasms of her contractions. But finally, with a sigh, she raised her body from his. Venute became aware of the roar of the assembly. Then in a swift movement, Aduna, dressed now in a flame-red sagum, swept her hand under Cartimandua's buttocks and held aloft what she had stolen. The fluid, mingled male and female essence, glittered in the sunshine. Part of it ran down her arm. She quickly daubed it into the mazelike carvings on the altar stone then a little into the Crookstone, the Star Guider.

"Thus, the Great Mother takes Her tithe, gives Her blessing. You are man and woman joined, queen and consort."

7

Near Llanymynech, Mid Wales
Third moon of Imbolc, waxing: late April, AD 51

ALL WAS ACTIVITY IN THE hasty camp Ostorius Scapula, Governor of Britain, had set up in the water meadow by the slim silver of Afon Afyrnwy, the Vrynwy river.

The cold dawn had brought a soft cloudy drizzle out of the north, which gathered in a blear on his breastplate and hung heavy in his dark eyebrows.

The commander stood, thick legs apart, and stared at the fortress of Llanymynech on the opposite bank. Behind him, a contingent of the Second Augusta fidgeted with their helmets and tightened their leggings.

The fort was in shadow, overlooked by steep, crumbling cliffs. Atop these, silhouetted heads moved. Behind the thick triple wall of staves that ringed Llanymynech's central enclosure, there was a grim tense silence. At least the trickle of reinforcements—individual Cymri scrambling like spiders down crevices and paths known only to their tribe into the fortress's enclave from above—had ceased.

No more defenders for this last major battle for Mid Wales would be forthcoming. Rome held the southern territories of the Silures, tightening its stranglehold from the fort at Caerleon, and now only Llanymynech stood between the governor and the north.

"He has the skill of a devil." Scapula grimaced, turned to his legate, Marcus Severus. "What are you thinking, Marcus?"

"This is no ordinary hillfort, or I would have suggested the techniques developed by Commander Vespasianus in the south—rams for the gate under shields after a slow advance towards the ramparts and a quick follow-through with the testudos formation," said the legate carefully after a pause.

"Nothing wrong with the testudos. If we took the hill behind?"

Marcus sniffed. "It would take forever to clear the groves on the far side of those cliffs. The Ordovices have bowmen hidden everywhere. They're without a commander as far as we can tell, but it's a fair bet they have instructions to pick off anything, and everything that looks remotely Roman. Even if we could get two, three centuries up there, we'd need ropes, grappling hooks, armed cover. We'd be hellishly exposed."

"How about a pincer movement—forces under the cliffs from left and right?" probed Ostorius.

Marcus shot him a swift look of approbation. The gap between river and cliff on either side of the camp was narrow. Even if the stone wall defences could be breached, the gaps could be defended by a few Welsh against many. It was not the governor's style to sacrifice men for little gain. Then, inwardly, he smiled. It was the Governor's style to tease forth military strategy. Trial and error. But in word only, not in deed. Truly, this man deserved his rank and position. Marcus felt a surge of loyalty, tinged with the frustration of knowing he was on trial.

"Sir, his strongest point is also his weakest." Marcus pointed to the river Afyrnwy, bowing round Caratacus's defence works in a huge semicircle. "I suggest we attack frontally across the river and fire the fences one after the other under shield cover. It will cost lives, but I can't see how else we can break in."

"You're right. This will cost us dearly in men. No matter how quickly we cross the river, we will be totally exposed." Ostorius sighed. "But I agree. A frontal assault it is. At noon we cross the river. Bring up every ballista we have now, and back them with the Syrian and Parthian archers, though at this range, they'll be useful only if Caratacus ventures outside his own walls. Turn this spring day into a winter of hailstones, Marcus: soften him up thoroughly from now until noon."

"Ho, Ostorius Scapula!"

A huge voice echoed across the river, ricocheting off the cliffs. There was a sudden whir, and a long-shafted arrow buried itself at the commander's feet. His men leapt backwards, but Scapula held his ground.

"Fetch me the Pretani translator," he barked. The command echoed back through the ranks.

But Caradoc's laughter filled the valley, and he spoke in soldier's Latin, learned in the southern Romanised court of his father Cunobelin.

"Go home, Ostorius Scapula, and take your pig-men with you. When you fail here, we will come after you one by one, and not one of you will see his homeland again. I am the Prince of Wales. I have spoken."

"Caratacus, Prince of the Catuvellauni, you are no Prince of Wales," shouted Scapula. "And you are a fool if you think the might of Rome can be stayed by a few rows of wooden stakes and an earthwork. You will all be slaughtered. I offer you amnesty. I will not offer it again."

The laughter rang out, this time joined by the hoarse cries of hundreds of men within Llanymynech's walls. Caratacus addressed his men, translating no doubt in their own tongue, and though the words could not be distinguished, the sarcasm in his tone was abundantly evident.

"At least let your women and children go. I, Ostorius Scapula, guarantee their safety."

"Go to hell on the end of my spear, Ostorius Scapula!"

Out of the cliff's shadows rose a dragon's breath of metre-long arrows, hissing as they curved through the air. Legates and centurions ordered their legionaries' shields overhead, but for many, the command was either too late or unnecessary. One black-feathered shaft tugged at Scapula's tunic as he raised his shield; the screams of his men behind indicated many of the Welsh barbs had found their mark.

"The bastard," breathed Scapula. "Marcus—"

But Marcus Severus lay in a crumpled heap at his side. An arrow had slit the legate's shoulder strap over his clavicle and plunged deep into his heart.

Scapula knelt, stroked the legate's forehead. His heavy jaw knotted, his eyes glassed in fury. "Your death will be avenged a hundredfold today, dear friend," he said. "I promise."

"Here they come."

Caradoc, resistance leader of all the Pretani, held his spear and shield aloft atop a low stone-and-turf wall in the compound. It was an exposed position—see and be seen, hear and be heard. He was an immense bull of a man, barrel-chested with arms and thighs like stripped oak bough. Yellow-haired when not in war garb, his long locks and bushy moustache had been lime-starched, and his hair stood out from his head in a huge grey spiky mass, half-halo, half-mane. His face, torso, and legs were a complex map of woad and lime, the symbols of eternity and the marks of those gods Caradoc knew were protecting him and his people in this struggle against the barbarian.

But his eyes were his most striking feature, wide-set and burning brown, brooking no distraction even beneath their twin rings of charcoal. The muscles of his great jaw worked.

"They're halfway across the river. Slingshots!"

The Second Augusta were coming on in tight formation, the locked shields above their heads wavering only as they hit deep water and were in danger of losing their footing in the surge.

Two hundred arms whirled, and river pebbles whined with uncanny accuracy into the ranks of the approaching legionaries. Cymric slingsmen were considered for military service only when they could hit a sparrow at a score of paces. Not even the Cretans, whose skill with the sling was feared across the Empire, could compete. Screams and wails echoed against the cliffs. Discarded Roman shields floated east, and bodies bobbed in the waters. Still they came.

"Slingshots! Save your arrows!"

Caradoc turned to his younger brothers Congal and Brychan. Slimmer than their older sibling, they were both skilful warriors and would—so the prince hoped—carry on the resistance with Caradoc's wife Rhianydd if anything were to happen to him.

Which it wouldn't.

"Where's Rhianydd?"

"At the outer palisade," shouted Congal, tossing his blond hair.

"Support her. Take fifty men. No, a hundred. Slingshots, bowmen. If they break through, it'll be right in front of our eyes. They must not destroy the outer palisade. Understand?"

Congal nodded and leapt from the wall.

"Brychan—your best sword hands. Can you go out through the west tunnel and flank these Roman swine?"

Dark-eyed like Caradoc and battle-fired, Brychan nodded. "Rely on me, brother."

Caradoc turned to his waiting bowmen. "Pick your targets and fire at will. Make every arrow count," he bellowed.

Stocky and mostly dark-haired, they were what remained of the southern Silurian forces who had accompanied him north through the hills a few weeks earlier, augmented by eight or nine hundred of the local Ordovices, the Welsh "hammer fighters," and minor tribes—a force totalling somewhat more than twelve hundred. With the specialist sling, sword and spearsmen, trackers, snipers, Druid priest/herbalists, quartermasters, women and children, the Welsh resistance numbered a little over two thousand souls.

They were ranked against the Second Augusta at its full strength of 5,000 infantry, backed by a cavalry unit of over 120 horses anxiously awaiting their call to action on the far bank of the Afyrnwy, plus supplies, weapons, and engineering support.

The barrage of stones from the tight line of Roman catapults, the feared ballista, hissing over their heads as the first cohorts edged slowly across the river, had wreaked havoc inside Llanymynech. Thatched huts, nestling against the mountain wall on narrow serried terraces, were roof-stoved and ruined, and the crushed bodies of dozens of his forces, men and women, lay everywhere. Priests ministered to the wounded or dragged bodies beneath the cliff wall, where they lay in uneven lines, uncovered.

But Caradoc held Fortress Llanymynech, and the river was red with Roman blood. This would be no Battle of the River Medway, from which Caradoc was forced to retreat, and in which his beloved older brother Tycaedmon was killed.

Today, the stakes were higher. We'll win here and sweep southwards, gathering the once-cowed Welsh as we go, Caradoc told himself, and Rome's boar standard will be lowered for good on the land of the Cymri.

And then we'll drive these Roman bastards into the sea.

As the sun rose higher towards noon, the chorus of horns repeatedly called Scapula's forces into retreat, back over the bloodied Afyrnwy. Each time, they rallied, regrouped, tried a different course over the river's stony churn; and each time they drove nearer the bank under the wall of flesh-eager staves. Finally, under a constant hail of slingshot that thundered and echoed dully on the roof of their shields, an ever-growing force of legionaries established a bridgehead on the only available spit of land before the first of the triple fences that protected Llanymynech fort.

A huge shield wall was built and held without motion. Stones and spears and arrows rattled uselessly against it.

Suddenly, clouds of smoke rose at the palisades. Through it, Caradoc saw the neat lines of sharpened staves that comprised the outer barricade waver and tumble. The call went up—"The Romans are through the outer defences!"

"They will not give up, no matter what it costs," growled Caradoc to himself. To the Welsh tribesmen before him, his bull voice rose over the consternation. "This is our hour, great warriors of the Cymri!" And with a roar and a shake of spear, he led his main force through hidden gateways in the inner ringworks into the breach.

8

Brigantia
Third moon of Imbolc, waning: May, AD 51

"**I**'M DYING, PRINCE."

Caradoc reached over in the saddle and hauled on the Welsh pony's reins. He searched his companion's drawn face, noted the brown crust of blood on his flushed, fever-damp forehead, the way his rough splinted arm hung painfully.

"I think not, Dewi. But let's rest. Enough is enough." The prince turned to the stragglers. "Ordovices! No more riding for today! We're within spitting distance of Cartimandua's court, and we have no pursuers. Let's wash, feast, and warm ourselves tonight. The queen must see us at our best in the morning."

The travel-stained warriors dismounted. Caradoc rode among them as they cleared the glade of brush, built fire, and spread out their meagre provisions.

"Feast," said Dewi to a fellow rider, Gwdyr. He grimaced with pain. "Rabbit, dried horsemeat, and cheese rinds. How can he be so cheerful, with all Cymru and his own family in chains?"

"You could be dead in the ruins of Llanymynech," muttered Gwydyr tiredly, shaking his long dark hair as he unclasped his saddle and threw it on to the banking. The orange ball of the sun was westering through the May-green birch copse.

"That might have been the better fate," said Dewi. There is the pain of cold death in my arm, and my head is full of sour thunder."

"You're a warrior, Dewi," said Gwydyr encouragingly. "Your name is already in the roll of history. The gods will welcome you into their halls. But in the meantime, make yourself useful. Play the woman—fetch water from the stream yonder."

"I can't." Dewi collapsed on the ground and feebly drew his cloak around him. Shaking his head, Gwydyr took a leather bucket from his comrade's saddle.

They were in the shallow lee of a long ridge. Prince Caradoc rode his fine dappled Arab—stolen from a Scythian mercenary after a skirmish the previous year on the Silures' borders—to its southern edge and stared across the rolling forests in the valley. The glint of a river could be seen in the valley bottom, bounded by patches of lurid green marshland. And before him, rising out of the viridescent sea of the forest, the bare whaleback of a mount known as Rampart Hill, Celtic Cadradaon, "Battle Ramparts Height," or as generations much later would call it, Castle Hill, site of the largest Iron Age fort in Yorkshire.

The heartland of the Brigantes.

Behind him, the noises of soldiers making camp faded.

In my dreams, I saw you again, Rhianydd. I saw your eyes as I led the charge from Llanymynech. We both knew I might not return, yet you refused to leave the Cymri. And in your eyes was the All-Mother, Brigid, and on your shoulder, the Great Rook Hroc, harbinger, urging me on—to what?

And in his mind's eye, he saw that moment when the shield-locked lines of Romans wove unhindered across the river and the Welsh fell before their stubborn discipline, the breach in his carefully prepared defences widening and widening. He saw the sky darken with stones as the ballistae loosed their deadly

loads, heard their thud, and crashed in the compound, the smash
of bones and flesh as the great rocks snuffed out the rebels one
by one. He saw the rain of arrows from the deadly short bows of
the Syrian auxiliaries—warriors spinning to the ground, clutching
limbs and heads and guts as the shafts found their targets.

He saw himself from without, a raging animal, rallying his
troops, riding wildly across the breach, scattering Romans left and
right, stabbing with his spear until its head broke inside a centurion's
ribcage, shouting until he was hoarse. He remembered gathering
all those with mounts to his side, shaking his sword until it sang
in his hand; he remembered seeing his nemesis, Ostorius Scapula,
standing on the riverbank unscathed under the hated boar and the
Second Augusta standards, ordering more and yet more centuries
into the swirling waters of Afon Afyrnwy. He remembered the
blind, blind hate, pierced only by Rhianydd's eyes and the briefest
of waves—whether for help or as a farewell—from Congal in the
press of fighting as he and a dozen horsemen forced their way
through, the icy plunge into the river, a voice his own yet not his
own, an arm thrusting and slashing with a sword so busy he was
oiled with gore to the armpit. The look on the governor's face as
Caradoc and his men bore down on him. The legionaries forming
a wall. A miracle not one soldier thought to skewer his horse.
Hacking at the standard-bearer. The standard teetering. Harsh
cheers from dead men. The legionaries closing ranks. Ostorius
Scapula nowhere to be seen.

And the cavalry. Rome's finest butchers, wheeling in from the
right flank. Caradoc's Welsh outnumbered ten to one and in the
open. Ride, ride!

And then all was blank.

The escapees from the debacle at Llanymynech now numbered six, of whom only two, Caradoc and Gwydyr, were uninjured. A band of one hundred had ridden from the fortress of Llanymynech promising reinforcements, only to be to be ambushed by a century at the crossing of the River Ceirog ten miles north. Their retreat cut off, and the Marches swarming with legionaries' patrols, Caradoc had decided to press north-northeast into the territories of the Brigantes' last stronghold before the invading might of the Roman army.

He had expected to find the queen at Uellacaern, Ilkley. But the fort was manned only lightly, and the mareschal told him the queen and her retinue were on their summer progression. He headed south.

In his heart of hearts, he was not optimistic. Even Brigantia was a client state, rumour had it, no better than the mongrel Iceni, the Belgi, the snivelling Atrebates. Cartimandua had betrayed her Goddess and her people for a few Roman trinkets and the promise of protection, it was said. She seemed unaware that inside the bastard Roman kid glove was a fist of tempered steel. Caradoc shook his shaggy head sadly. Such a fool!

What, then, would be his reception at the queen's court? Was he riding from a lesser danger into a greater?

The warrior Dewi developed a consuming fever in the night and died with a great rattling sigh as the first lark rose in the gloom of the next morning. There were those among the warriors who said they saw his shade rise, survey the glorious countryside, and depart sadly for the land of his birth, riding the great black stallion that Donn, god of the dead, provides for the long journey to his dark halls.

His companions built a cairn over Dewi's body on windswept ground on the top of the ridge. Caradoc prayed to the morning star, Venus, eye of heaven, into whose light the light of Dewi's soul had been absorbed; and he commended Dewi's soul to Gofannon, he who strikes sparks in the forge of the sky's vault, known as Goibniu the Smith to the Brigantes, in whose land Dewi's bones now dwelt forever.

On routine inspection of the defences of Rampart Hill that morning, Venute caught the glimmer of armour, of burnished breastplate and sullen red of Imperial capes on the high hills to the south. The ridgeway was a known trading route, but armour meant the approach of Romans or mercenary forces allied to them or emissaries under military escort.

His fist was white-knuckled on the hilt of his sword. "Great Mother! We have been here less than a month, and the eye of Rome is already on us," said Venute to the wind. "More bribes from Ostorius Scapula, no doubt. May the Goddess forgive my queen for this . . . betrayal."

At Venute's advice and so that the southern tribes in the Brigantian confederation might offer tribute and their resources be more easily assessed, the queen of all the Brigantes had moved her court south from Uellacaern into the densely wooded valleys of the territories of the Denovii, Venute's and Vellocate's homeland. Now she and her palace guard, retinue, bards, temple ministrants, workers, slaves, and camp followers were ensconced for the summer on the commanding site of Rampart Hill, where a double palisade had been built to reinforce the ancient triple earthworks.

Already, a grove of circular dwellings had appeared— workpeople's summer huts, clumsily mounded turf walls topped with thatching, a weaving shed, a threshing and drying floor, pig huts, and sheep pens. In the centre towered the thatch of the queen's palace-cum-temple, in which the Goddess Brigid and her earthly minister Cartimandua dwelt. A choked well had been cleared, middens dug, and a kitchen garden planted in untidy rows, watered and weeded by a small army of children. The hillside had been denuded of scrub and a ring of sharpened staves had been buried aggressively, like a monk's tonsure or splay teeth, above the outer ditch. A simple wooden gate and watchtower completed the works.

Rampart Hill had been a site for defence for at least six hundred years already. It commanded the entire river valley from the bleak scrub and moorland tops southwards to the lush forested valley spread impenetrably below, with the occasional clearing or tended water meadow visible as a gleam of yellow-green or dark shadow north, east, and west.

The high plateau to the southwest lee of Rampart Hill had been cleared of scrub and forest much earlier, and the conical thatches of three roundhouse farms studded the well-tended land. There, Vellocate's family held a moderately prosperous homestead or *tref* on the crest of a rounded bluff a mile or two beyond the plateau and obscured now from Venute's gaze by the plateau's rim.

Vellocate had been given spring leave to put his house in order and clear more land and was gone from Venute's side.

The sky was high and clear today, with cirruslike careless brushstrokes and a sharp spring breeze from which, on the nab of Cadradaon, there could be little shelter. From this height, the distant skyline was a blue-grey smudge of bluffs—the wall of the Du Cant, Dark Edge, at the head of the river valley, which forty generations later would come to be called Holme Moss—and Pen Cadair, Cradle Hill—later, West Nab and Deer Hill—where the summer sun sets, being the major landscape features.

And from these largely untamed and untrammelled wildlands, the queen's hunters brought wild boar and mountain hares, deer, and hedgehogs daily; and those farmsteaders living nearby and with surpluses were already establishing terms with their new neighbours.

No sooner had Prince Venute ordered a doubling of the guards and despatched a party of scouts to shadow the approaching force that an alarum came from warriors stationed on the western approaches. He rode below the row of staved defence work to meet them.

"More riders, m'lord," said one youngster, pointing north across the tangled valleys.

"Tribespeople," said another. "Six horses, one riderless."

Venute stood in his saddle, shielded his eyes.

"By the great mallet of Sucellos! I know that yellow hair. It's Caradoc," he breathed to himself. "It can surely be no other. The scouts were right, then; a huge defeat in Cymru and every Roman in the Midlands chasing Caradoc the ghost. No surprise he turns up here eventually and from the north. He's been to Uellacaern first, of course; that's where he thought the queen would be. This could be interesting! Two visiting parties in one day. Coincidence? We'll see what the Roman dogs say. The bastards' eyes will tell me all I need to know."

He turned to the guards.

"That's Caradoc down there, my boys! Yes, Calum—Prince Caradoc. Don't look so astounded. You knew he'd turn up here sooner or later, didn't you? Roman emissaries and the soul of Pretanic resistance together under one roof! You heard me—Romans approaching from the south. Two of you fetch Vellocate immediately. His holiday ends here. If there's bloody work this day, I'll need my sergeant at my side."

"Let's see how my queen deals with this," breathed Venute to himself, turning his horse towards the inner gate. "This will tax to the limit the diplomacy she claims not to have."

Unaware of each other, the pitiful remnants of Prince Caradoc's army and a deputation from the British governor Ostorius Scapula's new camp at Castra Devana, Chester, were converging on Rampart Hill.

"My lord Venute, all is prepared as you ordered. But may I speak?" The royal household's mareschal, Ewan, stood in the doorway of Venute's chamber, resting a great tattooed ham of a forearm on the willow-woven screen.

Silently, Venute beckoned him into the chamber. Little light reached into the room, even at noon, so Venute kept three oil lamps burning day and night.

"Well? What is it, Ewan? You have always spoken your mind. Has silver-tongued Ogmios withdrawn His favours all of a sudden?"

There was an embarrassed silence. Ewan shuffled his feet.

"My lord. I serve both you and the high queen, this you know."

"The queen and I differ, Ewan. We differ on many things." Venute sighed. "The gossip is true. Everybody knows it. Speak out."

"The Romans. They're bringing more gifts. How long before gifts become trade, and trade becomes obligation? We shouldn't be dealing with the Romans, m'lord. Not at all. The Fifteen Tribes have wind of this, and I hear from travellers too—murmurs of resentment are everywhere."

"I know. You bring me no new news. I hear it from every *tref*, every village, every fort throughout Brigantia."

For eight years, Venute had ridden far and wide, promising alliances and support, trade deals and intercessions up to and beyond his capacity to fulfil them, just to keep the tribes under one banner. But Cartimandua undermined this; she was flattered by Ostorius Scapula's personal attention, his letters, the stream of gifts from the south—wines, pottery, mirrors, skins from Africa Byzacena, sculptures, even slaves.

Venute had begun negotiating with the tribes on his own behalf. If a storm came, he would not be without allies. The peace that had settled on the land was a false one; for three years now, Rome's tentacles had been wrapping themselves insidiously round the very heart of Brigantia—and the queen could not see it, would not accept it.

Very soon, those tentacles would harden their grip. Brigantia was on the brink of becoming just another client state of Rome, and Cartimandua just another puppet of the emperor.

Perhaps it was already too late.

"I just thought you should know," mumbled Ewan. "If the storm breaks, I'm on your side, and so are the palace guard here and at the royal households from coast to coast. We're on your side, and may the Goddess have mercy on us."

"Rest easy," said Venute, slapping his shoulder. "The Goddess goes with the righteous. We have not spoken, Ewan. Go to your duty."

9

Cadradaon: Castle Hill, West Yorkshire

VENUTE WATCHED THE ROMAN GROUP from within the gate as it made its way slowly up the winding path out of the forest to the hillfort. Ornate, rich harness clinked and glittered in the sunlight; shod hooves clattered on stone.

Slingsmen had been stationed within easy casting distance on both sides of the path; the prince didn't care that the visitors saw mistrust and hostility and strength of arms whichever way they looked. In fact, he wanted them to know that, no matter how civil their reception, they were and always would be unwelcome intruders in a foreign land.

He had borrowed a hooded sagum from a warrior and loosened his hair to disguise his status. He needed to learn everything he could about his enemy, preferably without their knowing. He needed to catch and keep them wrong-footed.

Meanwhile, horsemen had been despatched to head off Prince Caradoc's party; if there was a confrontation, it was to be where he, Venute, could control and manage it.

Warning Ewan with a flattened palm not to acknowledge his presence, he urged the man forwards to meet Ostorius Scapula's delegation at the gates. Ewan's instructions were to stable their

horses, set aside a pair of huts for their use, provide the usual
hospitality there, and bring any messages to the queen. He was to
ask them to prepare for a midday audience.

Venute tallied the party:

— A guard of four legionaries, one of whom carried a spear
  tied with a white cloth. We come in peace.
— A bareheaded white-haired man, clearly a retired soldier
  or centurion by his bearing and manner of riding—the
  emissary, the word dealer, Ogmios the Eloquent. Who did
  the Romans worship? Mercury. A man of Mercury.
— A shaggy bowed creature in a long cape, shielding his eyes
  from the spring sunshine. A translator?
— A string of six laden ponies led by a fifth legionary.
— And two oxen driven by a hunchbacked creature of
  apparently Belgic extraction, small and swarthy and
  with the intense close-set eyes typical of the continental
  flatlanders, sycophantic mules the lot of them. The oxen
  hauled a creaking flatbed cart heavy with crates and boxes,
  a mountain of sackcloth and straining rope.

More gifts from Rome under the guise of trading. Always the
eagle-eyed soldiers, the military strategist, the spies and calculators
weighing up our strengths and weaknesses much more efficiently
than we theirs. *Bugger the rules of hospitality—I should dangle their
heads at my belt and send their bodies back to Rome,* Venute thought,
suddenly overcome with frustration.

What made him most angry was what left him least powerful—
the knowledge that Scapula's arm could reach so swiftly and
surely—so casually—into the Pennine wilderness and locate the
new summer camp. Venute had suggested the move to Rampart
Hill barely two moons ago as part of a long-term project to
reinforce and unify the middle marches of Brigantian territory.

True, the denuded hump of gritstone was visible for miles around, but Brigantian territory covered thousands of square miles, mostly of trackless oak and birch forest in which the gods and their true people roamed freely, and Venute liked to think this huge natural barrier protected the Brigantians' movements from prying eyes.

This was clearly not so. And Scapula—may Lugh's long arm reach out and squeeze the breath from his body—Scapula's delegation had been sent with a message that screamed out, "We know where you are, we know what you're doing, we can come for you any time we like."

The delegation disappeared inside the gates.

Prince Caradoc too had seen the approach of the Roman delegation. He watched with mounting anger as the party wound up the hillside and entered the fortress between the double watchtowers.

"So it's true!" he shouted to his men. "Sleek Pony is in the thrall of Rome." He spun his horse round so hard it reared. He reined in at Gwydyr's side. "I'd take heads this day in the absence of the gods' vengeance on this—this blasphemy. By my birth sign and stars, by all the walking spirits of Samhain, by Blessed Brigid—"

"Stay, Prince." said Gwydyr urgently. "Anger and bloodshed will tip the balance here. And not in your favour. Why not shame the queen in front of her new friends?"

Caradoc frowned. "In front of these bloody invaders? I am no soft-tongued priest or fawning Belgian. What do you mean by this southern talk, Gwydyr?"

The Welshman was unbowed. "It is custom that no weapons are drawn in the courts of the Pretani. Under this protection, if you stay calm, you have a chance to push the queen into a choice—for

Rome or for Pretan. These Romans are here to report whatever they see, whatever they hear, directly back to Scapula. If you played this thing right, the rallying of the north could start this day—either that or the queen could be removed from power by her own people."

"Too subtle for me, friend. And I suspect too ambitious, too naive. But in one thing, you're right; I no longer command an army. Bloodshed is no option." His eye roved over his companions, the proud but bedraggled warriors of Cymru.

"Lads!" he called. "Today, we storm the high queen's palace on yonder little hillock. By my reckoning, there are barely three hundred warriors within, so we should be finished by noon. To celebrate our victory, I'm planning a pig roast—you find the apples, and leave me to dress the Romans for the spit."

The men's laughter was cut short as sunlit branches parted, and horsemen with the shield bosses of Brigantia pounded to a halt in front of Caradoc and his men.

"Hail, Prince Caradoc!"

The riders' leader, one Edrun, raised a palm in greeting. "I am sent by Prince Venute, consort of the High Queen Cartimandua, to welcome you . . ."

Slowly, Caradoc rode his large mare round Edrun's pony, disconcerting him. "An armed welcoming party? This is unusual. I had heard the Brigantians were the soul of hospitality. Do you want to tell me something? That your guest houses are full, perhaps?"

Edrun cleared his throat. "It's true, m'lord, that your arrival, er—"

"Is not well timed. And who is the queen entertaining at present that my party must wait in the wings? A goddess or two, perhaps? The assembled princes of the north? I would guess the *Romans*"—he hurled the word in Edrun's cringing ear—"are here to pay tribute, to beg for mercy, to tell the great queen they are so impressed by her strength of arms that they are leaving Pretan altogether, by the next boat from Rutupiaea?" Caradoc used the Roman name for Richborough, where the Roman invasion force first landed.

Edrun shook his head angrily. "I like this no more than you do, Prince. I—we—cannot say how we feel and remain loyal. The queen is the queen, and she is the Great Goddess's voice on earth. There is an old saying—'Punishing the bearer of bad news doesn't change the news.'"

Caradoc slapped the man on the back so hard his pony started forwards. "I know what you're saying. I apologise."

"Sir—would you lead us against Rome?" said one of the warriors accompanying Edrun. It was echoed on the faces of the others.

"If you would follow, boy, I would lead you *into* Rome. What do you call this place?"

"Rampart Hill, m'lord."

"Very impressive. Shall we go?" And without waiting for his protesting Brigantian guard, he signalled the Cymri forwards.

The audience with Rome had commenced. Cartimandua, her long raven hair braided with beads and a bronze tiara on her head, played nervously with the torc at her smooth neck. Though she tried to concentrate, her eyes were drawn downwards to where Hroc's eyes blazed accusingly, angry pinpoints of red.

Venute was at her side but in the shadows, determined to read every Roman inflexion and expression and equally determined they should not read his. This had been his and the queen's agreed modus operandi since the visits had started.

Vellocate, his skin bronzed from his work clearing land on his family's nearby *tref*, stood impassively behind the throne, both hands resting on the hilt of a huge sword whose point rested on a block of wood on the stone-flagged floor. As royal armour-bearer, his was the only weapon allowed unsheathed in the audience chamber.

A low backless chair had been placed centrally, and on it, straight-shouldered, sat the leader of the Roman delegation, white-haired Gaius Horventa. He was flanked by four of the soldiers, who, as custom demanded, remained in full uniform.

The shaggy man, a scribe and translator as Venute had correctly surmised, had cut a new quill, wetted a small pot of ink, and was poised over a piece of parchment. He translated Gaius Horventa's words into Celtic:

"My lady, those people known to us as Corieltauvi, to the south of Brigantia, continue to be troublesome to both of us. Ostorius Scapula bids me to tell you that a force of four centuries has been despatched with instructions to set up a marching fort in their heartland. From here, troops will be able to deal swiftly with the raiding parties we both find so, er, inconvenient."

Cartimandua stirred from her reverie. "This is good, but we must be compensated for the cattle and sheep the Corieltauvi have stolen. Our farmers in the south report that eighty head of cattle and two hundred sheep of the Midlands breed have been taken, and according to last year's agreement with the governor—"

There was a commotion in the palace forecourt. Cartimandua signalled Ewan to investigate. He rushed back into the gloomy hall. "Your pardon, my lady, but—"

He was thrust roughly aside by Caradoc, who burst into the room, his yellow mane flowing, his barrel chest bared in defiance of convention. His longsword in its ash wood sheath banged at his thigh.

"This is appalling!" started Cartimandua, but Venute's glance cauterised further protest.

The prince, who had anticipated something like this, leapt forwards and barred Caradoc's path to the queen's throne.

"Old friend," he said loudly, gripping Caradoc's immense forearm and wrist, loosening and clasping his thumb in the time-honoured Celtic way.

Caradoc responded—no Celt would spurn such a gesture—but recognition was slow to dawn in the deep brown pits of his tired eyes. Then a broad smile crept across his travel-stained face.

"You! Damn you, you're the little fellow with his nose into everything at the palace. You knew everything that happened inside and out of Camulod, *Colchester*. I don't know what my father, Cynobelin, saw in you, scraggy little northerner. I recall you broke my harp when I was—this high!"

"A harp is no toy for a boy. I was protecting your interests." There was laughter in Venute's eyes.

"Venute? Oh, Venute." Caradoc took the prince in his arms and crushed him breathless. "I could play that harp well. You wrecked my career as a bard. I should pull your head off."

Caradoc held his childhood friend Venute at arm's length.

Gaius Horventa, rising with dignity from his seat, had no trouble recognising the man before him; he was in the presence of Pretan's most wanted rebel.

The prize was at hand! Come, Scapula, now, and claim it!

Nor had his guards failed to identify the dishevelled yellow-haired giant. Their hands crept slowly to the hilts of their shortswords, searching for a signal from Horventa. But with his eyes and an almost imperceptible shake of his head, the envoy warned them against action.

"These—shits—seem to think you are a friend of Rome, my queen," said Caradoc, striding into the midst of the Roman delegation and enjoying their consternation. "What might have given them that impression?"

"I thank you for your gifts, Gaius Horventa. You may go. We will continue this audience later. There is much to discuss . . ."

The white-haired emissary stepped forwards. "My lady—"

Venute was at his side in an instant. "You have been thanked, and you have been given permission to leave," he whispered in his ear, stepping quickly aside.

Horventa stood rigidly before the throne for an awkward moment, considering his options. Then he nodded acquiescence, turned sharply, and left. The scribe, dropping ink and pen, followed. The sweep of a guard's cloak spread the ink across the floor. The queen started; the ink was in the shape of a rook, Hroc, wings spread, cruel beak opened, coming towards her . . . Cartimandua stared directly ahead, her thoughts in turmoil. She felt Hroc's claws tightening on her shoulder, tightening, digging into her skin; she felt the skin puncture and hot blood flow forth . . .

10

"A PITY YOU DISMISSED THEM, my lady. I should
have liked to insult those pigs some more." Caradoc
grinned, thumbs aggressively stuck in his broad leather belt.

A shaft of sunlight played on drifting motes, the thick blue
curl of fire smoke in the central hearth. Queen Cartimandua's
polished nails drummed on the arm of her throne, and tiny muscles
twitched in her jaw.

"You barbarian!" she shouted. "Your manners are worse than
the Romans you condemn! How dare you behave so in the
presence of your queen!"

Caradoc grinned, thumbs in belt. "You are not my queen, my
queen. You will be my queen when you join me in throwing the
Roman invaders into the sea. Then I will happily be your faithful
servant, your most cringing vassal."

Venute stood at Cartimandua's side. "I doubt it," he said, eyes
suddenly cold. "Even in defeat, you are the proudest of men. And
by the holy sword of warlike Camulos, you've had more than your
share of defeats."

"We've had many victories," said Caradoc, drawing himself
up to his full height. "We would have had more if help had not
evaporated when we placed our trust in it, if friends upon whom

we relied had not turned out to be in Rome's pay. You are a warrior like me, Queen Cartimandua."

"I may be a warrior," said Cartimandua. "But foremost, I am the protectress of my people, as representative of the Great Mother. I have my duty to my people and to the Goddess, and that is to prevent them from dashing themselves uselessly against a force so mighty it has subdued the world. You are a child in these matters, Caradoc."

The warrior stirred with anger, his forced humour no longer a shield. When he spoke, it was quietly and with steely menace.

"Your Goddess, it is said, has commanded you to drive out the boar standards," he said. "By pandering to these Roman swine, you have betrayed the Mother, betrayed your people, betrayed the Pretani. Word is you are a puppet, no better than the fawning Belgi, the southern mongrels."

Venute stepped forwards, hand firm on his sword's hilt. "You insult the high queen. Curb your tongue in this room, or this sword will curb it for you."

Caradoc turned to him slowly, brown eyes glittering. Fire seemed to dance between their locked eyes. Then the Cymri's adopted prince turned back to the queen. "The Fifteen Tribes have the strength to drive the Romans from these isles. But have they the will?"

"What is the point of fighting forces far superior to your own?" said Venute calmly. "Every trick you play, they counter. Every minor victory is followed by a crushing defeat, every small gain followed by huge loss. Your family, Caradoc. Your man Gwydyr has told me they are captured, held prisoner, and for all you know, are now dead. You have no army, no wealth, no land, no subjects."

Cartimandua added, "We have heard you come fresh from the slaughter of your last allies, the Ordovices, hopeful that the Brigantes will as willingly lay down their lives to satisfy your pride. Let me tell you, Caradoc—I have Roman soldiers fight for *me*!"

Caradoc's laughter was harsh. "And what does the Mother Goddess think of that, I wonder? You're supposed to defend Her, keep Her people pure. Yet you have surrounded yourself with Roman favours, Roman trinkets."

He strode to the low table and picked up her mirror. The guards tensed and moved forwards. Caradoc hurled the mirror into a corner, and before Vellocate and the guards could restrain him, he picked up a full amphora of wine from its resting place near the wall and smashed it on the palace floor. Wine splashed everywhere, ran like blood. Venute motioned the guards not to restrain Caradoc but did not send them back. They stood rooted at Venute's side.

"Betrayal! What do *you* think of all this, Venute?"

"She is my queen." Quietly, eyes down.

"And you are no king, Venute. I wonder if you are a man, even, or some snivelling eunuch. Do you too lick the crumbs from the Romans' table?"

"Enough!" The raw hiss of iron against ash scabbard filled the echoing hall as Venute, the guard, and Caradoc all drew their swords simultaneously. For a terrible moment, all was poised like a tableau—Vellocate in front of the throne, his great notched longsword at shoulder height, protecting the queen; firelight flashing from the guards' blades; Venute's slimmer weapon held out to Caradoc's throat but one vital pace too far for the stroke; the darkening spreading wine; Caradoc's battle sword high over his head, poised to swing on anything and everything.

"Lay down your weapon, Caradoc." Venute spoke quietly into the electric air. "This has gone too far."

"That you should ask a warrior to lay down his arms," growled Caradoc, the muscles in his jaw twitching. "What kind of miserable, cheap Roman bollocks is that? I will *never* lay down my arms!"

Caradoc's terrible two-handed sword flashed in the firelight, connecting with Venute's and slinging it sideways. The first guard to reach him took a powerful kick in the groin and went down like a pricked bladder, his sword clanging and slapping on the wine-sodden ground. Another swing and Vellocate's blade showered sparks against Caradoc's weapon; Caradoc powered his sword under Vellocate's and flipped it over and over into the gloom. The arc of the Catuvellaunian's stroke continued, and the flat connected dully with the side of Vellocate's head. The armour-bearer crashed to his knees, sightless and stunned.

Venute and the second guard struck at the same time. Again, sparks flew, and Caradoc, misfooted, slipped in the attempt to fend off the two strokes. The guard dropped his sword and managed to get his arm round Caradoc's bull-like neck. The hilt of the prince's sword rose smartly under his chin and broke his jaw.

As the guard fell away with a groan, spitting blood, Cartimandua sprang past Venute. Her jabbing shortsword slit Caradoc's tunic sleeve and bloodied his arm. With eyes on fire and a roar that rattled the rafters, Caradoc whirled his sword round his head for a fatal stroke on his attacker—but the blade's tip flashed into the chain that held the cooking pot above the fire. The pot tipped crazily, and broth spilled into the flames. Clouds of aromatic steam rose.

In the confusion, Venute leapt through the vapour and drove the point of his sword into Caradoc's shoulder. The Catuvellaunian dropped his sword with a look of surprise.

"Let *me* kill him!" screamed Cartimandua, lunging forwards. Venute tripped her deftly, and her blade slithered across the floor.

By now, the door wardens, spears in hand, had run into the room. Caradoc punched one hard in the face and scrabbled for the man's dropped spear. The kicked guard, first into the conflict, grabbed Caradoc's ankle, and the unbalanced giant toppled, hitting his head on the cooking pot. For a few moments, a pile of bodies, kicking and punching, became more and more tangled.

"Fetch binding cords!" shouted Venute to the next face to emerge into the room. "Quickly!" It was the mareschal Ewan.

Speedily, he fetched willow-bark cord as the guards and Venute struggled to hold the big man down. He was growling like a cornered bear and convulsing in an attempt to break free. They turned him on his side, slippery with blood, and finally strapped his wrists together, then his ankles.

"I could have let her kill you, old friend," breathed Venute into Caradoc's ear and nodding towards the crumpled, sobbing heap that was the queen. "I should have. You're a bloody fool." He spat a gob of blood onto the flags. "That's a tooth you've broken."

"Nobody has ever pricked me like you did. I must be getting old."

"It was seven to one."

"At those odds, you should all have been lying bound, and I the free man. I'm ashamed of myself." Caradoc shuffled into a sitting position, still restrained by the guards. "So what next?"

"I get the priests to dress your wounds. We disarm your Welshmen. We send you all, bound either in oath or cord, to somewhere safe, deep in the forest, until we see which way the Romans will jump. I'm working on the details."

"You're a good man, Venute. Your wife, however, is a bitch. May the Goddess desert you as you have deserted her!" he shouted at Cartimandua.

"Silence, you animal!" Catlike, Cartimandua got to her feet. She picked up one of the discarded swords. "This is a palace, a temple to the great Goddess Brigid—and look what you have done to it. This desecration demands a sacrifice. I want your *head*, Caradoc," she hissed.

"The Romans want my head too," growled Caradoc. "So yet again, you and Rome are in agreement."

"For the gods' sakes, stop this," said Venute, wiping his mouth. On the other side of the hearth, Vellocate stirred and groaned.

"There's nothing the Romans like better than to see us brawling. They have a phrase—'Divide and rule.'"

He stood up, turned to the guards.

"Take the prince Caradoc to the cereal store, and tie him firmly to the millstone. Captain—take a strong body of men quietly and quickly to the Welshmen's hut. Disarm and bind them, if at all possible without bloodshed. And send for Aduna or one of her priestesses to bind this man's jaw."

He staggered to his feet and grabbed Cartimandua's arms, as if to lift her to her feet. She was still staring at Caradoc and continued staring as the guards lifted and moved the Catuvellaunian at the spot near the hearth where he had been overpowered. Saliva drooled in a thin clear line from the corner of her mouth. Her whole body was shaking with murderous anger, her breast heaving, every muscle rigid. He shook her, but she was transfixed.

"And tell Aduna to bring those herbs that soothe and send to sleep." He kissed Cartimandua's forehead gently and sadly.

11

V ENUTE NODDED TO THE GUARD at the door of the
cereal store, and he opened its bark-woven door for the
prince.

"I've brought water."

"Your minions could have done that," spat Caradoc, shifting in
discomfort. Red weals round his wrists and ankles showed where
the Catuvellaunian had struggled against the twine that bound
him to the central millstone. "What do you really want?"

"You can't stay here," said Venute quietly, a finger to his lips.
"Our Roman guests know now where you are, and it's only a
matter of time before one of the legionaries of that fox Ostorius
Scapula knows too. The so-called governor is in the area. It wouldn't
surprise me if he turned up in person to cut you into pieces. In
fact, I think he'll get to know very quickly," he whispered, checking
Caradoc's bonds. "My mareschal-in-chief found a mirror in the
centurion Horventa's personal satchel. It's a sunny day today."

Caradoc grimaced with the pain from his wounds, sipped
from the wooden pan Venute had brought him. "You're making
no sense."

"The Romans have a coded language that can be transmitted
by the flashing of a mirror. I watched light going forth into the
forest from Horventa's mirror moments after he arrived and

light returning. What do you think our upright little soldier is doing right now? Chances are he's telling the watchers to come quickly—that a big prize is within their grasp."

"You have demons in your head, northerner."

"You still don't understand, do you? We are outpaced, outmatched, outweighed, outthought by the pig-men. Their military discipline, their way with machines, their intelligence and strategy. Whichever way we turn, they are always one step ahead. Caradoc, tell me—is this why you hate Rome so?"

"Because they are in some way better than us? Venute, give me credit! I admire strength of arms and military cunning. I admire their architects and road builders. I like the way they organise their *oppida, civitates, castra,* their *vici.* I even admired their bloody emperor Claudius's elephants, which I'll never forget seeing clumping into Camulod back in my father's time, and asked for one myself.

"By the gods, what we could learn—what we are learning— from these soldiers! No. What I hate is that they are arrogant, vicious thieves who have smashed their way into our house, raped our women, sold our children into slavery, seduced our sons and daughters, taken our corn and skins and all our chattels and turned to spit and laugh in our faces knowing—or thinking, Venute, *thinking*"—he hissed—"we are powerless to stop them. That they are *superior* to us. They have no right here. For better or worse, this is our land to deal with as we please for the benefit of the people we have ruled for endless years.

"But do you know what really makes me feel the lights are going out all over Pretan? The death of our gods. When I hear the whisper of oak leaves in the breeze, I hear the voice of the blessed Medb and see the Horned One, Cernunnos Himself, guardian of all the forest's teeming life. In the work of our potters and tinsmiths and bronze smelters, I see and worship Lugh Samildanach, most skilled in the arts. When Sucellos beats out the thunder on his shield and his consort Nantosuelta prepares the forked fire and when Arianrhod's silver bowl, the moon, shines at night . . . I weep for their dying, Venute.

"For die, they will—these brutal, mindless Romans will crucify Teutates and Taranis, Esus and Epona. They'll rip out Ogmios' tongue and burn Grannus and Sequana's healing herbs, and only Donn, dark god of the dead, will stalk our naked fields and empty homes. I've seen Brigid, Venute. Seen Brigid in the face of my wife and in the faces of a thousand women. I've worshipped at her breasts and between her thighs, and I've seen her tears and had her eyes burn my soul, and she says just one thing—Rid—my—land—of—Rome."

There were tears in Caradoc's eyes now too, and he blinked them away. Venute gripped his arm.

"Believe me, friend, I hate it as much as you do. But fighting them is like hitting our heads against a wall. You must see that."

"No!" said Caradoc, struggling against his bonds. "You can muster fifteen thousand warriors if you choose. That is more than enough to turn the tide. Do you think the subjugated tribes like Roman rule? There's grumbling at taxes and tributes throughout Pretan, even among the most Romanised client states of the Atrebates and Cantii. The Iceni and Trinovantes are just waiting for an excuse to break free. Don't you realise how easy it would be to get rid of Rome forever?"

Venute considered Caradoc's words. Sunlight filtered through the rough thatch, tiny glittering shards. Somewhere, a cooking pot clanged, a dog barked, a wag's mumbled witticism drew a gust of laughter from his warrior comrades. He could hear the thud of arrows hitting their straw targets at the butts on the flat hilltop south of the main encampment. He saw in his mind's eye, further afield and across the vast rolling territories of Brigantia, men and women clearing the forests and tilling the soil, raising families, building villages; good harvests, good weather, peace, prosperity.

"Don't humiliate us any further, Venute," pleaded Caradoc, shaking his matted golden hair. Give me leave to speak to the Fifteen Tribes."

"No!" he hissed. "I haven't spent these last ten years binding the Brigantian federation together to have it torn apart by you! What we Brigantians do, we do together. That is our strength."

"Then call a council."

Venute stared into Caradoc's eyes for a long time. Finally, he sighed.

"If you will bury yourself in the woods with your Welshmen until riders can go out and call the chieftains in, yes, I'll do that. And I'll abide by the decision they make."

"It's all I ask. Oh, that and a skinful of wine."

"Sorry." Venute shrugged. "You spilt it all. Remember?"

The high priestess Aduna surveyed the scene, horror in her heart. Her queen sat on the floor of the throne room, rocking back and forth. Slaves, fearful, worked round her to clean away the spilled blood and wine and ink and scattered utensils, to replace weapons, to help the injured guards. Vellocate, groaning and shaking his big head, lay at the foot of the throne, and two slaves were gingerly helping him to his feet.

Come quickly, Mother, they'd said. Bring simples, medicine, for the queen and her guard are injured. And as she came to the queen's house, she'd seen warriors surround the Welshmen's hut, burst in, struggle with its occupants; she'd heard their curses, their frenzied accusations of betrayal as they were disarmed and bound. Oh, holy Mother! She sensed a change in the winds, an embittering of the spring air, leaves curling and dying on the trees. Roman horse and harness in the stables, the murmuring of foreign tongues. Suddenly, Rampart Hill was exposed, cold, visible to the greater world. The eyes of the gods were upon them and all their doings; and the taint of Rome had sullied the temple, the home of the Goddess, at the centre of which was this wrecked and distraught queen, the very soul of the All-Mother on earth.

Suddenly, Aduna was terrified. The delicate balance of her land, in which the spirits and souls of the gods mingled with those of humans, was in upset, careering into the mire. There was no time for prayer and ritual, no time for appeasement and sacrifice. Dignity and order lay ruined on this bald hilltop, and evil crept up the slopes from the darkest regions of the forest. She feared the night, the soft cruel eye of the owl, the leather-winged bat, the blazing anger of Brigid in the unlit groves, the hammer of Sucellos unleashed in the heavens, the long arm of Lugh reaching through the silver clouds to snap limbs, crush skulls, pluck lives, exact burning vengeance. Could it be that the Goddess had chosen ill? That this queen was not the daughter of her mother Cybella, that she is a changeling? Brigid, who lives within our hearts, must know.

And so Aduna at least must hold on, hold on—protect the living vessel of the threefold Goddess, manifest in this crumpled, whimpering bundle on the throne room floor.

She hastened to the queen's side.

———————◦◦◦———————

Later, Cartimandua lay in the dimness of her inner chamber. Aduna had lit tall lamps, and the smoke curled up into the high thatched ceiling. Healing balms were burning on a bronze brazier, and the air was heavily scented. Two priestesses chanted softly by her bedside.

"You must deal with the Roman delegation," the high priestess was saying. "Send them away."

"I must deal with the Romans," murmured Cartimandua, her eyes glazed.

"We must find out what the Goddess wants. There is much to put right."

"The Goddess wants."

"Lady, listen to me. Prince Caradoc and his men are in danger. You must find a place of safety for them. The storm clouds are brewing on the far hills. I feel it, know it—danger everywhere."

"Safety?" Cartimandua whispered. "Oh, sweet Aduna, there is no safe place in this world for the likes of Caradoc. And now he has brought danger and ruin to us and our people. What shall we do, Aduna? What shall we do?"

"You are queen and daughter of the Great Goddess. Ask Holy Brigid Herself."

She silently handed Cartimandua a tiny phial of the same drug administered to her on the eve of her initiation long years ago in Uellacaern. "Pray with me, and together we will enter the land of the Goddess."

The day's shadows lengthened, and mountains of cloud had built on the horizon. The huge bruised yellow ball of the sun glared fitfully through the cumulonimbus, and swathes of shadow billowed over the forest below. In Vellocate's thudding head, they appeared to be the shadows of celestial war chariots.

Venute and he had, of their own volition, sought to placate the Romans with many diplomatic gestures and the promise of a feast. "It goes against the grain," Venute had said, his arm round his armour-bearer's broad shoulders, "and I don't expect you to understand, but our Roman friends must be kept occupied."

"Roman *friends*, my prince?" Vellocate, bemused, had rubbed his heavily bruised broad forehead.

"It's a manner of speech, Vellocate. Tonight, when the Romans have abandoned their senses, you must take Caradoc and his men away. South. To the hillmen in the white peaks. I'll send a messenger at the moon's first quarter."

Now wrapped against the evening chill and waiting for his master Venute's signal, the armour-bearer stood on the hillside watching the westering sun. Behind him, Brigantian and Roman voices, muffled by the daub walls of the great hall and the streaming wind, mingled and grew looser, more crass. A druid bard chanted one of the cruder legends of past victories, martial triumphs, and the clatter and thump of a mead cup and bass beat of knife and spoon handles on the low tables reverberated dully in the thin air.

Suddenly, he was aware he was not alone.

"Are you all right, Vellocate?" said a voice softly.

Startled, he saw the queen beside him, a smile playing on her noble lips. Her eyes glowed like sun-flecked oceans of blue. She was washed and her raven hair combed and pinned, and the sun was turning the bones of her cheeks and her smooth forehead the hue of meadow buttercup. The fur-lined collar of her cape was upturned against the breeze, but in the hollow of her neck glowed the torc, the symbol of her power and majesty. The Great Rook Hroc's piercing red eyes rayed out over the tumbled forest below.

I would worship my queen for her queenliness, thought Vellocate, awed. *But I would worship her for her womanliness even if she were no queen. And herein is the trouble, the mystery—*

"You are in pain. Let me tend you." She turned to him, smiling, and ran her hands gently over the rippling muscles of his shoulders.

"Not here, my lady. How many times? The prince has watchers everywhere." Vellocate froze at her touch, looking around as if he and the queen were about to walk into an ambush.

"Who cares what my husband thinks or does? Am I not queen, and does not the Goddess move within me? I can feel her moving within me, Vellocate." Cartimandua sighed achingly, slim fingers on the smooth mound of her belly, reaching downwards. "In all our years together, Venute has not got me with child."

And neither have I, thank the gods, thought Vellocate.

"If you were to stir my cauldron one more time, perhaps . . ." Her hand caressed his groin, and despite himself, a hot hard erection forced itself against his tunic. His own farm-calloused hand enclosed hers and cautiously moved it away.

"I cannot. We cannot. The Romans—the Welsh. And Venute has asked me to take Caradoc and his men into the wilds."

"Has he? Has he now? And this must be done immediately? Have you no time to satisfy your queen?" Cartimandua's eyes blazed.

"I . . . I . . ." Vellocate was torn.

"This—"—she reached beneath his cloak and caressed his aching penis—"this tells me everything I need to know about you, armour-bearer. Go to my chamber. I will follow. Then afterwards, you will take Caradoc to your brother's farm. There, they can take provisions without our Roman guests noticing." She kissed him tenderly on the lips, stroked his taut body. His lust for her was overwhelming, but he was confused, confused.

"My queen, this is not what my master wants. He has asked that I take—"

Cartimandua suddenly gripped his testicles hard, drew him lower, breathed into the warrior's pained face. "If I command, and Venute countercommands, whom should you obey, Vellocate? Who is your queen? In whose name do I speak, by whose power do I command?"

"By the Goddess, my lady."

"You have your answer." She released him.

"And then what, my lady, when Caradoc is . . . secure?"

"Wait and see."

12

UNDER THE INFLUENCE OF THE swirling powers bestowed upon her by Aduna's potion, the queen was a frenetic and demanding lover. Not for the first time Vellocate was drawn into the arms of a creature whose sexual ferocity made his head spin and taxed his skills to the limit.

Their congress had become a game played on several levels. Cartimandua achieved satisfaction by attack and conquest; repeatedly, Vellocate found himself holding back, defending. This element of the game had its own exquisite piquancy since the queen was unrelenting and possessed of endless energy, while Vellocate discovered he could summon hitherto unused reserves of self-control.

There was the element of risk, obviously, and the queen had lately taken greater and greater ones. Where they had once slipped away into the forest together or, disguised, borrowed a nearby homestead or byre, the queen would now deliberately seek to flaunt propriety, dragging the massive warrior to his knees in the grain store and forcing him into cunnilingus or fellating him behind the screens that separated the weaving alcove from the palace audience chamber.

The betrayal of his master's trust racked the armour-bearer sorely. But the more he resisted the queen, the more insistent she became. The more his body demonstrated its guilt, the harder the queen worked to bring him to tumescence and orgasm.

It was certain in Vellocate's mind that Venute knew of this and the queen's other frequent indiscretions, and as a result, the relationship between the prince and his armour-bearer had completely lost its warmth and spontaneity. It was now stiff and formal. They were no longer comrades—merely an aristocrat and his loyal servant. It was beyond Vellocate's limited intellectual powers to determine whether it was his own guilt or the prince's response to the adultery that had brought about this sea-change.

The queen said he was a better lover than Venute. The queen said that should Venute ever die—"*Die, Vellocate*—are you listening to me?"—there would be no question as to whom she would take as her consort. Cartimandua had spoken with the Goddess on this many a time, and there could be no misunderstanding; the Goddess approved. "Do you understand what I'm saying, Vellocate, my big, strong, hard darling?"

The last light had long left the sky when the bemused and aching armour-bearer left the palace building stealthily to do as he had been bidden.

It was near midnight when Venute strode into the queen's chambers, brushing aside the guards, his face a mask of rage, lips the thinnest of lines.

Cartimandua was absentmindedly combing her hair and turned lazily towards him, smiling.

"This room smells of sperm and sweat and cheap Roman perfume. Where is the prince Caradoc?"

"I sent him to the governor."

"The governor? Ostorius Scapula? Do not make jokes."

Cartimandua turned back to her highly polished bronze mirror, apparently unaware that its image, following the damage done to it by Caradoc's outburst, was warped. She said nothing, merely smiled the more.

"Tell me you are joking."

When Cartimandua still made no reply, Venute grasped her shoulders roughly and spun her round. He held her chin in his hands. Her pupils were pins of darkness.

"Where—is—he?"

The high queen's eyes suddenly focused. "He is a bloodthirsty fool. Thousands of Pretan's finest warriors are dead because of him."

"Better to die honourably as a freeman than to live as a slave," hissed Venute in his wife's face. He watched her eyes.

"You really mean it. You really have betrayed him," he whispered. He stood straight. "I can't believe you have betrayed one of our own. Tell me this is a jest. Don't you realise what Caradoc means to the people? He is their light, their hope, their last great warrior. Can you imagine what the Fifteen Tribes will think of this? Many of them would have laid down their lives for him. He is the spirit and soul of Pretan."

"No. I am. Listen to me, Venute—"

"When word of what you have done travels, all we have worked for for years will disappear like water on sand. You cannot hope to command the Brigantes now as a force. The Isogores, Belisidan, Dobni—they'll all go their own way. All that work for nothing. And you call yourself a diplomat!"

Cartimandua slapped Venute's face.

"Don't speak to me like this! I never called myself a diplomat! That was your job! While I maintained the peace, you have been preparing for war. Why else have you bound the tribes together? Yet you know as well as I that where there has been resistance elsewhere in Pretan, the Romans have put the priesthood to the torch, burned down the sacred groves, smashed the images of our gods, killed our livestock, burned our grain. I have spent my time preserving our Goddess, her people, and our ways. And we are wealthy—Brigantia is the richest, largest kingdom in Pretan. I am the queen. I am guided in all I do by the Goddess."

A deep fear grew in Venute's heart. His queen was possessed but by no god or demon Venute recognised. Their world was crumbling before his eyes; Caradoc's words earlier in the day sprang into his mind. He knelt by Cartimandua's side; she smiled lopsidedly, insanely, and her hand reached to touch his face only to fall limply to her side.

"Where is Vellocate?" he whispered.

The queen's eyes emptied. There was no reply.

And then a tiny shift of the pieces of his intelligence created a new and horrific picture. He drew a long breath.

Venute snapped. "You animal! You have betrayed the Goddess. That you should seduce Vellocate's body is crime enough and one to which I have turned a blind eye. But that you should pervert his mind, his loyalty! And I'll bet all in the name of the Goddess. You are no longer fit to wear this—" He snatched the torc from her neck.

"Give me that back!" screamed the queen, completely distraught, trying to rise, held back by Venute's arm. "May the Goddess strike you deaf and blind! This is blasphemy, blasphemy! O holy Goddess, strike him down!"

Venute looked at the glittering talisman in his hand, suddenly aware that, other than Cartimandua and the high priestess, no human being touched the torc. Or if they did—and the stories were whispered—they died instantly and horribly. The powers of its blessing and curse were in equilibrium, balanced like the moon and stars in the heavens.

He was alive. Nothing happened. There was a frightful sense of nothing happening. As if the torc was waiting, waiting.

"Where is Vellocate?" Venute hissed again.

Cartimandua's response was oiled with venom. "Vellocate always does as I ask. He is altogether a more pleasant, a more amenable man than you. He is a prince in nature, whereas you are a prince in name only. Give me back my torc."

"And what's that supposed to mean?"

Cartimandua smiled through her tears, wheadling. "Give me the torc, and I'll tell you."

"You are pathetic! I know all about you and your sordid rutting. Do you see no message from the Goddess that no amount of seed will awaken in your ground? That your womb is made of stone?"

The queen's face hardened. "Your armour-bearer is a fine man, a noble man. In all things, a better man than you. When I call him to my service at any time of the day or night, he obeys. He obeys me implicitly. The Goddess will bless us in a matter of time." Her lip curled. "Give me the torc!"

"Oathbreaker!"

Venute moved swiftly to the weapons on the wall and took down his sword and scabbard. "You did it—this—because Caradoc insulted you. Wealth and comfort! Is Caradoc to die so that you can preserve your wealth and comfort? I must ride now to stop this treachery. Where have you sent him?"

"If you do, Venute, you ride into exile."

Venute froze at the door. He slowly turned to face Cartimandua. When he spoke, his words thickened in his throat. His face was hard, his eyes cold steel. "So that is how it will be?"

"How dare you challenge your queen's decisions!" shrilled the queen. "What I have done, I have done."

Queen and prince faced each other across the dim room, lamplight flickering on their faces.

"Then it is over," said Venute. He turned and left the chamber, shouting wildly for his armour-bearer.

Warriors, hearing the commotion, came forwards outside the great hall. "M'lord, Vellocate left with the prisoner and an armed guard."

"You didn't stop them? Where did they go?"

"Southeastwards," said one. "To Vellocate's homestead?" ventured another, flinching.

"Ride with me." Venute was on his way to the stables, ordering servants to saddle his mare.

"Sir, we can't," they said, running alongside him. "We're on duty. The queen will—"

"The queen is a traitor. You no longer owe her allegiance. She has betrayed the prince Caradoc. Ride with me!"

Alone in the throne room, images of Caradoc and Venute and Vellocate swam and mingled in the queen's mind. *Strong but stupid and unsubtle, all of them. Not one of them has the Goddess's ear, you see. They are just pawns.* Her oval face softened, and gentle light played on the blue oceans of her eyes, turning to tears of sadness and regret. Caradoc's face predominated. *Those burning brown eyes . . . such a handsome man—not like the hairless boys of my husband's model army, his collection of toy soldiers. Would Venute—or Vellocate—be jealous if they knew how I felt?*

She sighed, stroked the tops of her thighs. *But I could have killed him, the bastard, for desecrating the holy confines of the Great Mother's temple and my throne room. I could have cut off his head and carried it into the courtyard on this sword, heavy though it is, and thrown it to the dogs. No, I could have had it put up on a pole above the entrance. I could have kissed its cold lips and glazed eyes . . . What shall I do, Goddess? You said I could have anything I wanted. Shall I have Venute*—she stabbed a dagger into the low table in front of her—*or Vellocate*—worked it loose, stabbed again—*or Caradoc*—another stab—*or Rome? Or all of them, one—after—the—other?*

I, Hroc, stared down on her from my perch on a bossed shield on the wall. I preened my pinions with my pitted grey beak and suddenly flapped onto the table, pecking inquisitively at the blade embedded in the wood, cawing and chuckling to myself. She's coming, coming . . .

A dim drumbeat started up in the distance and drew nearer, louder.

Then it stopped. Silence.

Cartimandua looked quickly around. "Brigid?"

"I've been loyal—kept the covenant, the religious feasts, honoured the priesthood, sacrificed in the groves—to the last letter of our creed. Oh, my holy Mother, I have not deserted you!" she shouted. The sound echoed in the stillness.

I eyed her, head on one side, watching her without emotion.

"That stupid bull of a warrior wanted me to sacrifice the tribes for his further glory. Rome has asked for nothing. At my request, they crushed the Parisii and sent a force against the northerners. True, they have sent flattering gifts. Should I send them back?" Her voice was wheedling, pathetic.

But the Goddess was silent. And the silence, to Cartimandua, was more horrifying than a visitation from the deity.

And then it seemed the rook spoke.

"Where is the symbol of our pact, my lovely Cartimandua?"

Brigid emerged from the shadows. In the light, it was impossible to tell her age; in the flicker of the lamp, she looked like a smooth-skinned maiden; in the light from the brazier, a full-fleshed mother; yet in profile and in the long cast of her shadow, a wrinkled, stooped crone. Hroc cawed loudly in greeting and flapped clumsily onto her shoulder. She stroked his gnarled claws.

"Oh, my Goddess, it's you! I have waited so long."

"Where is the torc I gave you?"

"Venute. He stole it." She wept.

"Oh, my daughter, how disappointed I am. You failed me. The torc goes in relay, and he who bears it now takes it to the one who may yet save Pretan and all its true souls. For you have passed the burden on."

Cartimandua blinked back her tears. "Not so, holy Mother. I am the true bearer of the torc. It is mine, with all its pain and glory. You gave it to me."

"What a goddess gives, she can take away."

Hroc rose from the Goddess's shoulder, growing huge and black, his wings eclipsing the rafters. Wherever his shadow touched the walls, armour—spears, shields, swords, daggers—tumbled and clanged to the ground. The lamps sputtered and died, and the brazier's flame turned to ash and cinders. Cartimandua fancied she heard the rotting heads on the poles outside the chamber scream hollowly from whatever hell they inhabited—*Come/come with/ come with me/with me.* A thin blue flame danced round Brigid's head, and her eyes were deep wells in which the world's souls writhed and struggled. Cartimandua closed her eyes. Hroc leapt down, his claws clutching the flesh of her face, dragging her eyelid down, slipping her lip into an involuntary snarl. She smelled old feathers, the dankness of nest and mute, the breath of maggots and spiders.

"On the floor, bitch!"

Claws held her down, though in her horror, Cartimandua could not tell whether they were those of the Goddess or Hroc. Stars wheeled around her head; she hardly heard her fate.

"I could kill you now. But that is not my way. If you leave this life now, that would be merciful, and I am anything but merciful. You punishment is not the release of death but the burden of life. Slut that you are, I give you Rome. All of it. Every common soldier who demands your body shall have it. You will not be able to resist. You have sold your soul to Rome. Rome shall have your body too. Release you? Not until your degradation and humiliation is complete. You will suffer long years for this betrayal, a travesty of the Goddess you have pretended to be to my people all these years—maiden, mother, and crone. Your beauty will evaporate, your hitherto barren belly will be filled endlessly with mongrel bastards, and finally, you will creep on the earth, a toothless hag begging me for death.

"Hear my words. They are my last to you, traitoress."

13

THE RISING MOON WAS AN oily orange, huge and myopic over the heavy canopy of oak, elm, and ash, a delicate tracery of hazel beneath, the air cool and still and perfumed with new greenery. Struggling silver trunks of birch twisted upwards. The party made its way down a shallow but deepening cleft into the tangled woodland. A stream gurgled and hissed somewhere below them. Guards outrode left and right, alert, their ponies' ironshod hooves occasionally snapping twigs, clinking on stones.

Once they were half way down the slope, out of earshot of Rampart Hill's watchmen, Vellocate unloosed the cloths that stuffed and bound Caradoc's mouth. He instantly regretted it.

"Where are you taking me? Where's Gwydyr and my Welsh guard? Answer me, you moss-brained log!"

Vellocate's face was grim. "A safe place."

"On whose orders?"

"On the queen's orders."

"On Venute's orders, you mean? You are Venute's armour-bearer?"

"On the queen's orders," repeated Vellocate.

Caradoc felt a shiver run down his spine. The queen's catlike form, hunched and tense and deformed with rage in the throne room, hovered in his mind. Her hatred had been palpable, and

Vellocate's stubborn insistence that tonight's journey was at the queen's instigation, not Venute's, had him fear the worst.

"Unbind my hands, you bastard. I can't guide this pathetic nag down this steep slope with just my thighs, for Medb's sake! Now my wound's bleeding again. By all the silly little gods of the Romans—"

"Be silent!"

An owl hooted, and its call was answered far across the dark valley.

Queen and princedom lost and the night dark and foreign around him, Venute cast himself into the care of Cernunnos, lord of the forest; the bear goddess Artio; and the lesser gods of tree and stone and running water. Under his breath, he asked for forgiveness for his trespass; the Denovii were forest folk, true, but in the wan light of Arianrhod's lunar lamp, the spirits roamed free, their powers to bewitch and harm enhanced and indiscriminate.

Cursing himself for his fear, he pushed his warriors at haste into the depths of the river valley, trusting that Hu and Ailleann, who lived as man and wife on a farmstead not far from Vellocate's *tref,* would find their usual passage across the river. Danain, a young palace guard, rode by his side, with Hu and Ailleann scouting ahead.

The woods were silent. No trace of the passage of his armour-bearer and his prisoner, Caradoc, could be found.

"It was only a guess, my lord," whispered a troubled Danain. "They might have taken Prince Caradoc to the Roman hill road or sunrise-side to the fort on the plains."

"Unlikely," said Venute. "Listen! We're near the river. If Caradoc is not at Vellocate's farmstead, we'll—"

A hiss and thud, and a spear hit Danain in the cruck of his collarbone. With a rattling cough, the young warrior disappeared off the back of his pony and crashed into the undergrowth. Venute's mount reared, and he hauled it round. Another spear whistled past his head.

"Ailleann! Hu! Ambush!"

It seemed the undergrowth was alive with sound. Branches cracked to the left; with a despairing cry, Venute drew his sword and charged. Two, three, four Roman legionaries burst forth to meet him from bushes near the riverbank, shields held high, lances poised to skewer his pony; but his was a trained mount, and within striking distance, he pulled the animal round. With two mighty sweeps of his blade, he killed one soldier outright and maimed another, rode a third down, and leaned over to plunge his sword into his chest.

Instinctively, Venute leapt from his pony's back and ran to the nearest large oak, pressing his back to its rough bark for protection.

"Hu! Ailleann!"

"My lord!"

The world slowed, as if played underwater—black shadows; glistening steel-coloured leaves weaving darkness; the flickering of a breastplate, blade, or spearhead; a grunt of exertion; the hiss of branches swept aside. Hu's pony burst from the trees, and he galloped wildly forwards; a spear whistled from the forest mass, thumped into the warrior's back, emerged from his chest in a shower of black blood. Venute saw his eyes roll white as his death spasm threw him to the forest floor.

A hand grabbed his arm. He spun round, driving his blade horizontally into the helmet of the fourth Roman who had crept behind Venute's protective tree, but two more were four paces away and charging, and others he vaguely glimpsed beyond, their shortswords winking evilly in the moonlight. Over to the right, a scream tore the night—Ailleann!

And then the leading soldiers stumbled and fell, their weapons tumbling uselessly into the brambles and old bracken. Elsewhere, the forest echoed with wailing. In the canopy, huge wings crashed, and human cries mingled with the cawing of some great invisible bird.

Venute froze. Starlight and clouds, black leaves and outthrust branches. The cries faded to whimpers, the whimpers to silence.

The prince heard his heart thumping wildly, a counterpoint to the invisible river's powerful gurgle and hiss below and to his left. He gripped the satchel at his side, felt the rough shape of the torc; it was hot through the leather. His mouth was dry; he wanted to call out but could not.

Picking her way over fallen branches past glimmering rocks, her silver sagum gleaming in the tapestry of cold light, a figure approached, stopping here and there over the fallen foetally-curled figures of Rome.

"They see what they fear most in this world and the next. You, Venute, see what you desire most."

In all his years with the queen, Venute's awareness of the Goddess's presence had been eye-corner—the rustle and flap of Hroc's wings, perhaps, reminding him of that rainy night when he first sought audience with Brigid's handmaiden; or a sense at the ceremonies and feasts of a swirling of the air, of being watched or touched so that the hairs on his neck would stand on end; or smoke would form patterns vaguely human. And sometimes, when they made love, Cartimandua's face would be transformed, and he would imagine the Goddess lived behind the queen's soft skin and radiant eyes.

The creature that moved through the trees brought with her another timeless world, in whose presence all nature bowed and was silent. The Goddess Brigid had taken the form of Cartimandua yet was not she.

"My Goddess! All-Mother, Brigid, have mercy! My queen!" he whispered.

The creature smiled. But when she spoke, her lips did not move. *"Not your queen, but perhaps what your queen should have been, dear Venute. What we read in the stars and what we vowed at the Stones does not always come to pass. Our journey on Earth is a mutual one, and I am seeing now that our lives and fates are bound most closely together."*

Queen Cartimandua it was—light shimmering around her, her beautiful oval face a light in the depths of the night—yet not the queen he had married all those years ago when he was but a struggling prince of a small tribe, and she the nascent goddess-queen of all Brigantia. Softer, warmer, gentler. This was how he had imagined Cartimandua to be, hoped she was, dreamed she would become.

No more beautiful creature existed on Earth than the one that stood before him.

He was moved to offer her the torc, shuffling it out of its satchel, where it glowed with a pale inner fire, but she shook her head sadly.

"My heart bleeds that you should clutch the torc as if it were a thief's booty."

She approached him, stroked his sweating taut face with fingers as light as gossamer.

"Let me ride with you, guide you, Venute. As long as I am by your side, no harm can come to you."

As if in a dream, he fetched and remounted his pony, held out an arm to the Goddess. She grasped it and lightly swung onto the pony's back behind him—so light she was almost not there.

"There are times when not even the gods can foresee the future—when for brief moments, human beings perforce must sit astride both worlds. This is one. You carry a blessing and a curse, Venute. You have done no wrong. The soul of Pretan rests with him to whom you deliver the torc, symbol of my power on earth." The words pounded in his head.

"I am a warrior. I am no priest, no sage. You ask too much." His voice sounded like the croaking of frogs, hers like silvery bells.

"For a few brief moments of your life, you carry the chalice of life and death, the heart and soul of all that makes this island unique. Think of it as an honour. Take me to Caradoc."

They plunged into the cold river, spray sparkling like diamonds. Venute's pony struggled up the far back through the slap of alder leaves, a thick grove at the river's edge. Wild boar snuffled invisibly in the thicket. A wolf howled on the distant moors.

They came to a low wall of upturned tree roots and dead branches, tumbled stone—plough's clearance—that marked the boundary of Vellocate's family's homestead. Beyond grew meadow grass—hay and silage for the family's livestock; and near the crest, a ring wall and single line of staves, more of a fence than defence, was just visible in the moonlight. As they rode upwards though the field, the Goddess firmly holding his waist as they rode, Venute saw ploughed land south of the enclosure, already green with barley and bean rows, beetroot; a patch of herbs; pollarded trees for fencing; a duckpen and pig and sheep enclosures.

They dismounted out of earshot of the farm buildings, which huddled beneath a huge, dense stand of oak on the brow of the hill. Venute tied his pony's reins to a fence stave.

The night was still and ethereal—a picture, a dream. The prince's mind swirled, his body tensed. They trod silently into Vellocate's yard. The main farm building was a solid hut to the left, and a testimony to industry and wealth of his armour-bearer's clan was a huge round barn, threshing floor and byre to the right.

"They see what they most fear," said Cartimandua, smiling and touching his arm. *"Remember."*

Venute drew his sword quietly and crept to the wicker door. Lights were within. Aiming for the leathern latch, he kicked it open.

Vellocate, sitting at a long oak table with benches, was instantly on his feet, reaching for a dagger. The flat of the prince's blade pinned his arm swiftly to the table; two men, the armour-bearer's younger brothers or farmhands, rose but backed off the far wall, their eyes wide with fear.

The prince took in the scene in an instant. On the wall behind, cooking implements hung. Bunches of herbs drying. An ornate empty cauldron, booty from some skirmish in the south hanging over a hearth in which embers glowed. A loom, a spinning wheel, a beehive oven with embers still glowing within, and the warm musty smell of freshly baked bread. Smoke spiralling to the hole in the thatched roof.

A woman and children, wrapped in blankets, stumbled out from behind a wattle screen—the bedroom—followed by two grumbling elders. All stopped, aghast at the tableau before them.

"The perfect domicile." Venute's voice was low. His eyes flickered into every corner. "Who else is here?"

"No one, my prince. You're cutting my arm."

"I thought of you as my friend."

"And so I am, my lord."

Venute's eyes glittered. "Friend you are not. What are you, Vellocate? A farmer? An armour-bearer? A queen's lover? Or a traitor?"

"I serve you, my queen, the Goddess, my family. I don't know which should come first, which last. Please—let—my—arm—free."

"Oh, you served your queen, Vellocate," said a soft voice from the portal.

"My lady!"

"It is time to serve her again. I would see your prisoner. Where is he?"

The image of Cartimandua stepped forwards into the light, perfect glowing majesty. And Vellocate sensed a discrepancy, a wrongness for which he could find no explanation.

The queen, yet not the queen.

He gulped, his mouth suddenly dry, eyes wide. He made no answer.

"Well," sighed Venute, "you have made your choice. I cannot govern or direct your conscience. Give me Caradoc, go free. I want no more from you—ever."

"Behind you, Prince," the armour-bearer managed to say.

Venute turned swiftly, sword flashing in the lamplight, but the blade was stopped by a burly legionary's shortsword and viciously rasped downwards. Leatherclad soldiers of Rome piled in behind, pinioned his arms tightly behind his back, and forced him face down over the creaking table.

14

"WELL DONE, CAPTAIN CATULLUS. HOLD him firmly—that man is as slippery as a fish."

Ostorius Scapula himself was framed at the doorway, helmet under his arm. He ducked beneath the lintel and entered, sniffing with disdain. Soldiers with many torches moved behind him out into the room, binding at the Governor's gesture all but Vellocate, who slumped back to the table, head in hands. "The Goddess, it was the Goddess," he murmured frantically.

"What have you seen, heathen?" said Scapula suspiciously. "I heard a woman's voice. Not one of these peasants, a cultured voice. Check the room." Soldiers spread through the farmhouse.

"Perhaps you wonder why I came in person, Venutius," said Scapula to the prince in Latin. "The prize your servant holds is worth the journey."

"Do not think I am unable to understand you," returned Venute, also in the speech of Rome. "I was born and raised in Camulodunum, and know your barbaric tongue of old. There is no-one here worth your attention."

"Barbaric? An interesting use of the word. I know you know Latin, Venutius. I know much more than you think. I think for instance, you're mistaken about there being no-one here worthy of my attention." He turned to the quivering armour-bearer and placed his shortsword next to the man's head.

"Vellocates, Vellocatus, whatever!"

Vellocate rose with a clatter of kitchen implements.

Scapula sniffed and looked round the room. "There is no-one I want in this pigsty, it's true. But you have a barn, have you not, armour-bearer? And I am told by my watchers that in the barn there is a beast of considerable value."

"Latin is lost on him," said Venute, playing for time. "Let me go. I am no threat to you. I am a soldier like you, Scapula—I know when I'm outnumbered."

The soldiers released him at a nod from the governor.

"They say you are a shrewd man for a Celt," said Ostorius. "How is it in your language? *"Wily"*? In my world, one who is a mad queen's errand-boy and cuckold is not wily, but stupid. I could kill you now, but it hardly seems worth it. I fancy seeing the capture of your Caratacus will be heartbreaking enough, and I would like you to share that moment with me, *Prince* Venutius."

"Is—your prisoner—in the barn?" Venute asked Vellocate in the Celtic tongue. The armour-bearer nodded, tears in his eyes, the full realisation of his part in Caradoc's betrayal now dawning. "My Prince, I would not have done this if I'd known—"

Venute bowed his head. "I know." He turned to the Roman. "Humour me, Scapula," he asked the British governor quietly. "Who brought you here?"

Scapula shrugged. "I was in the area. Gaius Horventa brought me, I suppose. But who brought Gaius Horventa?"

No-one needed to ask. The flat acid reality of betrayal sagged like a shroud and in it, tangled and lifeless, hung Cartimandua's name.

"Well, it's getting late," said Scapula cheerily. "Bring our friends to the barn. Him and him. You and you—guard the rest. Catullus, er—" and he nodded towards the door. "Fetch the insurance."

The captain grinned and exited with two men. Venute, Vellocate, Scapula and torch-bearing guards crossed the yard to the barn.

No help. On my own. Where's the Goddess? thought Venute desperately.

A single smoking lamp illuminated the barn's immense and gloomy interior. In the centre, tied to the huge oak load-bearing pillar, sat a dishevelled Caradoc, his clothes still bloodstained, sweat-darkened hair hanging over his face. A threshing floor of hardened earth lay to one side; to the other, a row of large earthenware grain pits, huge lidded storage pots sunk into the ground. Cattle were byred and horses stabled in an adjacent shed; their humid dungy smell mingled with the sweat of scythed grass.

"Ah, Ostorius Scapula!" shouted Caradoc, raising his shaggy head. His bull voice, unquenched, echoed round the barn. "I'd recognise that ugly face anywhere." With a great effort, he shuffled his bonds up the pole and stood upright.

"You are not a pretty sight yourself, Prince Caratacus. Have you been fighting with your, er, friends?"

Caradoc ignored the taunt. "So what is it to be, Scapula? Torture? Murder? All the fun of the circus? You've brought an audience, I see. What has Rome in mind for me do you think, Venute, Vellocate? Thumbs up, or thumbs down?"

"My dear Caratacus, none of those. I've come to take you to Rome."

"Rome? I'd die first." Caradoc spat.

"I think not, noble prince. The Emperor Claudius has specifically requested your presence in the Capitol. He apparently thinks you're a bit special. And I think you will go . . . peaceably."

"Piss off!" roared Caradoc.

"It is my hope that you will not be a difficult prisoner on the journey, stirring slaves and suchlike to rebellion," chided Scapula.

"So I have brought along insurance for me, company for you. It's a long way to Rome."

He snapped his fingers. Into the light came a tall, big-boned woman, bearing herself as proudly as her heavy chains would allow; and behind her, stumbling, but unchained, holding each other, two men, one blond, one dark—

"By the Great Mother. Rhyanydd! Congal! Brychan!" Caradoc struggled with his bond, lashing to and fro. "But what have they done to . . ."

Caradoc's brothers held each other's arms, pitifully shuffling forward. It seemed they took in the scene before them; but this was impossible, since their eyes were pierced and sightless. Congal tilted his head slightly.

"Caradoc. We thought you were dead," he said softly.

Caradoc strained against his bonds until the great bowed muscles of his shoulders bulged taut and shiny. Blood sprang afresh from his shoulder wound. His noble face was twisted into a rictus of agony and anger. A low growl rose in the pillar of his throat.

"Oh, Scapula, you slimy piece of pig-shit. Oh, no, NO." Caradoc's huge frame shuddered.

"Your brothers, Caradoc," said Rhyanydd gently. "They've brought your brothers to see you." And a tear ran down her cheek, glittering in the light of the torches.

Brychan hauled himself up to his full height and stretched out his hands, his scarred sockets searching pitifully to recognise a face now in memory only.

"Caradoc? These bastards told me I'd never see you again. I thought they meant by that they were going to kill me, or you. I didn't think they'd do—this—to us."

"Families are a nuisance, aren't they?" said Scapula, patting the men on their backs. Brychan lashed out uselessly; Scapula deftly stepped out of the way. "But less so, we think, if they are sightless. These two have been no trouble, and curiously enough, neither has their sister in law, ever since . . . Well, enough said. Let's be about our business. Guards!"

Venute felt light fingers loosen the bond at his wrists. "*You still have the Torc. Caradoc must have it. He will know how to use its power. He is of the blood. Can you do this?*" The Goddess's voice whispered in his ear.

"For Pretan. For you. For what might yet be," breathed Venute, tears of fury in his eyes. "Divert them."

From the flickering shadows emerged the Goddess, in the likeness of Queen Cartimandua, perfect in every way, regal, glorious, a smile playing on her noble lips. She spoke in court Latin.

"Ostorius Scapula, you are an uninvited guest on my sovereign territory. You have no jurisdiction here, and this is ratified by your treaty. Shall I quote?"

She walked towards him, stood proudly before him. The governor of all Britain stood his ground, but only just; a thin line of sweat appeared on his shaven top lip.

"And worse, you are a thief in the night. It is my experience that Romans do their thieving by day."

"My Lady. This is an unexpected surprise," said Scapula, frowning. His quick eyes darted left, right, suspiciously. He gripped the bronze hilt of his shortsword. "But as you can see, there are instances when military expedience must come first. I must consider the security of these isles. We have here a traitor and criminal, and whether you wish it or not, we are taking Caratacus to Rome—"

"*We see.*" The Goddess's voice came not from her smiling image, but from every corner of the cavernous barn. "*Come, my winged ones, join the fray.*"

The clattering of feathers, the scratch of claws and beaks filled the rafters. Out of the roof-joists fell a flock of heavy, black-winged birds as if released from a cage, talons stretched, feathers swirling, their targets the guards, who fell and writhed, claws embedded in scalps and faces. Torches whirled and fell; some plunged into the dry hay, where columns of smoke and flames soon leapt upwards. Shouts of alarm turned rapidly to screams as Scapula's guards sought unsuccessfully to fend off their corvid attackers.

In the confusion Venute slipped his bonds, took the Torc out of his satchel and plunged through smoke and flailing bodies to the barn's centre. Loosing the dirk he kept in his boot he severed Caradoc's willow-bark manacles.

"By the gods, Venute, this has been a day to remember!" Sooty tears streaked Caradoc's cheeks and his face was twisted with anguish, grief and failure.

"Use this!" hissed Venute through the howls of pain, the rising crackle of flames, the noise of terrified beasts and the cries of fleeing prisoners and soldiers.

What is it? By the Blessed Mother, Venute—you stole this from Cartimandua? This is the torc of—"

"It's yours. Use it now!"

The torc glowed in the gloom. Fire flickered on its golden surfaces, flames beckoning seductively. Caradoc's bloodied, filthy fingers slowly reached for the necklet, then swiftly withdrew. "I cannot be Brigid's emissary," he said, gasping. "I am no druid! I am an ordinary man, a warrior. The torc was meant for you, Venute."

"By the Mother, Caradoc! What future for Pretan if you refuse this gift? You are our only hope. Wear it—and call the Goddess!" Venute tried to clasp the torc round Caradoc's huge neck, but the giant brushed his hand aside.

"You wear it," he growled. "My strength is in what I can see."

A sword blade deftly flicked the torc out of Venute's proferring hands and sent it whirling into the darkness, where it struck a grain pot hollowly. That same sword was at Caradoc's throat before he could move out of its range. Scapula's face, scored and bloodied by clawmarks, leaned into theirs.

Catullus, Scapula's captain, who had also managed to beat off the frenzied talons and bills of the birds that mauled him, stood at the governor's shoulder. Breathless and bleeding, he held another blade at Venute's throat, preventing him from recovering the precious torc. It was becoming hard to breathe in the smoke-logged barn, and flames flickered everywhere.

"Gentlemen, this is no time for exchanges of jewellery," coughed Scapula. "I have chased this man the length and breadth of your stinking land. If you think a few conjuring tricks, a flock of tame crows and a burning barn are going to deflect me now, you've misjudged your man. Take them both."

"You bastard!" Venute flung himself at the Roman. Captain Catullus clubbed him heavily with the hilt of his sword and the prince crumpled to the hard earth. Catullus crouched by Venute's body, a piece of sackcloth pressed to his mouth in an attempt to prevent the smoke scouring his lungs.

"Let him burn, Catullus," coughed Scapula. "This is the prize. Let's get him out before we suffocate."

Stumbling in the murk, Scapula and Catullus took Caradoc at swordpoint through the smoke.

"If you value your lives, get out of here now!" he shouted hoarsely to those guards still stumbling among the showers of lit reeds that cascaded from the roof. "And if you find that bloody woman, run her through!"

It seemed to Venute that he was walking between the fires of the living and dead. Images of blind Congal and Brychan in the flicker of flames, the glint of a spear emerging from Hu's chest, the fear of a dense dark forest, the face of Cartimandua burning away to reveal a dry, black-eyed, long-toothed skull; all these coursed through his dream, and there seemed no escape.

And ever the voice of the Goddess was with him, though her words were lost, and her form obscured by mist.

He woke to the gentle splash of morning rain and the smell of cinders and soot. A toothless old woman, her head cowled and her thin grey hair in rat-tails plastered to her wrinkled forehead, leaned over him. With a cloth she stroked his aching head. Above them, in the scorched oaks, rooks cawed disconsolately as if mourning their dead. The sky was grey and his pallet—straw piled in the corner of a twisted, leaning wattle fence, part of some outhouse wall—was damp.

He rose on his elbow, only to fall back, the egg-sized bruise on his head throbbing. The Romans had wreaked bloody vengeance on those who remained in Vellocate's family *tref* and fired the farmhouse. It and the barn were smouldering ruins. The recent dry spell and a hilltop breeze had fanned the conflagration and destroyed the settlement utterly.

Vellocate, Caradoc and his, Scapula and his legionaries, were nowhere to be seen. The odour of death and smoke and soot hung over the scene like a shroud.

"I must find the torc," he said. His voice was as rough as Hroc's.

The old woman smiled sadly, patted his arm. No words passed her lips but they formed clearly in his head: "*No, Venute. The threads I sought to draw together are now unravelled and destroyed, and from this night onwards the land is sliding into the hands of Rome. So dies the House of the Ram, and so rises the House of the Fish. Oh, they'll fight on for many years yet; but the Heart of Pretan is lost. The torc is cursed: you must let it lie.*"

"Then I must rescue Caradoc," he coughed. "Why did they let me live? Where is my sword?"

"Some soldier took your sword as a trophy. They let you live because they enjoyed the thought of your burning. They imagine you are a pawn of the Queen. You and I know different.

"And how will you rescue Caradoc? You are wounded, the Welshmen scattered, and your armour-bearer scurries back to your Queen, who wanders witless on Rampart Hill. Caradoc is in chains and is being borne to Rome with six cohorts as his guard."

"I'll rally the Fifteen Tribes—"

The old woman sighed, and her eyes rolled. *"That you will. I see it. And so will Queen Boudica, great Victoria, in the south, and many nameless others. But the world is changing, and the gods are departing."*

Venute struggled to his feet, dizzy and wearied, half in and half out of sleep. He was suddenly very thirsty. "Who are you, old woman? Is there a well or stream nearby?"

The crone gave him a bowl of clear cold water. *"They see what they most fear, but you, Venute, see what you most desire."* She cackled at the irony.

Venute stared. Then cold sweat broke out on his discoloured brow and he slithered backward to the wattle and straw in a faint. She seemed just another withered old hag; but of course—the Goddess was virgin, mother and crone, all ages of womanhood.

"Forgive me, Mother," he said, and passed out.

"Leave the Soul of Pretan where it lies, Venute. You have done all you can."

She stroked his brow tenderly.

"I too am tired and worn. Rome has yet one more poisonous gift to your people, a cup so potent it will close the door to the gods for many long years. I can see the future only dimly, but I sense that Heaven will slumber, and the paths of gods and mankind will be sundered. My own powers are fading, and the fields and lakes and rivers and forests, the sun, moon, stars and clouds will lose their magic, mystery, power. There is a new Roman God arriving in His fiery chariot, riding on the backs of the legions, and He will close your minds, and you will sleep for millennia,

while they who know me are persecuted and burned, and will be forced to hide their knowledge of me, to disguise the truth.

"What remains of me will sleep with the Torc, and may your kind never happen upon it again. May it lie forever in the earth that has been cursed and trampled by Roman feet. The bond between us is broken."

And the Goddess's image faded and blew away in a swirl of rain-blackened ash, as if she had never been.

15

CARADOC AND HIS FAMILY RODE side by side and spoke among themselves in the Gaelic they knew their captors could not understand. Their horses were tied together, though they themselves rode free; two dark-bearded Syrian auxiliaries rode behind and held bows that could be trained at a moment's notice on Caradoc's broad back, should the prince choose to make a bid for freedom. And this was enough, Scapula deemed.

By early light, the party paused and made camp on a hilltop south, cloaks damp and heavy with the sullen rain that steamed their horses and bedewed the bush and scrub on all sides.

Talk among the legionaries was hushed, and many a sidelong glance was cast at dark crags and glades and back at the deep rain-gloomed valley where so many of their companions had dreamed and died. Those who remained of the party that ambushed Venute's group and the men who witnessed the strange events in the barn and survived were like haunted men, wounded and troubled where no sword could touch, afraid to sleep, or tossing and moaning in their wrapped cloaks and hastily erected tents. Scapula was angry and puzzled, demanding his captains put an end to the whispers, threatening waverers with beatings. Only Catullus, a hardened and simple soldier, seemed unaffected, swaggering here and there through the camp, joking with his men.

The governor had arranged beforehand to meet Gaius Horventa and his party here and anticipated at least a day's wait. The bullock cart of gifts for Cartimandua, relieved of its load, would still make heavy going through the untracked countryside, especially now the rain had turned dust to mud.

Below them in the rain-haze, a column of grey smoke still rose from the destruction of Vellocate's family *tref* to be whipped away by a stiff breeze in the upper airs. Rampart Hill stood gloomy and silent a little to the east; its watchers would have noted the blaze and guessed at the fear-driven insensate slaughter and rapine that had counterpointed its destruction.

Scapula doubted there would be reprisals. Nevertheless, he posted a tailguard of scouts on strong horses who crisscrossed the valleys and streams behind them, alert and watchful of ambush.

When fires were burning and cooking pots swinging, Scapula rode to the outcrop where Caradoc sat watching the plume of distant smoke. The Romans' doctor had cleansed and cauterised the warrior's wound—with Caradoc howling in protest—and was grinding antiseptic sulphur as a dressing. With gestures, Rhianydd was offering a herb compress at which the physician, a wiry grey-haired Greek, was sniffing cautiously.

"Nobody will come, Caratacus. The rebellion's over."

"You truly are a nasty little man, Scapula. You are also far from home and in enemy territory."

Scapula shrugged and grinned. As governor of Britain, any other human being who spoke to him like that would have been lashed or castrated. But he had so wanted to be present at Caratacus's capture, he happily dismissed the insult, this brazen lack of a humility he had grown to accept from all others. He dismounted, crouched on his haunches next to Caradoc, looked out over the broad valley towards the smoke.

"You were a noble opponent, Caratacus." he said. "Even now, in total defeat and pouring rain, your spirit is unquenched. I admire that. But you know that Cartimandua and Venutius and Vellocates are roast meat, and the fine warriors of Rampart Hill are cowering inside their straw huts leaderless. What do you see out there? Legions of trained fighters rallying to your aid?" he asked.

"I see the Goddess Brigid haunting you wherever you go, even in your dreams. I saw your face last night."

Scapula shifted uneasily. "Last night? Hmmm. I was going to ask you about that. Your Cartimandua is—was—a powerful woman. Not as I imagined her."

"The queen Cartimandua?" Caradoc laughed harshly. "That wasn't the queen, you bow-legged old fool."

Scapula rose. "Then who was it, savage?" he said scornfully. "Give me a little credit. I am not prey to your superstitions."

"Nor I to yours. You'll never know who you spoke to in the barn because you haven't the sight." He tapped the side of his shaggy head. "You're all straight lines and—what do you call it? Greek logic."

Whoever she was, thought Scapula, *she and Venutius cost me a dozen good men and addled the brains of a dozen more. Hades, but that woman's powerful. I'll be glad to get out of this bewitched land. Back to civilisation.*

He shuddered and blew a droplet of rain from the end of his nose.

"Superstition, Caratacus. Just superstition. We'll wipe all this nonsense away. The whole land will bow to Rome. They'll embrace our culture and our ways. They'll forget their gutteral lingo and speak Latin like the rest of the empire."

"In your dreams, Scapula. Nowhere else."

"Look at the smoke, savage, and tell me whose dreams are in ashes now."

Caradoc's jaw set grimly.

Rhianydd approached, her head hooded.

"Out of my way, Roman," she said. "Let me apply this poultice."

Caradoc translated. Scapula stepped to one side and bowed in mockery. "By all means, my lady," he said sarcastically. "A fine big wife you have there."

Caradoc ignored the remark, started with pain as the poultice was applied. "Woman, take great care," said Caradoc in his native tongue. "This ugly fellow has developed a passion for real women and would pin you to his bed given half a chance."

Rhianydd roared with laughter. "And would he tickle me with this?" She waggled an extended little finger in front of the governor's face.

"Gaius Horventa's party in the valley four stadia east," called a guard.

The governor acknowledged the message. "Just one thing more, Caratacus. I'm curious to know what trinket Venute was so keen to pass on to you. It seemed to be of gold. A charm bracelet, perhaps? An amulet to ward off evil spirits?"

"You'll never know, Scapula. You'll never know."

<hr />

The rain blew over, and a weak sunshine filtered through the pale clouds as the day wore on. Horventa's men joined the party towards dusk, labouring up the hillside, several looking distinctly hung over on the honey-sweetened wheat ale that so often stupefied or incited the Celt and which had provided lubrication the night before.

The emissary, Gaius Horventa, reported that Cartimandua was distraught, enraged, and in no fit mood to continue negotiations; that he would return in a month's time to complete them; and that rumour had it that the prince Venutius had survived the torching of the homestead, for several of his most loyal supporters had abandoned their queen and the hillfort was in undisguised turmoil.

"Messengers went out this morning as soon as the events of the night became known, sir," said the old man. "I fear the Fifteen Tribes will know of this before long. If, as is rumoured, the prince Venutius *has* survived—"

"We may have another Caratacus on our hands," Scapula finished. "I wish I'd run the bastard through last night just to be certain. These people's heroes spring up like weeds . . ." He left the thought open.

On this information, Scapula resolved to build a marching fort in the area. The site of Vellocates' homestead commanded a good view of the Brigantians' headquarters and would be as good as any. There were unclaimed crops and cleared land recently vacated . . . and there was nothing like rubbing the savages' noses in the dirt.

In the meantime, he instructed Horventa to double the next consignment of "gifts" to Queen Cartimandua.

"She has done us good service, caught us a fine fish," he said, nodding towards Caradoc's group. "A bounteous reward should tie the woman more closely to us and split the Brigantian federation even further asunder."

He laughed, clapped the frail Horventa on his bony shoulder. "All in all, a good day's work."

South and then west they rode the next day, pausing only for the engineers to take readings and measurements for the road Ostorius Scapula intended to drive through the humped barren hills east from Castra Devana, the new fort at Chester.

16

QUEEN CARTIMANDUA ABANDONED RAMPART HILL shortly after the feast at the beginning of high summer, of Lughnasa, and the cereal harvest had been homed. She never returned. She and her court moved to the well-established fortress town of Venta Ysur, known to the Romans as Isurium, and which would later become Aldborough, North Yorkshire.

The news of the destruction at the Hill and the banishing of her husband sent waves of unease rippling through the tribes, and Venute's strength grew as he roved among the Brigantes like a tiger, assuming the mantle of the lost Caradoc and rallying the tribes with a kind of mad energy the likes of which the Brigantian chieftains had not seen before. This time, he told them, there was a new enemy—his wife, the Romans' doll, the slut and traitor Cartimandua.

Behind him strode the influential druidic priesthood, proclaiming him heir to the soul of Pretan and disowning Cartimandua. Publicly, the prince embraced their support, but his faith no longer gave him comfort. Inside, he felt uninhabited.

For him, the gods were already dead.

And thus were the tribes split. Some were secretly seduced by the wealth and security that Cartimandua courted and so were either her allies or neutral. Others were drawn to Venute's charismatic insurgence and prepared to die for their lands, freedom, and religion.

But Venute had been betrayed and rejected by the queen he had loved with all his heart, abandoned by his Goddess, and deprived of the simple, strong virtues of his lifelong companion Vellocate, who now sat at Cartimandua's side, an outlaw consort to a queen sinking further into madness and depravity. Vellocate, he heard, was calling himself king; a simple man bewitched and enthralled, powerless but deluded and seduced by the trappings of power. Venute could imagine Cartimandua's secret delight as she manipulated this sorry puppet of hers, and the prince sorrowed over her gain and his loss. He felt a terrible loneliness in the seat of his soul which he could fill only by exacting terrible vengeance on Rome, looting its supply trains, sacking and burning its wayforts, harrying each cohort and century he came across.

But in time, the cold hatred he felt for Vellocate burned itself out. He came to see how the trusting armour-bearer had been torn apart by conflicting loyalties—between his master and friend, his queen and the seduction she exerted over him using those powers and gifts bestowed upon her by the Goddess, and the ties of the land which bound him to his family in the shadow of Rampart Hill.

That winter, he returned with a small band of warriors to the frost-rimed blackened ruins of his friend's farmstead. He stood, head bowed, shivering amid the invading brambles and weeds and charred posts, while the rooks cawed disconsolately in the leafless trees above him.

He was not tempted to search for the torc, for he heeded the Goddess's curse on it and all that touched it. But he wept for lost Pretan and resolved to mark the death of those, here and throughout the island, who had fought to honour the Goddess and hold in their heads and hearts the mystery and majesty of life's great wheel.

He ordered a howe to be raised on the site, a great low mound of soil. "Let there be no stones to mark these graves," he said, "for stones will attract stone breakers. Let the Earth reclaim her own. Let them rest in peace."

And finally, he enjoined Hroc, the Great Rook, to watch over the land. "I give you guardianship of the torc and those who died in its name, noble birds!" he shouted into the silent rookery. "Let no man disturb their peace."

Then he left, never to return.

<hr />

Ostorius Scapula's health declined rapidly, and he was dead by the spirit festival of Samhain in November the following year, racked with horrors, unable to sleep, his limbs bound and his joints invaded by Pretan's invidious damp and cold.

Upon him, the curse of the torc rested most heavily, and in every nightmare, he saw the face of Cartimandua, her hands like talons clawing at his eyes, her voice a harsh crowing of anger and savagery.

His place as Governor of Britannia was taken by Aulus Didus Gallus, who took upon himself Scapula's desire to link Castra Devana with the new fort at Eboracum, York. Parts of the road had already been built, but a viable link through the bandit country of the Pennines had yet to be established.

As a temporary measure, he strengthened parts of the ancient track used by Scapula on his retreat to Castra Devana, establishing small way stations by means of the map his predecessor's engineers had drawn.

One such way station was on a mounded howe southwest of Rampart Hill.

Saturnalia, AD 58

"I hate this place. I truly believe it to be haunted," sniffed Marcus Tullian, hauling his thick woollen cloak tighter round his narrow shoulders and clamping his leather-sided helmet more firmly onto his tight-curled head. "I wonder what we did to receive this commission."

"Absolutely nothing. And that's the problem," growled his companion Artemori, a cleft-jawed, pug-nosed, swarthy Thracian auxiliary. "Had we distinguished ourselves in the summer campaigns, we would have been feasting like heroes in the halls of the plains, not freezing to death on the world's roof."

Flurries of snow flicked and swirled, misting the valley and lashing the sentries' faces. Daylight, such as it was, was leaking from the leaden sky. The road from Castra Devana snaked dimly into the black trees before it rounded a spur and climbed upwards into the scrub. It was deserted. Preparations for December's chief festival had cut the flow of visitors to the marching fort to a trickle; the last legionaries out of Cheshire, on their way to Eboracum, had passed this way two weeks earlier, stopping merely to rest and reshoe their horses, mend a broken cartwheel and axle, reprovision and rest.

"Do you think they'll ever build a proper road?" asked Tullian.

"Through here? Unlikely," said Artemori. "The action's all in the north these days."

They walked to and fro on the raised wooden walkway behind the palisade, stamping numb feet, fumbling with stiff hands for the small warmth to be found in their armpits beneath their cloaks and leather-bound breastplates.

"Haunted? You called this place haunted?" the Thracian asked, screwing up his eyes against the snow.

Tullian banged wet sleet from his mittens and tried to scrub a little warmth into his face.

"Notice how the locals steer clear. There's been trouble of one sort or another at every other fort on this route—marauding parties, pleas for help from that harridan Cartimandua, even the occasional drinking bout and orgy up and down the line—but not here. What do we get here? Skinners and salters and knife grinders. Craven fur-bound savages trying to sell us skinny mountain hares and then scuttling off into the mists faster than their prey ever did."

"That means nothing. The gods have forsaken this land—"

"No, they haven't. I can feel it."

"Oh, mighty Rome!" sighed Artemori theatrically. "I hail from a superstitious land, but you native-born Italians beat us all hands down. Ghosts hiding behind every tree bole, every standing stone. Boo!"

"So you pay no heed to the stories about this place—the very place where Caratacus was finally brought to heel? The place where Governor Ostorious Scapula himself was fatally cursed?"

The Thracian sniffed pensively. "Not so much haunted as deserted. The only birds that sing here are those damned death crows, and I'd hardly call that singing."

"What about that new latrine we started to dig yesterday then? The moment we struck into the earth, those very birds set up such a screeching and wheeling it was impossible to hear oneself think."

Artemori shrugged and laughed. "They're birds, for god's sake. That's what birds do."

Alone with their thoughts, the sentries stomped in opposite directions round the square walkway. Artemori was first to return to the northernmost corner above the fort's wooden gate.

"Ho, Marcus Tullian!" He gestured vigorously. "We have a visitor."

A black-cloaked and hooded figure, fighting the wind and hung with grey snow, struggled towards them on the rough-stoned road. It stopped and looked upwards towards the fort. The soldiers glimpsed a pale white face smeared with long dark strands of hair.

"It's a woman," breathed Artemori. "My Saturnalia gift!"

"Be quiet, satyr."

The girl located the winding footpath that led out of the defile and began to climb. After a while, they could hear her laboured breath. She stopped at the palisade and stared upwards.

"Hail, traveller!" shouted Tullian mockingly into the gathering gloom. The girl did not respond.

"*Loquarisne latine, puella?* Do you speak Latin, girl?"

"A little."

The girl spoke wearily, apparently searching for words in the soldiers' tongue. "Food and a bed. Please. I am tired."

"This is no taverna. Go on your way."

"Are you mad, Tullian?" hissed Artemori. He leaned over the parapet. "My friend is inhospitable. Wait there. Our commander is an honourable man and may be persuaded to allow you within our walls."

The girl leaned heavily against the palisade and, with a rattling sigh, slithered to a crumpled heap at its base.

"By the gods, Artemori!" seethed the Roman. "She is a spy. Or a demon. Linnius will crucify you!"

Artemori, heedless, scrambled like a monkey down the ladder into the fort's quadrangle.

"Bind her," ordered Captain Plautius Aulis Linnius. "Take her into the messroom. Artemori—she is your ward. The first hint of trouble and two things will happen—she will be executed, and you will dig her grave—on the northern hill, alone, and at night. Do you understand?"

"I do, Captain."

"How is she? Still unconscious?"

"Cold as death, sir." The legionaries in the messroom—merely an open area with a stone-chimneyed fire in the centre, same long hut as the First Platoon's dormitory—had gathered round the traveller. The Thracian was chafing the girl's hands, a lascivious grin on his swarthy face.

"Who'll have her first? We must cast lots," he said.

Captain Linnius gripped the Thracian's arm hard. "Men, even in its furthest coldest reaches, a citizen of Rome behaves with honour and decorum. If and when this girl returns to her senses, I want her brought to my office immediately for questioning."

Their commander turned and left.

"Pompous old bastard," muttered Guthrun, a Belgic auxiliary, wrapping a cloak round his torso and throwing another over his shoulder, clasping it tightly. "Wants her for himself. Just my luck too—I'm on duty. C'mon, Quintillus—time for a walk on the walls."

A gentle voice spoke: "Stay a while, Romans. Don't leave me. Take a little warmth with you first."

Thus it was in Babylon, in the burnt dust of ancient cities, in the bare marble-floored temples, by fountains sparkling with cool water brought from the mountains where the gods crouched and frowned.

The woman slipped her bonds as if they were of dried grass. She rose swiftly to her feet, unclasped her damp cloak. Artemori fell over, eyes glazed. She slipped delicately, gracefully out of her simple shift, smiling. Her naked body gleamed in the firelight, white and golden, her breasts full, nipples dark, the black triangle of her pubic hair mysterious, her thighs long and pale.

In paintings laboriously applied by rough and speechless savages in the hidden furthest reaches of underground caverns, where the leys of the earth met and were focused in the artist's fevered imagination, he painted and daubed, his greasy lamp flickering, consumed not by bison and stag but by the spirit essence of the creatures upon whose flesh his tribe relied—consumed not by woman, but by womanhood itself.

The soldiers stared, open-mouthed, rooted to the spot.

"I believe I am in love," whispered Quintillus.

And I walked with the queen, with the long line of her ancestors, in whose frail and trembling souls burned a holy flame, a chain of starlight flickering down the ages, a delicate bridge from the cold clay of Earth to the wild spiralling of eternity.

"It is the whore Cartimandua! Bewitchment and death!" gasped Guthrun, gripping Quintillus's arm.

So might she imagine the truth no longer exists; that she might turn her back on vows made in blood and spirit; that the might of her own will and flesh is greater than mine; that these sorry, lonely men and their ants' empire hold the key to higher and better things than the worship of the world's womb, the gathering of the harvest of fruit and souls.

The woman smiled calmly, pointed to Guthrun. "Go raise every man. This night, each one of you will walk in Arcadia."

In this way, I tell the world: You have broken my heart, unpicked the weave of many lifetimes, destroyed the tumbling harmonies and resonance of life itself. Each of you should have listened to your inner voices, then you would have known that I have cursed and hallowed this land for all time. On this land, tonight, death shall walk tall, and tomorrow, my birds will feed on your blind eyes.

The Belgian stumbled into the night, bewitched, dreaming, sleepwalking, driven. Already, like his fellow legionaries, and though he could hardly imagine the manner of it, he was a dead man.

PART TWO

17

FOR TWENTY CENTURIES, NO HUMAN has looked into the eye of Hroc, lord of all rooks.

This huge bird, black as lamp soot, rules all the kin, the community of Hroca, rookdom, from the heart of a rookery five thousand nests strong.

On the isolated bleak northern slopes of the Lammermuir Hills, a thousand wing-beats sunwards of Dunbar, the Lord has been protected and hidden. Five thousand nests burden the dark trees, the core so dense the light can barely penetrate, so knitted and knotted a body can hop from nest to nest, tree to tree for nigh on a field's watch, never once setting air to pinion.

This great rookery, the largest in Pretan, has outlying nests scattered over eighty, ninety, a hundred upwind wing-beats, over a great swathe of dark forest, a whaleback of wooded mountain, with the Lord's phalanx-guarded throne four hundred wingspans deep in its noisy heart.

No upwright—the rooks' name for human beings—ventures far into this labyrinth of trees. The air always seems laden and ominous and secretive. Hostile eyes follow every upwright movement in malevolent silence. No rook has cause to love the upwright with his guns and nets, scarecrows and noise machines, and when nine thousand birds turn their disdain and mistrust upon the stumbling and benighted hiker, farmhand, or sportsman, even the least sensitive among them feels uneasy and seeks escape.

No upwright has reached the heart of the Lord's rookery. No upwright, even in these materialistic times, has the will, the inclination, the reason. Or the courage.

Here, he who is the soul of all the kin, mind and memory, lore lord and eldest, sits and watches, while messengers wing their way across all Pretan to do his bidding, fetch him tidings of all that lives and moves within the mist-bound realm.

That big bird rarely has need to make a sound, his gunmetal beak pitted vulcanically with the distant flame of a score of centuries, there in the tall weaving branches. With the move of a minor pinion—slightest in the breeze, smallest pinion in the great ragged fan of his deathless wing—he directs the flock, his aye and naw the be-all and end-all.

It was he, the Rooklord Hroc, who watched over the shabby movements of the strange small dark upwrights who peopled those cold drab regions in times beyond our furthest remembered grandsires, who saw fur-clad and shivering Pict and Scot making their cautious furtive way over the hills, their arrow-packed quivers clinking in the still air.

And it was he with whom the Great Goddess, our sweet Lady of the Earth, made a pact:

"You shall rule every rookery in Pretan from this day on," She said. "Every member of the kin, from youngest squab to oldest elder and wisest master throughout the misty lands, shall own you as Lord, and you shall be their life and death. Your life as Master of Masters for as long as the mists rise from the soil, until I call you once again to my breast, blessed Hroc," She said.

And in return, sir, your guardianship of my deepest secret . . .

Now the Rooklord stirs, knowing some great matter is afoot. Out of the far beyond, in the racket of rumour and tittle-tattle that washes through the suburbia of the Lord's rookery, he detects a turning of events, tiny moving specks in the most distant field on the mistiest horizon.

And they are moving nearer.

"Keeneye, Greybeak, Airchurner. Come."

"Sire?" The three birds, the Master of Masters' closest and most trusted guardians, clattered down through the crooked branches at Hroc's croaking call, standing round the huge black-twigged nest in which Hroc lay. The big bird rose stiffly, blinked, filled his nostrils, stretched wide his huge grizzled beak. The racket of a busy rookery continued unabated round them.

"Isn't there something different in the Air today?"

The guardians looked at each other.

"I don't mean the mists have lifted. There's more snow on the way, this time from sunrise-side. One of the old fort crows has died in his sleep. All this I know. Something else. You, Hawberry Mac Greybeak—I detect the Lady's sight runs in you more strongly than in these other two. Tell me what is in the wind?"

"M'lord I . . . I am no seer," Greybeak stuttered.

Hroc stepped ponderously over to Greybeak, and the bird flapped awkwardly, gripping his perch. Hroc stared him in the face, first with one eye then the other, his great beak brushing the other's cheek feathers. Greybeak blinked rapidly.

"Your mate is called Cobweb, and you will be choosing a new nest site when the days start to lengthen and peck is easier to find. You will not rebuild in your ancestors' tree following the storm damage the moon after Samhain but will move up the slopes maybe ten wing-beats. It's a wise move. Less crowded up there."

"Th-thank you, sire."

Hroc moved even closer. "Don't thank me. This will not happen. These are merely your plans. But in the star-glimmering

nights, when the frost nearly binds your feet to the branches of the
roost tree, you are disturbed by dreams you dare not even tell your
mate. Tell me what you see. Give *me* a sign, Greybeak."

Chaw-ich-cha. Greybeak was flustered. *Chaw-ich-cha,* give us a
sign, give us a sign.

The sun broke briefly through heavy banks of cloud, turning
the bare net of twigs above the birds' heads to pure silver. The
rising wind shivered through them, and droplets of ice-cold rain
fell, splashing and showering like fine mist. Into this fine, clear
cold world, a goddess might descend, perhaps the Lady herself,
and it would be fitting that Hroc, he who has kept faith in this
world while the Lady is banished into the world beyond, should
rise to meet her. Will She come from the Air, the invisible blue
reaches where the eagles may not venture? Or may She be called
to the accursed spot in which She was betrayed, where the gift lies
buried and where She left the Earth, her bond with the upwright
broken?

"Interesting," said Hroc, nuzzling the younger bird with his
pitted beak. "There *is* something in the Air after all. And you think
I should go to meet it since it will not come to me?"

"I don't know, sire. I don't know what I said. I—"

"You are one of those rare creatures who can see through the
mists, Greybeak. I shall be making my last journey in this life soon,
this much is now clear. I too hear the distant call of the Lady. I
should be honoured if you and your spouse were to accompany
me. It will mean no nest, no eggs, no squabs this year. Speak with
your Cobweb before sun-zenith and return with your answer
before it sets.

"Meanwhile, guard duties call for you all. Go!"

18

IT HAD BEEN AN EXCELLENT day for peck.

The fields on the plateau beneath Rampart Hill broke through the grey mantle of snow that had covered them for a moon's waning—indeed, since the year's turn—to reveal pressed grass that smelled of dung and damp and growth.

Scouts from the rookery of Safehaven spotted the newly exposed feeding ground at dawn and returned with the news, heavy-winged through half-light and persistent sleet. An impromptu council of the *hroca* assembled, begun by the tree elders but joined quickly by the entire congeries, hungry and anxious since the nearer Colden water meadow was looking pecked out. After debate, quartermasters were nominated and peck squads assembled.

Mildhollow and Ashneagh rookery scouts had made the same discovery, not unsurprisingly, and there was harsh talk between the quartermasters of the respective kins *in situ* before feeding areas were apportioned.

The warmer damp weather had brought peck to the surface in huge quantities, though, and there was plenty for all. Each rook took his quarter—about twenty square metres in upright terms—and, largely unhindered and unthreatened, filled belly and pouch with earthworm and centipede, leatherjacket, quick spider and beetle. Disputes were few. Occasionally, overeager males fought females for space, quite against rule of congeries, and the quartermasters were quick to leave their roosts on fencepost, gate, and dry stone wall to arbitrate with sharp bill and fierce lowering and rattling of wing.

In an attempt to extract the most from the snowmelt opportunity, Safehaven's birds were last to leave the Rampart Hill fields. Tree moot and counts took place in deep dusk, and thus, the kin of Safehaven joined the parish roost late, after the last scintilla of light had disappeared from the sky.

Though *hroca* have good night sight, there were crash landings and disturbances, much pushing and flapping and pecking and shoving, the *chrrks* and *aachs* of grumble and muttered insult.

As the murmurs died away, one youngster's mind was unable to rest, to sink into that watchful timeless state given to fishes and birds but denied dogs and humans.

"Didn't we ever talk to upwrights?" asked yearling Bruton, son of Westray and Sunrise Airchurner.

"It's dark," chipped Westray impatiently, taking his head out from under his wing. "Don't you youngsters ever get tired?"

"*Aaar,* give it a rest, kid," added Gifford Hangclaw from his roost nearby.

Chrrr, Sunrise chided her mate. And she lolloped nearer to her son. "At first light, I shall tell you the story of our inheritance—though I dare say your father, or Gifford here, or better still, Safehaven's master, Caspian Surebill, could make his usual poetry from it."

He's done it often enough before," said Hangclaw. "Surebill could talk the talons off a kee, *kestrel.* Get him started, and you'll never stop him."

"Please to be silent," churred one of the kith, a jackdaw, sleepily in broken *cromark.* "Likely horrid long day coming very soon, so shut tongue inside bill, yes?"

"The Mother from whom all flows came to this land borne on the wings of Her favourites, the Kin (that's us. Shh.) Five held the fingers of her right hand, five held the fingers of her left, five each for her feet, and thus, as a star she appeared in the Air over Pretan.

"And here, She landed, on a mighty throne of twigs black and thick and locked solid, where the God Cernunnos, recognising her superior power, bowed down and worshipped Her, He and all His panoply.

"And He said, 'By what name shall we call you?'

"And She said, 'Call me Brigid, bride of the Earth, She who calls sleeping life awake, She who sustains it, and She who reaps a terrible harvest.'

"So one by one they came to worship—Sucellos and Medb, Taranis and Goibniu, Lugh, Mannannon and Don, Grainne and Belenus, and so on, and so on. And the upwrights who watched said, 'Surely if all the gods of the field and forest, of water and Air, of land and fruit of the land, of peck and forage worship Her, then we should worship Her too.'

"And they brought Her gifts, pearled hunting horns, sheaves of finest barley, bright swords, a cauldron. Brigid blessed each item and said, 'I thank you for your gifts, but gods have no need of such things, and I give them back to you.'

"For this horn will call friends from anywhere in Pretan in time of aid, and this sheaf of barley will multiply a thousandfold, and its grain shall be big as apples, and none of your kin shall go hungry; and this sword, no enemy shall hold lest he be struck dead, and no sword shall strike this sword and remain itself in one piece; and this cauldron shall never be emptied, no matter how many guests call on your house . . . and so on, and so on, and so on.

"Then the birds of the Air, seeing how the gods and upwrights worshipped at the foot of Brigid and brought her gifts, brought their own tokens—a feather, a prized twig, a leatherjacket, the shell out of which their largest squab had emerged.

"And each gift, She blessed and returned—for the feather, She bestowed firm untiring flight; for the twig, a nest that stays firm-placed no matter how hard the storm; for a leatherjacket, rich peck in the fields for a year and a day; for the shell, a vow no eggs this year and next would be addled.

"But Hroc, who had seen all this, determined on a better course and one which was to change his people's lives forever.

"'Our Kin have carried You from the ends of the earth, the hot lands and the cold, the bare lands and the rich,' he said. 'We have so little to pledge to Your service, so we pledge ourselves as Your servants.'

"And Brigid nodded. This is a fine and sacrificial gift. But I have blessed and returned all gifts. How shall I return this one?

"'That we should move freely as You move between the lands of the immortal to the mortal is sufficient,' said Hroc proudly. It would be enough that we should be able to see as You see.

"'So it shall be,' said Mother Brigid, clapping her hands with delight at Hroc's audacity. 'Come sit on my shoulder, Hroc, proud bird. Not earth, wind, fire nor water, nor the light that threads through all things, shall separate us until the bridge between the worlds is shattered.'

"And thus it was and is that Hroc and his Kin are guardians of the gateway from the eternal lands to the misty kingdom of Pretan."

"Yes," said Sunrise. "We were haruspices once."

"Haruspices? What are those?" asked Bruton.

"Er, tellers of the future. But only because we had Brigid. She was a goddess, you know. We were Her special flock."

"What, Safehaven?"

"No, the Kin. But Hroc, you know, Her special envoy—he's still alive, old beyond telling."

"Where? Where does he live?"

"Oh, a moon's waxing of wing-beats, away from the sun."

"So what happened?" said Bruton.

"Well, the bridge between the worlds was shattered. And Hroc, immortal though he was, was parted from the Great Mother. Both live on, but the Mother is in Her world, and Hroc is in this. He waits, in the heart of the greatest congeries on earth, for Her call."

"No doubt they pine for each other."

"No doubt."

"How did it happen?"

"How did what happen?"

"How was the bridge broken?"

"This is the sad part. The Great Goddess Brigid put her trust in the upright. Never trust the upright. An ancient queen, whose line of ancestors ran back to the beginnings of time, became the bearer of a gift, a magic token—one might say the bridge between the worlds itself. Pretan itself became the pearl in the world's shell, and this earthly queen became the seed inside the pearl.

"At that time, those who worshipped other gods came to Pretan and bent this precious land to their purposes. They felled trees, trampled the sacred groves, sent roads sprawling across the land, killed those who worshipped the old gods and put up stone roosts for the new. Their rape of the land started then and is going on now, and you see below you the wild world penned in and stoned over and burned, clipped and poisoned, withered and reduced.

"This queen was seduced by the newcomers and their ways and gave homage to the newcomers rather than to the Goddess.

In fury, the Goddess broke Her pact with the queen and cursed the gift. 'Let it lie in the soil until the world changes,' She said. The gift to the queen was lost. And we—yes, we in Safehaven—are the guardians of its final resting place."

"*Worrch,* I've heard that before," said Gifford Hangclaw. "There isn't a congeries in the land that doesn't believe its tree roots guard the Lady's gift."

"But those who fought the soldiers on this very hill and died by fire and sword, Gifford Hangclaw. You remember their names from elementary classes?"

But Bruton leapt in proudly before Hangclaw could answer. "Strongtalon, Coalfeather, Dreadcalmer, Surebill, Highnester, Blackflight, Greybeak. Names carried down to this present day, the names of honourable Safehaven families."

"*Chek chek chek.*" Hangclaw yawned, rolled his eyes. "These are names found in every congeries."

"Oh shush," said Startle Coalfeather. "Just because no Hangclaw is on the roll of martyrs."

19

ALONE, ANTLIKE, THE CHILD THREADS his way through the cornfields.

He's heading towards the ridge, whose low upturned keel is barnacle-clustered with limestone outcrop, the crumbled jutting bleached bones of the earth. Between the child and the ridge, the land is insubstantial, the wind making an ocean of the heavy swaying grain, cloud shadows passing over like grey and purple bruises.

High and invisible in the hissing air, a lark thinly telegraphs the boy's passage.

The cerulean summer canopy is closing—down east, pressed vividly against the boiling darkness of an impending thunderstorm. A perfect double rainbow arches over soft green Wensleydale, high above Aysgarth, a crock of gold each for the pretty villages of Carperby and West Burton, Britons' tun, village of the Celts. The westering sun covers the fells with intense gilt and green and the bleach white of limestone, each tumbled boulder angry and sharp, each crag clean and bright like sea foam.

From the ridge, he can look down on the copse in the valley, the fist of windbreak that grips the clutter of buildings called High Rigg Farm.

Over his head flap a pair of dark rags, rooks returning to roost in the copse. A single caw passes between them. The boy's binoculars sweep upwards, pinning their forms to the bruised sky. He knows where they are going.

He has mapped their flight-paths, knows where they feed, how many, what times of the day. He is acutely aware of their caw and chuck behind the dense mat of summer leaves at High Rigg, their harsh call-signs in the bare trees of winter, their flight paths, the site of their spring and autumn roosts, their preening and mating gestures.

He knows it so well he feels part of the complex pattern of their lives. And there is another feeling beneath.

A feeling that he is being left out.

This complexity and wealth of knowledge excommunicates him from his fellow pupils, to whom the birds are of no interest. But it is more than that; Richard is too intense, too single-minded, too serious for them. In the schoolyard, he plays halfheartedly, which is worse than not playing at all.

The first or second time he trekked to the farm, he'd been there a matter of minutes before Mrs. Outhwaite came toiling up the slope, all red and blotchy and exerted, white apron over bobbled slacks, walrus thighs, fleshy hammocks slung beneath her upper arms. He was terrified she'd turn him off the land—you're trespassing! But she had no motive other than curiosity. What is the boy doing here?

Perhaps Mrs. Outhwaite, whose husband was High Rigg's tenant farmer, saw him as the grandson she never had. When Kevin was out in the fields or in the milking parlour, she'd take Richard a scone thick with cream and strawberry jam.

"Who's your best friend?" she asked once, fretful that the boy was always alone.

"Don't have one," said Richard.

"Why don't you come in for tea?"

Richard shook his head vigorously. "Got to watch the rooks."

"They'll still be there after."

"Got to watch the rooks."

"I was always fascinated by them. They're thought to be the most intelligent of birds, rooks. About as far as birds can go without evolving into something else, something perhaps more sinister. As a child, I imagined them in their city, a metropolis of swirling branches notched with big untidy nests. There was a rookery behind the farm. The people who held the farm were called the Outhwaites, I think. I'd spend hours watching those nests. Dad solemnly gave me a good pair of binoculars for my eighth birthday."

"These?" Sarah put the coffee mug down and ran her finger over the worn rim of a lens as they lay on the workstation, ready to hand a huge clumsy war surplus eight-by-thirty-two millimetre Zeiss with its wrinkled casing bare and silver at the edges, the leather case patched and shiny.

Richard Cleeve nodded. He reached out, tracing the ridge of Sarah's finger to the neatly trimmed oval of the nail.

She made a little breathy sound that meant "that tickles" or "thanks for touching." Or maybe even a "not now."

"But you grew up."

"Mostly."

Sarah looked at the side of his earnest face, tried to imagine him as an eight-year-old. She saw the emergence of black bristles on the pale skin of his neat pointed jaw and the silky black hair with barely a hint of wave and just the start of a recession at the smooth temple. No eight-year-old here. Instead, she saw the marks of his thirty-two years—tiny wrinkles in the corner of his eye, of laughter or tiredness or endless ornithological squinting or frustration at the quotidian nature of his teaching job at the local high school, or a little of all of those. And the eyes themselves, as he turned to her smiling, were clean blue behind unfashionable round spectacles, their colour dazzling and charismatic and intense, too intense—as ready to fill with emotion at a banal movie on television as to reach into hers in the twilight of their bedroom, whispering, "I love you."

"What are you looking at?" A tilted questing glance, lips laughing.

She shrugged. "Just looking."

"I really meant, 'What are you thinking?'"

But she shook her head ever so slightly. "I don't want to talk, to think. It's enough just to be." She stroked a wisp of hair from his forehead.

"You staying tonight?"

"If you'll have me."

"'If I'll have you?'" He touched the end her nose with a long finger and grimaced theatrically. In a thick Gloucestershire accent: "Oi'll 'ave you awroight, m'dear. Oi'll jest fetch me implements."

"What are you on about?" she said, mock-angry, mock-puzzled.

"If I'll have you?"

"Oh. Hah. Well, we could get totally pissed and pretend to watch TV all night instead."

"No-o-o, that sounds like a bad idea. I think I'll have you instead."

"Good. 'Cause I'm going to have you whether you like it or not."

"Settled."

Sarah turned, clattered down the stairs. He watched her go, an almost sad smile playing with the corner of his lips then turned back to the glowing screen.

From Richard Cleeve's first love, rooks, had come a love
of ornithology in general—from ornithology, roaming the
countryside; from roaming came the discovery of the Dales'
wealth of Iron and Bronze Age and medieval village sites; and
from that, an interest in history developed. It provided a simplistic
explanation of what he had become, and Richard liked it for its
neatness, the way it fitted well on his CV, though the truth is
always more complex.

He was much more cautious of history's causality. He tended
to view history as a series of rich tableaux; the tapestry always
seemed more interesting than the weave.

If you closed your eyes, you could *see* them—fur-clad hunters
returning to the campfires with strings of hare or squirrel, hedgehog
or snipe, a fallow deer—its legs strapped to a stave, head lolling, eyes
saintly blind—the mysteries and rituals, gods of river and waterfall,
elder and mistletoe, of gloomy crag and shivering mountain, of sky
and thunder, of the four seasons and their changes, the dancing,
chanting, the glitter of arrowhead and the polished haft of spear,
the whorls and mazes on worshipped stone, the insistent, soporific
beat of skin drum, skirl of pipe and echoing blast of horn . . .

They came alive for him, these characters from the misty past.
More than that, sometimes. Sometimes he scared himself. He lived
with them, touched and smelled and felt them, stared into their
dark eyes. Drumbeat and pipe would echo round the room after
he woke, even after daydreaming, letting his mind wander.

And every so often, his vision would corrupt. He saw things
then in grey/blue/black, the entire world in fish-eye, a great gloomy
panorama, his brain someone's—something else's—vision.

It was this spirit—this excitement, though not the intensity,
the fear—he conveyed to his pupils. Many who lived in the bright
light of the twentieth century were repulsed or simply puzzled
by his enthusiasm, the strange, bloodthirsty, filthy, lyrical mental
pictures he painted.

So he settled for igniting their enthusiasm. Making them see that the past wasn't some textbook exercise, a list of names and dates, some dry and dusty excursion into lands and times and people that never existed or, if they did, had nothing to say that couldn't and didn't echo down the ages.

An old favourite was the ancient history of his own adopted village in the Colden Valley, Kirkbretton. A ring-back file lay open on the workstation. He was carefully, painstakingly, slowly moving a decade of tattered yellowing notes into hard disk files.

> *There is no archaeological proof that Cartimandua established a base at Castle Hill (SE153141), the principal periods of occupation being during the neolithic period, Bronze Age, and medieval era. Pottery finds and radiocarbon dating on oak timbers both indicate occupation in the Iron Age (fifth century BC), but no evidence for occupation exists from the fourth century BC until the Middle Ages. The castle—or the site of the castle, which may have been derelict or in ruins—was occupied well into the fourteenth century (Dr. W. J. Varley).*

He made a note in another file for the History Club:

> Dougie Allen: *find out all you can about Cartimandua.*

> Khalia Hussain: *rough dates for (a) neolithic period, (b) Bronze Age, (c) Iron Age. Why do they have these names?*

> Annette Preston: *research the medieval history of Castle Hill. When was the castle built? When and why was it destroyed?*

He clicked his laptop's window down to an icon at the foot of the screen and, on impulse, clicked another file open. Another unfinished piece for inspiration, written several years earlier, a cul-de-sac of local history research:

Venutius, consort of Cartimandua, is thought to have died with his troops at Stanwick Camp (NZ179112), 5 m (8 km) WSW of Darlington, possibly after the collapse of a line of defence at Becca Banks, Aberford, which Professor Alcock suggests were of Iron Age provenance and had a military purpose. The Stanwick site, excavated in the 1950s by Sir Mortimer Wheeler, was first fortified in the early first century AD in a 17-acre (10-hectare) area today called the Tofts. In about AD 50, a further 130 acres (53 ha) was enclosed north of the Tofts, and in about AD 70—when Venutius was preparing for his last stand—a further 600 acres (240 ha) in the south were enclosed by earth walls.

Bloody hell. Seven hundred and forty-seven acres.

If the defences collapsed inwards, the Tofts is the spot where the remnants of the Brigantian resistance met their death. A three-foot longsword in its ash wood scabbard, horse trappings, including a splendid bronze horse mask and chariot fittings, were uncovered.

✥

He pushed the window of his gable-end study open, and the echoing caws of the rooks as they circled the bare trees filled the room.

He sighed again. He hated pressure, deadlines. It was March, a cold crisp Saturday morning, sky uniform grey, coming up to the Easter break. The air refreshed him, chuckled the pages of a reference book on his overcrowded desk. Must get these notes done, photocopied before end of term. Harrop's silly bloody idea to call the upper school's tiny group of archaeology nuts the History Club. Sounds like the Tufty Club, remember that? Year 10 upwards kids at Colden Valley High were cool. "History Club" is uncool.

When Harrop retires and they give me head of department—*if* they give me head of department—History Club becomes Colden Valley Archaeological Unit. Let's see how many members we get then. Co-opt outsiders, experts, somebody from the West Yorkshire Archaeological Unit, some of our guys from the village History Society. Involve the kids in real digs.

We could start on Bride Hill. Sure we saw the corner of a fort. Or something.

Richard's mind wandered.

Gordon O'Connell, drinking mate, amateur pilot, and engineer, took Richard up from Crosland Moor airfield in his two-seater microlight late one summer evening the previous year. They'd overflown Bride Hill, a gritstone-capped wasteland prominence round which the village of Kirkbretton clustered in a southerly crescent. Crumbling soot-blackened cliff to the east overlooking Dean Beck. Church of Saint Bride's on the western slope, graveyard running west right down to the old water meadows of the River Colden.

Funny they didn't build the church on the brow of the hill. Off to the side. Almost as if the place was *too* hallowed, older than Christianity somehow, older *and more respected*.

The idea was to provide a Hockney-like serial map of the area for a History Club show for parents' evening. But Richard had spotted—*thought* he had spotted—the line of a wall or shallow ditch. Linear banks meeting at right angles. A corner . . .

Ideal spot for defence works, Bride Hill. Not as prominent as Castle Hill, sure, but. Iron Age? Roman? The 1860 Ordnance Survey called Bride Hill "glebeland," church-owned. Richard, therefore, asked the vicar of Saint Bride's, Alistair Sutton, for permission to field-walk the land.

Sutton had shrugged. "Of course. No problem. Local history? Always been fascinated. Didn't even realise it was church land. Not the kind of thing one needs to know. Must look into that. Mmm. Go ahead."

Richard found nothing.

That autumn, the club's members had mounted an exhibition—"The Iron Age in Kirkbretton." Local finds—mostly borrowed from the Tolson Museum at Moldgreen—relief models, maps, crop and field-marked photographs Richard had taken from O'Connell's microlight that summer evening. An Iron Age hut whose roof lifted off—bit of a cheat, that, because the detailed modelling had been done by Bruce Sykes, fifth former, Kathryn Sykes's dad and a secretary of the Kirkbretton History Society. Kathryn herself was showing precious little interest in the club and rather too much in some talentless but clean-looking band of pubescent boys with a couple of hit songs and—more seriously—a slaphead rugby player called Wayne. Kathryn later failed her history GCSE.

Win some, lose some.

Sarah had videoed interviews with the group, Harrop's inane and condescending comments. "We're trying to involve these youngsters in their own, ah, *heritage*, something that, ah, *belongs* to them, something they feel, ah, *rooted* in. This area is rich in, ah, *heritage*, blah blah blah." Richard had backed off, declaring an interest. Or, as Sarah later called it, a *dis*interest.

"We want to combine it with work in other schools. Harry has a West Yorkshire schools project going. He's calling it Making History," Sarah told him when the stuff didn't materialise instantly.

Harry Tasker was Sarah's partner in the video enterprise.

"All sorts of exciting things happening, you wouldn't believe. We've phoned and mailed every secondary school. Would you script the commentary? You can see the rushes so far if you like."

Rushes? Wasn't this a video? Sarah had shrugged.

"Do you want me to bring it or not?"

"Please, of course. Soonest. Money?"

"Some, she'd said. I'll talk to Harry."

Richard didn't like Harry but wasn't sure that this was because he was with Sarah most of the working day. Smug bastard, always had to have the last word. Financial smart-ass, flowchart-mad, handsome as hell, confident, older than Sarah, possible father figure. Business—and pleasure?

Richard shuddered.

The rooks wheeled overhead. Some carried twigs foraged from the Dean Beck woods. Nesting time. *Some pairs will have eggs already*, thought Richard. Corvids are among the earliest birds to lay.

Richard lived alone, though Sarah Lewis, when the mood was upon her, came to stay irregularly, casually. It was an oddly unsatisfactory relationship for Richard. He wanted more. Not the company, the sex, or rather, not just the company and the sex. It was the notion of sharing and supporting that appealed to him. The little things you do together, like shopping, driving your partner to the newsagents or the hospital or the theatre, going to sleep and waking up next to someone, watching the rabbits and smelling the bluebells in Kirkbretton Old Wood, swapping sections of the Sunday newspaper.

Continuity.

Even if she stayed a weekend, Sarah always seemed to be looking at the clock—things to do, people to see, places to go.

He had no need of any woman but Sarah. Perhaps she needed other men, other company, company she could not or would not share with him. It was a taboo between them. Richard found it too painful to consider.

"Why don't you move in?"

"No. We've been through this. I'm not ready."

"Save a lot of money. One place. Anyway, when *will* you be ready?"

"I'm ready now." And she would whisk round the edge of the lumpy, creaking, overstuffed old sofa, giggling, and plump herself in his lap, her hands swiftly inside his shirt . . .

The house was overstuffed like the sofa, Grade II-listed, seventeenth-century yeoman clothier's; overgrown, ivy threatening the mullioned windows at the back, a gnarled wisteria slinging out wild shoots and magnificent summer-blue clusters of bloom twice a year at the front. A cobbled yard, Farrar's Fold, behind, space to park his elderly open-top MG. No garden, just Shepley blue sandstone flags and huge tubs of petunia, pelargoniums, aubrietia, pansies and primula in winter.

The previous tenant had knocked the kitchen/dining room and lounge into one and put in a broad arch. Wisely, she'd kept the huge ornate—almost gargoyled—black-leaded stove, which Richard had thoroughly cleaned when he moved in but had never used. One day, he heard a rook from the Saint Bride's graveyard rookery on the other side of Cliff Street talking to itself quietly on the chimney pot way up above. The sound was amplified hollowly, as if the bird were actually sitting in the fireplace. For Richard, the sound confirmed that rooks had a profound intelligence.

English Heritage don't allow you to change any external feature of the house—according to a note left by the previous tenant when Richard moved in. So who would want to? It was enough that doors kept slewing off the cheap kitchen units. He should replace them. Money, money. He'd framed dozens of old charters, acts of parliament, tinted maps, a series of landscape lithographs on the staircase to the first floor, master bedroom, guest room, small bathroom, and shower. There was a narrow staircase to the third bedroom—top of the house, Richard's den—converted to a study, booklined, cluttered, untidy, smelling of exercise books and faint armpit, the laptop dominating. The walls' pine panelling he'd stripped and waxed; similarly, the doors throughout the house, wrenching off the hardboard panels tacked there in the 1960s as was the trend then.

It was a good house, full of memories of when Sarah and he first met.

20

SARAH'S SIDE OF IT IS this:

I helped Richard decorate the house on Cliff Street. Seven years ago! I can hardly believe it.

It was as if we were building our own world from scratch. Richard was recovering from a painful divorce or, rather, from a childless marriage that lasted two years. As far as I can gather, Claire—that's his former wife—turned out to be a nasty piece of work, a sarcastic, sulking, materialistic bitch who made his life a misery. I've met her twice; on both occasions, she was utterly charming. Possibly that's how Richard was ensnared.

Anyway, I think there was relief all round when she met some rich guy who ran a chain of furniture stores. She just cut loose, left him a house, a kind of guilt payment, which he sold and bought the Cliff Street place outright.

We met at a wedding. I was a photographer's assistant, badly and irregularly paid by a sordid little bloke called Clifford with roving fingers and a very dangerous darkroom. I put up with him because he was good at his job and taught me well.

Richard was an usher at the wedding, which was of a junior schoolteacher friend who went to live with his new wife in Zimbabwe and whom Richard never saw again. I can't remember his name. I doubt if Richard can.

I too was recovering from a broken relationship. Lars was a Dane who discovered, when I was pregnant with his child, that he was homosexual. He disappeared back to Denmark, and I had an abortion. I don't regret it. At twenty, I was just too young to be a good mother—a mother of any kind.

What attracted me to Richard, and what still does, is his patience, his gentleness, his devotion and loyalty, his sense of humour. If there's a barrier, it's one I put in place. I can't let him have all of me. I wonder if it's because there's been betrayal in my life. Lars and I had a great time. We did extravagant and unusual things, things of which Richard would disapprove. In my innocence, I gave him everything. You can't keep on doing that. You need something in reserve.

I've always hedged questions about that period in my life. And we've a kind of silent pact here. He doesn't talk about Claire, I don't talk about Lars. I think he's curious, though.

I won't move in with Richard. Not yet. I think I'm moving towards it. And it would, as Richard so often points out, make sound financial sense. I'm an oboeist with the Leeds Philharmonic, and I share a flat in Meanwood, which is very useful for rehearsals. Annie has the run of the place most weekends, and I still pay half.

Harry Tasker, who owns the Huddersfield educational video business where I work, recently made me a partner. We get on well together. He's quirky, sophisticated, comes from a family with an extraordinarily cavalier attitude to money. Lots of brothers and sisters, always lending each other thousands. He'll push cash at a project on a whim, and usually, it works, makes a profit—but he's not in the slightest bothered if something crashes and doesn't seem to care much if it's a runaway success either. Strange.

I have my own budget, but I don't have Harry's brashness. I plan my ideas carefully, cost them out, try to build fallback positions, and so on.

I think Harry sees me as the "younger woman." Not that he's married. I boost his ego. It's another reason why I need the flat; Richard hates Harry, I'm sure, sees him as a rival. It's not true. I might think briefly about it if Harry asked me to marry him. I'd be flattered. Harry's exciting, unconventional, but if you're going to marry, better to a solid, kind man like Richard than a flash, dangerous man like Harry. Richard would win.

I know my seeing Harry hurts Richard. He sees it as a form of adultery. I do question my motives. I *am* selfish. I want it all—danger yet a good solid relationship with an adoring and adorable man to fall back on. I'm too young, too restless. I don't want to miss anything.

It's not that Richard isn't exciting in his own way. Some weekends, my sides ache with laughing. He has a very dry, self-deprecating sense of humour. In bed, he'll sometimes penetrate me suddenly while we're hooting with laughter over some staffroom or playground tale, and if that's happened to you, you'll know what a turn-on it can be.

What does he like about me? He says my eyes are the green of beech leaves in May. Very poetic! I'm slim—in the mirror, I seem to be short and narrow-bodied, my legs too long, my boobs too big, but Richard says this is a lack of perspective. I wore my very wavy brown hair bobbed when I first met him. Now that it's grown out, I look like Medusa. I never dye or tint or highlight.

He tells me he loves me, and I believe him. I love him, despite his village outlook, his limited ambition. Amateur historian and bird-watcher says it all. I used to go with him on his twitching expeditions. But whiling away the hours in a hide with an anorak, a flask, and a pair of binoculars is not my idea of fun. I used to persuade him to take breaks from that, and what we did as a consequence would make the reed warblers and sand martins blush.

But there's something else about Richard. As if he's not always there. He'll get totally absorbed in a school project. He has to know everything about a subject. He's very conscientious. But it's more than that. He'll tell a fireside story from the depths of history as though he's there, seeing it unfold with his own eyes, like a minstrel or druid or troubadour. I started counting recently how often he slipped from "they" to "me" or "us" when he's telling one of his tales. It sounds silly, but that can be quite scary—as if you're with a time traveller, somebody possessed, somebody *on* something. Just don't let him turn out the lights for atmosphere. It's the weirdest party trick.

Me, I'm committed about nothing; he commits to everything he's involved in—archaeology, bird-watching, the schoolkids. He's committed to me. He deserves promotion, deserves success.

He deserves more from me. Perhaps he deserves more *than* me.

21

I T WAS EARLY FEBRUARY, EARLY morning, before the consecration of earth known as plough's first turn. A brilliant cold sun made a frosted foil of ivy leaves, which glittered like spilled coins in the dead and mute-splashed undergrowth beneath the Safehaven rookery.

Most of the Safehaven kin had formed two peck squads that dawn. One was a group of a dozen one- and two-year-old birds that had settled on a raid on a freshly muck-spread field on the slopes below Rampart Hill. The other, a party of twenty older members of Safehaven, including most of the tree elders and the rookery master himself, Caspian Surebill, had gone left of sunwards, flying over the church of Saint Bride's and its sad, silent graveyard to quarter the old water meadow by the side of the River Colden.

Several of the kin, mostly solo guards and newly bonded couples who had decided to make a start on their nests, lingered in the bare branches of the Safehaven trees. One such was Startle Coalfeather, who had inspected the winter storm damage on the vicarage lawn and had found what appeared to be a perfect nesting twig, a wingspan long, elm, flexible, with bark already shredding for lining material. Bearing it proudly with a triumphant *whaaark!* into her chosen elm, she was now pulling and twisting distractedly at it, her tail feathers flicking and bouncing. Rattling it like a bow across a violin's bridge, she began to subject it absently to the Five Tests to ascertain its suitability for nest material. But halfway through, it slipped from her beak, tumbling with a *thwick* into the rusty brambles below.

Startle batted dust from her wings, tutted at the loss, and was about to return to the search when a shriek jarred the air. She hopped clumsily to face the east wind in time to see her mate Dryden barrelling over the High Roost, the rooks' name for Saint Bride's bell tower, like an incoming Hercules transport, seventh and eighth pinions imperceptibly manipulating the cut-glass air, missing the stone pinnacles by a centimetre.

"The bird's a total fool," she said lovingly.

"You're right there," hawked Gifford Hangclaw from a higher perch in the next tree. "A total fool, *chh*. No sense of responsibility. You should have chosen me." And he hopped a branch closer, lowering his wings in an altogether menacing and sexual way.

"As I recall from council, you're on watch this quarter moon, Hangclaw. And don't eavesdrop. It's coarse as crow feathers." Haughtily upright so as to give the sentry no encouragement, Startle dropped like a deadweight a good two wingspans to meet her mate.

A frenzy of courtship and mating left the rookery unsettled, edgy; Gifford Hangclaw was one of several birds whose hormones, enflamed by the lengthening of the days and stoked by the occasional warmth of a still bleak sun, were tweaking him to frustration.

But now, finally, for Startle and Dryden at least, if not for Hangclaw, vows had been taken and progress was being made.

Startle Coalfeather and Dryden Dreadcalmer had sat close on a high branch many a late afternoon before the call to roost, arguing endlessly and gently for this tree, against that, for this fork and angle, against the other. They were conscious that other Safehaven citizens had paired, many of them as early as mid-January and were already building or repairing nests in the trees around them.

They had located the site of a former stack by the presence of two brittle rotten twigs and sadly faded beak marks—house signs—in the bark where the stack must once have proudly rested. It was clear to Dryden, who knew his congeries history well, that distant relatives had nested here, perhaps ten years earlier.

No runes indicated sadness; the line, an inconspicuous branch of the Dreadcalmer family, had merely died out, its last male heir (according to the marks) taking his spouse and two fledglings down to the congeries at Mildhollow two hundred wing-beats or so away from the sun at zenith. Mildhollow—a rookery the upwrights would recognise as Kirkbretton crossroads—had accepted the family, Dryden assumed, since there were no signs to the contrary. After much display of erudition, posturing, humming, and chawing, Dryden announced that a Dreadcalmer by the name of Amroth had left his mark.

"Don't you think the nest is a little too far from the main rookery, dear?" asked Startle.

"Let's not go through all that again, *crrrch*," said Dryden, exasperated. "If you want to gossip, you hop here, here . . . and here. Then a swoop across the *chwaagh*way, *road,* and you're in Caliban Dawncaller's own tree," he called, ignoring the angry croaks and *churrs* from neighbouring nest builders.

"And what if I start a dread?" asked Startle when Dryden returned to their tree. A dread or outflight is when tension is released by a sudden explosive exodus of most of the birds from the rookery. The birds circle noisily, sometimes chasing each other in tight circles, until nervous energies have been expended. The trigger for the outflight may be little more than a sudden movement of a congeries member from one tree to another.

"Then you start a dread. Someone has to." Not for nothing was he of the family Dreadcalmer.

Dryden was the youngest scion of a respectable family, pillars of Safehaven society for years beyond count. The Dreadcalmers had produced two rookery masters and one mistress within living memory. But like many a young rook fresh out of his second year, fire and enthusiasm often pushed common sense out of the nest.

"Dryden, he's a wild one, as were many of us," rasped Calvin Airchurner during council one crisp evening earlier that month. "But he's from good stock and bears a true heart. When this partnership with the Coalfeather youngster is consummated, we should see a solid Safehaven citizen emerge, mark my perch."

To Startle, he was brave and loyal, solemn and earnest. His feathers were glossy, his neck and bill strong and thick. He was from good stock. Startle believed she could make something of him.

"Where've you been, you horror?" she churred, only slightly miffed.

"I can't see the mother-to-be of our squabs go without food," he said, waddling a little and quickly dipping his beak under his wing. "I have gapeworm, beetles, and two small but sweet earthworms from the streambank here in my bill-pouch, and I'd like you to share them with me. Also, something's happening the other side of the High Roost, up on the Haunted Hill."

Startle lowered her wings, rattled her tail flights in anticipation.

"I know," she said quietly.

"You know? How?"

"I—I don't know. I just thought I did." Startle hopped a twig higher than her mate, bent her neck low, ran her beak along Dryden's back between his wings.

"How romantic," sneered Gifford Hangclaw.

Dryden lowered his back aggressively, gave him a serious warning *waarrk*. Hangclaw flapped wildly and rose to one of the topmost branches, where he hacked the three notes of the "all clear" quite unnecessarily and wobbled, wings batting the cold air for balance.

The couple shared food like the lovers they were, their black-clad shoulders close on the bleak branch, many a small churring noise passing between them. Dryden's scaly foot clenched and unclenched with impatience. Startle ate slowly, deliberately, her mischievous grey eyes rolling.

"Tell, then," she said at length.

"Tell what?" Dryden fidgeted nervously on the branch, paddling this way then that.

"What is happening the other side of the High Roost, up on the Haunted Hill."

"I thought you said you knew."

Startle shuffled. "I just—know—when something's in the Air. I don't know what it is, as a rule. But you can just tell—can't you?"

"No, I can't," said Dryden hurriedly. "Sounds to me as though you might be a bit, you know . . ."

"What? Seerish? I don't think so, Dryden, sweetheart."

"Well then. If you don't know what's going on up the Haunted Hill, come with me and see."

"I'm busy."

"Forty wing-beats, no more, and a long glide back on the wind. Come with me." He gently cuffed the side of her head with his beak.

"Just for a moment then," said Startle, secretly relishing the chance to stretch her wings.

With harsh cries, they plunged from the branch so violently that bare twigs yammered together at their passing. A rash of alarmed chucking and hawing broke out across the rookery, and several younger birds tried an outflight, but so many were busy with nest building that the dread did not catch on, and the fliers returned abashed to their perches.

One small whey-faced creature the kin called upwrights, humans, armed with sticky tape, had bound white notices to the boles of two outlying trees in Safehaven Rookery.

He had arrived in the gloom of early morning, before full light, and his body language spoke to Dryden of stealth, stalking, pursuit, and death.

The upwright had climbed out of a small black *chwaagh* with red stripes and left it in the lemon-tinged sunlight at the entrance to the leaf-carpeted walk behind Saint Bride's Church.

His action had alerted a pair of magpies, kith to the Safehaven kin, whose frantic warning chatter was racketing through the bare trees. The pair were planning to nest in the hawthorn hedge in the garden of the tobacconists at Dean Bridge, just by the derelict mill.

Dryden and Startle descended to the capstones in the quiet early morning to see what could be seen.

And indeed, the magpies, a pair, male and female, had made a quick recovery from their scare and had returned to lolloping loudly into the road, tails low, black eyes greedy, and hot for a mess of road pickings. Dryden called them the death squads.

"Nice, it should be pulverised and in easy to pick morsels. But we're not equipped to get out of the *chwaagh*'s way," said he, extending the "aagh" of *chwaagh* ludicrously for effect. "Big floppy wings, ch, great heavy bodies. Let's face it, *hworcch,* we're not built for speed. If the Hroc had wanted us to scrape squashed rabbit and hedgehog off the road, don't you think he'd have given us a shorter alert-to-takeoff interval?"

Startle chuffed up a wing, pushed her gunmetal beak into Dryden's neck ruff and extracted an imaginary louse, pretending her gesture hadn't happened.

Then her eye caught movement. "Hullo, what's this? A yellow-topped upright. What do we know about yellow-topped uprights?"

"This is my news," said Dryden, blinking in the sunlight. "This is what I saw on my way from the streambank. Upwrights. Where upwrights should not be."

He's on the Haunted Hill. The Lady will be angry.

He's coming this way, and both rooks hastily and heavily flapped upwards, bowing westerly, to get a better view of the intruder.

"He has a stick," chawed Startle. "Is it a gun or other killing thing?" She paddled on the branch nervously.

"No, dear. Almost certainly not. The stick is the wrong colour and has too many other pieces attached. Besides, the yellow-topped upright is making too much noise." The realisation that death was not about to strike them down was a relief to Dryden, who involuntarily flapped and cawed and jumped a little at the discovery.

"That's true," said Startle. "Funny, isn't it, that you can always tell when an upright is wanting to shoot something dead? He creeps. This one isn't creeping at all. Look, he's putting the stick down."

"Spreading its legs. It's a kind of stork he's got there. Look at the stork's head. Oh, and look down by the lane. Another upright has emerged. They are talking loudly, cawing across the Air. This other upright is yellow-headed too."

And so Startle and Dryden discussed the arrival of surveyor and surveyor's assistant and their theodolite at Safehaven that fine February morning, when so much else had to be done. Finally, ashamed of their gossip when their work was being delayed and the nest remained unbuilt, they agreed to bring the matter to the dusk eldermoot and flapped off to speak with their tree elder and representative on the full rookery council, Caliban Dawncaller.

The old bird had a tendency to wax hysterical in his dotage, and Startle had said to Dryden, "Leave this to me. We mustn't panic him."

"Elder Caliban," said Startle carefully, while Dryden hung about on an outer branch, bending twigs embarrassedly, choughing and keen to say his piece. "Elder Caliban, strange things are going on—"

"Behind the High Roost, I know. While the sun was yet low, we had it from the ceri, *starlings*, terrible gossips, never did learn anything but the most rudimentary cromark. But thank you all the same, *chhrr*." Caliban fidgeted. "Oh yes. I was to tell you all later at eldermoot, but eldermoot's cancelled in any case, and you're here now, and it's not supposed to be a secret or, if it is, the good master Surebill did not indicate—"

"Eldermoot's cancelled? But that means—" Dryden crew irritably from his perch above. Startle shushed him with a twitch of her glossy wing.

"The good master Surebill called council when the sun was claw-high, after the peck squads left for the downwind fields. Safehaven will meet at twilight in the topmost tree. You might do me a favour when the others come in from peck. I might miss them, forget. You know me. I forgot you, didn't I?"

The old bird chuckled, rubbed the side of his beak with a gnarled claw. But then he stretched his neck nervously, blinked, drew in air, seemed about to take flight. A cold breeze drifted like a ghost between the branches.

"Something's not right, *ch-chraw*, or I'm fodder for Hroc," Caliban Dawncaller mumbled.

22

THE SUN DIPPED WEAK AND red behind the hump of Wessenden Head and thrust a torch into high mackerel clouds, leaving them the colour of weals and bruises. A ghostlike, almost-luminous mist rose, hiding the sluggish Colden in its bower of leaf-strewn banks and black-barked trees. It crept like death over the water meadow, slimed the lichen-green wall of the graveyard and pearled the cobwebs that festooned the gravestones of Saint Bride's.

The last of Safehaven's kin flapped homeward above it, flight-calling the single *aarch* that speaks of full belly and bill and binds a squad's complex and loose formation together. Older and younger groups met and mingled, swirling in the air above the rookery, exchanging news—no moots tonight and we roost here, not at the parish convocation; rookery master Caspian Surebill has called full council.

The birds, young and old, all three score and eight of them, gathered expectantly in the council tree, a mighty, grey-boled beech that leaned over Saint Bride's vicarage.

Master Surebill, a fine, heavy bird of twelve summers, glossy and sleek and powerful and Master of Safehaven for three good years, brought the congeries to order. He spoke sonorously, crimping off each phrase with a nasal *hff*, as every rookery master has done since time's beginning.

Chack? Chaw. Chack? Chaw. Chack? Chaw. All present and correct. They made so much noise an upwright, the one the kin called the Oystercatcher, because he wore black with a white collar, came out of his red-roofed roost and pointed his white face at the sky.

"Bracken Nightwing has the full story, gathered at peck and from those who ventured over the High Roost today. Bring us up to date, Bracken," he said.

The kin cawed, "Hear! Hear! Tell us."

Bracken explained about the upwrights, puffing out her chest and giving it a quick wipe, left and right, with her rather long beak. Surebill's choice of informant was shrewd; Bracken combined the rooks' natural talent for gossip with an unerring accuracy—a somewhat rare quality, Surebill had silently noted, among Safehaven's community.

From the *ceri* and the Kith—the *chakachit*—magpie pair, she'd had warning that mischief was afoot; from Startle and Dryden, she'd had news of the upwrights' deeds beneath the trees on the Haunted Hill; from Caerleon and his mate Elderflower, a report that the upwrights had later "muted" or "marked" two trees, whatever that might mean, before they had reentered their *chwaagh* and departed.

Bracken's story over, the rookery once again erupted in noisy speculation. Surebill called his congeries to order and said, "The business before us is a matter for information. But something tells me this is not peck for gossip. I feel ill at ease. Who knows what travels through the upwright's mind? This could be a game or some tactic about which we know nothing. I open this council for free debate."

"What if they plan to bring down Safehaven? They could be planning to build stone roosts. Yellow-topped upwrights were seen in the river fields, and shortly after, the earth was wounded to its heart, much deeper than the plough that turns our peck," said Calvin Airchurner, an elderly rook with a cloudy eye.

"We are observers only. There is nothing we can do. There has never been anything we can do about the upright," said an elder from one of the sycamores in Bride Hill quarry.

"This has come at a bad time of the year. It's bound to cause uncertainty and addle the eggs," said one of the two-year-old Nightwing females, Bracken's nieces.

"Come, come," said Startle Dreadcalmer. "This is panicmongering." This caused pained chattering and one clearly audible "Little Miss Bravery" piece of sarcasm.

"Why should the uprights mute our trees? Do we know which ones, Bracken?" asked a querulous youngster of two summers, Thornton One-Claw. His family name belied reality; Thornton had two fine strong feet. Perhaps a distant ancestor was hatched deformed or was the victim of a tragedy.

Bracken consulted with a crony. "The twin-trunked sycamore next to the *chwaagh*way left of sunwards at the edge of Haunted Hill and the beech with the broken branch, home to Elder Halley Coalfeather here and six pairs."

There was a burst of cawing silenced by Surebill, who looked at the elder in question.

"I came here directly from peck," said Halley gruffly. "I have nothing to say."

"We're building nests. The Air's getting warmer, the sun higher each day. Eggs and then chicks," said Dryden impatiently. There were caws and chacks of approval throughout the tree. "There must be something we can do. Should we stop building? Should we move?" He lowered his voice. "Master, we need an answer. Give us a sign."

Give us a sign. *Chaw-ich-cha.*

At this, Dryden, realising his error, sought hastily and impossibly to recall his words from the damp Air, wishing to his last unpicked bone he had never opened his beak. And those of the congeries within earshot rocked and crowed in dismay on their slippery perches, yawing and flapping, and within seconds, the whole rookery was advised of Dryden's rash utterance.

It seemed, for one dense moment, that the misty sky descended and enfolded the assembly of kin, gloomy and ominous, the great drum of its invisible ear cocked for the slightest sound behind the soft crown feathers of the Air.

Now it is little known outside the Kin that the words "give us a sign" have aweful potency. *Chaw-ich-cha,* as the upwrights would render it. Herein is a challenge, one of the darkest in the corvid lexicon, dating no doubt from those days when a rook would sit brooding and prophetic on the shoulder of some mighty and obscure wizard, some manic and desperate king.

It is a call from which there is no turning back, and Dryden, in his abject manner, knew full well the import of his utterance. Those who call upon the mantic invested in the master of a rookery do so at their peril, for they are bound to play a part in the destiny thus unfolded.

"Give us a sign." Surebill shuddered to his tenth pinion, and his beady brown-flecked eyes rolled. In a huge yawing gesture, his great wings opened, and he rocked on his branch unsteadily.

Yet not for nothing was he seer of congeries at Safehaven. Only on rare occasions in his long life had call been made on his auguric powers, these that are invested upon the master of a rookery at his initiation or at least given rein, revealed, enhanced on that occasion.

Now, as ever, he trusted to that which he could never touch, never understand; he put his faith in the Ley, the great theme that runs invisibly through all living matter, and is focused and channelled in some indefinable way via the soft electrically sensitive matter inside our heads.

"You have asked, and you shall receive," said Caspian Surebill, Master of Safehaven, his voice harsh in the still air, black eyes rolling insanely.

Beneath him, even the chaffinches, chasing each other for mates in the underbrush, ceased their game. A great tit stood to attention like a black-medalled sergeant-major in the chestnut boughs; a dozen starlings at whistling practice were instantly silenced and cocked their silly punk heads anxiously at each other in the gutter above the sign that said Palfreyman's Butchers 1927.

On a slate roof by the post office, three pot-bellied magpies paused midguffaw, lowering their proud tails respectfully, straining to catch the master's words. And all the wide world saw Safehaven at cusp.

"You have asked, and you shall receive, Dryden Dreadcalmer. And may the feathered emperor of the North Kingdom guard and keep your soul from harm in the telling.

"I see a fifth part of Safehaven in smoke and the drumming of a thousand upwright drums. I see the land laid bare to its bones. And I see the Lady's gift unveiled, its dreadful curse enacted after the ages and our guardianship ended."

"What did he say? What does he mean? How did it start?" Birds shuffled along branches to catch the augury. More, alerted by the pool of stillness as its waves rolled outwards over hedge and garden, lane and gable, homed in, wings burring with unseemly haste, and landed as Surebill's harsh words faded, and the air's silence gathered like thunder gloom.

"What did he say? What does he mean? How did it start?"

—∞∞∞—

"You are stupid beyond belief," said Startle to Dryden as they leaned together in the dripping indigo of dusk. "That a partner of mine should utter *those words* unthinkingly. There'll be dreads at the drop of a tail feather for weeks now. You've well and truly darkened the Air."

"Warned you," said Hangclaw from a half-wrecked nest in the next tree. Both birds responded simultaneously: "*Shut up!*" And Dryden added, "This is not your affair, Hangclaw. Why don't you fly backwards into a wall?"

"All right, all right," soothed Startle. "I've said my piece, Dryden. You know how I feel. We can't untwig this particular nest."

"I think you were *very* brave," churred Caliban Dawncaller amicably from above his large, four-season nest, where mate Sapphire nestled and slept. "I hate to think of Safehaven damaged, and I do wonder which fifth will come down—but you see, we'd have *none* of this information if you hadn't made your, *tch,* mistake, young Dryden."

"A fifth of Safehaven in smoke. We could survive that," said Dryden with more optimism than he felt. 'The bones of the earth laid bare. That means more upwrights' stone nests. We've survived that before. We tell our youngsters stories of when there were no chwaaghs and the chwaaghways were mud tracks; when all the fields were open for us to quarter; when Safehaven boasted a hundred trees, not thirty; four hundred Kin, not sixty. But Safehaven has always been here, ever since the Lady's time. We are here to guard Her gift, which lies buried under the Haunted Hill. She won't let anything happen to us. She'll protect us."

"Why should She protect us?" called Gifford Hangclaw. "When was the last time you saw Her? She left Pretan for good when the pact between Her and the upright queen was broken, so the legends say. She won't be back. The world has changed too much since then."

"Gifford has a point, *chh*," said Caliban. "And one is bound to wonder how we might guard the Lady's gift if the upwrights start to destroy Safehaven. Will we attack them, gouge and claw their eyes, as we are told our ancestors gouged and clawed in the fight on Haunted Hill? I think I might be a little too old for that sort of thing."

"What do you think the Lady's gift really is?" said Startle to Dryden.

"I really don't know. *Arr,* some kind of upwright thing, a glittering thing perhaps, one of those things the *chackawi*, jackdaws, take to decorate their nests sometimes."

"Not like the mutes on the trees, then?" asked Startle.

"Do they glitter?"

"I had a word with Elderflower—what's her name, Longfeather?—Longpinion, that's it, after council, and she said they glittered as the sun went down. You saw how distressed my father was when Bracken said it was his tree with the uprights' mark on it."

"I don't know what you're saying, dear," chacked Dryden irritably. "It's late, virtually pitch-black. Perhaps we should roost."

"I think I have an idea to save Safehaven," said Startle.

23

T HERE IS A MOMENT IN the Earth's gentle cycle when the spring's vessels of life begin to thicken and stir, fed by the dense old blood of the previous autumn. It is the moment when the couch grass root feels the sun's warmth in the black earth and flexes its muscle. The moment when the first vivid green points of bluebell burst through the leaf mould and make a star, catching a perfect cold crystal of rainwater.

That moment is marked by a rich, foetid, delicious, rotten, rainsodden, frost-crushed, toadstool-and-dung warmth odour. It sets the rooks' mating, planning, outflying, arguing. It fills them with enthusiasm and wild ideas. And after a raw winter like this one, it fills their bellies and bill-pouches. Rich peck, indeed, in every field and copse and bridleway and hillside, plough, pasture, and common land.

Dryden, Gifford, and half a dozen others, alerted by a scout's report that a plough's turn in the high steep fields above Kirkbretton offered a wealth of food, formed a squad the next day, and balanced in the topmost branches of one of the quarry sycamores as daylight swelled.

"Coming, dear?" Dryden asked his mate.

Startle tutted and clicked frustratedly. "Dryden, we have a nest to build. I can find peck round here. Time's running out. If you stay to get this—and this—bit built, I'll go."

"We can both go. We don't need to stay all day. *Chhk, whaw,* please, Startle. We'll both work on the stack when we get back."

The squad, meanwhile, had taken to the air and were circling lazily. "Dryden!" called their quartermaster, one Cherry Highnester, Levenworth's widow. "Are you with us or not?"

Dryden gestured helplessly.

"For the Lady's sake, go. Your turn to nest-build tomorrow."

"You have a deal," said Dryden, much relieved. "I'm going to bring you back the most delicious, fattest, juiciest—" And then his voice was lost with the others as they rowdily built a flight order, took directions, and argued quarter with Cherry.

Startle waited until Highnester's squad and a much larger one, bound for the Colden water meadows, had left the rookery to the nest makers and sentries.

Then she took to flight with the long lazy strokes which told the rest of the congeries, "I'm going nowhere, doing nothing, just exercising." A long banked glide brought her to the capstones and within sight of the first of the upwrights' "mutes," tightly taped to the tree at the edge of Haunted Hill, Bride Hill.

"Mutes"? Startle cocked her head, blinked. "Upwright marks. Upwright hain." She batted her wings at the idea. Upwright hain, upwright speech. Like the marks that spiders make when they walk across a damp leaf. The spiders' feet say, "I'm going here. And here. Quickly. Or slowly." The upwrights' signs will say, "Cut me down." But if I can take the upwright hain away, how will the yellow-heads know which tree to cut down? They might pass by altogether and cut nothing down, for there would be no sign to say, "Do this, do that."

She flew at the tree, trying to grip the notice that began Town and Country Planning Act . . . But there was no purchase on the tightly bound tape for her talons, and after two attempts, she retired to the wall, breathing heavily.

"Well, bugger me. Just look at that." Shaun grabbed his mate's shoulder and shook it vigorously. Both lads had had a little more than enough to drink postmatch down at the George Inn.

"Wha'? Gerroff."

"Look! That crow. It's havin' a go at that notice. Look, on that tree. It's just done it again."

"S'shiny, s'what. Crows like shiny things. Shaun, m'boy, I've left me kit in the George."

"Bloody 'ell. What a tit you are, Jason, what are yer?"

"A'll 'affta go back for it."

"Am not waitin' for yer. Sal's gointa rip me 'ead off anyway. Dinner'll be ruined. See yer at practice then, Thursday."

"Yeah, see yer." Jason trotted unevenly back down the road towards the centre of Kirkbretton and the George Inn for his forgotten football kit. Shaun looked both ways, past the vicarage, down the hill towards Dean Brook, then urinated against the wall.

Startle saw him and flapped away to a nearby horse chestnut tree to consider her failure.

"If it's this bugger you're after, you're welcome to it," shouted Shaun after her. He reached over the low wall, pulled and tugged at the planners' notice. Finally, it came loose. He screwed it up and hurled it into the air. "Can't do this, can't do that. Bruddy blurocrats—bureaucrats, pardon." He giggled. "Well, just look down there, Mr. Crow. There's another o' them notices. Would yah like that one as well?"

24

"WHO IS THIS UPWRIGHT?"

Bruton and Dryden were in the tall unnested sycamore that leered dangerously out over the alleyway behind Saint Bride's Church. Unnested, it has to be said, because the Safehaven community was convinced a storm would bring the tree down; if you live intimately with them, the noises trees make can tell you when they are approaching the end of their life.

The young rooks were on alert. Easy peck. Children from Colden High School had scattered a lunch break bag of chips on the bright green patch of grass that separated the church from the vicarage, and if the upwright who now watched them would move away . . .

"He won't go," said Dryden. "Mute him, Bruton."

"Well, that's a little unkind, wouldn't you say?" sloughed Brittle Blackflight, who was a dozen or so wingspans away on an outhouse roof. "Mute him! Just like that!"

"Mute him!" screamed Halley Coalfeather, Startle's father, from another tree. "These are the creatures that plan to flatten our Safehaven, don't you forget."

And Bruton, with a flick of the tail feathers, sent a white shower of droplets downwards. The upwright stepped hastily out of the way, a mumbled curse on his lips.

"Their voices are a dead weight in the Air," cackled Dryden, stretching a dusty wing and thrusting his beak viciously at some imagined tick beneath it. "Pity you missed."

"Why do we hate them, Dryden?" asked Bruton, fidgety.

"If you have to ask, you probably don't," said Dryden. "But in general—we hate them because they foul the Air with their noise and smoke, because they cut down our trees, because they throw stones at us and bring the death-from-a-distance—"

Brittle interrupted with a harsh call and a clapping of her wings. "But they also turn the ground with their *chwaaghs* at Imbolc and Samhain, and then it's banquet time for all the kin. And their animals' dung—"

"I've heard it all before," said Dryden. Out of one eye, he was watching the upright, who'd moved into the relative shelter of an ivied wall but whose white oval of a face still stared blankly upwards into the bare trees.

We just don't understand them at all, even after all these millennia, he sighed. Long gone are the days when we'd sit on their shoulders and whisper our advice in their ear. Long gone are the days when we had any advice worth listening to! The powers that the Lord Hroc and his kind must have felt in the roots of their feathers, in the caves of their bones, when the bridge between us was open and when the pact between god and upright and animal was unbroken!

When the Ley ran through us like Giobniu's fire, and every stone, lake, bird, beast, god, and upright felt the steady beat of the Earth's heart!

No, we can't read their signs. This one could be plotting to uproot Safehaven. Or plotting to prevent some other upright from uprooting Safehaven. Or more likely, he is just curious. I know him of old. This one is always looking up at us. I call him Crow-head for his dark hair. He walks across the Haunted Hill. He's a strange one.

Maybe he knows the Lady. Maybe he knows where the gift is hidden. Maybe he wants to know where the gift is hidden. Maybe he is trying to read our signs, as we try to read his. In which case, what will he think of little Bruton's trick?

"Do—you—speak—hrocain? Cromark?" cawed Dryden. The pasty face still stared upwards. Rook/Kith, talk? Corvid/Kin, talk? "Bilhain, then, the common language of all birds?"

The upwright nodded in affirmation; I understand all too well. Ye gods! thought Dryden. That couldn't be—

Halley Coalfeather haw-hawed. "Listen to you, Dryden Dreadcalmer, son-in-lore. Talking to the landbound, the earthstar, the stupid wax-faced upwright. Go talk instead to Levenworth's widow, whose mate was killed from a distance or Thornton One-Claw about how his family got the name or any of the Rivenlea congeries, whose rookery is smouldering logs and dead twig and whose Air is filled with so many upwright stone roosts and sounds and hard furlong, you traitor to your kin."

"Dryden is no traitor, Halley," called Caspian Surebill, swirling magnificently through the bare branches to land with a clatter in the leaning sycamore above their heads.

"I, for one, would have no objection if, by some magic, we were able to talk to the upwright again. I admire your attempt, Dryden," he said, turning to the unfortunate bird, "and good luck with it. They are totally alone, you know, these upwrights. Not only are they alienated from the Earth that created them, they are alone from each other. When the Lady threw down the bridge, they lost their sense of belonging. This beautiful place became something to fight against, not fight for. Their hrocain—sorry, their language, whatever it is called—is so complicated it hides more than it reveals.

"Our creature down there—I know what you feel for him. You know he's different. So do I. There's a connection between him and the Lady, and I don't know what it is. But you can see, can't you? It's almost a pain that he should be in the body of an upwright. I sense he wants to fly. I once heard from Master Airchurner, my predecessor who spoke, he said, to birds who travelled from lands before the sun rises and learned a rumour that any creature that can feel its heart beat may at some time or another live within the body of another creature. That would be a bat as an upwright, an upwright as a rook, a rook as a frog, a frog as a rabbit. This is a worrying thought."

Chek, chek? said Surebill to the upwright below.

Waark, waark? added Dryden.

What *are* they up to? In the same way that he heard whispers from the distant past as if they were the lowered voices of lovers in the next room, Richard Cleeve, standing beneath the clamour of the rookery, could hear rumours, intimations, hints of meaning—fragments of a broken mirror, tiny shards of a smashed pot, a footprint in grass, evidence that is almost no evidence at all—that the rooks of Saint Bride's were in possession of some great secret.

That modern ornithology and bird-watching are shallow crude fascinations tapping lightly at the door of an infinitely more profound mystery.

That perhaps, in their black-feathered impenetrable way, the rooks knew more about him than he about them, knew more about him than he knew about himself.

That they knew who he really was.

25

H E HEARD THE CLATTER OF footsteps on the flags, what he guessed was an overnight bag clumped down in front of the door, then the fuss of a key in the lock—Sarah.

"I'm upstairs," he called as the door opened.

Surely, he heard her mumble, "As usual."

Thumping up the stairs, humming Mahler. Symphony Five. The big bit from near the end. The Adagietto?

"Good to see you. How was work?"

"Hff," she said. There were flakes of snow in her hair, turning to stars, droplets. How's the book doing?" Sarah stroked his head. He turned and gently pushed her bomber jacket aside, kissed her slim midriff, warm through cotton.

"Hell, Sarah, it's not a book. How many times? Just some stuff for the History Club."

"Nice welcome. You *should* do a book. History of Kirkbretton. Fancy a pot of tea?"

"A chilled can would be better. There's one in the fridge. Sarah—" Their fingers slipped apart.

"Bloody cold out," she said, her voice muffled, already one floor down.

The phone rang.

"I'll get it on this line." "OK" drifted up from the kitchen. Richard dug into an unsteady deck of papers, notes, bills, and extracted the extension phone.

A pot clanged; the fridge door clunked open and shut.

"Have you seen the local paper?"

Whoever was ringing had a mouthful of food.

"Who is this?"

"Peter Sutcliffe. Dr. Crippen. Gandhi. Who the hell do you think—"

"Eddie."

Eddie Chesterman. For Richard and Sarah, Eddie perpetuated the chemical mystery of relationships. Neither knew why Eddie had attached himself so tenaciously to the couple. A biology teacher at Colden High, he had thrown his corpulent, wildly ginger-haired, pig-eyed, pockmarked, bandy-legged self at his new colleague on Richard's first day of the first term at lunch break, stealing the chips from his plate while delivering a stream of acidly bizarre observations, advice, abuse, jokes. Eddie turned out to be a loyal and persistent friend, always there when needed, rarely when not; and wryly, Sarah and Richard reciprocated, though Eddie was a nightmare to be with in public—no reserve, no modesty, no subtlety, no respect, no manners . . . insensitive and wildly comical, crass and perceptive, generous and cruel, and above all, unpredictable. Eddie brought to the feast a passion for education, a common interest in ornithology, and an unending string of the ugliest, least intelligent, downright unpleasant girlfriends ever assembled in the UK.

"Have you got Friday's paper? I'm amazed you haven't seen it."

"Yes. Somewhere. Wait a minute. Seen what?"

"Bottom of page 7. Got it?"

"Hang on." The *Express* was on the floor, rucked by the wheels of his office chair. "OK, where am I looking?"

Incoherent mumblings of disgust. "Included in planning applications submitted to Kirklees Council are the following . . ."

and, at the bottom, under "P ASSED: Burgeon Builders Ltd. outline permission for eight detached dwellings and detached garages at Glebelands, off Bridegate Lane, Kirkbretton . . ."

"Bloody hell."

"Across the way from you, eh? Bet that'll block the view. Aren't you supposed to put notices on lampposts or something? I'm astonished this is the first you've heard of it. Head so far up your arse, perhaps—"

"I can't believe it."

Burgeon was a farmer turned builder—the kind of man to grub out hedgerows, get permission for barns and build a house, then get permission to convert the "barn" to a house; a couple of years ago, he was prosecuted for pumping sludge into a birchwood copse then draining a mill pond Kirkbretton Junior and Infant school had adopted as a wildlife reserve.

And there were rumours he baited badgers and organised dogfights, though this Richard put down to pub talk—no evidence.

"I'm not sure he can do this, Eddie. That's church land, has been for centuries. The church commissioners can't have let it go."

'The stock market crash buggered them up, didn't it? They're supposed to be desperate for cash. They'd sell if the price was right."

"Leave it with me. Thanks for being your usual observant self."

Eddie coughed with false modesty. "You're welcome. Just thought you ought to know. See you Monday."

Richard found the phone directory, located Dr. A. Sutton, The Vicarage, Bridegate Lane.

"I'm afraid Mr. Burgeon went over my head. I have to say, it would have been courteous of him to let me know what his intentions were. All of Kirkbretton has seen that land as "common," it seems, for generations." Dr. Sutton, vicar of Kirkbretton, sounded half-miffed, half-apologetic. As if he'd been interrupted or caught out.

"So you have no say over what happens to the land?"

"None at all. It's not been part of the Kirkbretton living for more than a century. If you think the word *glebelands*—"

"I'm sorry?"

"The parish records say there used to be an income to Saint Bride's, albeit small, from pasturing and quarry rights on the cliff itself and Bride Hill. That's what's meant by *glebelands*. Land from which the church derives an income. That income would often become part of the money on which the parish priest would live. Hence 'living.'"

Yes, thank you, vicar, I am *a history teacher.*

"But it's still technically church land? I mean, you gave me permission to field-walk it last year."

"That was you, was it? I knew your face. Not awfully good with names, though. You're not a churchgoer, are you?" Sutton sucked air through his teeth. "You see, if there had been a regular income from the land, the commissioners would have been more reluctant to part with it."

"So you're saying the church no longer owns Bride Hill?"

The vicar cleared his throat. "I'm afraid I didn't exactly follow it up at the time. But I spoke with a friend at the commissioners' office this morning, Mr. Cleeve, immediately after I'd seen the same newspaper item you saw. For the last year, the owner of the land has been Burgeon Builders Ltd."

"Mr. Sutton, can I ask you a straight question?"

"Of course." That miffed tone again. *If there is a God, why does He allow so much misery? Come on, vicar.*

"If I were to, ah, fight, this planning permission—would you be behind me?"

There was a short silence. "Yes, I would. On several grounds—"

One of which would be loss of a certain vicar's visual amenity, peace and quiet, thought Richard. The vicarage overlooked the site too. He invited him to next Friday's History Society meeting and put the phone down.

"Chilled can, as requested." Sarah plonked the Boddingtons into a nest of bank statements and stood behind him, massaging his neck. "Who was on the phone?"

"Mmm, that feels damned good . . . Eddie, to tell me they're going to build a housing estate on Bride Hill, would you believe? Then the vicar across the way—I rang him. He might add his name to a petition, but I'm not going to hold my breath. Over my dead body, Sarah, before they build on that hill."

Sarah smiled a crooked smile. "'Bulldozers squash protester.' I can see the headlines."

"It's not funny. I've told you before the hill's probably the site of a Roman fort or an Iron Age settlement. If they build there, it's gone forever."

Sarah continued to stroke his neck and leaned to look out through the attic window up the hill. "It's wasteland, isn't it? Do you think anybody cares? Do you think there's anything you can do?"

"Watch me."

"I love you, tough guy."

Richard blinked, sighed, stood, threw Sarah's arms round his neck. "Are you stopping this weekend?"

"Oh yes," she purred. "I'll need the weekend to get over the chili con carne and tossed salad with very expensive balsamic vinegar and very sticky baklava you and I are going to force our way through this suppertime."

"I think this beer needs to warm up a little—"

"As it happens, the mince needs to defrost too."

"Then perhaps we should go down one level."

"Ooooh, Master Richard, you are a one! That be the bedroom level you be a-speakin' of."

He cupped the rounded warmth of her groin in his hand, kissed the end of her nose lightly. "Lust's a wonderful thing, isn't it?" he whispered.

26

THE BUZZER THAT ENDED THE official school day rang everywhere through the elderly faded building. The school emptied as if magically drained of life. Only Richard remained, it seemed, though Tuesday was History Club night, and Dougie and Khalia and Annette should be on their way through the labyrinth to RC2, a lofty 1940s vintage-style room painted the kind of green Richard always associated with hospitals. Light from the school pond flickered on the stained ceiling.

Dougie, year 11, Khalia and Annette, year 12, edged into the room with a nonchalant hi.

Richard had hitched himself on the corner of his desk, playing listlessly with the forms he'd photocopied. He looked up, welcomed his team, folded the papers in two, turned them face down.

"Did you know there are plans to build on Bride Hill?" He showed them the cutting from the *Express*. They didn't know.

"But, sir, if planning permission has been granted, you're kinduv stuffed . . ."

"Outline permission, Dougie. Big difference. It means Kirklees has no objections in principle and at present. It also means they don't see the site as being of archaeological interest. If nobody tells them . . ." He shrugged.

"Sir, I don't mean to be rude, but—it in't. Of archaeological interest, I mean," said Annette Preston, gangling blonde, eyes rather close together, a cold sore on her top lip. Khalia Hussain laughed and nudged her friend. "It's just a blackberry patch and a corner of the rookery."

"Right. Remember I told you I took some aerial pictures last summer over the village?" Richard spread them on a desktop. "Here—and here, but fainter, coming out of the wood—two lines. We were about four hundred feet up, so I'd guess from their width these are collapsed or eroded linear banks. But further out, look from where the cliff starts to the boundary wall of the Sunday school. Must be fifty metres. A curving line—very, very faint. Narrow. Like a wall."

"Could be an old farm wall. Maybe the top of the hill was a pound or summat." Annette frowned.

"Good thought, Annette. Hmm. Maybe. On the downside, I have to say the second line isn't visible on the ground. When I walked it last year, I'm pretty sure I could detect the inner linear banks, though they're pretty much covered with heather and brambles."

"Still a bit boring," grumbled Dougie.

"OK. You know this is all about evidence? You build it up like it was a crime scene. Before your time—in fact, well before my time here—the sixth form history students produced a booklet called *Kirkbretton Down the Ages*. Printed in 1978. There are four copies in the library, and I have them all here." Richard handed them round. "Look at page 26. Read the second paragraph down, Annette. After the bit about subscriptions."

When the excavations were made for St Bride's Sunday School and Parish Rooms in 1910 an undamaged beehive quern, a bronze brooch and three corroded Roman coins were found in what was known as Banks Corner, together with post-holes that were thought

to be those of the foundations of a circular medieval farm dwelling.
The quern—said to be the best example of its kind found in West
Yorkshire—is probably Iron Age or Roman. The brooch was in the
Celtic style and featured a horse. The coins have yet to be accurately
dated, though they are probably pre-Flavian. All the finds have
been given by the Vicar to Tolson Memorial Museum.

"Still don't know what you're getting so excited about, sir,"
said Dougie. "What's a beehive thing anyway?"

"A quern? It's a device for grinding corn. Pour the corn in
at the top, twirl it round with a couple of wooden handles fitted
into holes, and Bob's your uncle—out comes flour. The point is,
my little History Clubbers, that we're looking at an important
site that was almost certainly occupied in the first century AD."
He listed the clues: "Celtic brooch, quern, coins from the right
period—pre-Flavian means before AD80. Flavius was emperor
from then until about AD117, I think. And circular post-holes.
Unlikely to be medieval. Also, now I think of it, Banks Corner.
That not a cash bank. For banks read earthworks, an Iron Age
palisade."

He scribbled BROOCH, QUERN, COINS, POST-HOLES,
BANKS on the board.

"I don't know, sir," said Khalia. "They ditn't do anything about
it in the 1970s. Why should they hold up a building site now?"

"Well, times have changed. We're a bit more careful about what
we destroy these days. Also, you didn't have the same network
of county and borough archaeologists and archaeological units at
universities. It was all down to enthusiastic amateurs like ourselves
and the Kirkbretton History Society. Look, we're studying the
period anyway, planning the model of Castle Hill. Let's see if it isn't
worth switching to Bride Hill. We could go out there for a field
study—trowels, that sort of thing." He winked conspiratorially.

"Private land, sir—naughty, naughty." Dougie chuckled.

"Come on, man, let's live dangerously for a change. Tell you what. There's a History Society meeting on Friday night in the George. Come along if you want. Bring your parents. Doesn't matter—you'll just hear me tell them what I've told you. Then I'm going to suggest mass trespass."

Khalia's eyes lit up. "Civil disobedience. Whoa."

"My dad says Burgeon is handy with a gun," said Dougie.

"Scared, then, Dougie?"

"Me? You're kiddin', sir."

"I need you on my side, Harold."

Harold Moorhouse, president of Kirkbretton History Society, tended to be reelected year after year. He was a sage, crusty man in his midseventies, with a scalp as bald and mottled as a lapwing's egg, pebble lenses in horn-rimmed frames, limbs like flails. He beckoned the George's barmaid over.

"Get this lad a pint, Sandra. He looks undressed without. By which you mean," he growled, turning to Richard, "you want the society on your side."

"Of course."

"Times have changed since Toomey's day. We lose more than we win. Had you joined when we lost the Scotland Quarries enquiry and they ripped out the cairns in Kirkbretton Old Wood?"

"Cheers, Sandra—Harold. Yes—and I know." Richard nodded, sipped his beer. That had not been a happy time. Of the ten Bronze Age cairns and two hearths discovered, all but two cairns had gone. In their place, a forty-foot deep chasm, the land ground up for gravel and building sand. Harold lived in the golden age of local archaeology, referring to it constantly; his big claim to fame and his right to declare himself an authority on local prehistoric sites rested on his work with J. P. Toomey on the 1960-67 digs at Oldfield Hill and Royd Edge, Meltham in the neighbouring Holme Valley.

"We've tangled with that bugger Burgeon more than once before and lost too."

"No reason not to try, Harold."

The historian's thin moustache was edged with foam. He smacked his bluish lips. "Good ale, Sandra. Oh, we will. I favour the common land approach. All that stuff about querns and coins and *maybe* palisades isn't going to convince the planners. And it's not in our remit to rattle on about loss of amenity *unless* we've got a permissive footpath or bridleway across the land, which we ain't. Or *unless* somebody can come up with a sound archaeological case for stopping the development. Which you can't."

"Not yet I can't. But I still have field-walking permission from the vicar—"

"Tut-tut," said Harold. He thought for a moment. "The outline application goes to Kirkbretton Parish Council for approval, doesn't it?"

"That's the next step," Richard confirmed.

"Who do we know on the planning committee?"

"Wallace. Brandon-Wallace. Lib-Dem, Kirkbretton—ah—East, I think, but also on Kirklees for Colden North Ward. Dougie! And Annette, Khalia. This is a surprise. Good for you."

Dougie Allen had an arm round each girl, smiling broadly, the girls less enthusiastic. All three were framed in the stained glass lights of the doorway. Annette Preston muffled almost to the eyeballs in a red scarf. Khalia Hussain looking pretty, shy.

"Forgot to mention I'd invited them. Sorry. Harold, meet Colden Valley High History Club. My guests. Potential recruits." Richard, slightly awkward, introduced them to the president, explained the reason for their visit, and bought them drinks—hooch, two breezers.

"Hi, Bruce. How's Kathryn doing?"

Enter Bruce Sykes, breathless, checking his watch, grimacing.

"OK, thanks. Architecture suits her. She's planning to go to college this autumn."

"Delighted," said Richard. "Still playing rugby?"

"Don't mention it, just don't mention it. Not late, am I?" Kathryn's father, the society's secretary. A man with unbrushed, wiry hair thinning at the temples and a slight harelip that gave him an unwarranted sneer. Partner in an architectural practice in Huddersfield. Kathryn working there, still seeing Mr. Muscles Kevin by the sound of it.

More introductions.

The Kemp sisters edged into the George. "Sherries as usual, ladies?" said Harold, towering over them, booming. "I'm in the chair, and your arrival, ladies, gives us our quorum. Sandra, a pint of mild for Mr. Sykes here and two medium dry sherries is it, yes, for Katie and Joyce. We'll be in the snug if anyone else turns up."

No vicar, thought Richard. *Waiting to see which way the wind blows, probably.*

27

"BURGEON BUILDERS HAVE ACTUALLY PUT forward a very, mmm, sympathetic plan that has been approved by the Kirklees officers, Mr.—mmm—Cleeve. Eight luxury houses on that land is not a lot," said Mark Brandon-Wallace, councillor.

Richard cringed at Brandon-Wallace's accent—flat Barnsley vowels struggling out like flagstones from under an unevenly laid Home Counties screed or what the councillor imagined was Home Counties. False as his double-barrelled name, Richard speculated.

"The common will be wiped out."

"As you yourself admit, Bride Hill is not common land. If it were [he pronounced it 'wear'], we wouldn't have given him the green light, actually. He appears to have satisfied our officers with regard to access from Bridgate Lane, and the argument that the development is infill, rather than an encroachment into green or white land, I have to say, actually carried some weight. Bride Hill was earmarked for potential development in the Kirklees LDP—local development plan—two years ago. And as a safety measure, Kirklees has applied for, and will get, let me assure you, preservation orders on the trees in the, mmm, north part of the site. At this moment in time, I can't see, actually, any reason why the plans shouldn't go ahead."

"Yes, and as soon as the plans are confirmed, he'll put forward an application to vary, and those eight will become ten or twelve." Richard was getting snappy.

Brandon-Wallace sighed. "That's a little unfair, actually. You don't know that."

"He's done it before. Successfully." Richard had done some research. He mentioned three earlier plans for Burgeon developments in and around Kirkbretton.

"Well, I don't know about those personally, actually. They don't ring a bell. Chances are, anyway, such an application would be turned down at parish or Kirklees level. I certainly wouldn't be in favour. I'm not sure what else I can say. Thank you for bringing this to my attention."

"Actually, actually, actually," mouthed Richard, putting the phone down.

The History Society's letter was ignored or, as the planning department put it, "objections noted." Brandon-Wallace, according to the press report of the parish council, said nothing when the item came up for approval. The *Express* didn't pick up the story.

Richard rang the editor.

"Apparently, no mention was made that Bride Hill is an archaeological site. There were letters of objection, I'm told. Just a second.

"How many? Three? OK. What grounds? Yes, yes, mmm. The editor sounded as though he'd muffled the handset to confer with a reporter.

"Three letters. One from Reverend Sutton, two others—one yours, I suppose?—loss of amenity, mention of extra burden on resources. One wanted assurances the quarry would be fenced off and made safe."

"I know, I read your report. So no mention at all that this could be the site of a settlement or Roman encampment?"

"Just a second." More mumbling, hand covering the receiver. "Nothing on those lines. But if you know different—"

Richard listed the 1910 finds. He'd repeated them so often he felt ennui in his own voice. *I'm convincing no one.*

"Anything since then you know about?"

He admitted not. The editor urged him to write a letter. A sodding letter! "The plans are due to go through on the nod at Kirklees in two weeks' time. Knowing Burgeon Builders, they'll be making a start the following week. Early May."

"Perhaps the diggers'll uncover something."

"Chances are, by then, they'll have wrecked the site completely."

"We can't stop them." The editor sounded bruised. "We'll monitor it from this end, of course, and please get back to us straight away, Mr. Cleese, if they do find anything. I don't suppose the builders will tell us."

"You bet they won't."

They took his number at home and at work.

Mr. bloody Cleese. I mentioned the war, but I think I got away with it.

For the fifth weekend in a row, Richard was out with a spade and trowel on Bride Hill, early morning. The wind puckered his anorak and bent his hair. Last year's horny arms of blackberry plucked at his legs, tore the back of his hands. He'd seen the curtains flickering at the vicarage—Sutton or his wife wondering what the hell's going on. He felt like an alien. The hilltop was terribly exposed. He was probably getting a reputation, one he could ill afford as a known local teacher.

And goddammit, the rooks were watching. Sometimes in eerie silence.

The History Society seemed to have lost interest, regarded Burgeon's building scheme as a fait accompli. "That old bastard'll blow you away one of these days. Found anything?" Sarah asked. Richard said no; the palisade, if he had located it, appeared to be plough's turn stones—Annette's compound wall, perhaps. And at the windy brow of Bride Hill. All he could say was that it was perhaps unnaturally raised, but just earth—packed disturbed earth—two, maybe three feet deep. He dared not dig deeper, desperate though he was. The banks? mounded rubble, massively overgrown with stinging nettles, brambles, stubborn bilberry. Nothing definite.

"Oi, thee! What's ta doin'?"

"Looking for blackberries."

"Sure. In bloody April? I'm Burgeon. Who the bloody 'ell are you and what yer doin' on ma land?" The builder trundled over in shirtsleeves and braces and porkpie hat, shirt taut across his gut like a tea clipper's sail. Walking the dog. "Stay, Butch." The German shepherd slunk to his feet. No shotgun, thank God.

"Richard Cleeve. Pleased to meet you. I'm looking for evidence that Bride Hill is the site of an Iron Age settlement, possibly also a Roman fort."

"Y've no right." The builder stared beetle-browed at Richard's extended hand as if he'd never seen one before. Butch growled. "Down, boy—for now. Iron Age fort? What bollocks. This is just an 'ill."

"Things have been found here that say you're wrong."

"What things? Where are they?" Burgeon cocked his bull-like head to one side, as if Richard were hiding the evidence behind his back.

"Artefacts from the period."

"Arty-farty. It's all bollocks to me, lad."

Richard tried another tack. "I'm also a member of the local history society. We think you might be destroying an archaeo—a historical site. If we could—"

"A sympathise, A really do. Look, A'm not a villain of the piece, watcher call it. Ev'rythin's above board. Just earning a livin' lahke you, no cookin' t'books. Assumin' y'*do* work."

"History teacher at Colden Valley High."

"Educated, huh? Then y'should know better." Burgeon's bottom lip swallowed his upper and nearly ate his strawberry nose.

"Educator," Richard couldn't help correcting.

"Smart-ass," mumbled Burgeon. He suddenly looked as if he'd had a little too much conversation for the day. "Yer on ma land. JCBs move in Monday morning, fort or no fort, 'nuff said. Butch!"

The dog growled, inched forwards. Richard found himself fascinated by the Alsatian's teeth. So long, so yellow. "Good boy."

"Good *boy* to you," growled Burgeon, though Richard couldn't make out if the remark was sarcasm, a mishearing, or an attempt at a pun.

"See you Monday morning then," he said over his shoulder, desperately hoping Butch didn't take a liking to his ankles.

"Do yer no good, lad. Waste o'time."

Yes, it probably was. But fortunately, it was half term. If the bulldozers uncovered something, it was important—vital—someone was there to spot it.

28

Safehaven: April 25

AN UNRELENTING WIND FROM THE southwest brought tremulous, shivering gusts of rain and silent explosions of stratocumulus.

Dryden had been out with the peck squad at Colden meadows from sun's rising, returning with a full pouch more times than he cared to remember. Quarter—the time-honoured system whereby each foraging member of the kin is allocated his or her own area of feeding ground and must stay within it, an arrangement policed by elected quartermasters—had been difficult to maintain with so many parents fighting for the best peck. "No quarter" had been declared, finally, and loud rioting had broken out almost immediately, the field full of birds threatening each other, leaping and flapping and cawing. The whole thing was unsettling, especially under this pall of dark and threatening weather.

"And the worst thing is that there's enough for all," he complained to Startle as she crouched over the chicks to protect them from the rain, which pattered and splashed over the unfurling canopy of leaves above them. "Last year, you were lucky to find half a dozen leatherjackets per quarter, sunrise to sunfall. This year, we're falling over them."

Dryden and Startle's chicks, born exactly two moon cycles after Imbolc, were now (as the upwright would say) five weeks old. Early death had taken two, but three ugly and ever-growing offspring gaped their bright crimson and pale orange mouths upwards, haranguing their exhausted parents with their constant che-che-che-che for forage upwards of fifty times a day.

"Yecch. I hate this," said Startle, shaking her bill vigorously to rid it of a chick's mute. "So acidy." In an attempt to keep the nest reasonably clean, adult rooks prod their chicks' bottoms to make them defecate.

"Only one more quarter moon, darling, and they'll be doing this for themselves," said Dryden through a pouch of ground worm. "Have a portion."

"Bless you." They clattered bills, Startle reaching into her mate's mouth for the rich soup.

"Your turn for the battlefield. I'll take over here. Che-che-che-che to you too. Move over," he chided the squabs.

'There's a lot of movement on the chwaaghway this morning, wouldn't you say?" said Startle, hopping higher into the canopy.

"Not yellow-heads, I hope."

"Hardly likely, dear. I told you how I put paid to their little tricks."

"I think the fermented-smelling upwrights had some part to play in that, according to the way you tell the story," said Dryden drily.

"Oh, by the Lady's hell!" Startle screamed.

"What's the matter? Tell me."

"Just look. Yellow-heads. Upwrights. Just look at those chwaaaghs."

"What is it? What is it?" Incubating couples throughout the tree began to panic. Dryden came off his chicks, leaving them to thrust and waggle and blink at the rainy sky.

"I see a fifth part of Safehaven in smoke." Gifford Hangclaw and Dryden plunged from the tree, rattling branches as they went; then Startle and a dozen other birds, Caliban and Sapphire Dawncaller, young Bruton then, in quick succession; parents Westray and Sunrise and the next tree and the next, tumbling forth in outflight, crying, *'Waar, waar, waar!'* the dread upon them. "What is it? What is it?"

"Waar, waar, waar! Alarm! Alarm!"

———⊲⊳———

A powerful excavator made its way slowly up Bridegate Lane, its stack belching blue smoke, its steelshod caterpillar tracks screeching and grinding on the tarmac. Near the crest of the hill, it stopped, and its bucket scoop, held aloft as if in triumph, now lowered like the head of a bull about to charge. More screeching, and the excavator turned sideways. Its bucket crashed onto the wall, buckling it, sending stones chattering and rolling into the road.

In a few swift drives, the wall and its banking were ochre mud, and the excavator was clawing its way up into Bride's Hill, glebelands, pushing a wall of bracken and bramble back, scouring the earth beneath. A second digger arrived behind it, then a lorry, then several vans which spilled out a dozen or more men.

Soon, fires were springing up, and the air was rent with the crack and splinter of wood, the sweet smell of sap, the wrack of turned earth. And the noise! The grind and howl of tortured stone, the thrum of diesel engines, clouds of poisonous blue smoke, shouting.

Safehaven kin returning from peck swelled the dread, but finally, the call began to go out—"We can't abandon our chicks." And braver birds alighted to comfort their youngsters.

"This is the end. They're going to fell our tree and bring our babies to earth, I just know it!" wailed Startle. "By our Lady, oh, come to us now in our need!"

In Dryden's heart, there was terror, an unfounded, unmarked, uncharted horror of what was happening.

He knew more than the others; he began to perceive dimly. There was a pattern, a destiny, that seemed to have been written indelibly behind his head. He was condemned never to be able to see it, merely to feel its ever-present threat—that he was the one chosen, the one who stumbled, who called upon the Ley that runs through all life; and Surebill, a servant of that Ley, may have been no more than the messenger.

Nevertheless, it was Safehaven's master, Caspian Surebill, who spiralled down from the Air and landed with great skill in the branches above him.

"What should we do?" Dryden was desperate.

"For the Lady's sake, don't—you know—say *those words* again. You've no idea how it takes it out of me." The Master ducked his head a couple of times, blinked, tried to see what was going on below him. "There's nothing, Dryden. You *know* there's nothing can be done."

"Are you saying we should retreat? That we should just give up?"

"Well," said Surebill, "we can attack, like our ancestor heroes did before us. But I wonder what message we'd be giving the upwright. I think he'd go for the kill-from-a-distance, don't you? I think he'd get guns. This is what I think, Dryden—if our legends are true—if the Lady really is on our side, if we really are the guardians of Pretan's honour and the Lady's gift—then She will be here sooner or later. She will not endure silently this slur, this desecration. Shall we leave it in Her hands?"

"Crow-head is here again," said Dryden.

"He wants the yellow-heads to go away," murmured Startle.

"He cannot fly," said Surebill. He was musing, not talking to Dryden, who was left to shuffle on his perch, looking at first one then the other bird.

"Maybe he can crow louder than the yellow-heads, then."

"He cannot fly and doesn't know if he is bird or upwright. All his life, he has dreamed of flying and cursed his feet for being anchored to the soil. This much is certain from his eyes. There is no malice in him, but I doubt there is much power."

"Maybe his voice will drive away the yellow-heads."

"Where there should be wings, there are weak limbs; where there should be feathers, there are soft small talons. If there is any power in him, we should look for it behind the eyes."

"Excuse me," said Dryden, edging impatiently down his branch, "but can anyone join in?"

Surebill looked at him, head cocked. "You'll have a part to play in due course, Dryden Loose-tongue. Look after him, Startle. Meantime, we have our young to feed. I'll get the elders to set watch, and we'll swear in new quartermasters. Life must go on."

"Gods, how can he be so calm and practical?" spluttered Dryden after the Master of Congeries had flown.

"How do you think he feels inside, Dryden? But if the master loses his nerve, Safehaven will fall no matter what the upwright does."

29

THE BULLDOZERS MOVED IN THAT Monday morning at 8:00 a.m., knocking down a thirty-metre section of the dry stone wall on Bridegate Lane, their great stacks heaving diesel soot into the air, tracks slithering in the yellow mud that soon spilled into the road. Their first task—skimming the brush. Fires were lit, linnets and skylarks leaving their nests for good. Hedgehogs crushed in their leaf-balls, rabbits trapped in their warrens; Richard shuddered over his cornflakes.

Burgeon's lot were working well. He couldn't help but admire the man's almost military coordination. Richard went to the shop at the corner of Cliff Street and Bridge Road for eggs and bread, and there were diversion signs—Access Only. Back up the road just past the turning space for Saint Bride's were big yellow triangles. Road Closed: Sorry for the Inconvenience. All the utilities, services had turned out as if for a trade show. Transco for gas, Kenyons for water, some local contractor for electricity. Even the telecom and cable network vans. Getting in each other's way, the air occasionally blue.

Of Burgeon himself, no sight.

From his garret, Richard could see most of the action but still felt it necessary to go out, restless to check progress. The JCBs were making their way up to the brow of the hill, peeling back the vegetation effortlessly. Workmen with chainsaws were reducing the tougher brush to matchwood, and the huge bonfires grew, their furious crackling adding to whine and hum and grind and roar of machinery all over the hill.

Barely an hour had passed, and the place looked like the Somme. He wandered up the road to survey the mess at close quarters.

A battle-scarred yellow digger lurched drunkenly into a forty-foot sycamore, tearing off a great hull of bark. Before Richard's astonished eyes, a T-shirted navvy had the thing down with his chainsaw in a great flurry of yellow dust and chippings.

"You can't do that!" he shouted over the roar of diesel engines. "All these trees have preservation orders on them."

"Sorry, mate, we just did!" roared a square-topped bruiser with bullocks' biceps, a crucifix tattooed on his forehead and enough earrings to set up a New Age stall. Laughing, cheerful. "Don't know nowt about preservation orders."

"Anyhow, who says?" sniffed a snub-nosed boy, also on the work team. "Where's it say that, Brian?"

"Shurrup, Nige. You an environmentalist then?" Brian returned.

"Greenie?" added Nige, sniggering.

"You make it sound like a disease. No, I'm an archaeologist," he lied.

"Then watcha interested in trees for, then?" Nige couldn't resist interjecting.

Richard, looking theatrically over his spectacles, subjected Nige to a silent sneer.

"After buried treasure, then." Brian looked smug, as if he'd just finished the *Times* crossword.

Richard shouted over the noise of the engines and saws. "Look, I live in the house with the wisteria—the big climber—just over the brow, down Cliff Street—"

"Ooooooh, posh," said Nige, not unkindly. "Wass mysteria?"

"If you do find anything, please let me know. It won't be gold, Nige, just some rusty thing. Oh, I don't know."

"If it's gold coins, we keep it, don't we, Brian? Treasure."

"Ignorant little bastard." Brian spat through a large gap in his teeth, grinned hugely. "OK, squire, it's a deal. See ya."

Richard dragged himself homewards, took off his begrimed CAT boots, hung some washing out in Farrar's Fold, filled the dishwasher and set it rumbling, considered wandering up the village to the George for a pint and a sandwich, counted his change and decided against it, made a pot of tea and an omelette, rang Sarah at work.

Harry Tasker's oily self-confident condescension: "She's not in, Richard, but she said she'd be over your place for lunch. Get that stove going!"

"Thank you, Harry. Get stuffed, Harry."

Then . . .

A knock on the door.

Nige. Carrying a heavy bundle in a diesel-stained cloth.

"Found this on't site. Brian says to show it you. Old pan, really, innit?"

Richard peeped inside.

"Bloody hell. Come in." He spread newspapers on the kitchen table. Found a stiff brush. Nige unwrapped his parcel gingerly.

"Was it this shape?" whispered Richard.

Nige put his finger to his lip, then took it away, frowned at it. "Dunno what shape it wor. Digger ran ovver it, far as I could see. 'Orrible screeching noise. Wurf a lot, then?"

"You have no idea."

The yellow clay came off in lumps. A bright score, presumably the track of an excavator tooth. Bronze. Badly corroded for a third of its diameter at the base, so thin it was little more than twisted tracery. But the rim had survived. Ornamented holes for hooks and a chain or an arched handle. Celtic. Definitely Celtic. Round the rim, animals—a stag, a pig, a long-horned cow. The face of a god or goddess. A god, clay brushed from a beard. And horns. Cross-legged. Cernunnos, lord of the hunt.

"My God. You've just crushed a Gundestrup replica. Sorry—they found a cauldron like this in Denmark last century. Nige, this is probably two thousand years old. You just crushed a two-thousand-year-old cooking pot."

Nige was impressed despite himself.

"Shit. Ditn't mean to."

Sergeant Grantham: tall and narrow-shouldered but with hands like lobster claws. An uneven face, one eyebrow significantly higher than the other at the best of times—now half an inch separated them, and the gap was growing.

"This is not strictly the kind of thing we get involved in," he was saying in Richard's kitchen, holding his flattop hat as if he'd discovered his flies were open but couldn't get round to doing them up. "You made it sound like they'd dug up a body. A little misleading, your call, sir. 'Specially on 999."

"I'm sorry. Bodies? Believe me, it's not out of the question. There could be graves, all sorts." *Bullshit, bullshit.*

The sergeant's eyebrow cranked itself a little higher still.

"I didn't know how to deal with this. I just knew that the more they cleared the site, the more they'd wreck. I just had to get it stopped. Look, I could be overenthusiastic about this, but cauldrons like this are extremely rare."

The cooking pot, bruised and filthy, lay on the kitchen table like a relic in a shrine. Sergeant Grantham tapped it gingerly with his thumbnail. It made a dull *thung*. "Kind of interested in this sort of thing myself, sir. I'd say this was treasure trove, wouldn't you?"

Yes, thought Richard desperately. *My grannie's walled up in the cellar, and I have a teenage vice ring in the small bedroom. God, why do they always make one feel guilty?*

"Yes, of course. Absolutely priceless. I've already rung the West Yorkshire Archaeological Unit and they're sending someone over. God knows what else might be on the site."

"Well, you'll be pleased to know work's stopped up there. There's some pretty heavy swearing going on on that site right now, I'll tell you."

"That's nothing to what Burgeon will say."

"Burgeon? Burgeon Builders? That old vill—sorry, sir. Forget I said anything." Grantham tried to invest in a shamefaced grin of complicity, but the result gave him the aspect of one who skins live cats for weekend fun.

"You didn't."

The policeman shot Richard a glance that seemed to say, "OK, deal. We're in this together, united against a common enemy."

But then again, maybe not. You never could tell with the cops.

"I'd love to see his face." Grantham chuckled.

"Sooner than you think, Sergeant. He just passed the window."

The officer rubbed his palms together vigorously, grinning like a lunatic. Heavy rapping on the door. Grantham sucked in a roomful of air. "Right. Now, Mr. Cleeve, no provoking him. I can handle this."

"You bastard. I knew you wor trouble first tahm Ah set eyes on yer." Burgeon, spittle on the side of his face, pushed the door open into Richard's nose. His eyes were like gobstoppers.

"Steady on," said Richard, off his balance.

Then Burgeon spotted the officer. "Oh. It's you." Burgeon turned to Richard: "'Hidin' beyind a policeman now, are ya, ya fuckin' nuisance?"

"Less of that, Jack."

"'E started this. I could kick 'is bollocks down 'is—"

"Causing an affray, Jack. Think on it."

"Bloody busybody. Greenpeace summat. Fuckin' teacher. Ye'll ruin ma lively'ood for a bit o' bloody tin pan, bloody smart-ass uppity—"

"Last warning, Mr. Burgeon, then it's a caution and down to the station. Sit down, Jack, take the weight off your head. If you don't mind, Mr. Cleeve, beg pardon. Would you fetch him a cup of water?"

Burgeon was red, going on purple, a huge vein throbbing in the concave of his temple, sweat springing from every pore. "Just waitin' to cause me trouble. Got it in for me," he rumbled. "Ah'll get you yet."

Richard dashed for the taps. Sprayed water over his shirt. Noticed his hand was trembling. He couldn't determine whether the principal cause was the cauldron on his table or Burgeon's force-fed testicles offer. Sergeant Grantham was having a quiet word in Burgeon's bulging ear. He couldn't catch the words, but it sounded fairly minatory. The builder's menace was subsiding; he didn't look much more harmful than a locomotive with a head of steam, which was a definite improvement. Huff, puff, mumble, bastard, mumble, get him.

The door catch went.

"Oh."

Enter Sarah, tousled, a big cardboard box of groceries cradled in her freckled arms. "Guests, Richard."

"Absolutely. Sergeant Grantham—" Sarah put the groceries on the worktop. They shook hands. "Pleased to meet you."

"And Mr. Jack Burgeon of Burgeon Builders."

"Hff," said Burgeon, blowing a collapsed sweaty scrapeover out of his face.

"We'll be going now, Jack, won't we, unless you have anything else to say to Mr. Cleeve that doesn't involve effing and blinding. Leave it to us, Mr. Cleeve. We'll sort it out. Bye for now. C'mon, Jack."

With Grantham's muscular hand on his elbow, Burgeon was steered to the door.

"Mr. Burgeon. Listen, I really am sorry about this—"

"Fuck off. Pardon me, girl, no offence. I'll see you in court, Cleeve, mark ma words. Worked 'ard for every penny, then this clever little . . ." And the sounds bubbled off into the distance.

"Phew, nice friends. So that's the archdemon Burgeon. Richard!"

"What?"

"What the hell's that thing on our kitchen table?" She pointed to the cauldron.

"What? That? Oh, only the most significant archaeological find in Britain this decade. Vindicated! *Yes!*"

And he made an uncharacteristically enthusiastic gesture like grabbing a fly in front of his face. Sarah was sure she'd seen something similar on some football match on the telly.

30

"BRENTWOOD, AH. WE, AH, SPOKE. On the phone. West Yorkshire Archaeological Survey, County Hall, Wakefield."

A small balding pink-skinned man with earnest eyes swimming behind horn-rimmed lenses stood in the doorway, tiny limp hand extended. Richard shook it.

"Delighted you could come. That you came so quickly. You'll not be sorry you did, I think."

Richard ushered Dr. Brentwood in and looked both ways along the street. *No Burgeon. Thank God. I'm going to have nightmares about that fellow.*

"I got over as quickly as I could," he said as Richard offered to take his fur-lined and somewhat stained anorak. Brentwood shook his head vigorously, thrusting his hands deeply, stubbornly into his pockets. His body language said, "If this is a wild goose chase. If all we have is a gypsy cooking pot, circa 1850—"

Then Brentwood's eye fell on the cauldron. He lunged at it.

"My. My-my. I say. You haven't washed it or anything?" Dr. Brentwood's tone was suddenly brisker, his manner businesslike.

"Just lightly removed some clay and soil. With this."

"Good. And this damage—"

"I'm told an excavator ran over it."

"Dear me." Brentwood sucked his teeth. Removed his spectacles and frowned at the cauldron closely. There was a long silence.

"Well, Mr. Cleeve, your first guess is correct as far as I can see, unless it's a very clever reproduction, a fake. And why would anyone want to do that?" Brentwood rolled his eyes at the ceiling in self-deprecation, as if the very thought were unworthy. "This is Iron Age, a century either side of year dot. That's our dear friend the horned god Herne or, as they called him then, Cernunnos. Pan."

"Pot."

"Pardon? I said Pan. Oh, ha-ha. Pot and pan." A polite laugh. Brentwood looked at Richard strangely. Richard smiled as if palsied and looked for a hole to crawl into. "Sorry, just a joke. Very excited."

"Right. First. Can I use your phone? I need to make a couple of calls. We'll need to get an injunction preventing further work on the site—*whether* or not we need it ultimately—until we've given it a thorough going over, and ah, I'll have to invite the Tolson Memorial Museum curator to the party. His patch, y'see. Also, English Heritage need to be informed pronto. It's possible they'll send someone over."

"Sure. Go ahead."

Dr. Brentwood made his calls.

Then briskly rubbing his hands together, he said, "OK, that's sorted out. Now let's visit the site. Is it far?"

"No, just up the road. You'll need strong footwear."

"That's OK. I always carry wellies and a hard hat in the car. Am I safe to park outside the church gates?"

They donned boots—Brentwood from the rear of his hatchback, Richard in the hallway.

"I have to say, Mr. Cleeve, this is most exciting." The little man's eyes glistened.

"You're not kidding." The two men grinned like idiots at each other then, embarrassed, coughed simultaneously.

They walked up the road. Vans with workmen smoked, read the papers. Brian gave him a wave from a lorry. "Sorry, the lads squashed it. Nige says it's a gold one. Didn't look gold to me."

"Gold one? Gold one . . . no no no, *cauldron*."

"Oh, cauldron." Brian looked sadder but none the wiser.

"Friends of yours?" said Brentwood.

"Professional archaeologists to a man."

Again, that strange sideways look. Richard was beginning to discern that humour means different things to different people.

The utilities were still hard at it, perhaps because their preliminary work involved roadworks only. Richard was glad that Burgeon was nowhere to be found; maybe Sergeant Grantham's hard word had penetrated.

"The local archaeological society? You were saying you're a member?" asked Brentwood, puffing a little. "Kirkbretton what, History Society? Seem to remember I came to speak to you last year sometime."

"That's right. We've only one member with any experience of a professional dig—the president—Harold Moorhouse. Nice guy, in his seventies, though. Only about ten members, most of those getting on. They could work under supervision, I guess . . . then there's Colden High School's history club, they'd be keen to help." Richard flushed, aware suddenly he was prattling.

"Moorhouse. Pleasant chap. Hmm. We're going to need some serious input. It's not a criticism. Really, every bit of help will be welcome. I can organise a site marquee. But we're getting ahead of ourselves. We might be looking at a lone find, a stray," said Dr. Brentwood.

A long twig, pushed into the raked soil and clay, marked the spot where the cauldron had been unearthed. Brentwood pushed it further in, put a cluster of heavy stones round it. His eye roved over the site.

"The best we can manage is a rescue dig, you do realise that? This is not open land. The builder will be suing for loss of earnings and so on. That means we have a stay of execution. A month, maybe six weeks."

"But if this really is an important site—" protested Richard.

"Makes no difference. We can't buy it. We can't fight a protracted court battle, though no doubt if we threw a few feints, we could extend the dig period a week or two, a month at the outside."

"Ten weeks."

"Maximum. This is why we need to put out a call for volunteers. It's coming up to summer—the universities are a splendid source. Huddersfield, Bradford, Leeds, ah, Sheffield, York. Bit late for this year's dissertations, but if this site turns out well, could be a real feather in the cap for first and second years, bachelors, masters, that sort of thing. Hmm."

Brentwood took out a penknife and scraped a piece of mud from the side of his boot. "This is undisturbed soil, a clayey podzol. Very barren. Leached soil. But this—"—he gingerly picked up a handful of broken earth from the hill itself—"this is mound soil. A real mixture. Bits of sandstone and gritstone bedrock, peaty stuff, all mixed in with the podzol. The diggers haven't done this."

"So who did?"

Brentwood shrugged.

"I thought an old warren, perhaps, but then there isn't a monastic establishment, no large estate nearby. Burial mound?"

"Unlikely. Too extensive, too low. It's as if something's been covered over, nearly half an acre. But this."

Brentwood marched over, taking out his notebook.

"This is linear ditch and bank, no mistaking it. They've ruined it, of course—something that's lain undisturbed for two millennia destroyed in half a day. However, they didn't uproot the trees, and the bank is undisturbed for what—fifteen, twenty metres. And by God, that's a corner. Look where they've cleared the undergrowth. It's square. It's virtually a perfect ninety degrees. Whatever else this site might have been, it has been overlaid with something most probably of Roman provenance, Mr. Cleeve."

"A marching fort?"

"Marching fort, possibly. Very small, a temporary garrison. I can't see through the trees, but I'd guess the site offered a good view up and down the valley, good signalling visibility from Castle Hill . . . we'll need coins, pottery fragments, buckles and clasps, armour pieces, weapons, bones, a waste dump or latrine—something like that for confirmation. First thing is we measure the entire site, photograph it all just as it is. I'll see to that as soon as we get back." Brentwood checked his watch. "It's getting late to have a professional out now. First thing in the morning. Second thing: a soil resistivity test. Bradford University's Department of Archaeological Science will send a team out. They'll cover the whole site; if we push 'em, we'll have the first results back in two to three days. Now let's see—pollen analysis, radiocarbon dating, pottery and glassware boffins, recorder, surveyor, photographer we've thought of . . . . you've no idea how complicated this sort of thing is." Brentwood's speech was getting faster and faster.

"I'm picking it up quickly."

"But this is fascinating too. These stones. It looks as though they might run right round the mound site. It's a collapsed wall, perhaps a boundary . . ."

"Plough's clearance?" said Richard, chuffed.

"A paddock or pound, more likely." *Good old Annette. Limelight stealer.* "I'm not saying that for sure. Just a guess, Mr. Cleeve."

"Richard."

"Richard. But here and here—this is a circular bank or what remains of one. We'll find traces all the way round, except over there, where quarry's chewed out a lump, and here, where the foundation walls of the Roman station have obliterated it. They overlap, by the looks of it. These are early days, but I imagine we'll take a sampler cut or sondage through the ringwork and banking here . . . and then perhaps the stratigraphic clearance of a quarter to a half of the central site here . . . to here . . . the area most likely to involve overlap and then trial pits in one or two other strategic locations."

Richard was following Brentwood round as if they were attached by bungee. Twang, twang.

"Astonishing. It is a really big if. But if this initial survey has any substance, we could be looking at something that as far as I know is unique in West Yorkshire—a Roman marching fort built partially over a Celtic hill settlement."

Two mighty cultures, the mechanical overlaying the mystical, right on his doorstep. Like winning the lottery.

It was then he noticed the rooks in the newly leaved trees above them. Not cawing. Not outflying—what the books call a "dread" or rookery disturbance.

Row on row, on the branches . . .

"Like something from Hitchcock's *The Birds*, isn't it?" Brentwood said, following his eyes. "We're going to have to map the whole site centimetre by centimetre . . . Richard? Mr. Cleeve?"

Just muttering to themselves.

31

MY LADY'S FACE DISTORTED IN the bronze shield, fire flickering on its bosses. Her form twisted on the ivoried eyeball of the warrior, her mystery revealed in the maze and fylfot in the shape of the black-pressed stars, the glittering mica in moonlit stones. Her kiss on my great dusty wing, my bill buried in her raven-black hair, my claws buried in the flesh of her shoulder, her hand stroking the feathers of my breast. All I know is that I am guided ever closer, that Her gift screams from its grave to be released, like one who wakens from deepest sleep to find himself buried with his life's treasures in the stone tombs of the hills. Guide me, my lady, for my sight fails and my will falters . . .

The sky was a dark, rich blue. Already, an opalescent moon was stitching the wind-wracked clouds with mother-of-pearl. Far below, the bend of a river flashed silver, and streetlights suddenly winked on, their dusky red brightening quickly to orange—strings of pearls meshing the gloomy hills.

Cobweb and Hawberry Greybeak, flying with measured beat either side of the Rooklord against a constant crosswind, could see the old bird was flagging. The tension in his shoulders, the feathering of outer greater primaries, the unsteady rocking of tail primaries and coverts all signalled near exhaustion.

"My lord."

"Greybeak." Hroc's voice was deep and harsh.

"My lord, it will be dark soon."

"And we must rest, I know. I can fly no further. Find us a community of the faithful and a sheltered roost. Stay with me, Cobweb."

"As my lord wishes."

Cobweb and Hroc lay on the easterly, coasting lightly, pinions and coverts splayed, Hawberry's mate pacing the Rooklord in his descent. Hawberry broke formation and spiralled down. It had been a warm day, and the scents of the fields, exhaling in the dusk, rose like a blessing to greet him, a gust of rich farmland, soft mud, the dankness of ponds and streams in the gloaming.

He cruised, gliding downwind, using each updraught of warm air, practised eye seeking out the local congeries, giving the travellers' call sign—*aarh-chekh! Aarh-chekh!*

Then suddenly, he was answered from a copse of Scots pine. Always one eye on the pair above, and he saw them alight in a tall beech tree, forty, fifty wings to the sunfall.

"Welcome to Lowhills. I'm Calum Dawncaller, master of eleven trees. How many in your party?"

Flapping rapidly up to meet him was an old rook, fierce-eyed and raggy-winged. The two birds fell into a spiral glide together.

"In the Air, I and two others," cawed Greybeak, following the protocols. "Our gratitude for your shelter. I'm Hawberry Mac Greybeak. Is there peck to be had nearby?"

"After sunfall?" The old bird cackled. "Only if you have no fear of Rahrara." The Fox.

"We fear nothing. I guard the Master of Masters."

Calum Dawncaller looked sideways at his visitor. "In a sense, we all do, Hawberry Mac Greybeak," he said cautiously.

"Hroc is with us."

"Master of Masters? Hroc? Forgive me, did I hear you correctly? This—this is difficult. You are tired. You've obviously travelled many thousand wings today. Perhaps—"

"I guard the Master of Masters," Greybeak repeated wearily. "Calum Dawncaller, I urge you to believe what you hear. Come with me." The Rooklord's guardian banked steeply and beat towards the beech tree, closely followed by Dawncaller.

Dawncaller was persistent. "And what would lure the Rooklord from his sunfurthest lair? Are we at the end of time?"

"Maybe you should ask him personally," called Greybeak, landing below his master.

Dawncaller was about to land too but suddenly saw Hroc's menacing bulk in the branches below. With a shriek, he tumbled madly away, flapping wildly this way and that. "Gods, it's the Rooklord himself! We are all to die!" And so loudly and frantically did he call that his congeries broke from their nests in outflight, cawing and chacking in a deafening chorus, their scouts rocketing into the moonlit turquoise to see where their missing master might be—for there is a legend among the kin that Hroc, the Rook of Passage, appears to those who are about to depart this life, to cross the bridge into the eternal land of the old gods.

"You are not to die," called Greybeak. "My lord calls upon you to play a part in the unfolding of events. He calls upon you not as a disembodied spirit but as a creature of feather and flesh, of claw and beak."

"Wonders, wonders. Legend comes alive. My lord! I am Calum Dawncaller of Lowhills congeries. We are your servants."

"Have you seen the Lady?" came Hroc's hoarse call.

"The Lady? No, Master of Masters." When Hroc looked into the distance, he turned to Greybeak, whispering, "The Lady?"

Guided by Lowhill's astonished silent elders of tree, Hroc came to roost in a tall lone pine on a jagged bare branch just below the canopy. Cobweb and Hawberry were shown a damp meadow rich in peck. They vitchelled for themselves first then packed forage and fed their Lord as they would a fledgling, taking the rich proteins of spider, leatherjacket, and earthworm in a soup in their bill-pouches. Then, in the quiet darkness, they fell to roost alongside him.

"My brave and loyal friends," murmured the ancient rook, rubbing his beak gently against each of them. The wind moaned forlornly over the rustling top of the pine. The moon slid in and out of mist and cloud.

Have you kept faith, Hroc? Have you kept faith?

My lady, I am so tired. I look out on a world that grows lighter each day. Wherever I look the fabric of this world is parting.

Have you kept faith, Hroc?

I am so old, my lady.

Do you remember?

Oh, I remember. I remember the way you used to fold down my wing when we went into battle, promising me the sightless eyes of the dead . . . or when we watched the world revolve from the pinnacles or soared over the bridge into the Golden Land. There I was a god among gods.

Hroc listened to the Ley; he saw the web of the land spread before him, as only the birds can, the Air being their territory. He gathered the glimmering lines in his aged claw, holding, caressing them. And heard that whispering thread speak one word:

Dudeldera.

The dark meadow of the oaks. They were wing-beats away from Dudeldera.

The Romans, they of the boar standard, the bull worshippers, had no name for this place, or if they had, Hroc never heard it and could not identify it from the ageless echoes of the stones or the whispering of the trees. But their ghosts mingled with those of the Pretani, the children of Brigid, lost children, their faces and limbs black with moonstruck blood.

Now they call this place of death Stanwick.

The lie of the land is right, the shape and feel and Air of it. The high banks and stave-filled ditches are gone, the bloodied field is no longer strewn with bodies as far as the eye can see; the fires no longer burn. But the screams of the wounded and dying are merely muted, not gone; such agony is imprinted on the stones and soil forever. Manicured trees and neat hedges have grown where the oakbound meadows lay in AD 71, and everywhere are the glittering lights of the upwright, the smooth *chwaagh*ways, the stone roosts, the tamed roost meadows with their florid masses of imprisoned and foreign blooms . . .

He to whom You entrusted the gift—Venute—I followed him, my lady. I followed him as You asked, watched him from the gallows, from high in the circling air, from the bluff dark walls of fort and forest fence. Your light settled upon him, though he worshipped not. But his people—slave and servant, warrior and seer, lord and chieftain—followed him, dedicated their lives to him, willingly threw themselves upon the Romans' swords to save him.

He was the last of his people to bear Your gift and remain unscathed. Yet its cold glitter had burned itself onto the insides if his eyelids, and he was never free, not until the day of his death, and You came for him.

The ranks of his followers swelled in number until fifty thousand marched behind him. I listened to their talk—they planned to descend on the castra, oppida, and villi of the south and destroy utterly all that was not born and reared from Pretan's soil. He called the cream of the Fifteen Tribes to the place they now call Stanwick, Dudeldera, this very place, in one vast assembly under his command. But into the camp marched warriors of the Scoti, Parisii, Picti, Carveti, and fighters from tribes of whose names and very existence the Brigantes were unaware until that moment. There, he trained his warriors in the arts of battle and set their commanders, loyal and stout, each man and woman, in one mind, and that the mind of Venute alone.

And he struck terror in each Roman and Romanised heart. Word of Venute's plans reached the Ninth Legion's headquarters in Eboracum. They mobilised within days and bore down on Stanwick from all sides.

Hearing that the Romans were nearby, Venute's army hastily threw up walls and ditches round the camp, where no defence was expected; but their scouts were captured, their intelligence poor, and I could do nothing, my lady, to warn them that the legions were nearer than they thought.

Oh, Hroc, you have seen so much, too much. Would that I could have taken you into the Golden Land.

Our pact, my lady. The guardianship.

Yet I was there, Hroc the oathkeeper. I saw the legions and their mercenaries, column after column. They burst upon the Brigantes. The finest, relying on chariots, were driven into marshy ground or herded together by mounted bowmen, faster and more agile, where they were stuck and pricked and speared until they bristled with weapons buried to the hilt in their loyal flesh, more like a boar surrounded in a thicket, a hedgehog with its quills.

Venute's cavalry were then outpaced and outmanoeuvred by Scythian horse archers and Galatian javelin hurlers, mercenaries to a man; Nervii and Tungrians from Belgium, Batavii from Holland, Asturians and Vardulli from Spain, Dalmatians and Ulpians from the Balkans; and his infantry clashed repeatedly with the invincible testudos, their carapaces of tough shields belying the deadly sting of shortsword that issued repeatedly from beneath.

They fought hard and long through the day and into the night and were still fighting the next morning. But the battlefield was scarlet with blood, and not an inch of that vast field that was not covered with the eviscerated, the dismembered, the dying and dead—with their disembowelled and broken-backed horses, their smashed chariots—the wailing and the stench!

They cornered Venute and his elite guard finally at noon and cut them down with a hail of arrows, rushing in with gladius and hosta to finish their bloody work.

My lady, I followed still. After the slaughter, they slashed Venute's broken and pierced body into pieces and bore his several parts aloft on spears then scattered and burned them. He was a remarkable man blessed with physical strength, with his ancestors' madness, with your own fury, and with the love of his people. So no part of him should remain, the Romans intended; but by some miracle in which, perhaps, I saw your hand, my lady, his warriors recovered Venute's head, battered and bruised though it was, and kept it safe.

It is said that at the wake held in his honour, it spoke to them and demanded to be buried on a hill in Londinium where, as boys, wards of the Catuvellaunian court, watching the merchant ships of the Veneti arrive laden from Gaul, he and Caradoc swore the finest oaths of loyalty to each other and to their country.

And it was so—Venute's head was taken to Londinium and buried in a place called the White Hill, and our kith—the *Chraaka,* the ravens—have guarded it ever since. There it will remain, the very essence and spirit of true Pretan, the final resting place and inviolable sanctuary of the soul of these islands. And maybe, my lady, you shall permit Venute to speak once again for the proud and free people of this land they now call Britain, for though tongues change, your people, those our kin call the upwright, have not entirely forgotten their pact with You.

Nor have you, sweet Hroc. Soon, friend. Soon.

Oh, my lady, I have seen with these eyes and with the dimming eyes of the Ley, all directions at once. Your gift comes to a few *hroca* each generation but weakly now, it seems; few can walk with the gods as You and I did. And I have looked for Your return. I have sent the message down the line, and all *hroca* in Pretan know they are guardians of the truth. The legends are strong, the bond and promise unbroken.

We have kept faith, my lady.

The time is nigh for your reward. I do not forget nor do I break oath.

32

"T̲AE BE HONEST, THE WHOLE place gives me the willies."

Alex and Paul, Bradford University student volunteers, stood under the awning of the sorting tent. The team nicknamed the pair the Celts. Alex and Paul returned the compliment but privately—the team were the Romans. The pair were camping in the lee of the hill with a motley crowd of students and jobbing dig freaks and had a subsistence arrangement with Saint Bride's. The reverend Sutton had rallied the Women's Group, several of whom remembered the Land Army and saw this as Dig for Victory revisited. Sandwiches, urns of tea, butterfly buns, a small contribution, if you please, to church funds.

"There's somethin' very wrang. A can feel et."

Before them, the site markers stretched away in lines, like the strips round policemen's helmets. Duckboards set on bricks creaked and twanged to footsteps and created a walkway maze through the site. Ropes and pegs marked off the pits in various levels of excavation. Mounds of sifted earth stood like guardians round the hilltop outside the site itself. Perhaps a dozen people of all ages working with palette knives, soft brushes, trowels, buckets, sieves, and garden griddles. Lost in their own world.

The sun was out now, and the awnings pulled back, fold on fold, roped and eyed and pulleyed so as to be hauled over the dig at a moment's notice, awnings marking site director Dr. Brentwood's determination to get as much done as possible, rain or shine. A rush of pottery finds the last three days and a noisy insufferable ceramics expert from Sheffield University was playing God at one end of the sorting tent. The air hot and brittle, drilled by the coming and going of insects. A photographer listlessly snapping the pits from the top of a tall aluminium stepladder, filling out location and time on a clipboard.

That time was running out.

"It's the air. Storm brewing."

Paul put his arm round her shoulder. Clumsy. Comforting. They weren't exactly *going* together, but the lanky psychology undergraduate felt quite warm and protective towards the spiky-haired plumpish worrier Alex. Taffy finds love with Jock. Jockess. Shared a laugh or two and a game of pool in the George. God, they'd *slept* together. Same tent for four weeks, inevitable really. Funny phrase, *slept together.*

"Scared of finding a skeleton, is it?"

"Och, ye daftie. I'm nae scared ae bones. It's thae bloody birrds." She shuddered. "Bloody craws. Bloody vultures mair like. Lookin' down ma blouse all the time."

"Can't say I blame 'um." Paul grinned, craning.

She shook him off. "Has the heat got to ye? A sometimes wonder if ye're a wee bit weird, Paul Owen." Nice blue eyes. Laugh wrinkled. He's OK, really. Could do worse. "Back tae work then, A suppose. Up the top end, start the last section, the prof says."

"I'm down yur, Alex. See you later. Goin' for a pint after, then, are we?"

"Mebbe, mebbe. If ye're payin'."

Alex trowelling then brushing earth from a spot between four markers. Thin layer of blackened soil, evidence of the big fire they'd found all over the central area of the dig. Brushed it carefully into one of her buckets. "Bucket full! No finds!" Shouting for the junior volunteers, day-trippers they called them, junior school. Heat on the back of her head. Ties her hair in headscarf. The tiniest mountain appears under the whisk of her brush. Bigger, bigger. Slightly curved.

Terracotta.

The air buzzes. She flicks away a bluebottle. She dons the surgical glove you're supposed to wear, pulls gently, back and forth. Stuck. A big shard. Her heart beats faster, she can hear it pounding in her chest. She works the palette knife furiously. A drop of sweat darkens the dust. Then another. It's huge! Jesus, it's a lid, here's the handle. Broken in three, four places, caved in. This is mine, mine. Nobody's watching. There's a cavity beneath. Burned grain, dry as a bone, little black pellets, barley? A granary bin, a huge, virtually undamaged granary bin.

"Found something, Alex?"

It's that history teacher from the local high school, Cleeve or something. Where did he spring from, the amateur?

"Alex?"

Warm grain? The sun, perhaps. But the lid fragments were cold. She reaches in, sifts the corn. Most of it has cemented itself together, but a few loose grains tumble and shift. Touches something hard. Hauls it out slowly, the grain rattling to the side like sand. It's gold. Good God, it's gold!

Huge bass drumcrack of thunder, softening into a tympanic roll. Voice says, muffled by earth banks, "Knew it couldn't last . . . summer storm . . . awning." Alex shaking, her head pounding. It's a necklace in perfect condition, bright as the day it was made, a torc—oh . . .

"What have you there?" The old woman knelt beside Alex. Alex blushed deeply, despite herself. Found out.

"Alex! Are you all right?" Cleeve's voice so distant now. Down a long tunnel.

"Ye should'nae be on the site, ye know," she said to the old woman.

The hag lifted the girl's face, looked closely into her eyes, searching. "Neither should you, girl. Neither should any of you. Gods, but I love your accent. Reminds me of . . ." Her breath was old, like the air from a body bag.

Holds out her withered hand. Alex sees the wrinkled, skinny, age-browned arm and thinks, *Tollund Man. Pete Moss.* "Let me have it. Come on, child."

"Ye shouldn'ae touch et wi'out gloves . . ."

"Fine workmanship. I remember it well," she said to herself. "Do you know what this is, child?"

"Well, no. It looks Celtic—"

"What's Celtic?" she said sharply. "Pretan?"

Alex frowned. "Brython, British, yes."

"Do you know who I am?"

Alexis was suddenly cold, scared, fixed to the spot. She stared wildly at the crone.

"No need to fear, my girl. I am the nearest thing to reality you are going to touch." As she spoke, her withered claw closed over Alex's wrist. Alex pulled; the old woman's grip was like steel. "Come with me. I have a most wonderful thing to show you."

"Alex!"

Richard raced along the access planks, shouting as he went. "Hey! What's going on?" The woman turned; he saw the glittering torc, frozen in time. "Just put that down right now. What have you done to the girl?"

He touched her arm. The woman recoiled. A cold sensation shot through his body, as if he'd touched electric ice. She stared. Muttered, "Winged ones, come. Come, my lovely Hroc. Come." Louder. "Leave me be, young man," she commanded. "You have done a thing for which the right way is death. Nevertheless, a thing done in ignorance may sometimes earn mercy. Besides, I think I know you. Hmm."

Alex found her irresistible. Disinterested, she watched Richard fall gently into the pit beside her. Two, then three rooks fell out of the sky, scrabbled with the torc, and finally lifted it out of the pit. One clutched it, tried to take off. It fell back. Another grabbed it. Then away, up into the trees. Then with the crone, she rose, leaving her body behind, and crossed the field, noticing with a kind of detached pleasure that, as she walked, the earth drew further and further away from her floating feet . . .

Buckets overturned. Mad scramble to the access planks. Katie and Joyce Kemp first to their side—Katie, former district nurse, feeling for Alex's pulse; Joyce, waving her handkerchief at Richard's death-pale face. "Phone for an ambulance." Junior schoolkid bursting into tears. Dr. Brentwood and the Sheffield man shouting, "What's going on out there? Richard? Look at those damned birds! What have they got?" Paul Owen shouting, "Alex! Alex! Alex! Alex! Alex!"

———⊗⊗⊗———

"This is a sorry mess," Sergeant Grantham scowled, his wandering eyebrow raised.

"The girl's dead. Dead. Richard's alive—but absolutely out cold. Like he's in a trance, a coma." Dr. Brentwood ran his hand through his thinning hair. "How can a thing like this happen?"

"It just does, sir," said Grantham. "Sometimes. I'm sure you took every precaution. Site safety and all. Your photographer got off a few shots, it seems. Grandstand view. We'll need to look at those pretty quick. Um. Do you have details of next of kin?"

"Alex? We'll have it on the register. Parents live in Scotland. We've a clocking card system in a cabinet in the church hall.

Richard? Girlfriend's called Sarah. Works in town. He lives just down the road."

"Oh yes." said Grantham. "Met her. Pretty woman. This is a sorry mess. Quietest, gentlest sort of thing to be involved in, normally, a dig?"

"God's sake, Sergeant, this is no time for philosophy." There was an abrupt interjection from the Sheffield ceramist Professor Arnold.

Grantham steeled his eyes, tight-lipped, furious. "No, sir, I suppose not. You won't be leaving the site just yet, then, Mr.—"

"Arnold. John Arnold. Look, officer, I was a bit—"

"I know, sir. Let's forget it. For now." Turned to Brentwood. "So you said Mr. Cleeve acted a bit strange just before the incident."

"Not so much acted strange as said something. He was angry with Alex. Told her to put what she'd found down. 'Put that down right now,' he said. Just like a teacher."

"But Alex had a right to touch it."

"Absolutely. Alex's only mistake was not calling an expert over thirty seconds earlier. But it's common enough among diggers, professional and amateur. A sense of possession, *my* find."

Grantham nodded. "Anything else?"

"I didn't, er, actually hear this, but the Kemp sisters and half a dozen others did, apparently. He said, 'What have you done to the girl?' Unquote."

"That's right. Right over the pit. He wasn't talking or looking at anybody else but Alex." Ben Shapiro of English Heritage, a tall birdlike man with a grey halo of wiry hair, confirmed Dr. Brentwood's statement.

"So who did what to the girl?" Grantham muttered, more to himself.

Brentwood called an emergency council in the sorting tent. An indigo dusk was falling. In the distance, the cawing of the rooks, the sky thick with their wings.

"The girl Alex was at the furthest corner of the dig, the last section. We'll get the granary bin out and call it a day. We're not going any further." Grim silence. "Christ, we've got two dozen coins, a hundred or so pieces of glassware, half a hundredweight of pottery, a sword hilt—"

"The cauldron."

"The cauldron, a dozen arrowheads, two brooches, timber and leather and textile fragments, remains of at least three unburied specimens, at least one Roman . . . I say we call a halt now and get out. We know what this place was, and it's now a graveyard."

"Please, no histrionics," said Professor Arnold.

Brentwood glared. "We'll tidy up, infill, the usual stuff."

"Don't forget the torc. The only precious metal artefact found. Massively significant." Dr. Jeremy Kingston, Leeds University, spoke. Wild-haired, a regular consultant on the BBC *Time Team* programmes, he was an Iron Age specialist, an expert on glassware and armour.

"That's crazy, getting out, now you know what's here," he continued. "You've at least another week. That torc could be just the first of many more prize items. On its own, it makes Bride Hill one of the prime archaeological sites in Yorkshire. There's a dozen papers in this and a feather in the cap for the University—for all your universities—"

"We don't have the torc. As far as we know, it's in the trees with those bloody rooks."

"That's about the strangest thing in all this."

"Say again, doctor. What's so strange?" asked John Arnold.

"The birds. Oh, forget it. Now Richard's, er, ill, any ornithologists here?"

"Did a bit of twitching in my youth," said Dr. Ben Shapiro. Muffled giggle from junior members of the team. Shapiro beamed through deep lenses. "Oh yes, that too. But that's not what I mean, boys and girls. Corvids are, by nature, thieves. All that glisters, yes. I, ah, never heard that rooks were particularly, ah. Usually jackdaws. Jays, occasionally."

"So if it's up there, how do we get it down?"

"A cull?"

"RSPCA likely to be slightly unhappy about that."

"Rooks are vermin, I believe. They needn't know anyway. Pop, pop, it's all over."

"Pellet damage? I won't hear of it. Besides, bloody cruel. Won't hear of it."

"Cut the trees down?"

"They're protected. Besides, who's to say the birds wouldn't take it somewhere else?"

"Sounds like you think they're intelligent. Deliberately keeping the item from us."

"Hello." A stir in the tent. "May I join you?" Richard, a plaster on his head, hair dishevelled. Sarah at his side. "He insisted." She shrugged helplessly.

You don't look too well, Richard," said Dr. Brentwood. "Are you sure—"

"Uh-huh. Really. Casualty wouldn't have let me go otherwise. I'm fine. Slight concussion. Don't mention the war." He saw their faces, felt trapped. "It's just a joke. Really, it's just a joke."

"You should go to bed," Brentwood said. "This must have been an horrific experience for you."

"Come on, Richard. They're right," Sarah said, holding his arm, somewhat put out by the lamp-lit faces staring at her.

"Shush. Now I know that when Alex . . . when . . . when the incident . . . what I want to know is, did anyone see an old woman with Alex?"

"The sisters, your History Society friends—"

"Apart from the Kemp sisters."

Brentwood looked round the table. "No. She was alone, Richard. You're tired. This has been a big strain on you. On us all. A trauma. Perhaps—"

"I hear from the police that the photographer was—"

"Yoo-hoo. I'm here." A voice from the darker recesses of the table. "She was talking to someone—I think. Saying, "Get off, you can't touch it" or something."

"Who was talking? Alex? You didn't see anyone?"

Out of his eye corner, Richard saw Dr. Brentwood start as if kicked. *If I'm talking to fresh air, then so was Alex. Can two-three— people suffer simultaneous delusions, doctor?*

"Sunstroke, mate. Long hours thinking. I see all sorts myself. Or maybe she was starting to hallucinate or babble or I don't know."

"The photos?"

"The police want them. I'm going to develop them tonight, drop them off in Huddersfield first thing. The investigating officer was most clear about that."

"OK. OK. I'll talk to him."

"Richard. Listen to me carefully. Bang on head. Rest." Brentwood tapped his own forehead.

"I touched something very old, very cold," said Richard.

"Pardon?" said Brentwood.

"Line of poetry, right?" The photographer looked round, grinning.

"OK. You're right. A good night's sleep. Sorry to have bothered you."

Sarah, apologetic again: "He's sorry to have bothered you."

The photographer blew her a kiss.

33

MASTER SUREBILL TOOK HIMSELF SPIRALLING to a great height and looked down on the devastation below him. To him, what the upwright did to the Haunted Hill—whether it be with heavy plant operators' excavators or archaeologists' soft-haired brushes and griddles—was still an unforgivable insult, apocalypse.

And he was powerless to stop it.

All had been horrific confusion from the moment the yellow-head upwrights and their machines had entered the sacred burial ground. But Safehaven was in turmoil for the loss of the best part of a generation of nestlings, the rooks tumbling out of the trees, shouting incoherently at each other, chicks losing their balance and falling into the undergrowth, parents trying to rescue them before the yellow-heads found them. Great *chwaaghs* starting up in clouds of filthy smoke. The Air vibrating with the whine, growl, and bite of chainsaws. The ground shaking with the thunder and scrape and screech of mechanical diggers.

They had called on the Lady to protect them, to cordon Safehaven, Air, and earthy sanctum beneath.

And briefly, it seemed, She had done. Dryden's raven-headed one, the mysterious upwright whom Surebill said had a *hroca* soul, who wanted to fly—had appeared. And soon after, the yellow *chwaaghs'* vicious thunder had ceased.

Then when the vehicles moved away, others arrived. As the days proceeded, Safehaven's noisy consternation gave way to a hollow dread; many birds virtually stopped feeding, hunching themselves in small silent groups on the uppermost branches, many of them bereaved and aimless. The routines and rituals that kept the kin busy during the lengthening days of summer were abandoned or halfheartedly performed. Those who did feed might set off in pairs, on impulse, to unfamiliar grounds at odd times of the day. The instruction of yearlings by experienced birds in sophisticated fly-glide technique was neglected. Visitors from other congeries were shooed away with a "No news! No news!" and dreads would start unaccountably, the rooks trailing each other round in disconsolate circles.

Tents were erected; holes in the ground began to appear.

Dryden, Startle, Surebill, two Nightwings, Gifford Hangclaw, and half a dozen others had gathered in a tall sycamore at the edge of the quarry. Tree elder Caerleon and his partner, Elderflower Longpinion, joined them.

"I was wrong about Crow-head, totally wrong. I thought he was a protector of the Lady's gift. Instead, he is just another grave robber, a *chakaw*," Dryden was saying. He shrieked loudly down at the site workers. "Go away!"

"Where's the Lady? This is total sacrilege! Can they do this?"

"They are doing," said Surebill grimly.

"Who can we tell?" fluttered one of the Nightwing sisters.

"Who is there to tell?" muttered Hangclaw. "We were always powerless, always on our own."

"*Chhh,* the Master of Masters is coming. We can tell him." All heads turned to Startle.

"What?" said Dryden. "Master of Masters? You mean Hroc himself? How do you know?"

"How does she know that?" echoed one Nightwing sister to the other.

"How *do* you know?" huffed Gifford Hangclaw.

She ducked her head with embarrassment a couple of times. "How do we know anything?" she said.

Dryden took a long look at her. And so, from his perch a little above, among the glittering green leaves, did Master Surebill. *She knows. She is a seer. A rookery mistress. If anything of Safehaven survives, that is,* he thought.

"Listen," said Startle urgently.

Dryden cocked his head to one side. The leaves? The digging noises? The coming storm?

"Oh, Dryden, something terrible is about to happen. I can feel it. I'm going down to the wall to have a look," she said. Without waiting for an answer, Startle half-dropped, half-flew, and finished with an accomplished glide, tipping onto the mossy uneven stones of the wall below.

"Is it safe? We'll stay here," said the Nightwing sisters.

"I'll come," said Dryden.

"Me too," said Surebill.

"Good luck to you," said Hangclaw, deliberately hopping a branch or two higher. "Somebody has to keep watch."

Nobody paid any attention to the three rooks on the wall, shielded as they were by the fluttering lime green of a low-slung beech branch. Startle had become frozen, rigid, as if the invisible leys of the air were bending together, focusing on her, passing through her body. Dryden and Surebill shuffled nearer, either side of her, unsure of how to protect her, what to do next.

"O help me, Lady, help me!"

"What is it, Startle, tell us!"

Dryden's mate was trembling, her tail feathers rattling drily together. "The upright in the hole has found the gift."

"You're overwrought," said Surebill sternly. "Let's fly back—"

Suddenly, there was an immense crash of thunder.

"And look, the Lady's here to reclaim it!" screamed Startle harshly.

"Where?" said Dryden. All he could see through the leaves was an upwright female, another upwright on a metal frame looking down on the site, two more in a hole nearby, and the crow-haired upwright running towards them.

"Crow-hair can see the Lady," flapped Startle. They watched, tense.

"Crow-hair touched the Goddess. Oh, Dryden, he shouldn't have done that. Nobody must *ever* do that. Come down with me *now!*"

Dryen looked terrified. "I can't go so close to upwrights. By the Lady, Startle, it's just not done!"

"Then I'll do it on my own." Startle glided from the wall silently, spreading primaries and secondaries and tail feathers at the last minute and rattling so low over the bare ground her passage raised dust.

"Oh, help me!" Dryden's mutes turned to water in his anxiety. But his indecision was overwhelmed by the need to protect his mate—perhaps to save face, perhaps because there exist between all members of the same kin almost imperceptible differences, hairline fractures in evolution, out of which momentous changes always pour. Do I fly down or watch from a distance? Bravery or cowardice.

With the insane breath of the seer within her, Startle was beyond help, driven and possessed, her actions not her own. Dryden was different—hostile to and scared of upwrights, full of the urges of survival and self-preservation, the loyalty to kin and congeries—in short, a citizen.

Whatever, he too plunged from the capstones a couple of seconds later and, with several strong wing-beats, drove powerfully to the clutch of upwrights enacting its mysterious drama in the excavations.

And there it glinted.

Clearly, the gift.

Startle was right. She had landed at the side of the excavation and was bobbing uncertainly back and forth—a step forwards, two nervous jumps to the side, a step back, a sudden flap. Dryden cruised in beside her. Nobody in the pit paid her the slightest attention.

Winged ones, come. Come, my lovely Hroc. All Dryden saw was the gift, shining golden in the sunshine. Startle saw the Lady hold it out to her, read her eyes: *Take it, take it now!*

"He'll come, Lady, *wa-aarch-che*. Hroc is on his way. We are his descendants. We are the guardians of the gift."

No! You take it! Take it, or the dead will once again litter this hilltop. I am not ready. Take it!

A black shadow flickered over the site, and Surebill's heavy *waark*, full of alarm and fear, echoed between the trees and over the bald, dusty earth. He thundered down out of the sky. "We must rescue the gift. We must honour our promise to the Lady."

At that moment, from the female upwright, there emerged that concentration of sparkling energy that creates a kind of warp or tuck in the Air, and Startle knew beyond a doubt that she was watching the death of an upwright. The Lady seemed to dissolve too; the two forces—the upwright female's shimmering self and the Goddess's pale, unearthly but clear outline, like the meniscus of water in glass—joined hands. And they seemed to walk away together, into the depths of the Air. Though both Startle and Surebill saw this, they could not say later how it was done.

As the gift fell, Surebill rose to meet it, claw outstretched. But he missed it, and down into the dusty pit it tumbled. With a clatter of wings, Safehaven's master grasped the torc from the floor of the pit and, flapping furiously, managed to raise it to the rim, where Startle also grasped it, held it firm.

"We have to get away," said Dryden urgently. "The upwrights are coming. I'm the strongest. Let me take it."

"I can manage," gasped old Surebill, beating his wings. But the gift was heavy, and Surebill's eyes rolled desperately in his head as he struggled into the air. With a violent, exasperated caw, he let the torc drop.

Dryden clutched it as it fell, already on a takeoff trajectory, Startle flew above him, shadowing his course. And gradually, he gained height as the hill fell away over the graveyard, the quarry edge, the green fluttering mass of the beeches and sycamores.

34

"IT'S SO HEAVY, MASTER. PHFFF, it seems to weigh more the further it goes from the ground."

"Be brave, Dryden," said Surebill. "If it becomes too much—"

"I—can—manage."

"Are you sure?" asked Startle. "I can take over. Really. I'm just as strong—"

"I *said*."

Dryden hopped clumsily upwards, branch to branch, the torc in his beak, accompanied by an anxious Surebill and Startle. Above them, the Safehaven rooks flocked and wheeled, the message passing from bird to bird—they have the gift. The Lady's gift. No! I don't believe it? Where is it then? Has She returned? Has *who* returned?

Dryden had no plan in mind. With great effort, he flew from tree to tree, pausing for breath between each, making his way to his and Startle's own nest, Startle accompanying him, tutting and clucking like an old hen.

As they approached, Dryden and Startle's chicks jabbered, scared and hungry. "Oh, please, be quiet," said Startle wearily. "Carew, eldest, help your brother and sister out of the nest. There. Go easy, Bran. Don't push him, Woodsorrel."

Dryden hopped closer, dropped the torc into the nest, turned quickly to his chicks. "We call this *roost*. Where, instead of lying in the nest, you rest on a comfortable branch for the night. Yes, here's a good place. One of your mother's favourite spots. You can all practise being at roost, just like your mother and me."

"But Mother, the Dawncallers aren't out of nest yet," complained Bran. "Why should we—"

"You're two days older. The Dawncallers will be up and about in two days, wait and see."

"What's that in the nest, Father? It's beautiful," said Carew.

"Something we must guard."

In the Air above, Surebill, keen to prevent further disruption of Safehaven, flew hither and thither to placate the dread that was pushing his flock to the edge of hysteria. His voice drifted down: "Be calm! Be calm! All clear! Call to full council *now*!"

Voices were raised: "In broad daylight, with half of Safehaven at peck?"

Surebill ignored them. "Elders, nominate scouts. Or fly yourselves. Bring all of Safehaven home."

Shadows were lengthening when the kin gathered in the council tree behind the vicarage, oblivious to the upwright mayhem beneath them on the Haunted Hill, the flashing lights of ambulance and police car.

"I saw the upwright die," murmured Startle. "I saw her die. I saw the Lady."

"Is it right, master? Is the Lady here? Where is the gift? We heard—"

"The gift is safe. There was a shadow . . . ," Surebill said uncertainly.

"We have to take it to the Master of Masters. We are unworthy of it. Hroc will know what to do with it."

"And where is he? Just more of the legend. Hroc's the ghoul-bird who comes to take you when you die, that's all," said Gifford Hangclaw.

"You Hangclaws are all the same. I knew your father. Bitter sour-feathered block-nostrilled old—"

"I can't believe we have the gift. The actual gift."

"Oh, you can tell. The power, the warmth, the weirdness. Surely you can feel it . . ."

"May I have a peep, just a little—"

"What does it do, Mother?"

"According to legend, it contains the spirit of our Lady."

"Has it crossed anybody's mind that this gold thing might just be a *chakaw*'s theft item?" said Gifford Hangclaw, unrelenting.

There was a silence, broken only by some yearling's nervous chuckle.

Surebill drew himself up to his full height. "By the power of the Goddess invested in me, I tell you that this is the gift of legend. This is the source of the curse upon the upright, the source of his blindness for five score of scores of years since the Lady last walked in the misty land of old Pretan. I know this in my old bones, I feel this beak-to-tail. And there are others in Safehaven who can feel the Ley, who know that I speak the truth. *Chaw cha-ich,* the sign is given."

"Who's the Lady then?" tittered a young female rook, Carmen Strongtalon, nervously.

"This is what happens when we abandon classes," tutted the gossip Bracken Nightwing. "Youngsters today . . . don't know the first thing . . ."

"There was a time," said her mother, Camomile, from the next branch, "when all creatures spoke together, when the web of life glistened with the precious jewels of the dawn . . ."

Surebill hopped nearer, gave Camomile a gentle push with his beak. "I'm impressed, Sister Strongtalon, truly, I am. But the catechism? Another time, perhaps."

"Sorry."

"It seems to me that we must take the gift to the Rooklord, to Hroc himself in the northern land," said Master Surebill. "At that point, our guardianship will end."

"Perhaps not," said Startle.

"Pardon?" Surebill was unused to a challenge. The rooks nearby looked ready to dread. Gifford Hangclaw, spluttering, one wing in the air, nearly lost his balance.

"Until now, our care of the gift and its resting place has been passive," continued Startle, making an embarrassed sound in her pouch. "Just an idea, a story, something to tell the juveniles about in class. Something to pass down the line from father to son, mother to daughter, *chaw-che-che*. None of us had ever seen it. Now it's real. We have the Lady's gift. We really have it, here in Safehaven. It's deathly unsafe where it is. I saw the Lady. And I feel the Rooklord drawing nearer."

"What are you now, Startle Coalfeather, but an ordinary *hroc*, our own kin, and you're seeing the Ley?"

"It's the madness she caught from Dryden here, old *Chaw-you-know-what*."

"Watch it!" warned Dryden in defence of his mate, thrusting his head down and forwards, splaying his tail feathers. Several birds tittered and flapped and took steps backwards, and Carmen Strongtalon plunged awkwardly from her perch to recover and flap noisily back.

"And she's taking over from our elected master Caspian Surebill—"

"Now enough of this," cawed Surebill above the rookery gossip. "As if we didn't need all the help we can get from whatever source."

"She says she saw the Lady."

"She did," said Surebill. "And so did I. The Lady offered me the gift, and I took it. And now we are set on a course that leads into mists and darkness."

"Nobody else did. Did you see? Did you . . . I didn't." The chatter went round the branches. "Where were we looking?" "What didn't we see?"

Surebill, head on one side, blinked, weighing Startle in his mind. Something about this bird . . . *Chaw-ich-cha* . . . give us a sign . . .

I have seen the Rooklord, Master of Masters.

"We should give the gift to the upright known as Crow-head."

Surebill was jolted back by Dryden's comment, and the screams of "I beg your pardon!" "Sacrilege!" "That bird's acting up again, remember the trouble last time!" echoed throughout the rookery.

"What is the reasoning behind this?" said the rookery master sternly.

"We cannot carry the gift more than a few wings at a time. It's too heavy. The upright, for all that he cannot fly, is strong. My feeling is that he will know what to do with the gift."

Horror!

"Crrrh, I can't believe you just said that, Dryden son-in-lore," cawed Halley Coalfeather. "The bloody uprights! You truly have fallen from your perch." And Halley hopped and flapped violently along the branch, striking at Dryden with his beak, to jeers and caws of approval.

The Master of Safehaven flew down, landing between them, forcing them apart with outstretched wings.

"What is this?" he cawed fiercely. "Don't let your hatred of the upwright close your mind to the truth, Halley Coalfeather. We know the crow-headed upwright must play his part in the final act. We know he, of all the flock of upwrights below us, was the only one to see the Lady, be touched by the Lady. And he is not dead. This must tell us something. The Lady's pact was with the upwright queen, the one we call the betrayer, before it was with *hroca*, the Kin. If, in our pride, we imagine the destiny of the gift is for us—and us only—to decide, then pride is deceiving us."

———— ✺ ————

Greybeak and Cobweb slept or, rather, roosted in that twilit avian world between waking and sleeping, that third plane of existence about which upwrights have forgotten almost everything they know.

Hroc, cursed by his Lady with eternal vigilance, stood guard a little way away on a crooked hawthorn branch as the pair shuffled and dream-flew on their high crumbling ledge of sandstone.

The creeks of dawn began to fill sluggishly with light's incoming tide.

With his long ancient beak, he marked out the land before him, the river below him, the way forwards. Near now. Very near.

In the land of my birth . . .

She speaks to the upwright, he who lies in the sodden straw beside the smouldering long hut. And to me. *Keep the gift safe. Let no one touch it.* We stand on the brink of a darkness that will last two thousand years. *How old are you, Hroc, my lovely?*

"I am so old, so old. Five score of scores of the lives of my kin, egg to fly-blown corpse and then more."

Have you kept the promise?

"You know I have, Lady."

What is your dearest wish, my lord Hroc?

"That I may come home. That I may come home at last."

"There it is! Just look at the size of that bird!"

"It's the escaped eagle. On the news."

"That's not an eagle. It's some kind of a raven, a crow."

Hroc eyed the upwrights dispassionately from his perch high on the crumbling cliffs above the Nidd at Knaresborough.

"What are they saying, master?" asked Greybeak.

"They think I am somewhat bigger than the average kin," said Hroc drily. "Several upwrights in the course of our flight have seen me. Upwrights keep birds from distant lands in places where there is no freedom, no Air, and since I look like nothing they have seen before, they assume I am one of those foreign birds and that I have escaped. I cannot see into their minds as well as I used." He yawned. "But, Greybeak and Cobweb, this is speculation. It gets us no nearer our destination. Are we ready to fly?"

"If you are, my lord."

"Then let's use the warm weather to climb high, maybe glide a little. The wind's in our favour, but there's a storm coming."

And sure enough, as the trio flew high over the great conurbations of West Yorkshire, Hroc's keen senses focusing on the Ley as they directed him to his destiny, huge bruised clouds gathered and tumbled, piling higher and higher.

Suddenly, the darkness ahead was riven with an acid flash of sheet lightning. A moment later, a great barrage of noise enveloped the travellers, a whiplash peal first and, on its heels, the rolling of heavy boulders over tin sheeting.

Hroc faltered and slid; his two companions plunged steeply after him.

"My lord, are you all right?" called Cobweb.

Hroc steadied himself. "The gift is unveiled. The Lady is here! Can you not feel Her, Hawberry Mac Greybeak?"

"I am lost, m'lord, far from my kin. You are my guide in these things."

"I can feel Her. She calls. Oh, children. We are nearly home. In the land of my birth, they have wakened the dead. It is the beginning of the end."

35

THE SPELL OF FINE WEATHER had broken, and drizzle clouded Richard's view of the site. He hadn't gone back. It was the embarrassment, the anticipation of strange looks. Alex and I were the only ones who saw the woman.

And Alex is dead.

Why were we the only ones?

But also, he didn't go back because he was *afraid*. Afraid of the rookery, the watching beady eyes.

In several dreams now, the rooks had been pecking at his eyes, their talons dangling the torc in front of him. He'd covered his ears in waking moments and, with a rush of vertigo, felt himself to be in the moonlit trees with the birds. He heard the dusty rustle of their feathers, their croaking and cawing assuming half-formed words. The chimney of the old fireplace seemed to echo with their whispering and chuckling. He wondered halfheartedly whether to board it up, but Sarah would think he'd cracked.

I haven't. I haven't.

By the number of cars parked in the church forecourt, he knew the archaeologists were still there, returning the site to some semblance of its former state, though the bulldozers would see to that, finally and absolutely. Then the Burgeons and Brians and Niges of this world could get back to earning a living, and the houses would go up, and middle class professionals with their spoiled brats would move in and furnish their rooms from IKEA and their gardens from B&Q. And no one will remember or care, except a few academics in their dusty ivory towers.

Bitter, bitter, bitter.

A wagon with the finds tent and stacks of trestle tables lumbered past below, leaving orange-brown mud on the damp tarmac. And minutes later, an excavator, its scoop raised in a yellow salute, made its way up Cliff Street. The phone rang.

"Mr. Cleeve?"

"Ye-es."

"Hello, Mr. Cleeve, it's Peter Robertshaw from the *Express*. I rang Colden High, and they told me you . . . well . . . you rang me a while ago about the building plans for Bride Hill . . ."

"Go on."

"Well, we got pictures of the dig in progress, spoke to a few people—Dr. Brentwood et cetera. I don't know if you were there? But we heard—pretty much on the grapevine, sort of—two things. From the police, of course, about Alex McVitie. But then, gossip in the village, you know. That you were, er—"

"Look, I'm not going to talk about that. There'll be an inquest."

"Yes. But two things, really. They said—I mean, this is the story—that you found a pot, a cauldron. And we had a word with the archaeology unit in Wakefield, and they said you were the one who originally identified it as Celtic. That it was a really important find. Mr. Cleeve?"

"It's for the experts to determine the cauldron's real value."

"But you were the one who found it."

"No, a JCB ran over it, nearly destroyed it. The workmen who found it brought it to me."

"Why did they bring it to you? Because you were the person who fought to stop work on the site?"

"I was nearest, I guess. No—I asked the site people to get in touch with me if they found anything. And they did."

"Mmmm. So you stopped them working on the site?"

"No. Dr. Brentwood stopped them. The professionals did it. I'm an amateur."

"How do *you* feel about the find?"

Richard found himself being drawn. Andy Warhol's fifteen minutes of fame for everyone.

"By itself, it would have been very exciting. Was very exciting. Things like this are found once in a blue moon. But the dig uncovered hundreds of artefacts, and it's much too early to say—"

"We were told one of those things was a necklace, a gold necklace."

"I don't know where you heard that."

"No problem with revealing our sources in this instance. John Arnold, the Sheffield Uni man. I spoke with him yesterday. Went on the record. Also, there's a photographer, Alan Foxcroft. He gave us some photographs. Can't use them, of course. No, we were also told that the necklace disappeared. That it was stolen from the site. That it was the most valuable thing found on Bride Hill . . . Mr. Cleeve?"

"I'm still here. Depends what you mean by stolen. Depends, also, what you mean by valuable. As part of the historical record? As a piece of gold? Look, I don't want to get into this—"

"That's OK. I understand. I just wondered, where do you think the necklace went?"

"There were birds on the site."

Silence. Then Richard heard a long drawn sigh on the other end of the line. "This is what we heard. Also, the photos. Frankly, Mr. Cleeve, it's a bit. A bit. I mean, jackdaws maybe. But a necklace. Must weigh a ton. We just wondered—"

"What did you wonder?"

"Well, you could speculate forever, couldn't you? It's just too, too odd to publish. I mean, it sounds . . . it sounds like a cover-up."

"For what?" Richard's patience suddenly snapped. "For what? You've got a conspiracy theory? And is there an accusation you'd like to make?"

"Look, I'm sorry, Mr. Cleeve. It's a good story, mystery and all, just too many loose ends. I thought you could tie—"

"Well, you were wrong. Good-bye."

Richard looked at his hands. They were shaking. His face was flushed and burning with anger.

The bastards.

He was off work. The mild headache and pain in his right arm and side where he'd touched the . . . where he'd fallen. And concussion. Yes, I'm very upset. And confused about the whole thing, doctor. The GP prescribed a mild sedative.

Sarah had decided to stay with him. Midweek, she moved a suitcase of things in, a couple a scripts to work on. A rough draft of the school's history script and an unedited tape. But she kept her distance mentally and physically. He caught her looking at him, sideways. Fidgeting.

"Lots of rest. Tea and sympathy. Work on the video—it'll take your mind off things," she said. Mothering made them both uncomfortable. It wasn't Sarah's forte, and they both knew it.

The television screen flickered, but the sound was down, and neither knew or cared what they were watching. Richard cradled a glass of wine. Sarah worked silently at the kitchen table taking in the waist of a silk gown; she was chief bridesmaid at a friend's wedding at the weekend. "You could save it for ours?" Richard's question had raised the bleakest of smiles.

Things had changed. Were changing.

She'd accused him of being "on something" at the time of the incident. "Like what?" he'd snapped. "Silk Cut?" Her green eyes caught his, impassive, impenetrable. Make a joke, take a joke. One of their phrases. "Lemonade, two glasses, Sunday school vintage if you must know," he'd muttered. Powerful stuff.

"Dr. Brentwood's pulled up the drawbridge. He's just pretending it didn't happen."

Sarah: "What? Oh, that's just a coping mechanism." Wearily. *Not this again.* "He blames himself for what happened, and it's the worst kind of guilt because it's unfounded, and he knows that, really. You too—you're feeling guilty. Neither of you did anything wrong."

"I know, it's not that—" Richard had started smoking again. He lit up. The match flame winked out in a nest of butts in the ashtray.

"He has a job to do. He's thinking about years of work the dig's created. Preoccupied. Leave him be. I don't care what your photographer or what anyone else heard. Richard. It was a hot day. Everybody was tired."

"And these? What about what Foxcroft caught *on film?*" Richard clicked off the TV, spread out the site photographer's enlargements.

She refused to look. "You can do anything with visual images these days. Foxcroft is a grubby little con man. I've told you—he's into child porn. Once and for all, Richard, stop it. Just don't talk to me about it. You're frightening me."

Suddenly angry. "Why the fuck are you so uptight about this? Why won't you just look at them?" He threw the photos on the table, grabbed her arm.

"Because—I—don't—need—to. You're sick. Now let me go."
She wrenched free.

The phone rang. Sergeant Grantham. His voice strained, stilted. "Thought you should know, Mr. Cleeve. Alex McVitie had a heart defect. Death from natural causes, though, as you probably know, this sort of thing has to go to inquest. So this is unofficial. I never spoke to you."

"Would a heart attack give her . . . hallucinations?"

A pause. "I don't know, Mr. Cleeve. I'm not a doctor."

"The eyewitnesses?"

"Stands to reason they'll be called. Or their statements used. A word of advice, sir. You're a prime witness. Don't discredit yourself. Have a thought for the girl's family."

"And the photographs? I ought to tell you, Alan Foxcroft dropped me off three photos. Plain envelope, hand-delivered. He's disappeared, won't answer my calls."

And Alex's last words on the back of an old time and location chart. But I'm saving that. Need time to think.

A silence.

"Are you still there, Sergeant?"

"We know he's disappeared. My advice is to drop it, sir. Those are fakes. They'll not be used in evidence. Fakes. Foxcroft is . . . unreliable."

"The team didn't think so. His work was exemplary."

"That's their business. I'll put it no stronger than this, sir, but Foxcroft is known to us."

"For faking photos?"

"Not, er . . . not faking them. As such. Look, Mr. Cleeve—"

"I understand. Well, I think I do."

Richard ended the call. He made himself and Sarah instant coffee. Felt Sarah's eyes burning into his back. *I'm still shaking. This is ridiculous.* Chewed his nails. *Nervous breakdown. But Jesus, I know what I saw. How can you know something and believe something else?*

Is that what a nervous breakdown, mental illness, is about? A new set of facts that won't nest in the old ones?

I know what I saw. He'd drawn the old woman several times. He was no artist, and the paper bin was full of failed attempts. The eyes always come out too big. She wasn't physically odd, just old. Horribly, immensely old. The shawl falls wrongly; her hair wasn't quite like that. Her hands like claws. Those skinny, wiry arms. Besides, his mind kept returning to the monochrome photographs, influencing the way he pictured the incident in the excavation pit.

One: Alex looking up into the sun, her face twisted. A shadow across her mouth. From what? What is she looking at? Staring into space. Is she in pain? There's a swirl of movement in the left third of the picture, and there's the torc. Not a good picture of the torc—part of the swirl obliterates its detail; the bright sun does the rest. Perhaps the swirl is dust blowing off the top of the pit? Rubbish—the day was perfectly still, that prickly waiting silence you get just before a downpour.

Two: The torc motionless in midair. Every detail perfect. Its arms, comprising four, maybe five thin gold wires, are twisted together firmly, the left clockwise, the right anticlockwise, and each ending in a grape cluster. The emblem is a spread-winged bird made, it looks like, from a curved plate of gold with gold wiring welded on top, holding pieces of jet or obsidian in place. The bird's head is gold, the eyes—by that tiny glint—some precious stones. His memory filled in—red. Ruby? Its shadow clear as a bell on the side of the pit. Makes it twenty, twenty-five centimetres clear—of anything. The swirl's still there, but a little further out of the frame. *Reaching out for the bracelet?* Foxcroft hasn't zoomed in; he wasn't using that kind of camera. Alex's eyes closed. By the slight blur here . . . and here on her face . . . she's starting to fall. Looks like there are two of her. Just possible, I suppose, the torc was falling, and Foxcroft caught it at the, what, the apex of its parabola, that moment when a thing appears to pause in the air.

Three: That's my back. I'm reaching for the old woman. She's the blur, still on the left. I'm blocking Alex out, except for this small area of her headscarf, extreme right. Top-left: the wing of one of those rooks. The torc higher this time. *Higher. But still motionless,* slightly different angle. The rook's reaching for it, talons extended. The blur's gone.

A wave of despondency swept over him. A huge mishmash of emotions—Alex dead or dying at the instant Foxcroft's shutter clicked, the moment the bomb went off, the bullet struck. The sheer strangeness of his sensations each time his eyes were drawn to shot 3, suddenly vibrant and present, the photo a mere stark black-and-white one-dimensional palimpsest upon which an invisible reality was imposed. But reality only in Richard's feverish mind. From another time in his life, another world. The pain in his arm—still a distant rheumatic sort of ache the doctor said was just the way he fell, hit himself on the side of the granary bin or the pit. I slipped. No, the old woman pulled me. I passed out.

God, another world.

Foxcroft's longhand: *The girl said this, the best I can remember: You shouldn't be on the site. Don't touch it without gloves. No, it looks Celtic, British. Then you said that stuff about putting it down and what have you done to the girl. That's all. I thought you should know. AF*

He folded the paper carefully, put it in a drawer.

Sarah had already sneaked a look at the pictures. Shit. Foxcroft must have worked through the night to doctor this stuff and reshoot it back onto negative. I wonder what kind of equipment he's got? And how he paid for it? Seamless work. The man could get a job with special effects if he wasn't so busy enticing little girls and boys.

Then the obvious, nagging, stupid, unanswerable question: why? Why on earth would Foxcroft go to all that trouble? What could there possibly be in it for him? Why twist the knife? It's pure absolute bloody-minded mischief. Sadism. No wonder the warped son of a bitch's dropped out of sight. You've got a lot to answer for, you evil little pervert.

Her practical mind refused to come to grips with what Richard had told her. Slid off it as if it were jelly. I know he believes it. Old woman, for God's sake. That knock on the head. Delusions. I've got to think of my own sanity. Somebody has to run the show. He needs to get better, back into school. He'll lose that head of department job he so wants.

No more Mr. Flaky, Richard.

Please. Please.

She felt miserable, helpless, angry.

———— ✺ ————

It's a moonless night. Sarah and he are cupped together, the soft curved flesh of her buttocks resting gently on his knees as they lie. She's breathing gently, a tiny regular hiss—the sound of a feather drawn across the windowpane. A streetlamp several doors down breathes faint yellow onto the beamed ceiling. His arm cradles her smooth neck, and his hand nestles in her armpit, the warm butts of her nipples nestling into the skin of his wrist. Her hair tumbles onto the pillow, black and forestlike in the shadows. "I love you," he whispers and gently draws the duvet over her naked shoulder. His own breathing deepens, steadies, the tiny spark that is *me* monitoring the onset of sleep from its hideaway in the fathomless caverns of the mind.

The old woman's face in the lie of the curtains, her eyes in the depths of the shadows behind the beams. *Come, winged ones. You have done a thing for which the right way is death. Nevertheless, a thing done in ignorance may sometimes earn mercy.*

What did I do?

You touched me. You touched me. You did not discover the torc. You did not lay hands on it. I am a giver and a taker of life. Mercy and vengeance, curse and blessing. The endless, wonderful, tragic circle of existence.

Besides, I think I know you.

Knows me, knows me. I know her too. She's Sarah. Cradled in my arms, I in hers. I'm a newborn; she cradles me, nurtures me. I'm her lover; she holds me close. I'm dying; she cradles me, lets me out of the world. The women who weave the swaddling bands, the wedding gown, the *tricoteurs* at the foot of the guillotine. Always there, always weaving. I love you, Sarah. Her face framed in the branches of trees, shining like the moon. Not Sarah, Alex. Not Alex, my mother.

You know me, then.

Sarah's breath like a feather on the windowpane. Tapping. Rain in the trees. The creak of twigs, the murmur of rooks at prayer. Tapping. Rustling.

In this dream, I feel the curtains hiss and click in the breeze, the chill on the back of my neck. I rise, carefully extricating my arm from behind Sarah's neck. She stirs but does not wake. I go to the window, naked. The rook is sitting on the windowsill, its black shoulder against the pane. In its right claw, it holds the torc, preventing it from slipping to the ground. Its dark eye stares at me, uncertain, nervous. It caws once, a quiet pleading croak. I open the window, careful not to dislodge bird or torc. The air is cold. I shiver. The necklace gleams with unearthly light. Yes, the eyes of the bird emblem are ruby, and if you stare too long at them, you could fall into their piercing light and be lost. Windows to another world. The bird backs away, claw and torc scraping the sill. "It's all right," I whisper. "I'm not going to hurt you." Take the torc? I can't. I can't touch it. Alex died, and so would I. Then follow? Follow what? The bird finally loses its nerve and flaps away, the weight of the torc plunging it groundwards into the silent street. It recovers, swoops upwards, and is lost in the night.

Hands curling arthritically, fingers long and blue and gnarled, nails hooked and flaky, flesh and nerve pared away. Face straining forwards into the armour.

"Richard?"

"Sorry, love. Didn't mean to wake you. I—the window. I was a bit cold."

Her voice low and purring with the gum of sleep. "Come back to bed. I'm missing you."

Then follow.

36

WESTRAY AIRCHURNER'S CHEST FEATHERS PUCKERED and burst, showered, and his blood mingled with the erupted cloud of down. The kill-from-a-distance lifted him from his branch; his wing aimlessly shot out to full span and collapsed. The little thunder rolled upwards from the ground as his talons closed and twitched; and down he came, slack and broken, like a burst bag, hissing and thumping through the leaves and branches.

The upwright reloaded.

"A bought Bride Hill, and A bought everythin' on it and in it, an' that bloody jewlery's mah'n, not some bloody archaeologist's 'n' them bloody crows mun bloody drop it back down 'ere or A'll bloody kill 'em all, spooky black bastards . . ."

"And then Hroc fetched Westray Airchurner, son of Calvin, father of Bruton, mate to Sunrise; Bracken Nightwing lies in the ivy, and her sister mourns in the distant trees; and the old bird came for Cherry Highnester too, gone now to join her mate Levenworth, both taken by the kill-from-a-distance and together at last in the Golden Land."

The day had dawned bloody, a fierce red sunrise that had set Startle twitching and mumbling. And it had stayed bloody. Eight birds were dead, shot in their nests or at roost before the vicar Sutton had called the police and Burgeon had been disarmed and arrested.

Now, though the little thunder had ceased, the birds were scared, subdued, almost silent; Elder Caliban Dawncaller had summoned a tree moot following a moot of Safehaven's elders in Surebill's tree.

After the roll of the dead had been called, Dawncaller pushed his head into his chest feathers and purred and clicked.

Dryden was embarrassed. "Where can we go? This is our home. Gifford Hangclaw's gone, along with three of the other mateless ones, to plead for Mildhollow membership; and I can't imagine, at this time of the year when the squabs are taking their first steps and the parents are occupied and peck is plentiful, that old Master Blackflight or the Mildhollow elders will turn them away."

"That's right, Dryden," interrupted Brittle Blackflight, a cousin of the master of Mildhollow. "Isn't it that the more birds there are in your congeries, the more territory you can claim for peck at the Grand Roost?"

"But most of us are not traitors; we are loyal to Safehaven. We were born here, and we'll die here," finished Dryden.

The members of Dawncaller's tree moot shuffled uneasily on their branches, thinking about birth and death.

"The upwright with the kill-at-a-distance—does he want the gift? Or have we taken peck from his fields? He is hugely angry." Carmen Strongtalon broke the silence.

"He is no upwright of the land," said Startle. "He is a creature who likes the fermented water and burnt leaf. Downwind, he is sour and smelling of the inside of stone roosts, not of greenery and dung as a lands creature does. He must want the Lady's gift."

"All the more reason to offer it to Crow-head," ventured Dryden.

"All the more reason *not* to offer it to Crow-head. Such action will never get my vote," said old Calvin Airchurner, shaking his wings. "The motives of the upwright are questionable and obscure. They kill us, so we give them that which we have guarded faithfully for scores of lifetimes. It makes no sense."

"They'll shoot my squabs. The upwright will come back. They get a taste for it. They always come back."

"The Lady will ask us, 'Where is it?' And what will we tell Her?"

"All our lives, we have trusted in the Ley. Our master is Master of Safehaven because he sees more than we do. I trust the Ley, and I trust him."

"We'll vote then," said Caspian Surebill. "How do we say? Who votes with Calvin Airchurner to keep the gift in Safehaven?"

"Aye. Aye."

"And for sending it to the crow-headed upwright?"

"Aye. Aye. Aye."

"Then we will send it to the crow-headed upwright. Would you, Dryden, do this extraordinary thing for Safehaven?"

Dryden's heart beat heavily in his chest. A voice almost overwhelmed him—a voice that said no. *You are no hero. Just get on with your life quietly. Say no. Take Startle and the chicks to Mildhollow or Ashneagh.*

Say no, Dryden.

"Reluctantly. But since I suggested it—"

"I wonder," interrupted Dawncaller pensively. "I wonder if any of us have a choice."

The sun went down as it had risen, in blood, great streaks of gory light piercing banks of sombre cloud, torn flags over a battlefield of the gods.

The last of Safehaven's birds wheeled into the dark trees that crowned the Haunted Hill, having snatched a final pouchful of peck for their ravenous squabs from the gloaming fields. And as they did, the fire sunwards died utterly, leaving a night black as pitch-black as the old bird's feathers, as poor dead Bracken Nightwing would have put it.

Dryden and Startle and the three squabs—Carew, Woodsorrel, and little Bran—sat on the branch, looking into the nest at the torc. The faintest of starlight limned it. And even Dryden, who would never lay claim to the Ley or any of its aspects, could feel its glow, its strangeness, its bloody past.

Finally, the squabs drifted off into a twilight of sleep, their ragged bodies heaving slumbrously.

"Oh, Startle, I can't talk to the upwright, whether or not he's our friend. The kin just don't do this sort of thing. Not these days," whispered Dryden.

"Then you shouldn't have volunteered. Tell Surebill tomorrow you couldn't do it."

"I'm bound."

"No, you're not."

"I'm bound by the same bonds that hold us to the gift and the promise we all made to the Lady. Anybody who swears on the gift holds to his word or dies."

"A bit dramatic, don't you think?"

Dryden shuffled. "You try it."

"I will if you want."

This said so softly that Dryden was forced to chuckle. "I made this vow. I'll keep it. But would you . . . ?"

"You'll not go alone. I'll go engard on the stone-roost-top where Crow-head roosts. Where the warm air rises."

Dryden ducked his head twice. "Thank you," he said.

———— ∞∞∞ ————

"I hate flying in the dark."

Startle and Dryden sat side by side on the ridge of Richard's cottage roof, having dragged the torc laboriously from tree to tree, then to the top of the concrete streetlamp over which leaves hovered like flat orange ghosts, then to a porch roof, and finally, to their present position. Both birds blinked with exhaustion.

"They have light in the stone roosts, but all the lights have gone," said Startle. "At least in Crow-head's roost. We see Crow-head's face at the opening near the top of the stone roost, with the light behind it sometimes, but usually the dark. This must be his nest. I think he has a mate."

"Crow-head is a he?" asked Dryden. "How can you tell their sex?"

"This is just to my way of thinking. There are two things—the first is that the adult male upwright has shorter head hair. Sometimes his hair is worn away on top, as if the upwright might suffer from our complaint, feather-drop. The second is that his voice is deeper. With the juveniles, it's impossible to tell which is which just by looking. You can tell only by being downwind."

"He must wish he could fly. I always feel sorrow when I think the upwright is bound to the soil, that he may never soar in the Air."

"That's not strictly true," said Startle. "I've seen air-*chwaaghs*, and all *chwaaghs* need an upwright to make them move."

Dryden considered this, picking small tufts of moss from the gaps between the roof tiles clumsily, since the heavy gift threatened at any moment to slither down. Conversation died. The two birds looked at each other.

"It's time I did my brave thing," said Dryden.

"You are the best. I'm glad you are my mate." Startle rubbed her beak in the feathers of his shoulder then under his pouch. "I'll be here, where the warm air comes out."

Dryden gripped the gift firmly, steeled himself, plunged in a low glide down the roof slates, flapped to lift himself—past the guttering, a sharp wheel inwards, a stall, then down! And a clumsy landing on Richard's narrow window ledge.

Dryden shuffled the gift until he could hold it firm with his claw twixt window frame, mastic and the crumbling sandstone of the sill. He reached forwards, uncertain of how to attract Crow-head's attention, tapped the pane tentatively with his beak. It made the sound of pebbles clicking in a stream.

Tap.

Tap-tap-tap.

Dryden felt vibration in the stone roost, the kind you felt on some of the larger roofs under which *chwaagh*-like engines grumbled all day long. No, not that kind of vibration—more uneven, getting nearer . . .

The window squeaked open, nearly dislodging him. And suddenly, within inches of his face, the face of Crow-head. *Aaach!*

Crow-head said something very gently, though it sounded to Dryden like a roar. He smelled *craf*, garlic on the upwright's breath, old burned *craf*, burned-leaf, just a hint of mint.

Take the gift! Take the gift! Dryden tried to move the torc nearer to the crow-head's face. *Take it!*

The upwright's mouth moved again, sorrowfully. Dryden crouched low on the windowsill, his nerve almost gone. *He's terrified if he touches it he'll die. You won't. Take a chance. Oh, please!*

A light came from Crow-head—a great sorrow, an overpowering sense of loss. Dryden looked for the first time into the upwright's eye, in the same way a man might look into a whale's eye and understood, finally, how the mind of this creature—and probably that of all his kind—was filled with the infinite detail of history, complex, labyrinthine, unknowable, like dense roiling cloud banks split unpredictably with the lightning of thought or action.

If you won't take it then follow. The cromark for "follow" is a sharp jerk of the beak over the shoulder. It is a sign known in similar form to every intelligent creature on the planet and understood as such, and it was not lost on Crow-head, Dryden was sure.

He did it again. *Then follow.*

Another upwright's voice came from inside the stone roost, and Dryden's nerve snapped. Clutching the gift, he hurtled from the windowsill, beating his wings madly as the glistening cobbles of the *chwaagway* hurtled up to meet him.

Startle was at his side.

Safehaven's Master Surebill caught the warm wind from the south as dawn broke, and the first daggers of sunlight turned the rookery's topmost leaves gold and silver. He rose high and lonely in the clean air, circling to a height where the stone roosts were clusters of grey studs and the *chwaagh*ways grey threads, and each tree and garden lawn a bright green dab of paint. Several birds were circling the trees below him, mere black pinheads against the greenery.

Then another bird broke from the flock, wheeled upwards; in a moment, he recognised young Dryden and triple-called a welcome.

"Caliban gave you my message, then?" asked the elder bird.

"I would have reported anyway—but yes," said Dryden. "Master, I don't believe I have ever flown so high. The sun seems harsher, the Air colder."

The birds circled, the chuckle and creak of rookspeak, *hrocain,* passing between them in the thin heights. It seemed to both that the green world rotated gently beneath them and that they were motionless, buoyed in the vastness of the Air their kind had made its own.

"I climb this high to think. Sometimes the racket of the congeries . . ."

"The squabs, especially," Dryden added ruefully. "Their clamour for peck, for knowledge—the older ones asking, 'When can I fly?' and the younger ones saying, 'You'll never get me out of this tree.'"

They cruised together, wingtip to wingtip, in silence.

"The upwright refused the gift last night," said Dryden eventually. "He fears it is a death dealer."

"I gathered as much. I never held much hope that help would be forthcoming from the upwrights, this one or any other. The world is changing, this much I know, but I am reading the Ley in the wrong way and am much saddened that my wisdom and intuition is so inadequate.

"This does not diminish your courage, Dryden Dreadcalmer. To my knowledge, no *hroc* has attempted communion with an upwright this side of the time of legends."

Dryden tightened the radius of his turn experimentally, slid beneath Surebill, braked with a tailspread, and regained altitude with a couple of wing-beats.

"We could try again," he said.

"I could not ask it of you. The elders reminded me that your expedition ran the risk of dropping the gift and that some other upwright might take it before you could retrieve it; I overruled them, but we cannot continue running that risk, especially since Crow-head has disappointed us once and would probably do so again. Give me time to think."

They floated, drifting sunfallwards, playing rooks' favourite summer morning game, watching the Air for signs of updraught and subtly splaying their feathers for best lift. Dryden, a less experienced flier than Surebill, was occasionally obliged to beat his wings to keep up.

Suddenly, the rookery master sideslipped and plunged earthwards, and Dryden tumbled after him, horrified that perhaps the Old Bird of Passage had taken his master's heart or that, as sometimes happens, the kill-from-a-distance had struck without warning.

With frantic strokes, he eventually drew level. Surebill stalled and crashed onto the roof ridge of the derelict mill beside the Dean Brook. Dryden whirled above him.

"Why was I so deaf and blind?" called Surebill hoarsely. "All I needed to do was listen to the Ley. Fetch Startle quickly, Dryden. I need her to confirm something."

Without a word, Dryden sped on his errand, wings clapping the Air madly.

Surebill paddled back and forth on the roof tiles. "The Lady—she's here. She's been here all the time."

37

THE OLD WOMAN'S FACE APPEARED at the caravan's smeared window, peering in. It was barely dawn.

Her voice was muffled. "Boys, will you help me one last time before I go? You must fetch me the man. I need to see him, to be sure. Meet me in my tent."

The two youngsters leaned out of their bunks, looked at each other. Before she goes? Where's Mam going?

"We'll get dressed. Wait a minute," mouthed Peter through the condensation. "Anyway, what man? Dad says not to talk to strangers."

But the woman was already gone.

"Is this another adventure? Where's she goin'?" whispered Michael.

"How should I know? Just get yer kecks on. And don't wake Dad—aw, Michael!"

A cock crowed on some distant allotment as they tumbled out into the half-light, hissing at each other, running grubby hands through tangled hair, and rubbing sleep from bleary eyes. Michael carefully shut the caravan door, and the two made damp tracks in the dew across the uncut grass to where the old lady's tent stood. They pushed aside the flap.

The old lady was arranging black feathers in a circle, quills inwards. She spat on her fingers, placed a dab on the tent floor at the centre of the circle, then quickly shuffled the feathers together, caught them up, placed them on her camp bed, looked up, gestured vigorously for them to come in. The morning breeze made the tent's stained canvas snap like the sails of a becalmed schooner.

"Where you goin', Mam?" Michael's eyes gleamed, but years of practice had warned him about showing emotion. He ground his teeth instead.

"*Mam!*" The old hag rolled the word around her gums. "I love it when you call me that. You've no idea how far back in time that word goes, what resonance it has. *Mam!*"

"We don't know what *rezzance* is," said Peter, pouting, catching his brother's mood. "We was hopin' you'd stay and tell us about it."

"Don't be silly now, boys. People will come and go throughout your lives. Grasp the swing as it passes." She tousled their dark heads, unafraid now to touch living flesh; times were changing.

"Yer said we 'ad to find a fella. Why can't yer just go to 'im yerssen an' say, 'Are you the one then?'" asked Michael.

"Boys! So practical, so down-to earth." She cackled. "I should go up to him, tap him on the shoulder? It would kill him. He is a Celt, but the Romans have had him in shackles for centuries, and he no longer knows who he really is. No, take it from me—the man comes to the Lady, not the other way round." And to herself she muttered, "He is a hybrid. He has dual nationality. If I had time, I would see how this can be, in time like this . . ."

Suddenly, she cocked her scarfed head to one side. Then without a word, she bustled, bent-backed, out of the tent into the slanting sunshine, shading her eyes. The lads followed her.

"There's something long awaited in the Air, boys, or I'm no haruspice."

"So this bloke—how will we know who he is?" asked Peter, holding a fistful of her rough skirt in his hand.

"Follow my bird," she said.

And out of the sky, flanked by two much smaller companions, wheeled a black bird big enough to throw a shadow. The smaller rooks settled together on a low branch at the side of the recreation ground, but Hroc glided powerfully in, scattering the boys, landing so heavily on the old woman's shoulder she staggered under the weight. Hroc could not fold his ragged left wing and rested it like a parasol on her head, until she swept it round to his side, stroking his neck and head. The ancient bird stroked the side of her wrinkled face with the side of his pitted gunmetal beak in a loving gesture, muttering in a language only she could understand.

The boys stepped back, astounded, mouths open.

"Welcome home, oathkeeper. Pfff, Hroc, either this world has tied weights to your feet or I am much diminished." And she whispered ancient words in a tongue the guardian of Britain had not heard in well nigh two thousand years.

"Bloody 'ell," said Peter to Michael.

<hr />

An early riser, Richard smashed his palm onto the alarm the moment it hit 7:00, grabbed some clothes, showered, and dressed in the bathroom to avoid waking Sarah. He went downstairs and ground some coffee and set the percolator huffing. The very ordinariness of daylight, the lingering odour of paella from last night's supper and its mingling with the rich sombre biscuit tang of coffee, the chattering of an ivy twig on the kitchen window protected him, his hands and mind performing the quotidian tasks that comprise and compose a day in the way a priest might tell a rosary.

Then follow.

He made his way carefully up the narrow staircase.

Sarah stirred, rolled over.

"Coffee on the dresser," he mumbled. "I'm going for a stroll. Want a paper? It's only 7:15." He stroked the hair out of her face.

"Mmm, bless you. How are you feeling? You look pale."

"OK, OK. Breath of fresh air."

He walked up the hill, not down into the village. The dig site looked pretty much the way he'd expected—the earth levelled, only the sondage trench exposed.

Deserted.

But he was not interested in the site. In every way, it was history. Alex's grave and the death of something inside him, perhaps the birth of something else.

Last night's dream wouldn't go away. So real. *If I had touched the torc, would I have woken up?*

What if the bird on the torc was—a rook? If it was—is—then what kind of coincidence is it that the birds of the rookery should make such a bold and unprecedented grab for it? What could it possibly mean to them? What force is directing them?

I would have no difficulty in putting all this to one side if I hadn't seen the old woman. Or if I had and Alex hadn't. Or if Foxcroft hadn't caught something so, so totally off the wall on his photographs. I could dismiss it all, return to normality, get back to school, get my head down, forget. Why all this denial? Dr. Brentwood—I saw his eyes in the tent. He made a connection he wished he hadn't. The sisters Kemp. Heads together after the event, convincing themselves they didn't actually hear Alex saying anything. Only Foxcroft asking questions, and him discredited.

They've all closed ranks. Closed eyes. Closed minds.

The mechanical engulfing the mystical, like an amoeba engulfing a food particle.

Why did I see her? Why me and nobody else except Alex? Why can I remember what she said to me only in my dreams? Who was she? What was she? Where is she now?

He felt completely alone.

The trees either side of the vicarage wall hissed in the breeze, their leaves fluttering, flashing their undersides like fish shoals in green water. He crossed the site, leaned on the wall, lit a cigarette, leaned back. Smudges of summer-white clouds, the sun on their bellies, drove overhead. In that trompe l'oeil familiar to sufferers of vertigo, the rookery seemed on the move, falling, endlessly falling, and the sky motionless.

The rooks were shedding their tail primaries. He picked one up, twirled it absently—nearly a foot long. Big bird. There was a dead rook in the vicarage drive, one wing moving idly like a windsurfer's sail. Waving.

No rookery racket, no movement in the trees. The large chestnut had a string of nests, one above the other, like a multistorey tenement. Just the occasional sad waark from the birds, a dirge or lament.

What do you want?

"Where's this then? Looks like a bum site."

"Dunno."

Two black-haired youngsters—probably brothers, nine and eleven, Richard guessed—were making their way across the site, picking up sticks and stones and hurling them, poking dirt mounds with their shabby untied trainers. Richard cleared his throat, announced his presence. The boys stopped, stared, side by side. Stared with the innocence of childhood, long and hard and without decorum or modesty. Laurel and Hardy. Richard smiled.

"You the priest?" said the elder, his greasy head on one side, grubby finger waving in the direction of Saint Bride's. He snorted, wiped snot on the back of his hand. His brother followed his gestures precisely.

"Do I look like a priest?"

"Don't talk to strangers," whispered the younger dramatically, tugging the baggy arm of his brother's T-shirt. The elder stood his ground.

"Can't tell these days. We had a priest came to the vans dressed like you—jeans and jumper. Had a cross thing, though."

"A Jesus," explained the younger.

"Well, they do," said Richard. "It's their trademark. No, I'm not a priest. I'm a teacher. Why aren't you at school?"

"Saturday, innit? 'Sides, we don't go to school. We're travellers." Proud.

"Travellers. He's Peter, I'm Michael."

"Shut your stupid face," hissed Peter. "Talk to strangers, talk to strangers."

"Oh. Vans. Caravans. Travellers go to school—sometimes—I think," said Richard.

"Doesn't know much for a teacher," said Michael to Peter, sniggering.

"This a graveyard then? Have they buried people here?" asked Peter.

"No," said Richard. "People have died here—but people die everywhere." He sighed. "No, this is a historical site. Thousands of years ago people lived and worked and died right here. Then some other people came along and dug around a bit to find out how they lived."

"Archaeologists," Michael said proudly. A statement, not a question.

"Yep," said Richard. "Who told you that?"

"I go to school sometimes."

"I do too."

"Where are you living?"

"Don't know. We're lost. Went to dam the stream up from the rec then saw a big crow hopping from tree to tree—"

"Really massive it was—huge, big as this—" Michael spread his arms.

A horripilation spread across Richard's shoulders. He shuddered.

"So we followed it. A really long way. Then up the hill. Then we lost it—"

"Back there—" the younger boy, wide-eyed, semaphored again.

"Then we came across some fields and the road, now here."

The boys exchanged stares. Did we say it right? Did we miss anything?

"You've come right round in a big circle. The rec's out of here and down the road. Come on, I'll show you. Come on."

"Strangers, strangers," jibed Michael. But both followed Richard into the road. He pointed to something down there. They stood, reluctant.

"What's the matter?"

Michael stared at the ground, shuffled. Peter looked frantically around. "Scared."

"Scared? What of?"

"Mother."

"Your mother?"

"Not our mam. Mam's dead. Mother."

"Grandmother then?"

"Sort of," said Michael.

"What's the problem? Won't she be glad to see you?"

Silence.

"Shiz goin'. She said shid look after us, and shiz goin'." Peter looked close to tears. Michael put his arm round his brother; Peter shrugged it off.

"I don't understand. Look, if it helps, I'll take you home." Richard glanced worriedly down the road towards the house where Sarah still slept. *It'll just take a few minutes*, he thought.

The three of them set off down the far side of Bride Hill— Richard in the middle, the boys picking their way down each gutter as if fearful of admitting their link with Richard—in the shadows of the blackened crag that was once a quarry for the stones that built the Dean Beck houses, now filled with a tangle of sycamores, the stand of tall beeches that bore the furthermost of the Saint Bride's rookery nests. Sun dappled the bent grasses, exploded the wood millet and Yorkshire fog into a dazzling carpet; dying bluebells rattled their seedcases in the breeze.

They crossed the beck's humpbacked bridge, turned right. A five-barred gate lay on its side, lifted off its hinges, bright yellow wood where it had been crowbarred. Shaggy horses were tethered on the recreation ground in the shelter of Dean Wood, and the travellers' caravans, wagons, and old buses clustered together at the far end. As always, there would be attempts to move them on; as always, they would be successful; as always, the travellers would be back, cutting the padlock on the gate or uprooting one of the concrete-embedded posts round the perimeter.

Michael and Peter edged out in front.

"You should go back now," said Michael.

"Where the hell have you been? With the old woman again?" A ponytailed man emerged from a dark green van and beckoned vigorously at the boys with a muscular tattooed arm. Then he saw Richard. "Who're you?" he asked.

"The kids were lost. I—"

"Thanks, pal. Get inside, you little buggers! I told you we were going to the boot sale. You've made me bloody late. Good of you to bother. I thought they were with that woman again, see. Mother. Comes from nowhere and fills my kids' heads with nonsense. Shut *up*, Michael."

"Not their mother, then."

The man looked at Richard suspiciously. "God, no. Their mother . . . anyway, none of your business."

"Sorry."

"There she is! Not one of us. Gypsy type." The man gestured at a woman who stood, arms on hips, at the door of a large oil-stained tent.

"Good of you to bring them back," the woman shouted across the green. The man huffed in exasperation, slammed the door of his van.

"That's OK," Richard shouted back, turned to go.

"Wait a minute." The woman shambled over to him. "Don't I know you from somewhere?"

"I don't think so. Look, I must be getting back—"

"I *do* know you. From the dig up on the hill."

And then Richard knew her too.

She was of indeterminate age, her skin darkened and etched with the sun and wind, but with widely spaced dark eyes set in elephant's leathery wrinkles. A headscarf of purple and tan silk revealed greying temples and held back all but a long hank of blue-black hair that twitched with the movement of a thick eyebrow. Her clothes were old, layered for warmth, but clean—probably Oxfam or Shelter. She smiled permanently—not the gross insouciance of the insane but of a creature well aware of harm and darkness in the way things are and determined not to find them.

And yet she was harm and darkness. The very nub and essence of it.

Richard found the courage to face her, the determination to hold his voice in pitch. Normal, normal. "The dig? I never saw you there."

"Oh, I follow them around." She flicked a black cape a little closer. Her hands were mottled, brown, shining. They reminded Richard of a tortoise's carapace. "I come from an old family of, ah, historians. Amazing things you can find in the earth." Her accent—a curious lilt.

"Yes. Well, it's all over now—"

"Bit of trouble up there, I heard."

"Yes. Anyway, I must be getting back."

"Come again!" shouted the woman. "Tell your fortune. Good at that."

"Maybe," said Richard, hurrying off the site.

Back over the bridge. His feet stumbling, the ordinary skill of walking taxing every effort, as if you suddenly couldn't remember how to drive or swim or button your shirt. In the shadows, out of sight of the rec, the woman—Richard stopped, leaned against the high lichen-stained gritstone wall, heart pounding. The artificiality of it all—the ruse, using kids. The crow, the boys' huge crow—the rook. Her bird, her familiar. She didn't look like the old woman who came to take Alex away, but by God, who else could it be? Or am I finally insane?

'Don't I know you?'

And . . .

'Besides, I think I know you.'

Fear prevented him from returning to the field, confronting the woman. Anger and frustration demanded he should. Why me? What did I do? This time, in this guise, everybody sees her, the kids, their father. Has she touched anybody, killed anybody? If she touched me or I touched her, would I be drawn through the veil that protects our sunshine world from hers? What does she want? What does she want from me?

Circles, enclosed circles, circles tightening their grip on his heart and mind. I am an island of the living in a sea of the dead.

The road lay silent and deserted, sun-dappled, tiny patches of lemon light roving the bruise-coloured tarmac like searchlights. Richard hurried back up the hill, past the site of the dig, knowing that his home was no longer a sanctuary and that the least mention of his contact with the old woman would estrange him completely from Sarah. He couldn't bear the thought. The cable of their relationship already seemed frayed to a strand. Paper, newspaper. Newsagents. Read the news. Put the kettle on. Daylight.

Daylight.

38

"WHERE THE HELL HAVE YOU been? I thought you said you were going for a paper."

Sarah in her dressing gown, showered, hair in a knotted towel, eyes flashing, the freckles in her cleavage like the shell of a farm egg.

"I—I forgot. Some travellers' kids were lost. I took 'em back to Dean Beck recreation ground."

He slumped into a chair.

"Waifs and strays, Richard. You're so soft. Are you all right? You look like you've seen a ghost. Oops. Sorry."

A pale dry laugh, almost a cough. "What's a ghost? Would I know one if I saw one? Would you?"

Sarah came over to him, held his head in her bosom. He felt the soft and rough of its texture, the gentle smell of talc.

Stroked his head. "I love you, sweetheart. You're off on your travels, though. Come back, oh, please come back." There was a catch in her voice.

He held her at arm's length. "You've no idea how much I love you. If I could come back, I would. I just don't know where I am. Dreaming and waking. The picture's breaking up. Oh, Sarah." His eyes filled with tears.

"I'll phone the doctor if you want. Go back to bed."

"That's no answer."

Sarah drew back, her face suddenly hard.

"Then for Christ's sake, tell me what is! All this fucking self-pity! You won't let me in, you can't keep me out. Won't. Won't keep me out. I've got to be involved. You've just got to involve me." She stormed to the fireplace, stroked its heavy black whorls, chewing the inside of her lip.

"You are involved. How could you not be?" Richard was pleading.

"Good question. I don't know the answer. I'm away next week."

Richard inhaled sharply. "Bit short notice."

"I forgot to mention it. Filming a conference in York University for the NAS/UWT. Is that right, the initials? Teaching union?"

"All next week?" Richard asked wearily. "Harry going, I suppose?"

"As it happens, yes. We're staying at the university. As it happens, all single rooms. Why are you so jealous? It's the one thing that really gets me about you. As if you don't trust me."

"I do trust you. But yes, I *am* jealous. Of the time you spend with him."

"It's my work. It earns me money, good money. That's all."

"Fine, fine."

"If you don't want me to go—"

"Please, Sarah, don't make that kind of sacrifice. Don't even offer it. Don't even use the offer as . . . look, I've got work to do, plenty to keep me busy. Research. I might go up to Bainbridge, see the family, touch base. Do some thinking, putting my house in order. There's stuff in the freezer—"

She stared at him, softened, let out a long sigh. "I'm sorry, Richard. Look, I—we've the wedding this afternoon—"

"Jeez, I forgot."

"Are you fit?"

Anything but, Sarah dear. But he took a deep breath, tried to flex those tiny arrangements of muscles over each cheekbone he'd read somewhere release good-mood chemicals—smile and the whole world smiles with you.

"Course. Get the suit out of mothballs. Do I get a fashion parade? Chief bridesmaid—Lordy, Lordy, Miss Sarah—ah, sure, do want to see yah fit that neat little waist of yours in dat tight corset."

Sarah chuckled. "Then y'all should come upstairs with me right away, young master," she said, sashaying and winking.

I can't hide the fear, and neither can he. I'm scared of him. I've never seen him like this. God knows what he's scared of. He doesn't know himself. But we can put it all to one side. Just like old times. Just for now. Please make him better. Please help him. He can't know it, but I need him more than ever. Now that . . . now that . . .

⬦⬦⬦

Bainbridge, North Yorkshire

"You're not looking after yourself, dear. What's Sarah thinking of?"

"Mum, I'm thirty-two. I go my own way. Besides, think about what you just said. Sarah's not my keeper."

They were sitting in Brian and Edith Cleeve's clean but cluttered farmhouse dining room—the room Edith always called the snug, just as she called the stone-flagged galley kitchen next door the scullery and the sitting room the parlour. The house was redolent with memories. It even smelled as Richard remembered it—faintly of wood smoke and pipe smoke and bacon, sweet pea blossom and Pears coal tar soap. Nothing much had changed since his childhood; the grandfather clock still nudged the low rough-hewn oak beams of the ceiling and still didn't work, though a walnut-cased timepiece on the age-blackened sideboard still clucked and chimed with startling energy to compensate. A leather sofa still had a rent on its shiny arm out of which there issued a wartlike tuft of horsehair. Sepia prints of longhorns up to their ankles in unnaturally still lakes and Victorians having picnics in poppy fields were scattered randomly across the somewhat faded wallpaper, and a dark badly executed oil of some fierce ancestor glared down from above the bare-bricked fireplace. The mullioned windows faced south; his mother was bathed in pale gold through which sparkling motes of dust drifted lazily. A great bronze trapezium of light shifted slowly across the lace tablecloth in front of them.

"Do you? Do you really go your own way?" Edith's sharp eyes glittered. "Trouble, then? Sarah and you still living together, not planning to get married?"

Richard stared at his mother, wondering how much to tell her. "You make it sound like a criticism."

"I know times have changed. And yes, I'm old enough and traditional enough not to feel ashamed about saying it—living together is putting the cart before the horse."

"Cliché."

Edith smiled. "That doesn't mean I don't love you. I want the best for you." She stroked his arm. "You look troubled. Drawn. Bags under your eyes. I've never seen you like this. If it's not Sarah, is it money? The job?"

"Mum." It was a gentle remonstrance. "None of those. I told you about the dig on Bride Hill?"

"Yes, dear. How exciting! Finding that cooking pot! Fame at last!"

"Hardly. A mention in the footnotes. No. I suppose . . . a girl died."

"You said. Was she, mmm, a friend?"

"Not really."

"You felt it was—your fault?"

"No. Just something I saw. I felt—something happened. Something old and evil. It's impossible to explain. Nobody else saw it. Like a genie let out of a bottle. Oh, this is ridiculous."

"Ah. Nobody else saw it." His mother's eyes glistened. She clicked her tongue, gently touched his face.

"What is it?"

Edith pursed her lips, eyes on the ceiling. Trying to sort out in her mind where to begin.

"Alison," she decided finally. "How often do you see your big sister? Your nephews?"

Richard screwed up his face. "Hardly ever. I spoke to her at Christmas—"

"It's May, dear, nearly June."

"And on her birthday in March. You know we're not close. I don't know what I did wrong. Something I did when I was a child, something so horrible it left deep psychological scars—Mum, shush, that's called irony. She's just got her own life, I suppose."

This was old hat. They'd covered this ground a dozen times. But this time, Edith had started. The ground had shifted. Richard frowned, puzzled, wondering where this was leading.

Alison was Richard's older sister by two years, a pharmacist living now in Sidenham, Kent, married with two girls. She was complex and somewhat cool, Richard thought—difficult to know, to understand, to warm to. His younger brother, Paul, on the other hand, was the cheerful no-nonsense sort who was glad to see Richard anytime for a pint and a joke up in the Crown Inn in Askrigg and who reciprocally dropped into Kirkbretton *almost* uninvited at irregular intervals. He had taken over the running of the farm while Dad, Brian, clung on to his Milk Marketing Board consultancy.

And yes, Richard was estranged from his sister. Why? Once, they'd talked about it. Five, six years ago.

"Alison said to me once, 'You were always Mother's favourite.' Said gently, almost whimsically, like she'd had many years to get used to the thought."

Like trying to remember the face of a loved one with whom one had had a spat, someone who'd died and deprived the living of a reconciliation. Regret. But Richard detected real hurt.

He protested to Alison, saying, "I wasn't mum's favourite. You know you were, really." And in his heart, he knew this to be a lie. Neither Paul nor Alison stood where Richard stood in mother Edith's affections.

"Is this the skeleton in the family cupboard?"

"Oh, I didn't know you'd started smoking again."

"Shall I put it out? Sorry."

"What, and your father filling the room with Saint Bruno? Pff!" She was cautious, edgy. "Look, Richard, I love you all, Paul and you and Alison. I never favoured one of you above the others, dear . . ."

"But?"

Edith shrugged.

"It should have passed to Alison."

Her hands stretched before her on the tablecloth, left thumb searching right palm. There was a heavy silence Richard did not know how to break; if he broke it, maybe everything would break.

Finally—"What should have? You make it sound like a disease, whatever it is."

"All your life, dear, you saw and heard things we didn't, couldn't. I lost the gift in my teens, if I ever had it. It all sounds so odd now, not really part of me. There were good trees and bad trees, see, and warm lines, sort of, that you could walk along; and streams and springs were alive, had names. And in some places, you could tell the people who had lived and walked there were not really dead yet, just in the shade a little, whispering, just out of sight. Like inside the Roman fort mound in Bainbridge Centre. We used to talk a lot about this when you were little—don't you remember? 'I can see the Roman soldiers,' you used to say. Oh, I can see you're laughing! We were just country folk, I suppose. My mother, your gran, had it all her life. Still has, the old witch. You know that young rook with the broken wing you brought her when you were ten or eleven? She still has it. They live to an incredible age. I reckon it'll outlive her. It sits on her shoulder—"

Sits on her shoulder.

His mother was saying—"Alison should have had it, by rights, but she didn't. It's supposed to pass down through the female line, but Gran used to say that that rule wasn't fixed. Sometimes the men had it."

Matrilineal descent . . .

"She reckoned they never passed it on, though. And God, Alison really wanted it. She knows exactly what it is. In here"—she pressed the side of her head—"but not here." Her heart. That's why she was so, so envious. I don't think she loves you any less. But that sense of being deprived—she saw you, sees you, as being favoured, blessed, set apart." Edith sighed. "Do you still . . . you know?"

"Do I still what? See things? Now you're really scaring me. Are you saying I'm psychic?"

"Oh, my love, I don't know what they call it. Gran calls it seeing things as they really are. You said on the dig site . . . I just thought . . . you've got to remember the family's been here for centuries—for all I know, thousands of years. Our bones are carved out of the limestone and return to it generation after generation. We're more Wensleydale than the cheese. I don't think we were ever tainted by the Vikings and those rude Germans the Angles and the Saxons didn't dare dawn nigh. There were Normans at

Middleham and Richmond, sure, but that's as far as they got. No, dear, I believe we're the real thing—we're true Celts."

Celts.

"Are you all right, dear?"

"What difference does it make? Being Celts?"

"Oh, no difference, probably. Except we own the land the way no other people do. We are part of the land the way no other people are."

Richard rose, agitated, pushed aside the roses-on-cream curtains, looked down the lane. He felt unaccountably angry. "Why have you never seen fit to tell me this before?"

"It's old, old stuff, folklore, not for the twenty-first century, dear. I thought if it—if it never bothered you, never came up in your life, then why make a mystery out of it, why worry you? But I've looked at you, Richard, and I know you better than any person alive, including Sarah, who doesn't seem to know you at all. And I know you're troubled, and I'm sure it's not the kind of trouble people normally have. There's a kind of shine on you, almost as if you're getting—what's the word?—translucent. Yes."

Richard stretched his unshaven face with his fingers, drawing his lower lids down. "I'm so tired, Mum. So tired. This will sound so strange, but given what you've just said, I'm going to tell you anyway. Be patient. I have to get some photographs from the car."

"I'll put the kettle on," she said. "Paul's in the back fields, and your father's in Durham, he said, until 6:00. We've hours."

Over the pictures, as Richard explained their provenance, Edith Cleeve's old fingers portcullised her mouth—not in horror but merely the way a mother might protect her son from her own innermost thoughts by disguising her expression. Her inhalation was a long hiss of air.

Richard's father, Brian, arrived home a few minutes after Paul, and drinks were proposed at the Crown Inn, following a steak and kidney pie dinner Richard and Edith Cleeve had prepared. Edith declined to join them for a drink.

"I'm tired. Lots to think about. I'll get an early night. Don't drink too much." She caught Richard's eye. *You can pretend for so long and to so many, but I can see your heart and its pain. Don't forget.*

Richard stored that image of his mother—a small, black-haired, elfin-faced woman in an old brown cardigan, sitting very upright next to the brick fireplace with her delicate veined hands in her lap and her sharp dark eyes glinting in the light of the coals. Whatever appalling curse travelled down the line from the irretrievable ancestral mists was at least shared, understood. But distance still stood between them; his was the burden, not hers. Her sympathy, her empathy was somehow inadequate. Her look said, "My concern is that my son is ill."

He nodded to his mother, shrugged his jacket on, put his arm round Brian's stooped shoulders, mock-punched Paul. "Still drinking Theakston's?"

"Is there another brewer?" said Paul, grinning.

"That's mah boy."

"Come on, son, it's an hour to closing time," said Brian, his voice chocolate-rich and tobacco-rough. "Race you to the pumps."

"That's mah dad." But though he attempted levity, the bonhomie was somehow strained. His father detected something in Richard's voice, cast him a sideways glance, then looked at Edith for an answer. A nod, the subtlest of gestures, passed between them. It said, "Tell you later."

39

Kirkbretton

"HOW WAS YOUR FAMILY?"
Sarah sounded distant.

"They're all fine. How are you? How's Harry?"

Pause. The call backgrounded by bar noises, voices and laughter. "I hardly imagine you really care," she said with edge.

"I care about you."

"I can look after myself. Look, this is a pay phone, I don't have much money."

"Am I taking up your time?"

He heard the hiss of her exasperation, realised the call was going wrong. Defences up, distances.

"I can't take much more of this, Richard. You're driving me out. You don't own me. When we've finished here, I'm going to take a break. A week off somewhere. I think we both need the space. You're not well. That's my last 20p. My mobile battery's flat."

"Everybody says I'm not well."

"Everybody's right. Please go to the doctor's. Get *psychiatric* help. Why won't you recognise it? You won't acknowledge it. That's the worst thing to live with—you actually think all this garbage about invisible killer women and sentient rooks is *real*. I can't handle it. I can't."

"Invisible women and sentient rooks. That's Harry-speak. You've been discussing me with him. For the last time, Sarah. I *know* what I saw. I can't lie, pretend."

"Well, maybe that's the problem. You've lost track of what's real and unreal. My money's running out."

"We'll talk about it when you get back. God, Sarah, don't make a mountain out of a molehill."

The line started rapidly beeping—out of money. "I'll call during the week. Must go."

"Sarah! Sarah!" But the line was dead.

In the draughty corridor in the hall of residence, Sarah slipped to the floor. Two passing students helped her to her feet. "It's OK," she said, brushing the back of her jeans. "I'm pregnant, that's all."

A footpath runs in a long curve between high walls, separating Saint Bride's vicarage and church from the graveyard. The path surfaces at one end between the butcher's shop and Kirkbretton post office, at the other in a small clutch of renovated houses and barns overlooking the Dean Beck and Colden River confluence. The church and graveyard are linked by a footbridge wide enough for four bearers to carry a coffin. At the bridge's eastern end, there is a lych-gate. Leaning on the gate is Richard, his pale, streaked face to the sky. Above him, the rooks are circling and cawing, going about their business.

"Looks like rain, doesn't it?"

"Pardon?" Richard jumps as if stung.

"I am sorry." Alistair Sutton, vicar of Saint Bride's. "Disturbed your reverie, did I?"

"You could say."

"Only normally, I make such a racket coming down the drive. Gravel, you see. Warns of my approach or departure."

Richard hauls the collar of his anorak, huddles further into its lined depths. "I'm watching the rooks."

The vicar glances upwards. "Astonishing birds, I've always thought. Organisation. Watch 'em for hours from my study window. Well, I'd better be. Er—Mr. Cleeve, isn't it? Involved with the dig, yes? Are you all right? I hope you don't mind my saying it, but . . ."

"I know. Death warmed up." Richard sighs, tears in his eyes. "I need to talk. Can I talk? Can we talk?"

Without thinking, the vicar pulls back his coat cuff, glances at his watch.

"Forget it." Richard half-turns to go.

Sutton reaches for his sleeve. "No no. Oh, look, of course. Stupid of me, just a nervous reaction, forgive me. Look, come inside now. Warm fire."

———❧———

The vicar hung their overcoats in the long sycamore-panelled hall. The study had leaded windows, mullions. Richard stumbled at first, and Sutton fiddled and umm-ed and aah-ed and then had an idea and went to a cabinet and withdrew a tall bottle of Glenfiddich, apologised for the lack of ice; but the fridge—on its last legs, a gift from the people in the last parish—had broken that morning on my way just then to half-inch the worktop fridge from the parish hall kitchen and . . . one finger or two?

A rook clattered down onto the vicarage lawn, bounced to an undignified halt, carefully folded its wings and goose-stepped to some morsel in the grass, nervously blinking and bobbing—Richard called it "shirking"—at some sound or movement, real or imagined.

Richard smiled at these familiar antics—antics he had known all his life. But the smile upturned only half his face, and Sutton saw it as a grimace. He leaned forwards, chair creaking, proffered the glass.

"You're a bird-watcher?"

"Rooks."

"Just rooks?"

"That's all, nowadays."

Richard sipped the whisky, shuddered as it burned his throat. He looked at Sutton, perched forwards, earnest, on his study chair, grey shirt, white dog collar, sallow-skinned, short white hair swept back. Ten, fifteen years older than himself. A puzzled, anxious, concerned look. What can you tell from all this? The light of a summer afternoon, all lemon zest and butter, catches the cleric's creased forehead.

Whether to trust this man? And if not, who? Sarah, off, unreachable. His mother, all gnomic, aaar, therr be ghosts. Some of the school clique, Gordon O'Connell, Eddie Chesterman—who, beneath all that bluster—was a good solid citizen, a mate. Even, perhaps, Harry Moorhouse at the History Society, who'd always treated Richard as a son?

I'm here now, by chance, on impulse. A wry flash—the boys: "*Don't talk to strangers.*"

He took a deep breath, began.

The rooks on the site on that first day after the bulldozers' destruction; the birds that took the torc from Alex's dying hand; the traveller boys' "big crow"; the rook on the window ledge on Cliff Street; and, of course, the woman *who thought she knew him,* the woman in the excavation trench, the woman who spoke to him in his dreams.

Sutton's face remained impassive. Impossible to tell what he was thinking. "Where is this woman now?"

"That's at the heart of it. She's everywhere and nowhere. Every woman you ever knew. She's neither evil nor good. She's just the chaotic, uncontrolled surge of life. And she's knocking at my door, Mr. Sutton. She's knocking at my door." He tapped his left eyebrow distractedly.

He took a long breath. "All my life, I feel to have known things, seen things, patterns, that other people haven't—not ghosts, just things that have happened. When I was twelve, I wrote a short story about a spring ceremony at Avebury four thousand years ago. I described what happened, what the people wore, how they spoke, what the stones looked like. My history teacher thought it was so realistic she sent it to English Historical Review or something. A history professor at Cambridge wrote to me personally after he'd seen the story. He told me I had a 'remarkable grasp of ancient history' and a 'vivid imagination,' and that he hoped he'd see me at Cambridge in a few years' time. I couldn't tell him we'd been on a school trip to Avebury, and I'd actually *seen* the festival. All I had to do was sit on a stone halfway down the avenue and partly shut my eyes. Father, I swear I never read a word about Avebury before the visit. There are dozens more incidents. I suppressed them all from the moment I realised that other people didn't have them."

"'A vivid imagination?' Would you put it at more than that, then?"

"I wouldn't have said it was more than that—until recently. Oh, this is so embarrassing."

"OK. Let's stop for a moment. Let me be absolutely honest with you, Mr. Cleeve. Er, can I call you, er—"

"Richard."

"Richard. I do voluntary work with a charity that counsels many mentally disturbed people. Please, please don't be . . . we use the term *mentally disturbed* because mentally ill is non-PC at present. Silly, I know, but. Now you are mentally disturbed. Not ill. Not ill. Things have happened to you, and your interpretation of them won't fit what the rest of us—and indeed what you, most of the time—see as normal, cosy, straightforward."

Sutton huffed with frustration. "This is so, so awkward. OK. When you look at what I and millions of other people believe—God sent His Son who died so that we, His followers, might have eternal life—you're bound to admit that belief takes some extraordinary shapes. God? A god with a son? A son that died? A concept called eternal life? You get the point? The problem you have is that, whereas there are millions of Christians, there is, at this moment, only one Richard Cleeve, and what he's seeing as reality is, um—"

Richard laughed mirthlessly. "You reject it then? Everything I told you is in here?" He tapped his head again.

Sutton spread his hands wide, clapped them on his knees. "Absolutely not! Yours is hardly a religious experience, but it's valid."

"You're patronising me."

"Far from it! But I *do* feel we're straying here. My fault entirely. You're desperately troubled, that's clear. That's the area of concern. The way you feel—validates—what you perceive to have happened, what you believe exists."

Richard's eyes, heavy-lidded, were closed. These were pat answers. They could not explain why he was drifting away from Sarah, drifting out of any sense of love, drifting out of reality.

He remembered his student days. You'd be round a table in a bar, all talking, drinking. The discussion would get heated, philosophical, profound. And there'd be a point where, if you were trying to explain your point of view or you thought you'd got a unique perspective on something, click! You'd be out of it. And your companions would look at you and say, "What are you talking about? You've lost it!" Or you'd be listening to somebody else, not taking part, and click! It would all become meaningless, nonsensical, futile—everybody getting angry and vociferous about nothing, everybody posturing.

Well, it was like that now. Sutton—a good man, honest. But it was meaningless. Nothing could touch Richard the actor. Just recite the lines. Richard the lover, son, teacher, historian, twitcher. Richard sitting in the confessional. Play the part.

"I'm not a heathen, Father. If I had a soul." He was weeping.

Sutton patted his hand, English reserve frustrating him.

"I can't see what you can see. That's a gift and a curse. But we can both see something that is invisible and eternal. Love."

The daylight had faded into evening. A lone blackbird poured its liquid notes into the gloaming from an invisible perch in the rhododendrons across the lawn.

"Love, Richard. Hold onto that. I'm sorry. I truly am."

❊

The house on Cliff Street, Bride Hill, had a neglected air. The wisteria had sent out masses of shoots—some reaching into the cobbled lane, others obscuring the windows. Under other circumstances, Richard would have got the ladder from the outhouse and trimmed it back to the wall; now it didn't seem to matter.

If he went out, it was for cash from Kirkbretton's only wall dispenser or for groceries to the off-licence in the gloom of dusk; he felt like a criminal, edging down the shadows of the gloom-filled lane or, better, out of Farrar's Fold and along a small unlit high-walled path between the gardens. If he met anyone he knew—pupils, parents, people from the George—the exchange was cursory. He avoided eye contact. He stopped shaving then started again when a rash developed and the itching became a distraction.

Richard worked through the night, not eating, surviving on instant coffee, dumping a new spoonful onto the dregs of the last, watching the brown stains spread. Cigarette butts piling up in unemptied ashtrays and the ash spilling over his keyboard, desk. The smoke burned his eyes and throat; there was a heavy harshness in his chest.

The laptop screen became the centre of his life, his reference books arrayed like votive gifts around its steady gaze.

He knew he was trying to drive out the ghosts which now crowded in from every side. He was tackling it the only way he knew.

He wanted it all—every reference to rooks, to Celtic life, their jewellery, artefacts, gods and goddesses. Paper covered with the intricate interwoven designs. He plundered Frazer's *Golden Bough,* half a dozen volumes on ancient Britain, everything in the house on the legends and mythology and archaeology of the area. He read meanings into each new snippet of information; old systems of knowledge collapsed under their own weight or diverged into new files, which again burgeoned with data and demanded cross-referencing. There was so much to do, so much to learn. Teaching, Sarah's warmth and immediacy, his family—all this had faded to a distant memory, something that might have happened to somebody else.

The phone was on answer.

Richard. Richard! I know you're there. I'm sorry about what I said from York. Please pick up the phone.

Richard, it's me again. It's, ah, 4:30, Tuesday. Are you in? You have my mobile number. Please *call.*

He ached with desire for her. Wanted to turn the clock back. Wanted passionately to be normal, ordinary, unburdened. "I can't, can't, can't," mumbled Richard to himself over the click and burr of the answering machine. He wanted to phone her, to say that everything was all right even though it wasn't. But he also wanted to spare her. I can't let her see this mess. Must get things into shape. The place stinks. I'll tidy the house first.

It's Eddie. How're you doing? Your door's always locked. Fancy a pint? It's Wednesday. See you in the George then. Hah. Or wherever. Give us a ring. Richard—I mean it. Do you good to get out.

Richard. It's 4:30, Thursday. Pick up the phone. Please. Don't shut me out.

But his research, not cleaning, came first. Dr. Franklin Coombs, *The Crows: A Study of the Corvids of Europe.* Suffolk Ornithological Group, *The Rook in Suffolk* by M. J. F. Jeanes and Reg Snook, 1976. G. K. Yeates, *Life of the Rook.* A mass of his own observations from yellowing notebooks going back to his childhood. Cross-referencing. Yeates says this, but Coombs says that.

Friday.

Finally, exhausted, he fell asleep on the sofa, a half-eaten tandoori from the takeaway congealing on the coffee table, unaware of the day, aware only that it was deepening dusk.

He is flying again with Gordon O'Connell in the little draughty microlight, hands frozen to the stanchions, the Dean Beck valley dark below them. Then swooping like a bird above the farm on Bride Hill, with its long byre and round huts, their thatches radiating like brown stars in the mist. Soldiers are bundling dejected prisoners across the muddy yard. Suddenly, the air is filled with other wings, diving and shrieking wildly, plummeting towards the byre. Richard is alone; the microlight is all feathers, quills, the hiss and lift of air; then fire and anger and turmoil; and upwards again into a sheaf of soft cloud, the mist stinging his face. They part, and below, where the farm was, is flattened earth. A lone figure stands at its edge, weeping for what is lost forever; then he too disappears in the mist, and a Roman marching station emerges, the soldiers on the palisade shading their eyes. An archer takes an arrow from the leather quiver on his back, sets it to his short bow, aims. Richard is frozen in the air. His wings are stiff—turning back into arms—he can only stare helplessly as the string tautens, the bow arches, the arrow's steel tip trembles before his heart.

And then the woman's face, the face he has known so many centuries, a face shifting like a reflection on water, through a veil of mist, in and out of focus. A smile, welcoming and seductive, cruel and deadly in turns as the light splinters and plays round it.

Time to go, Richard.

40

"HERE HE IS, LOOK! CROW-HEAD."
"Didn't take the gift then?"

"And what would he have done with it anyway?" churred Halley Coalfeather angrily. "All this trying to talk with the upright is a big mistake. Always has been. The number of times—"

"Yes yes, we all know your views," said Caerleon Longpinion impatiently.

The morning dew had brought a host of titbits to the surface of the dig site, and a group of Safehaven's opportunists were sitting in the middle branches of a dense sycamore at the edge, eyes peeled.

Richard appeared silently, his back to the vicarage wall, staring at the disturbed earth of the dig site. Michael and Peter shuffled over to him, and the rumble of words passed between them.

"I'm no expert on upright hain, but there's something unnatural about those juvenile uprights. A wrong smell. Fear. And Crow-head himself is almost a shining light," muttered Startle.

"*Chrrr,* I can't see a light from him," complained some bird from the depths of the fluttering leaves.

"I can't smell anything," murmured young Carmen Strongtalon. "Do you get fear-smell in your second year, then?"

"I can't smell anything either, dear," said Sorrel Nightwing, bereaved sister of Bracken, mournfully from a nearby branch. "But it could be a head cold."

The rooks watched Richard and the traveller's boys in silence, shuffling and hopping anxiously as the trio moved off towards Bridegate Lane.

"I think we should see where he goes."

"Why do you say that, Startle?" Calvin Airchurner looked slantways at her.

"You know how we peck a spider's web in the morning, hoping the creature will emerge from beneath its leaf and we can breakfast? We can't see the spider, but we just know she's there? Well, somebody or something is shaking our web right now. Somebody or something is calling."

"How do you know all this, Startle Coalfeather-Dreadcalmer?" asked Carmen Strongtalon enviously. "I wish I had your gift."

Carmen's manner of addressing Startle was a huge compliment, and Startle's ruff swelled out with pride. Rooks take a mate for a year, usually in September, during which the females retain their patronym. About half of those partnerships continue into a second year, and this marks the start of a lifetime commitment, signified by the adoption by the female bird of her mate's patronym. Carmen was, in effect, complimenting the strength of Startle and Dryden's relationship by anticipating they would make that commitment when the time came.

"Dear Carmen, thank you. But to see the shadows of one world in the sunlight of another is no gift. It is a burden you should hope is never yours."

You go, Startle, then," said Calvin. "But keep your distance. Juveniles can be handy stone throwers."

By skirting the old quarry in short flights and hopping from branch to branch in the dense woodland and shrubbery down towards the Dean Beck, Startle was able to keep the upwrights in view without leaving the protective cover of the trees.

But then the upwrights crossed the humpbacked bridge over Dean Beck and disappeared behind the derelict mill on the way to the recreation ground. Startle flapped upwards onto the mill's gable end and perched precariously on the mill's worn stone finial to reconnoitre.

"Good Lady!"

"Startle!"

"Master Surebill!"

The two birds padded towards each other, clicked bills.

"Dryden must have flown like the wind to give you my summons," said Surebill.

"I haven't seen him since the first light of dawn," she said, mystified." He flew to speak with you—to tell you about last night and Crow-head."

"And so he did. No matter. Other forces are driving you. I wanted you to tell me something. I want you to feel for the Ley."

"Master Surebill," she protested. "You know I—"

"It is one of life's mysteries that the talents and gifts of youth should be given to the young," said Surebill sternly, "when the elderly are so much in need of them."

"You are not old."

"Nor am I anywhere near as sure of my skills as a seer as you seem to think I am," he said, rasping his long beak into his chest feathers and under his heavy wing. "I need you. I need your natural abilities. I need to read the Ley. *Chaw-ich-cha.*"

Those dread words! *Give us a sign.* The mill roof swayed and spun. The morning sun, glancing now over the treetops into the valley, shook in the nest of the heavens, and clouds boiled on the horizon. Startle crouched, spread her body. Her eyes closed—oh,

Master Surebill, the cruelty! To see the worlds as they truly are, to feel their otherness streaming into your frail body, filling the hollows of your bones with unquiet, with the voices of the dead and distant! I am not ready, not fitted, not strong enough.

In the tumbling shapes of the clouds, there came a beckoning arm, a finely poised talon, a glorious face, a dark-spread wing—the slow resolution of an ethereal form but constant and light-limned, an aurora, a Shekinah, neither *hroc* nor upright.

And words . . .

"A trick of light separates my world from yours, and I was never far from you. I whisper in your ear as you whispered in mine. And yes, the Lady is alive. She is here. She comes to gather the harvest of that which was sown in anger and betrayal so many lives ago. She comes to waken the sleeping and to give rest to those who could not sleep."

"You did well, Startle. I know for sure now that the Lady is with us and that the final destiny of the gift is in Her safe hands."

Startle opened her eyes to see Surebill's beady brown eye close to hers—but behind him! Behind him loomed black night itself, the hugest rook Startle had ever seen.

It could be no other than Hroc, the feathered ruler of the north, Rooklord, chief and elder of elders of all *hroca,* Master of Masters. And the fear that inhabits every rook if they should see Hroc himself—the fear inculcated from their first tentative instruction in the nest until that moment when, in reality, the Rook of Passage actually does appear to take them home—that fear swelled within young Startle, and she cowered again on the rooftop in the slanting sun, believing that in invoking the Ley, she had crossed into forbidden territory, and the Great Rook had come to punish, death in his arched wings.

"Are you to take me to the Golden Land, my lord?" she whispered, forgetting that she herself had predicted the Rooklord's arrival.

"Not yet." The huge bird made no move.

Startle trembled, stuttered.

"Th-then you are here b-because the gift calls you."

"Startle, my dear, does the Ley still hold you, or—oh my, oh my Lady. Oh my. My lord. Forgive me." Surebill, suddenly aware of the looming shape behind him, suddenly and profoundly out of his depth, flapped, shuddered, nodded his head, looked appallingly embarrassed. "I should die too for this rudeness in the face of my own demise—oh my, oh, what shall I do?" he mumbled distractedly.

"Calm down, I beg of you," said Hroc gently. "'It is one of life's mysteries that the talents and gifts of youth should be given to the young, when the elderly are so much in need of them.' Perhaps you remember these words? Well, my kin, I echo them. My days stretch into the mists of time. It's true I have seen and heard astonishing things. But it is hope, optimism, joy, unmeditated courage, the seized moment, that will take this world into a new age—not the accumulated dust that you might call wisdom. I am yesterday's force and nearly spent. My own soul, one of the spans of the great bridge that will take me to the Golden Land, my soul that was lost among the upwrights, calls me urgently. We will be reunited, after all these aching years. No, you, my perfect guardians, you are tomorrow and tomorrow and tomorrow."

His great beak caressed the two Safehaven birds, who, in spite of themselves, lowered their backs and raised their feathers in fear at the Rooklord's touch.

"In respect of your question, Startle, I think the thing you name the gift called its owner, and its owner called me," said Hroc. "In my mind, these things are indistinguishable. But you, child—you can read the Ley? You are mistress of your congeries?"

"I feel the Ley's bright net around me, but I am no seer, my lord. The power and the answers lie deep in the mist. I am but a yearling, and no mistress of Safehaven. That honour and duty falls to my master, Caspian Surebill."

"Master of Safehaven, my lord. And your servant," mumbled Surebill.

"Accepted. Let me introduce Hawberry and Cobweb Greybeak, my travelling companions. Many a thousand wings have passed between my home in the sunfurthest."

And behind them—on a broken chimney decorated with the brittle ruins of last year's willow herb stems and the young unfurling shoots of this year's—were two other rooks, whose odour was of travel, of distance.

With a bright *chaw-chah,* the birds hopped forwards. They touched beaks politely. Startle and Surebill introduced themselves.

"Startle. My lord chose me because he says I am Leywise," said Hawberry, deferring to his master. "But you and I see only a small part of what my lord sees."

"These are old and failing senses, Hawberry Mac Greybeak," said Hroc, smiling wearily. "Do not belittle your powers—nor you either, Startle Coalfeather." The oldest rook's nictitating membrane shuttered his old black eyes.

"One thing you cannot see, so I will tell you—it will fall to you, Greybeak and Coalfeather, to guide the upwright to the Lady, and this in moonlit darkness. But by then, the upwright will have set foot on the bridge to the Golden Land. He will come to meet me, to end his pact, his long imprisonment. *Chaw-cha-ich,* a sign is given."

"My lord."

You have followed this upwright far enough, Startle Coalfeather. What goes on here is upwrights' business. Fly home to Safehaven, both of you, and herald my arrival. Startle, set your mate's mind at rest—at this moment, he is searching frantically for you, believing you to have been called by the Rook of Passage." Hroc chuckled deeply.

"The Lady has asked me to prepare you and your kin for your final task as guardians of Pretan's oldest truth. Call council."

Surebill called his elders, tree by tree, and they sent out messengers to those at peck in the Colden fields, on the slopes of Rampart Hill, and in the ploughlands and pastures sunfurthest and sunside, sunfall and sunrise.

"Council is called" was the message. "Return to Safehaven. The Master of Masters has arrived."

And at noon, Hroc spoke to his kin in the high weaving branches of a beech, Master Surebill's tree, behind the vicarage of Saint Bride's.

"You must not be confused by the term *gift*," the Rooklord told them. "It is a word that used to describe the Lady Brigid's contract with the upwrights' royal bloodline, with me, and with all our kin, once upon a time.

"But for many—*hroca* and upwright alike—the thing you call a gift has been anything but. It has been a curse and one that has taken lives and will continue to do so until the Lady Brigid chooses to remove it from this world. And She may not—She may, instead, decide that the violation of its resting place is cause to renew its death-dealing properties. This is in the hands of the gods and need not concern us."

"Who will avenge the deaths of our kin?" said Halley Coalfeather.

"You imagine the deaths of your kin were not part of that curse? You rightly call this the Haunted Hill. In the long lore of your congeries, the listing of masters, is there mention of any upwright living here?"

There was a murmuration of nos. Only Caspian Surebill, remembering the legends, kept his peace.

"Then is it time?" asked another Safehaven voice.

"Great forces are moving again in the Earth. I have been called to my destiny and await it in this sacred spot. You have fulfilled your task as guardians of the torc, which you know as the gift, and my lady, as you rightly divine, is here too, after countless lives of our kind. She has business with the uprights which need not concern us, and then I imagine She will reveal Herself to you."

"Pardon me, my lord, but I think all this *does* concern us," said Halley Coalfeather, shaking the feathers of his neck into a ruff. "We were appointed to guard this place and its gift. We have had nothing but heartache and trouble from the upwright, and I, for one—"

Hroc spoke with harsh tones. "Let's not speak of estrangement but of one purpose. There are matters for the upwright, and matters for the *hroca*—and you, kinscreature, presume too much if you imagine you know our Lady's mind and will in this."

And he turned, as if listening to the wind.

"I hear my lady calling. I must return to Her."

"My lord," said Dryden. "What should we do?"

"Hold on to the gift a little longer. Send messengers. Let them all know. When the moon is full, I shall return to bear it to the Lady. At that time, call all the Kin throughout the parish. Call all the Kith too. The passing of an age shall be witnessed by the chosen ones, but all those whose kingdom is the Air must know."

The Air was filled with the hiss and rattle of wings in the night. They came from Ashneagh and Mildhollow, the Rivenlea remnants and half a dozen congeries from Holme and Colden and Colne, waking the *chakawi* and *chakachitta* as they flew, calling them to the great convocation—some high, some low, some field-hopping, and many up in the clouds of the moon. The cry—what is it? What's going on? Join us, follow us! Great events, great changes!

And they settled in the trees of Kirkbretton Old Wood, black shadows, creatures that ruled the Air while man's ancestors were furry-tailed tree dwellers—thousands upon thousands of them, their wings brushing the trees, their bodies bending every branch—silent, taut with expectation in the blue cold moonlight.

"You have done a good job, oathkeeper," smiled Brigid, stroking his pitted beak. The Goddess swept her arm round the clearing. Her clear voice resounded.

"To all of you, but to the Kin of Safehaven especially—my dear birds, your instincts were right. The fires of the old religion may be rekindled in time. Estranged though they are from the soil from which they sprang, many upright hearts long to worship and stand in awe of their mother Earth again.

"Though you and I may never be called upon to renew our contracts with these creatures, I see the first faint streaks of dawn on the distant horizon. Hroc and I have fulfilled our destiny, and I shall take him home with me, noble bird and oldest friend. He has dreamed of being human and has always wondered why, and a line of upwrights has dreamed of being kin and always wondered why. It is time they were reunited and the paths of their destiny linked as they were when I ruled the Earth. The curse, your 'gift,' I remove. It has no place in this world or the one to come.

"You have been faithful guardians. When the dawn of this coming day breaks over Pretan, you shall be absolved of your guardianship. Meanwhile, bear witness."

41

*R*OOSTING AND FLOCKING: WINTER ROOSTS *break up within a few days in late February or early March, probably when egg laying begins. In other words, nest building takes place while the vast majority of the birds are still at roost. During the first few days of breakup, the rooks become increasingly anxious about leaving the nest colony with the jackdaws. Roosts often contain jackdaws, who use the rookeries as collecting points before flying with the rooks to roost, and can include carrion crows, ravens, and magpies. A few juveniles from some rookeries still use the winter roost. After nesting has started, the females use the nest as a roost, and the males use a branch nearby. When the young birds are big enough to accompany their parents, there's a choice—some return to the rookery, others to the winter roost. The roost is not necessarily near the rookery. The roost is rarely used by just one rookery and is known as a rook "parish." It can be four miles from the rookery. Rooks gather in late afternoon at their rookery assembly point. In Aberdeenshire, a roost once contained sixty-five thousand rooks.*

From these first collecting points, they fly, mainly along regular flight lines, to the fields and trees close to the actual roost. Here, rooks from all the different rookeries collect, many on the ground, in hedges, trees, and bushes near where the actual roost is situated. They feed for twenty to thirty minutes. The birds on the edge fidget. Then all feeding stops, and an uneasy calm descends, as if they're listening for the signal. Then the flight from these second assembly points begins quite suddenly. The species tend to separate. In the roost trees, there is constant noise and flights to and from, perhaps while the birds call to find their mates and suitable perches in the dim light. All this dies down, and birds can be seen roosting in pairs.

Dusk in, dawn out. At the crucial times of February/March and September/October, the birds disperse directly to their rookeries without stopping to feed; in winter, they stop to feed. Why roosts? Edwards (1962) reckons it's Malthusian; Ward (1965) says it's a food distribution negotiation . . .

He awoke with a start, his hand numb and tingling, a red pressure blotch on his forehead and wrist. The computer's fan whirred quietly and the screen saver was a starfield into which he was hurtling. He shook his head, quickly closed the files, clicked the power off.

He'd fallen asleep in summer evening light; now a huge moon had risen, nacreous through a chill summer mist, and great baleful pools of blue light spilled over his strewn desk. Small black shadows crossed the moon's face singly, in pairs. He rubbed his eyes. Bats? No. Too big, too purposeful in flight.

Rooks.

A summer convocation? A *midnight* convocation?

Impossible. Rooks rarely flew at night. So what was happening?

He stumbled to the door and went out into the street. Silently, except for the creak and rustle of their raggy wings and the occasional battering of leaves as they abandoned their trees, the birds were away.

This is rare. I must find out what's going on. Must. Mild night. Keys? Lock the door. Remember the times in Bainbridge when you'd follow the rooks across the Outhwaites' fields, Richard? It's just the same. Nothing changes. Adventure. Binoculars? No use. Too dark. Where are they going? Out of Kirkbretton—oh, wait, for God's sake! I'll never keep up. Too much drinking, smoking. A year ago, no problem, I could have done this easily. Phew!

Cold sweat soon stuck his shirt to his chest and back, and phlegm gathered like bloody glue in his mouth. But he found the energy to half-run, half-stumble, one eye on the birds' direction.

Beware folklore—when a rookery is abandoned, those who own the land are about to lose it.

He clattered through the silent streets of Kirkbretton, his shadow reaching crazily out behind him then before him as he passed beneath each streetlamp, stopping to catch his raucous breath and confirm the direction the rooks were taking. Left at the George Inn, past the junior school, stumbling, nearly crashing to his knees as the tarmac of the school approach ended in a stony lane, out into Moor Road and right, then up the hill . . .

A great arm of Kirkbretton Old Wood spurred into farmland two miles out on the Holmethorpe road, right on the ridge separating the Colden and Holme Valleys. A car swerved to avoid him as he ran past the last houses and up the incline towards the woodland. The headlights picked out walls with stones like gargoyles' faces, white posts with eyes like diamonds and rubies.

He knew now where they were going.

He turned into a farm track. A black bird, a silhouette in the night, a great river of moonlight on the ink-black of the feathers of its back, sat on a fencepost, flapping off as he approached.

He stooped, hands on thighs, the muscles in his legs rawly aching, trembling with the poison of burned energy, heart pounding in his neck and chest and temples, lungs hot and sore, sucking air.

Then he became aware of a susurration, an expectation in the gloom ahead. It was the rooks, their thousands of voices whispering quietly in the trees across the fields, where the lane petered out past a derelict farmhouse. In the dim glow of the streetlights over Sheffield, many miles to the south, he saw the denseness of the trees. They seemed weighted down.

He clutched his arms to his chest, shivered. The wind, hurtling over the ridge and whining through the trees, cut through his thin pullover. He buttoned his collar and sleeves. No voice urged, "What am I doing here? Why tonight? Why here?" The cold wind numbed his cheeks, but a colder wind anaesthetised his mind.

He had entered the world of the kin.

To Richard, that world was as black as feathers, black as a starless, moonless night, black as coal. Yet lights that were not lights danced in his head. He felt weightless like air, like someone who has walked for miles with a heavy rucksack between his shoulders and has finally released his load—a moonwalker, or younger by far, the years melting away.

In this world, all talks to all. He cocked his head on one side and listened to the Goddess, the rooks.

The thick rough grass soon soaked his jeans to the knees as he walked up the lane. The dense mass of the trees enveloped him; all around, there were whispers he half-understood.

He found a cold long stone, a fallen gatepost, brushed aside the dewy grass, sat down exhausted, a raw pain in his aching chest. The night took him, bathed his head in iced light.

I must rest. Must rest. But I'm here. This is where the rooks gather, their secret convocation, the Grand Roost. Just a little further, maybe. A little deeper into the woods. When I've got my breath back.

A rook landed on his left shoulder, startling him with its grip, its weight; but in this altered state, it was no more and no less than he expected. The bird struggled for a foothold, then another plumped clumsily onto his right shoulder. He smelled their old, old breath, the oil of their feathers, the smooth roundness of their bulky bodies against his cheek. And they indicated he should stand and move, directing him first one way then another through the blue-dappled silent trees.

"Oh, bless you!" he whispered, smiling. It felt like a dream coming true. How I always wanted to touch you, to show you I meant no harm, to fly with you, to share . . .

She stood in a shallow treeless depression before him filled with the dark backs of last year's oak and beech leaves, bathed in cold self-generated light. Her slender shoulder was gripped by the fierce gnarled claws of a majestic bird, Hroc, he of the legend, oldest and wisest of the feathered ones, gently caressing her long hair, winding it in his beak lovingly. Round her neck hung a jewelled torc.

The torc.

She smiled, beckoned him forwards. Birds crouched silent on every branch, her light a thousand stars in their attentive beady eyes.

"My silent witnesses," she laughed. "Drawn here to say good-bye. Don't be afraid, Thomas the Rhymer, child of earth. This is the last act, the finale. Come into the light."

Richard shook with cold or fear or both. She was how he imagined Cartimandua to have been—dazzling blue eyes, slim waist, black hair so smooth and luxuriant it glowed blue in the starlight.

"Who are you?" The wind whistled through the upper branches of the trees.

"You know who I am. People see what they want to see. And you know what this is." She fingered the torc, slowly unclipped it. Hroc flapped once, regaining his balance. She held the ancient token forth. To Richard, it seemed that the Goddess's hand, the grey bark of the trees, the hiss and rattle of the leaves, the gloss and beak and piercing eyes of the rooks all swirled into and out of torc, as if the visible and tactile were dragged like so many iron filings on a great black sheet of paper into the object's magnetic field like warped light on the edge of a black hole . . .

"*This belonged to Cartimandua, the great queen of the Brigantes,*" said the Goddess. "*Yes, your ancestor. It should have passed to Caradoc, whom you call Caratacus. But his destiny took him to Rome, where he too embraced the modern world and was lost. Take it. Take the torc. You've wanted to hold it since you first saw it.*"

But he dared not. Tears sprang to his eyes. He edged closer to the Goddess.

"If he receives it, he will be cursed," said a whisper from the trees.

"*It is my curse,*" said Brigid sternly, looking up into those dark branches. "*By what poor power I have left to me, I can make or break that curse. But if he should take it, he is bound to me.*"

Richard's hand stretched towards the torc. But he still dared not touch it. "This is a most beautiful piece of work. This was the piece in the trench, on my windowsill. Who made it?" he whispered.

"*The ancestors of the Celts of Pretan. Those whose blood mingled with Cartimandua's line. It is older, far older than you imagine—made with love and magic in a time lost, forged with skills beyond your comprehension.*" Her hands as she stroked the torc were young and slim, not mottled.

"If I touch this—if I touch you—the same thing will happen to me as happened to Cartimandua, the legionaries at the wayfort, to Alex at the dig—even to Ostorius Scapula—who You cursed in health and mind and who finally fell on the blade of the very sword that plucked that—that torc from Venutius' hand."

"*You read too much.*"

He shuddered with cold, and the tiny thread that held him in the real world shook like spiders' gossamer.

Brigid laughed harshly.

"*You're all so weak, so frail, so self-pitying. By all the gods, this world is getting too thin for me. From stew to broth, from broth to gruel,*

*gruel to water. Too thin by far. You can see right through the fabric of
people's souls these days.*

*"You can go back to your world and tell them. Turn around and go
home. Forget us. Your world is beautiful beyond belief, Richard, a pearl
in the sea of the skies. Listen to the call of the whale, the song of the
blackbird, the wind through the grass. Watch the sun dapple the fields,
feel it warm your cheek, see the fruit ripening, listen to the half-heard
conversation of the bees. Look at the canyons and peaks, the ice fields, the
panorama of the clouds. Just love it for what it is."*

And she sang, with her rooks in whispering chorus and echo:

> The gods are strong spears, hard-hurled from each soul;
> Born in the black cauldrons behind the eyes of the living.
> I am the hag, hauling the dead to their home,
> Burying my kin in the forked fires of worlds burning.

The pace of her words quickened.

> I used to ride at Cartimandua's side,
> Your kin one on each proud shoulder:
> Whoever told you it was ravens now?
> We'd ride into battle, and we'd shed blood together,
> She and I, and I could call down Cernunnos,
> Mr. Changer's white shafts of fire;
> Long-armed Lugh Samildanach,

And as each god and goddess was named, they briefly appeared
in the spectral light, a roll call of those who, long years ago, walked
with all creatures . . .

Most skilled in the arts, my dear cousins;
Their handsome son Cu Chulainn,
My own daughter Arianrhod, beautiful Silver Wheel;
And Taranis, the Wheel also;
Sucellos, the Thunderer, hammer at the ready,
His consort Nantosuelta;
Ramshead serpent Teutates, Esus;
Taranis, god of sky and thunder;
Cartimandua's own, Epona, pony goddess,
Blazing mane and sparkling hooves,
the Mare Goddess, fast as the wind.
Ogmios the god with the gift of tongues,
Limping Nuadu of the Silver Arm, Fisher King;
Goibniu the Smith, Gofannon to the Cymri,
Striking sparks in the forge of heaven;
Borvo with his beautiful and mysterious consort Damona,
Grannus and Sequana, with their healing touch:
And now all dead and gone down the roads of the sky.
Belenus, my, you've sparked my memory.
Belenus—the fire we lit for him,
God of herd and harvest, burning the straw
Given us by Lugh in the fullness of the year,
In two huge fires and driving the kine between them;
Mannanan, known by the Cymri as Manawydan;
Donn, god of the dead, my good friend in these dying days.
Bran the Blessed, Dagda, the youngest god, the good man,
Rosmerta, goddess of plenty.
Medb, she of the sacred oak, Artio with her bear . . .

Ah, the tall men, their hair stiff with lime
And combed in a huge mane, fire in their loins!
My, how they gave us pleasure after battle
And the celebratory feast! We rejoiced in them.

"And now it all ends. I never told Queen Cartimandua or any of those who rode with me at dawn from the scattered camps on into the field of victory or glory. It is something I never imparted to the countless seers and sages, bards and poets who worshipped me. But the curse is for eternity. To lift it, I must take it into eternity with me.

"I'm bringing the harvest home, Richard. Meet Hroc. Hroc, meet Richard. The burden of guardianship is lifted this night for both of you. You have done what was necessary in your sundered worlds, and you have done it well and patiently. Leave with me, and leave as one."

Richard saw the Rooklord then. Did the great bird bow his head to him? Then suddenly, he saw the world as Hroc saw it, and the memories crowded back, the dreams and nightmares, the *difference* that now, in a stroke under the dark trees, was no difference at all. Mystery solved.

Entranced, Richard found the decision simple. For the first time in weeks, it was all clear to him. He took a step forwards, gingerly took the torc from Brigid's hand. It was icy, deadly, deathly cold. He studied it, stroking the tiny golden carving of Hroc with his thumbs.

And then in a rush, the world he had just left tumbled back—the warmth, bustle, scents—of hyacinth and exhaust fumes; fresh-baked bread; paella and mimosa; moorland moss and rain on summer pavements; the echoing chatter and clatter of pupils as they streamed from lesson to lesson, ate in the dining hall, raced across the yard; Sarah's face and eyes, the freckles in the valley of her breasts; his mother in her brown cardigan, the tick and chime of the mantel clock in the Bainbridge farmhouse.

"Oh, Sarah, Sarah, Sarah, what have I done?" he sobbed.

"In one thing only in your miserable and uneventful life, have you excelled, Richard Cleeve, latest but not last in a long line. What did the Romans say? Amor vincit omnia? I take the curse of the torc into eternity. But the base metal is yours. Let the people who forged it have it. Let them

make of it what they will. Such power as it has is yours for a brief time. Use it."

She nuzzled the big bird's gleaming feathers. *"Now we have other business. Hroc and his kin have served as guardians of the torc far longer than he expected, and he is weary of this world. I'm taking him home. I'm taking you home, Richard."*

The lights died, and with slow, sad flapping in the thick darkness, the convocation dispersed.

42

EDDIE CHESTERMAN RAN HIS FINGER along the blinds. In the yard outside the single-bed ward, a flock of sparrows bounced in and out of a cotoneaster bush like grey notes in search of a tune.

"You could sing him 'Linden Lea'—the one you did for us that Christmas I was going out with Annette. Or was it Joyce?" he said. Out of the long silence, his voice sounded odd, muffled, subdued, with mysterious and unintended inflexions. He frowned briefly at this phenomenon.

Sarah didn't notice. "That would be one for you," she said softly, stroking Richard's lank hair. "Richard never liked it."

"I know." Eddie scrubbed his tired eyes. "I'm selfish."

"You're not at all."

The silence extended again like the distance between planets, broken only by the suck and collapse of the respirator and the ping and hum of the life support monitors. Eddie absently patted Richard's thin hand, picked it up, let it fall back onto the neat lemon-lit sheets.

"Do you think he knows we're here?"

Sarah just shook her head slowly, almost as if she were trying to relax the muscles of her neck. Pale October light crept through the blinds and fell in broad bands across Richard's bed. His hands lay peacefully at his sides. His musculature had atrophied with the months in hospital, months of perfect silence and stillness. Now his face was gaunt and sunless, and his complexion the colour of wax. The air was warm and musty with a swirl of odours—antiseptic and honeysuckle and Horlicks and rancid butter with an underlay of salt-nitrogen compounds, body wastes.

"Richard darling, I'm going to have our baby soon. It would be good if you could help me name her . . ." Sarah's voice rose, and her breath caught.

"Ah, Mrs.—?" Dr. Krisnamurti, a tall man with a willow's grace and expensive half-rimmed gold spectacles, pushed through the swing doors.

"Ms. Lewis. You always get that wrong."

"Yes, silly mistake of mine," he said, eyeing her distended stomach, shaking her hand, nodding to Eddie, who stayed by the window. "How are we today?"

Eddie and Sarah stared coldly, and the doctor was quick to detect the mood. His smile froze. "Could I talk to you?" His glance flashed between the two of them. "Yes, both of you if you wish, Ms. Lewis."

In a side room, the doctor took a deep breath and sat in a red plastic chair as far from Sarah and Eddie as possible, tapping the tips of his fingers together with nervous rapidity.

"Glad to have caught you. Now before you say anything, you must know that what I am about to tell you is perfectly obvious. There's been no change in Richard's condition in five months, none at all. The good news, then, is that his coma is not degenerative. The bad news is—well—"

"No signs of improvement either," Eddie finished the sentence for him impatiently. "Persistent vegetative state."

"Eddie," warned Sarah softly.

"I personally don't like the term *PVS*. No human being should be compared with a vegetable. But yes. No change. If we switched off his life support, he would not survive."

"What do you want me to do? Do you want me to try to persuade Mr. and Mrs. Cleeve to allow you to do that?" Sarah's voice was laden with menace. "Because if you do, you will have to speak to them yourself—"

"Dr. Krisnamurti's hands flapped up, palm outwards. "Good Lord, I wouldn't dream of it. I have spoken with Mr. and Mrs. Cleeve on numerous occasions on this very subject. It's just that I want you to know too that, medically speaking, there is almost no chance of any, er, of Richard . . . the point is that nobody would blame them. Remember too that life support of this nature is not cheap, and Mr. and Mrs. Cleeve cannot surely go on subsidising their son's care indefinitely—"

"I think if that's what they want to do, it should be their decision?" said Eddie.

"Eddie's right," said Sarah. "This is not my—"

"No no, I understand," said Dr. Krisnamurti. "But Ms. Lewis, may I ask, just out of interest—if it were your decision, what would *you* want?"

I would want him back.

For me, for our unborn child. For his poor, sad parents and his brother and sister, for everyone who knew and loved him.

But of course that's what we always want. We who are alive and moving. Never a thought for those for whom the clock has stopped. Never a thought for Richard, physically alive but mentally dead. Is he thinking and feeling at all? Is he trapped somewhere in the recesses of his flesh? Does some little spark flash every so often in the black cave of his mind? Or is it over for him? Maybe what he really is or was has long since departed. Maybe it left for good in the woods that night.

I would want him to know I love him. I would want one last chance to tell him that. When he needed me, I wasn't there. I've lost count of the times he comforted me when I was depressed or consoled me when I was angry, salved my ego when it was bruised, brought me down when I was on a silly high. I simply wasn't aware he was there—in that way—for me at the time. I took it all for granted.

I took him for granted.

And when he takes a dip, my first reaction is to run away. I'm critical, unsupportive, cruel, ignorant, and a coward. I saw what I thought were irrational reasons for his behaviour. I totally missed his pain, totally avoided it when I saw it, totally failed to address it when he needed me to.

I owe him. I'm in his debt. I'm so frustrated that even from—from wherever he is—he's made me feel guilty.

Wake up, Richard. There are reparations and apologies stacking high, waiting to cross the bridge, the divide.

But never mind that—the simple, belated truth is—I love you.

A farmer out shooting had found Richard on the Monday morning in the deserted stand of trees in Kirkbretton Old Wood, sunlight playing on his features then as now.

"He just seemed to be sleeping," the man told doctors, anxiously twirling a rook's primary feather nearly fifty centimetres long, blue-black and perfect, in his hand. "Oh, I found this at his side."

There had been a faint pulse. But brain activity had settled into the occasional random excitation, a quick blip on the EEG screen. The diagnosis had been brain damage from severe exposure.

All anyone could do, said the specialists, was to bathe Richard in familiar voices, pleasant sounds; to talk to him; to touch him; to play his favourite music.

And wait, hope, and pray.

Sarah looked for comfort, support from her boss and sometime lover, Harry Tasker, but Harry chose this time to tell her that at least Annie Shapiro took him seriously.

"Annie Shapiro, my flatmate? Takes you seriously?"

"So seriously, in fact, that she's agreed to marry me. That's more commitment than you were ever prepared to give me."

Sarah's astonishment flared almost immediately into an anger that knew no bounds and left her speechless. It was easy, therefore, for her to slam the door and walk away from Harry without revealing her utter revulsion. That revulsion did not subside; it grew until it mixed and fused with the anger she felt over Richard's intractable condition. All she knew was that each day with Harry's video company, she was an automaton. She started to look for another job. There was no way she could imagine continuing to work for such a pompous, deceitful, lightweight bastard. Yet now Richard was—ill—she had to stay. To earn. Do something.

"You should sit here," said the woman with the mottled hands and, curiously, a black veil. She patted the green paint of the park bench.

It was Sarah's custom, once or twice a week at lunchtime when weather permitted, to walk into Greenhead Park in Huddersfield, a short distance from Tasker Sightlines. Sandwiches, an apple, a banana.

Sarah shrugged, sat down anyway, but did not return the woman's smile, being disinclined by nature to exchange even pleasantries with strangers—and especially not now, now that Richard was . . . there was no humour, no generosity, no light-spiritedness in her.

But the presence of the woman unsettled her. The smile did not leave her face, darkened though it was by the veil; Sarah could see white teeth. Dentures, perhaps, since the woman was incalculably old and unlikely at her age to have her own. A Gypsy, Italian, Ukrainian, whatever. Did it matter?

The October sun was burning strongly, perhaps its last before the inevitable collapse into autumn. Yellowing leaves in the tall elms above them rustled sadly. Out of their dry, melancholy sound, Sarah began to distinguish the woman's mumbling . . .

"The line goes on. The magic never dies. Even in the darkest, most Roman of times—"

And assumed she was drunk or a mental hospital outpatient and then cursed herself for assuming.

"But *you*, dear." The harridan had shuffled along the bench, was gripping her knee. Sarah gingerly held the woman's wrist as if to remove it—but it was cold, clamped, and immutable. "But *you*, he loved. I'd like to show you the smallest part of the empire you could have commanded, but you haven't got what it takes. You don't know what a real woman is. You're just fat with child, a carrier. Nevertheless, he loved *you*."

"Let go, please. I don't know what the hell you're talking about. Just let go—now."

The old woman's hand sprang from Sarah's knee; signed pax, submission; subsided into her own black lap.

Sarah's heart thumped with anger and fear, that spurt of adrenaline that prepares a body for fight or flight. She should get up and go. She glanced at the old woman. Sitting there prim and mysterious, hands in her lap, upright, rigid, righteous like a Grandma Moses portrait. Something about her was pressing the release of her fury and frustration. What the woman had said passed completely over her, failed entirely to register.

"What do you want? Money?" she said hoarsely.

"Me, child? Nothing. I believe I hear the world's heart beat again. I want you to listen for it." The mottled hand reached forth a long slender finger, pointed it at Sarah's belly. With the other, the harridan flung back her veil. Sarah was caught like a rabbit in headlights. The woman leaned into her face, her breath as ancient and cold as unopened tombs.

"Listen for it."

"*Excuse* me. I said, are you all right?"

A shadow fell over her. A dapper tiny elderly man with white hair and moustache and an oversanguine face spoke with gentle concern. Sarah's eyes refocused and her mind tried to get a grip on the man's question.

"Hmmm. Yes. Yes, thank you. There was a lady here. Where's she gone?"

"No lady. I seet over there, watch you seet down here, get very agitato, agitated. I wonder she's all right iss all. You all right now, yes?"

"We've thought about it, and it makes sense. It's proper. We'd like you to look after the house, if you would. It's what Richard would want, I'm sure," said Edith Cleeve, her hand on Sarah's freckled arm.

"It's up to you, lass, though. Don't think we're pressing you," added Brian. "Richard said you had a place in Leeds." Richard's father had his back to the two women, ostensibly scanning the bookshelves in the lounge at the Cliff Street house.

Edith glanced in her husband's direction. "What he means is, this house is yours but only if you want it."

"It's very kind of you." Sarah spoke so that both could hear. "As it happens, I'd love to stay here permanently for a little while.

There's been a little trouble with the Leeds flat lately, and I was thinking of moving out."

"Then it's settled." Brian, thumbs in worn waistcoat pockets, came to the dining table and put a large hand on his wife's shoulders. He stared at Sarah; she thought it was in anger, until she caught the glisten of a tear in corner of his eye.

"You're a grand lass, standing by him. Many a lass would've beggared off, and who would have blamed 'em. We'd've bin proud to have had you as a daughter—"

"Brian," chided his wife, a twisted smile on her face. "You're embarrassing the girl."

"Well, as far as I'm concerned, we'll be its grandparents and—"

"Brian! This is not the time."

"It's OK. Really. I'm carrying Richard's child, and no matter what happens . . . you are my parents-in-law . . . if you see what I mean. The line goes on. The magic never dies."

"I'm sorry, Sarah? What was that?" Edith leaned closer, her eyes suddenly sharp. Sarah frowned. "What was what?"

"What you just said."

"I—I don't know."

After a meal and small talk in the George, Mr. and Mrs. Cleeve headed back for Bainbridge. Sarah wandered through the house. A thin layer of dust, an air of desolation, hung in Richard's garret study. She tidied the books, put them back on the bowed shelves, emptied the ashtrays, made neat piles of Richard's scrawled notes, tipped the contents of the waste bin into a black plastic bag, shut the lid of the laptop.

Standing back, she suddenly realised the symbolism of her gesture and wept, biting her knuckle until her saliva thickened and her voice was an inchoate creak, like the moan and sigh of wind in a shuttered room.

At the antique dressing table in their bedroom—*their* bedroom—she carefully brushed some of the tangle from her mass of brown hair, gently applied enough makeup to repair the runnels of her grief. Her own eyes, she avoided; she had no desire to revisit the anguish that crouched behind them.

And that anguish, she realised, was also fear. She knew now she was taking the first steps on a path Richard had travelled. She had tried to convince herself that the loss of Richard had created the illusion of the old woman on the park bench—that the incident was a disguised attempt to empathise with Richard's distress. The idea that the hag might exist, that she might be the same creature Richard saw at the dig on Bride Hill and on Dean Beck rec . . . Sarah shuddered.

I told myself I wanted something more exotic and dangerous than a history teacher, an ornithologist, a little narrow man of habits in a little narrow village. There was always another day. I'll commit myself tomorrow.

And now no more tomorrows.

"Come on, Sarah Lewis," she whispered to her image. "This is the real world."

And the hand on her shoulder was real too. Warm, gently kneading that beautiful smooth muscle that runs from the scapula into the scree slope of the neck

Look in the mirror.

Richard's pale angular face emerged from the shadows, blue eyes laughing behind the round spectacles he hadn't worn now for five months. The late afternoon sunlight struck silver and blue from his hair.

She had imagined this moment, the moment when the nightmare of Richard's coma became a dream that disappeared on waking. Perhaps once a thing is imagined, she told herself, its shock runs to earth. She felt calm, reached a hand up to reassure that Richard's was real. But dissenting voices in the parliament of her sanity ran off into corners and screamed.

You're hallucinating. Richard is in hospital. Richard is in an irreversible coma. There's something in the water. You're asleep. The old woman was Richard's bête noire. Everything Richard said was true. I'm pregnant, and they didn't tell me about *this* at prenatal class. This is a practical joke.

He waited at her side. Shudders—of fear or sorrow—racked her body.

Let's walk.

They crossed the road, Richard holding her hand; Sarah, the muscles of her legs like jelly, was desperate to see someone, anyone who might confirm she was not alone. Or that she was. But Cliff Street was deserted, and a bitter evening wind was sweeping away the last light whispers of warmth in the day.

They walked behind Saint Bride's, where a wilderness of rowan, brown-stemmed Himalayan balsam, and cow parsley hugged tilted gravestones. Chaffinches and blue tits clicked alarums. He put his arm round her shoulder, caressed her forehead the way he always did in life when comforting her.

Let's sit down. Here.

There was a bench with a dedicatory plaque, worn grey wood touched with tiny yellow lichen.

"Richard, I'm terrified," she whispered urgently. "I know you're not really . . . that you're . . . I can't believe you're really here. You have to understand—" She glanced up and caught that self-deprecatory half-smile that was. Absolutely. Him.

Truly, Madly, Deeply. Ghost. Sixth Sense. He laughed, a carefree sound that echoed against the deep-shadowed wall of the church tower. *We saw those films together, remember?*

"So what are you, Richard?" Sarah bit her lip. "This is cruel. You're driving me mad. What *are* you?" She tugged the sleeve of his ski jacket. The jacket behind the door on Church Street, a small insistent interior voice reminded her.

"I really don't know. Ever since that Friday night in the wood . . . ." He pushed his spectacles up his nose, scratched his chin. *"Life is episodic. There's no gap between then and now, but I've only to take one look at you to know that things have moved on here."* He patted Sarah's stomach. *"Call her Brigid. Or Sophia, Astarte, Inanna, Elath, Cybele, Ariadne, Artemis, Morigenos. One and the same. The woman. The mother who gives us life, the mate who sustains us, the crone who winds our shroud.* He sighed, but it might have been a sigh of contentment. *The name's not important. Brigid's nice, though."*

"Brigid? I'm carrying a girl? How do you know that? You're still in hospital, aren't you? This *is* a dream."

"If you believe that, I can't reach you. Look—one of the kin, hroca." A rook stalked a patch of leaf-strewn lawn nearby, turning leaves over in search of spiders and insects.

"You know how I loved rooks. Here, my lovely."

The bird flew clumsily onto the arm of the seat. Richard stroked the gloss of his back and wing coverts. The sound was of waxed armour. The rook made a nervous mumbling sound.

"This one's called . . . Dryden. It's a corruption of a Celtic phrase, but I forget what it means. I should have studied harder. Say hello, Dryden."

The bird blinked, dipped his beak twice.

"All right, that's enough. I'm going back." Sarah was in tears. The startled rook flapped heavily off into the tangle of undergrowth. Richard reached out for her, held her back.

"It's all right. I just wanted to tell you I love you and that I always will. No—don't. You'll put this down to a temporary derangement, wish fulfilment, and after a while, you'll tell yourself you were just emotionally overcharged, that it never really happened. That's fine. That's how we manage to live in the daylight.

"But the tide has turned. Life is pouring back into the world. The Celts? They believed that the lands of the living were an island in a sea of the dead . . ."

He squeezed her hand reassuringly, smiled.

"But don't worry. I found the torc. I suppose you could say I was its last victim. Nothing matters now—only you. But things are changing. This is the end of an era. It's not entirely clear to me because I still feel to be partly living here. I suppose that's the torc's last gift—or curse. I want you to take it now."

He reached into his jacket pocket and brought out the torc. Sarah recoiled from it with a sharp intake of breath.

"Take it."

He touched her face, smiled, gripped her hand, gently put the torc into her palm. It weighed a lot. Heavier than . . . the world. Sarah stared uncomprehendingly at the glittering piece of history, indiscriminate nemesis of guilty and innocent, token of humanity's simultaneous bondage to and freedom from the cruelly bounteous Earth.

"The Goddess drew off its power. It's just a piece of jewellery now. None of us can own it, and it can't own us. Not the way it used to. But I do suspect she's done something with it . . ."

"I can't keep this, Richard. Why are you giving it me?"

"For our daughter. When she grows up, she'll know exactly what to do with it. An heirloom. 'A gift from your father.'"

They stared ahead, holding hands, both lost in their separate worlds. Finally, Sarah turned to him.

"There's so much I—Richard, I'm sorry I let you down," she stammered. Her lip was trembling; tears welled like silver in her eyes. He fumbled for a handkerchief, dabbed them carefully.

"We don't know how much we value a thing until it's gone. I know. Been there. Look, I'll always love you. See you soon."

He kissed her lightly on the forehead.

She stood alone then, turning the torc over and over in her hands in the fading October light, knowing beyond doubt that her visits to the hospital where Richard lay were over.

She felt irrevocably damaged, irrevocably changed.

Irrevocably cleansed.

She was suddenly aware of the rooks, thousands of them, cawing and wheeling like ash from a bonfire, above her head.

The child stirred in her womb.

NOTES

*O*UT OF THE EARTH IS a story; I didn't set out to make this book either an historical or an ornithological treatise. Anybody who is interested in the way the Celts of the first century AD lived or rooks behave has not been misled deliberately in any serious way, though. I have slightly manipulated chronology, events, and locations in the Celtic section to suit the narrative but have been generous rather than economical with the truth.

Cartimandua, Venute (romanised to Venutius), Vellocate (romanised to Vellocates), Caradoc (romanised to Caratacus), and Ostorius Scapula were real people; Llanymynech, Ilkley, Castle Hill, and Stanwick are real places. In terms of landscape, what my characters are seeing, I have seen; though, of course, I have had to reclothe the hills in forest, demolish housing estates, cause the rivers to run without the restraint of corporation reservoirs in their headwaters, and rebuild the Celtic roundhouses in my mind's eye.

Publius Ostorius Scapula was governor of Britain from AD 47 to his death in AD 52.

Kirkbretton is not Kirkburton, my West Yorkshire birthplace, nor does the Colden Valley exist. I've imagined another valley between the Colne and Holme. Safehaven is more Honley than anywhere else, with Saint Mary's Parish Church as Saint Bride's and Green Cliff as Bride Hill, if you want to go and picture the scene for yourself. Many of the observations pertaining to rook behaviour are courtesy of my local rookery. I have even tried to match some of their vocalisations with their actions, though this has led to a high degree of guesswork . . .

Those who doubt that a rook's vocabulary is as varied as I suggest should attempt to get as near as possible to one. My baptism was like Richard's; I overheard one conducting a soliloquy on the chimney pot many years ago, and this amazingly complex sound was amplified into the bedroom.

Scholars have identified the names of about four hundred European/British Celtic deities, but about three hundred of these appear only once, which suggests that the majority were local. I have tended to mention the more popular and universal ones.

Celtic deities were observed by Julius Caesar, who recorded that the "Gauls" (continental Celts) worshipped Mercury as chief of the gods, honouring Apollo, Mars, Jupiter, and Minerva. He seemed to think no one would mind, least of all the conquered peoples of Europe if, on seeing a statue or carving or depiction of a Celtic god that appeared to have the attributes of Mercury, Caesar simply wrote something on the lines that "the local Celts worshipped Mercury." History is nearly always written by the victors for the victors.

I have stolen from Welsh, Irish, Scottish, and Cornish Celtic culture and language liberally, indiscriminately, and in that order of frequency. This is not the place to make a long list of confessions, so there are only three: the goddess Brigid did not, as far as I know, have a special relationship with rooks—though as a member of the matres (mother-goddess) triad, she had a close relationship with the messenger "crows" of destiny. These are, by tradition in many countries, the common raven, whose antisocial habits and huge weight—up to two kilograms (four pounds)—did not suit my story.

Cartimandua betrayed Caradoc at Ludlow, Shropshire, not near Castle Hill. The location of the conflict between Scapula's Roman forces and the Ordovices and Silures tribes of Wales is thought to have been somewhere along the River Severn, but nobody really knows. And Castle Hill (grid reference SE152140), first fortified in 550 BC in the early Iron Age, was never, as far as archaeologists can tell, a permanent Brigantian fortress. About the time of this story, however, its defences were briefly strengthened . . .

My rooks (it will come as no surprise) act much as rooks do throughout Europe, and with the exception of Startle's attack on the planning notices, I don't make them do anything they have not been observed to do, including attempting to "steal" substantial knickknacks. The reader's interpretation of their organisation, motives, and general culture is at least as viable as mine.

As a kind of postscript, I appear to make, I suppose, the assumption that the mysterious markings found to this day on the rocks of Baildon and Rombalds Moors above Ilkley, where Cartimandua accepts the Goddess and handfasts her husband, played a part in Celtic fertility rites. This may be true. It is one of a dozen theories.

I point the reader to the Cow and Calf Rocks a little further east—rocks covered with two centuries of lovers' initials. Cup and ring marks may be nothing more than doodles and vandalism more than two millennia old. Though I doubt it.

The Royal Society for the Protection of Birds (RSPB) was invaluable on several occasions in pointing me in the right direction during my collation of information on rooks, and three books that proved invaluable were *The Crows: A Study of the Corvids of Europe* by Dr. Franklin Coombs; *Life of the Rook* by G. K. Yeates; and P. H. Emerson's *Birds, Beasts, and Fishes of the Norfolk Broadland*.

Mr. W. E. Crosland, secretary of Huddersfield and District Archaeological Society at the time of my research, very kindly supplied me with a likely scenario of consequences following the discovery of a major archaeological site.

Thanks is no adequate word to offer to my wife, Philippa, whose unsentimental and nonpartisan margin notes let me know in no uncertain terms what readers might think of my attempts at storytelling but would be perhaps too polite to say.

GLOSSARY

THE ROOK CHARACTERS

Rook patronyms have been handed down for countless generations. The female rook takes the male's patronym in the second year of pairing, the first year being a "trial" partnership. Many pairs do not stay together after their first year; but if they go into a second together, they tend to be bonded for life.

THOSE WHO FOUGHT ON HAUNTED HILL

Strongtalon
Coalfeather
Dreadcalmer
Surebill
Highnester
Blackflight
Greybeak
(Forenames unknown)

LAMMERMUIR

Hroc	the Rooklord, Master of Masters, Feathered Ruler of the Northern Kingdom
Hawberry Mac Greybeak	guard of Hroc, with partial Ley-gift
Cobweb Greybeak	his mate
Dougal Keeneye	guard of Hroc
Badon Airchurner	guard of Hroc

STANWICK

Calum Dawncaller	Master of Lowhills congeries

SAFEHAVEN

Brittle Blackflight	
Caspian Surebill	Master of congeries
Halley Coalfeather	Irascible father of Startle, father-in-lore of Dryden, elder of tree (broken-branched beech)
Dryden Dreadcalmer	Impulsive but strong mate of Startle
Startle Coalfeather	Ley-gifted daughter of above, mate of Dryden
Carew, Bran and Woodsorrel	Dryden and Startle's squabs
Thornton One-claw	Strong, inquisitive two-year-old
Amroth Dreadcalmer	Moved with family to Mildhollow congeries; distant cousin of Dryden

Calvin Airchurner	Elderly, forgetful, cloudy-eyed from old injury
Westray Airchurner	Son of Calvin, father of Bruton; killed by Burgeon
Sunrise Airchurner	Westray's mate
Bruton Airchurner	Yearling, a companion and somewhat in awe of Dryden
Gifford Hangclaw	Unpleasant and cynical bachelor
Caerleon Longpinion	
Elderflower Longpinion	Caerleon's mate
Levenworth Highnester	Shot
Cherry Highnester	Levenworth's widow, shot by Burgeon
Bracken Nightwing	Safehaven gossip; long-beaked, knowledgeable; shot by Burgeon
Sorrel Nightwing	Sister of Bracken
Caliban Dawncaller	Elder of tree for Startle and Dryden, who live nearby
Sapphire Dawncaller	Caliban's mate
Carmen Strongtalon	naïve yearling
Camomile Strongtalon	Carmen's mother

ROOK TERMS

Air	= a.k.a. the Kingdom or Realm. The primary element.
Bilhain	= bird language. Includes hieroglyphs, bill and mute marks, international distress and alert calls, joysong, mating calls, kill calls, and taunts
Congeries	= the rookery. The word is singular.
Congronym	= the congeries' call sign

Council	= occasional convocation of the entire rookery to determine and ratify congeries law and to make decisions on matters affecting the rookery as a whole Almost always held at twilight. See *Eldermoot.*
Cromark	= kith sign language, itself a sophisticated element of bilhain, the language common to all birds
Elder of tree	= often a family head and usually a middle-aged to elderly bird (male or female), recognised by his tree as its spokesperson and thus as a member of Eldermoot (qv)
Eldermoot	= legislatory body of a rookery, headed by a rookery master or mistress
Engard	= watchfully sitting near the nest, daytime
Forage	= peck (qv) brought back to the nest, generally a sticky meal of grain, spiders, leatherjackets, carried in the bill-pouch and regurgitated
Furlong	= (a) measure of ground roughly equivalent to our own furlong, being one hundred wings (qv) in length, measured by a full grown rook on a still dry day; (b) colloquial for the ground, including rooftops and all other solid surfaces
Golden Land	"heaven": the place a rook is taken to by Hroc after death
Hroc	= the Rook of Passage, who appears to all of the kin immediately prior to their departure from this life; but he is a living creature, old beyond imagining, the Goddess's closest earthly confidant waiting for his final mission

Hrocain	= language peculiar to *Corvus frugilegus*, the rook
Joysong	= element of bilhain (qv). Birds peech delivering a paean to life
Kin	= other rooks
Kith	= the family Corvidae: rooks, crows, choughs, jackdaws, ravens, jays, and magpies
Longroost	= winter. Longroost night = the longest night of the year
Master/mistress	= the leading rook in a congeries. The position of leading rook is not for life; a master is reelected once a year at new plough's turn (qv) and is generally dependent on that rook's demonstration of at least mild auguric powers
Moon	= with season markers, the rook's measure of time
Moot	= the irregular meeting of the residents of a tree or close-knit group of trees within a rookery. In the average-sized rookery, there may be five or six moots.
New plough's turn	= season marker, equivalent to "spring"
No quarter	= order issued by quartermasters (qv) in circumstances where peck (qv) is concentrated and rich—carrion, spilled grain, insect or worm nests, etc. Can lead to squabbles
Old plough's turn	= season marker, equivalent to "autumn"
Peck	= feeding
Peck squad	= any group of feeding rooks; in winter, sometimes 95 percent of the rookery will form a peck squad. At other times, a squad might be only two to four birds.

Quarter	= (1) an individual rook's allocation of land for peck (qv), on level ground, about 250 sq. ft. (23 sq m)
	= (2) an individual rook's allocation of airspace during a mass manoeuvre
	= (3) rare, the area within a rookery deemed by a rook family to be its private territory
Quartering	= the act of dividing and allocation of land to individual rooks for the purposes of peck. Usually organised by quartermasters (qv)
Quartermarks	= cromark (qv) signs left by a rook to indicate that his quarter (qv) has been worked
Quartermaster	= temporary position passing in rotation through entire rookery population. Their principal duties are to identify a suitable peck ground, lead or direct the squad to it, overfly or quarter the ground while the rest of the squad watches, and allocate quarters (qv)
Safehaven	= Saint Bede's Rookery, Kirkbretton. Originally called Rawshoona
Roost	= literally "watchful sleep"
Shortroost	= summer. Shortroost night = midsummer eve
Scout	= usually a solo rook—a reliable juvenile or bachelor, occasionally a pair—sent by the rookery on any intelligence-gathering mission.
Sun	= used by the rook to give indication of (a) the passage of time and (b) direction. Thus, sunrise, suntop, sunfall; a hundred wings (qv) left of sunfall = 220 m southwesterly

Upwright	= human being, depicted in cromark (qv) as a four-armed star, presumably from a bird's-eye view of the human form
Vitchel	= peck (qv) eaten in situ
Wing	= a measure of distance, i.e., one full beat of a full-grown rook's wings in still air or about two yards (2.2 m)

USEFUL HROCAIN
(Language of the Kin)

Word/Phrase	Pronunciation	Meaning
aarh-chekh (repeated)	archek	we are travellers/ visitors/ strangers
ceri	see-ree	starlings
chakachit(ta)	chack-a-chit(-a)	magpie(s)
chakaw (s), chakawi (pl)	chack-or(-wee)	jackdaw(s)
chaw-cha-ich	chaw-chah-itch	a sign is given
chaw-ich-cha	chaw-itch-'ha	give us/me a sign
chraak(a)	crark(a)	raven(s)
chyffnaach	chiv-nark	weasel
chwaagh	whu-aa	motor vehicle
Hroc/hroc	'h-rukk	the Rooklord/a rook
hroca	'h-rukka	rookdom, the kin
hwfnaach	huff-nark	stoat
hwt(a)	hoot(a)	blackbird(s)
hytt(a)	heet(a)	sparrow(s)
kee	kee	kestrel (after its call)
rahrara	'hrah-'hra-'hra	fox (after its bark)
waagh!	wa-ar	alarm!

Making portrait and landscape oil paintings, working in a textile mill, slaughtering pigs, selling encyclopaedias, and publishing pub guides indicate that John Avison has not been too fussy in the past about how he has earned a crust.

Briefly, he was editor of two special-interest low-circulation national magazines and has written advertising copies extolling the virtues of anything from bath reenamelling to the Christmas presents in mail-order catalogues.

But he will be least remembered, perhaps, for his day job as a feature writer; art, film, and theatre critic; humour and gossip columnist; and letters page editor with local newspapers in Yorkshire.

He lives with Philippa in a tiny tree-encircled Yorkshire village, coincidentally only a mile or two from where he was born in 1949, and has a son, a daughter, and five grandchildren.